"Even when you're out of sorts, you're lovely,"

Creag said, enjoying the way light from the oil lamps penetrated the material of Jeanne's blouse and illuminated the shadows of her curves. "Do you know your eyes have golden sparks when you're angry?"

"If they do, then you have put them there," Jeanne declared.

"I could think of another way to make your eyes flash, Jeanne Donnachy," Creag murmured, leaving his seat and coming to stand before her. He reached out to gently capture her face in his large hands, tilting her chin upward so she had no choice but to return his stare.

Suddenly Jeanne was aware of Creag as she had never been aware of a man before. She watched in wonder as he began to drop his head toward hers.

"Shall I show you?" he murmured, his lips inches from her own....

Dear Reader,

The holidays are upon us and Harlequin Historicals is celebrating with a quartet of keepers!

First, *New York Times* bestselling author Elizabeth Lowell brings us *Reckless Love*. Janna Wayland is as untamed as the wild horses she trains. But when Ty Mackenzie comes into her life, her unbridled passion forces her to make a painful choice.

Margaret Moore, author of the Warrior series, takes us back to the age of Norsemen in her latest release. *The Viking* is Einar, a warrior whose decision to take Saxon woman Meradyce hostage changes his life forever. Filled with adventure and romance, this is a *must* read.

In *Providence,* Ananiah Snow—a woman with a scandalous past—risks everything when she hires handsome sea captain Sam Colburn to find her missing father. Yet losing her heart to Sam proves the greatest risk of all. Another swashbuckling, romantic tale on the high seas by popular author Miranda Jarrett.

And rounding out December is *Counterfeit Laird* by Erin Yorke. This charming tale about the people in a small Scottish village who trick American businessman Creag Blake into believing he is the long-lost laird is sure to please readers—especially when the sparks begin to fly between Creag and the old laird's granddaughter, Jeanne....

All of us at Harlequin wish you a happy and safe holiday season and best wishes for the new year!

Sincerely,

Tracy Farrell
Senior Editor

Erin Yorke

Counterfeit Laird

Harlequin Books

TORONTO • NEW YORK • LONDON
AMSTERDAM • PARIS • SYDNEY • HAMBURG
STOCKHOLM • ATHENS • TOKYO • MILAN
MADRID • WARSAW • BUDAPEST • AUCKLAND

ISBN 0-373-28802-6

COUNTERFEIT LAIRD

ERIN YORKE

is the pseudonym used by the writing team of Susan Yansick and Christine Healy. One half of the team is married, the mother of two sons and suburban, and the other is single, fancy-free and countrified, but they find that their differing lives and styles enrich their writing with a broader perspective.

For Brian Healy

With love and appreciation for being there

and

For Gloria McGovern Rabena

Your happy, loving nature has always made you
very special

Chapter One

Scottish Highlands,
1889

"Leslie, I thank you for your confidence, but what you suggest is entirely out of the question," Jeanne Donnachy told her companion with a rueful smile.

The two women stood just outside the main hall of the once grand manor house, the one a petite blond bit of femininity, her manner all nurturing softness, and the other tall and willowy with a thick mass of brown hair piled atop her head, her bearing as aristocratic as any Highland laird as she discounted the advice she had been offered.

With the difference in their looks and temperaments, a more unlikely pair was hard to imagine, yet Jeanne Donnachy had considered her distant relative, Leslie, her closest friend for as long as she could remember. Even now, the uncommon streak of obstinacy being exhibited by the usually quiet and gentle blonde was a loving attempt to spare Jeanne from the ordeal waiting beyond the doorway in the great hall.

"But I can't make sense of what you're doing," Leslie badgered, her large brown eyes beginning to water. "Think of what you stand to lose!"

"And what of everyone else?" Jeanne answered softly yet firmly. "What might their loss be if I did as you suggest?"

"Does it make a difference?" Leslie persisted, her small bow of a mouth starting to quiver. "It will probably happen anyway."

"But if it does, it won't be on my conscience," the taller and calmer of the two women replied patiently. "Would you really want me to commit such a grievous wrong, Leslie, and then have to live with it?"

"No, but..."

"Of course you wouldn't. Now go along and take a seat with the others. I'll need a friendly face inside."

Gently prodding the reluctant Leslie through the doorway, Jeanne heard the buzz of her neighbors' voices spilling from the large hall. By the sound of it, just about everyone from the small Scottish village of Linclachan, perched in the southern regions of the Highlands, had arrived.

Brushing a stubborn lock of reddish brown hair back from her furrowed brow, she listened to the hushed speculations of those assembled, and then wiped her damp palms in the folds of her dark green skirt. In an effort to bolster her courage, she needlessly adjusted the collar of her fitted white blouse and the sash of Donnachy plaid attached to one shoulder by an antique clan brooch. She had chosen her clothing carefully in order to appear serious, mature and confident. Yet despite her intent, her twenty-three years and her protestations to Leslie, Jeanne felt, at the moment, like nothing more than an inexperienced and hesitant bairn.

Now was not the time to give way to her own uncertainties, the Scottish beauty scolded herself. The issue could not be put off any longer. And so she straightened her back, lifted her chin, and went forth to deal with the latest and most dire of Linclachan's ever-increasing problems.

Fifty-odd heads turned in her direction and fifty-odd mouths drew together in consternation as Jeanne entered the room and began to make her way to the spot where Andrew Robertson, the local solicitor, stood, a small frown pinching his lips while his gaze traveled from the pocket watch held impatiently atop his soft, paunchy middle to Jeanne, and then pointedly back to his timepiece.

With the defiant pride so characteristic of her family and her own fiery nature, the young woman blatantly ignored this silent reprimand. Refusing to be hurried, she walked in a slow and stately manner, fixing her attention on the members of her clan, who had gathered for this all-too-somber occasion.

She had seen these same people come together numerous times to deal with other matters. But the familiarity of the faces surrounding her was small comfort to her at present. In fact, it was because she knew and cared for them all that she was willing to give up everything that was dear to her.

She spied Leslie, wearing a soft expression of concern, and next to her was seventy-year-old Maggie, Leslie's great-aunt and the little village's seamstress. Even now, when a decision had yet to be made, Maggie's eyes glistened with unspoken sympathy. This unexpected kindness coming from the usually abrupt old woman was almost more than Jeanne could bear. Before she could disgrace herself by giving way to her unsettled emotions, she moved on and turned to greet some of the others.

She nodded gravely to one of the manor's tenants, and then to the boisterous Jamie Robertson, a member of the council, who also owned and operated Linclachan's highly productive still. But even as she dipped her head in salutation, Jeanne was aware of the way in which the unruly curls of her upswept mane bobbed frivolously; she cursed her own foolishness in not wearing her hair long and loose as she usually did.

Attempting, now, to hold her head as erect as she possibly could, Jeanne finally reached Andrew Robertson's side, where she turned to face the others, her deep green eyes all too solemn for someone her age. But then, while she had known this day would eventually arrive, she had never thought it would be so soon. She wasn't ready to deal with it, even if she had no choice but to do so.

The council members, old as they were, moved forward quickly, their voluminous plaids stirring the otherwise still air of the room as they found their places at the council table that stood in the middle of the run-down hall. Besides Jamie Robertson, there was his brother Geordie, who made his meager living by brewing ale. In the old days, these men would have been warriors, but present-day circumstances had robbed them of that glory and reduced them to less than they were meant to be. Nevertheless, given their skills as makers of alcoholic spirits, the two brothers were held in relatively high esteem.

Next to Geordie sat Duncan Donnachy, Linclachan's only merchant, the owner of a sparsely stocked shop. And on his right was his ancient, dour second cousin, Malcolm Donnachy, whose function was to oversee the livestock of Lindall Manor.

While the council conferred quietly before addressing her, Jeanne noted grimly that every inhabitant of Linclachan and the manor lands was present. The only person missing was the clan's fierce hawk-nosed chieftain. Out of habit, and before she could stop herself, her eyes swept the sparsely furnished room to find him, as though, if she looked hard enough, Fergus Donnachy, fifth earl of Lindall and laird of both the village and Lindall Manor, would somehow materialize.

But even as she surveyed her shabby surroundings, where the ravages of time and the lack of funds had all but obliterated the grandeur of the hall, Jeanne knew that Fergus Donnachy would never again preside over the council sessions held here, listening to his advisers before making the decisions that affected Donnachy and Robertson lands. It had been almost a week since the laird, her grandfather, had died. And in spite of the innumerable arguments that had peppered her years in his household, Jeanne discovered that she missed him tremendously, nonetheless.

As the low, muttered conversation of the elders continued, Jeanne's eyes fell on her grandfather's vacant chair at the council table. Finally Duncan looked up, officially recognizing her presence while the rest of the men sat back stiffly in their seats.

Silence descended upon the hall as her kinsmen waited to see what Jeanne Donnachy would do. For a brief, tantalizing instant, the willowy young woman considered following Leslie's advice, an idea that had tempted Jeanne before her friend had ever mentioned it, if truth be told. All it would take was a few quick steps to stride past the others and brashly seat herself at the head of the table, her silent actions loudly declaring that she was the new ruler of this branch of Clan Donnachy.

But though she had served as her grandfather's steward since she had been fifteen, and knew more about the running of the manor and its property than anyone else, Jeanne was reluctant to assume responsibility for Linclachan and her kinsmen. It was not that she would ever consider shirking her duty to the clan; it was merely that she had some trepidation over which path that duty should take. Pride might urge her to sit in her grandfather's place, yet common sense and a genuine concern for the welfare of her extended family prohibited her from doing so. . . that was, unless the others demanded it.

"Will you be taking the laird's seat?" Jamie Robertson asked in an uncharacteristically quiet voice. "Or do you prefer to stand?"

"I should think that decision belongs to the council. But before you make your pronouncement, I must tell you that if you offer me this position, you offer it to a pauper. My grandfather's coffers are bare," she answered, her voice calm yet vibrant enough to be heard throughout the oversized hall.

The clarity of the young woman's words and her prepossessing manner sent murmurs of approval buzzing through the room. There was no doubt that Jeanne sprang from the old laird's stock. But the question remained, could one so young, and a penniless female at that, save a village that was on the verge of destitution? Was the lass, plucky as she was, strong enough to hold Linclachan and the manor together when a man as shrewd and fierce as her grandsire had had trouble stemming the tide of the land's deterioration?

"If you'll pardon my interruption," Andrew Robertson interjected in an imperious tone, blatantly annoyed that he was being overlooked, "I would think that before the council addresses the question, it should hear the last wishes of Fergus Donnachy."

"Aye," Geordie Robertson answered, fixing the solicitor with a piercing stare, "if what you're saying is that you have in your possession a paper dealing with the matter and signed in Fergus Donnachy's own hand. But if it's just your own opinions you'll be voicing, why then, man, you'll have to wait your turn to speak like everyone else."

"Of course I have such a document!" Andrew replied, his ire mounting, until a glance in Jeanne's direction caused him to remember the unruffled and pleasant demeanor he wished to maintain in front of her. The lass might not have a shilling to rattle around in the family strongbox, but there was still the land to be considered. Instantly his scowl disappeared and an unctuous smile slipped into place as the man of law turned his attentions to the recently deceased laird's fetching granddaughter.

"Of course, Jeanne dear, that is not to say that your grandfather did not confide in me as a friend, as well. Certainly he thought of me as more than his solicitor. During these last few months especially, we had many a long talk about his hopes for Lindall, as well as his wishes for your own future and the part he wanted me to play in your life."

Jeanne felt her cheeks burn with pique at Andrew Robertson's impudence. As though she would ever consider him anything more than an irritant. Why, the man was twenty years her senior, balding and ugly as sin! But more important, the solicitor was so filled with himself that he had no room in his heart for anyone or anything else; not her, not the manor and, above all, not the welfare of Linclachan.

"I'm sure you did," she answered sweetly, "but then Grandfather was delirious so often of late, that I'm certain he didn't ken just what he was saying."

A snicker ran along the back of the hall, and Andrew's face darkened. With effort he took hold of his emotions once more, reminding himself that there would be time enough for disciplining Jeanne Donnachy once he had wed her and been named earl of Lindall and laird of Linclachan. Then he could sell off the southern portions of Donnachy lands to the Campbells or, if they couldn't meet his price, to some wealthy English aristocrat. It made little difference to him that families would lose their homes. His own residence would be the manor, and the money from the sale of the parcel of land, added to what he had stolen from Fergus, would see him a rich man indeed, even after he had paid off the manor's debts. He was not about to permit such an opportunity to slip through his fingers.

"Still, he was of sound mind when he instructed me to draft this letter," Andrew continued doggedly, a self-satisfied smirk curling his lips as he held the document aloft for all to see. "As a member of the clan, and Fergus's legal representative, I demand the council take it under consideration before any decisions are made about the former laird's successor and the disposition of his lands."

The four gray heads of the clan elders drew together to argue the matter quietly before one of them took it upon himself to speak for them all.

"Aye, Andrew, we'll avail ourselves of Fergus's last bit of advice, even though he is speaking to us from beyond the grave. Read the damn letter and then go sit with the others and allow us to do what has to be done," Duncan Donnachy said impatiently.

Jeanne's stolid expression did nothing to betray her anxiety as she watched the pompous solicitor glance covetously at the laird's chair while he unfolded the document. That was the seat he wanted to take, there was no doubt of it, just as there was no question in the young woman's mind as to the gambit for power about to commence. Andrew wanted to be laird more than he wanted anything else. And while she did not wish the responsibility of the position herself, she had to find a way to stop him from snatching it.

For the next five minutes, Jeanne stood, her demeanor calm and her bearing as regal as that of any ancient queen, while Andrew Robertson wended through legal pronouncements and injunctions confusing enough to hide the meaning behind the words. And then suddenly, Jeanne heard her imperious grandfather's instructions being delivered in the solicitor's voice, Andrew's tone severely affected with his sense of self-importance.

"Since I leave no male issue to inherit my position and lands, my own son having seen fit to die before he could take my place and become laird of Lindall, I acknowledge that I have left the clan in an awkward situation. I wish to remind the council that in dealing with this problem, they have a few options. First, they could confer the title of laird upon my only immediate relative..."

Jeanne paled at the suggestion, until the silence of those gathered in the hall suddenly erupted and the elders once more bent their heads in hasty conference before speaking directly to their fellow clan members.

"While such a measure is highly unusual, it is not entirely without precedence," Duncan began. "After Culloden, there were a few instances wherein women, many of them as poor as Jeanne is now, took the reins of control."

"But that was only because there were no men to do so," Geordie countered gravely.

"Is the situation in Linclachan so very different?" boomed Jamie Robertson's voice.

"What Jamie suggests is true," Malcolm Donnachy, the oldest and most grizzled of those sitting at the table responded. "We all ken that if the monies Fergus borrowed in Glasgow are not repaid within a year, the manor and its holdings will become the property of those Lowland bloodsuckers who go by the name of banker. The lands are in a bad way, and have been for the last few generations, though the fault does not lie with Fergus and his family. Today, more than a hundred and forty years after Culloden, the ranks of our young men have been depleted by another foe—poverty. Most of them have been forced to leave their homes and seek their livings elsewhere, falling victim to the lure of industrialization to the south or the whispers of wealth across the ocean."

"Those of us remaining are too old and tired to be effective leaders," Duncan conceded. "Nor do we have the vision needed to save Linclachan. I ask you, who is left to guide us? How much worse off would we be, placing our future in young Jeanne's hands?"

"No worse off," shouted a fervent feminine voice that Jeanne recognized as Leslie's.

Noting that there were no immediate objections being made, a startled Andrew Robertson suppressed a sharp intake of breath at this surprising turn of events, and hurriedly pressed on.

"Please! Please! Allow me to continue," he interjected loudly, determined not to have his own aspirations wither as a result of the affection the villagers felt for Jeanne Donnachy. "You have not heard everything the old laird had to say."

"Go on then, man," called someone from the back of the room. "There's no sense taking all night about it."

His thick black brows clashing together in anger, Andrew readjusted his coat as the laughter died down and he struggled to regain his dignity. Comforting himself with the thought that he would command more respect when he became laird, the solicitor was finally ready to proceed.

"While a more intelligent and feisty lass than my granddaughter never drew breath, I am of the opinion that the problems of Linclachan are too much for young Jeanne to handle alone. To that end, I charge the council with finding her a husband, since I doubt the lass will be able to entrap one of her own, having failed to this point to have already done so. What is needed is a man strong enough to deal with both my own headstrong granddaughter and the troubles besetting Lindall Manor and its village."

From the corner of the hall, Jeanne heard a soft gasp of distress, most likely Leslie's, and then the crowd's reaction to the old laird's second option grew, becoming noisier and more excitable by the moment.

"Enough!" Jeanne ordered at last when the council members failed to act. Her clear, strong tones rang with the authority of a clan chief, though her crimson face indicated the outrage she felt as she silently condemned her grandfather for holding her up to ridicule before her kinsmen. "There will be no more talk among you of any marriage for me!"

"But surely you realize your situation," Andrew insisted, picturing the day he could climb into this lovely woman's bed should things go as he planned. "Your grandfather felt you could not shoulder the responsibility on your own, and should someone else other than your spouse become laird, you would be forced to leave the manor. Surely, marrying the new earl would present a happy compromise. You could remain in your home and have a loving husband besides."

"And where would I find such a man?" Jeanne snapped, anger igniting her green eyes with sparks of gold. "Though the members of the council are all worthy of bearing the title of laird, not one of them is younger than my grandfather was."

"Aye, and if the lass were to wed one of them, a few years from now would only see us in the same predicament—young Jeanne alone and no heir in sight," Maggie commented in dry exasperation as the council members reddened, reminded of their diminished virility, and squirmed in their chairs, too

cowardly to debate the woman they presently cursed as a med-
dling old crone.

"That is true," Andrew began smoothly, a self-satisfied
smile lighting his face. "They *are* too old to take Jeanne to wife.
But then, I myself—"

"I said there will be no more talk of marriage," Jeanne rebuked sharply, her manner more than a little reminiscent of
Fergus Donnachy. "If and when I wed, I will make the decision and no one else."

There was a burst of applause from one of the women of the
village before her husband's embarrassed glare caused her to
cease her support of the old laird's granddaughter. Then there
was a prolonged silence in the hall once more.

"It would appear we have reached an impasse," Malcolm
said morosely while the others shook their heads in agreement. "That is, of course, unless Fergus had anything else to
say. If he did, you might as well come out with it now, Andrew, and get it over with."

"Ahem . . . yes, there was," the solicitor replied after clearing his throat, his mind working feverishly to find some way to
make Jeanne Donnachy receptive to his suit. He knew only too
well that while Fergus's final suggestion didn't sever all his hope
of succeeding as laird, he stood a better chance of gaining the
acceptance of the clan if Jeanne chose him as her partner in
wedlock. However, among all the attentive faces before him,
Andrew did not find anyone who might become his ally in the
battle for that obstinate wench's hand. Why, even now, when
she was in danger of losing what little she had, the woman was
regarding him with nothing more than a cold and haughty
stare.

"On with it, then," Malcolm commanded, his already
wrinkled face puckering with impatience when the man of law
failed to proceed.

"Very well," Andrew said reluctantly as he held the letter up
once more to be read.

"Should my granddaughter, Jeanne Donnachy, continue
to be as stubborn after my death as she was during my
lifetime, and refuse to wed, I can only hope that the clan
will return to our ancient Scottish traditions, and look

among the Donnachys and Robertsons for the strongest and bravest male of the lot, and name him chief, laird of Linclachan, earl of Lindall.''

Immediately the room flew into noisy chaos, as the villagers considered such a possibility. If Fergus's position of authority did not pass to Jeanne or her husband, who would be the likely candidates? So few young men remained in Linclachan, and among those who had left to seek their fortunes elsewhere, was there any one of them who could be persuaded to return to the very problems he had sought to escape when he had left Scotland in the first place?

"Quiet! We need quiet," Jeanne insisted, attempting to impose a semblance of order when she heard ordinary talk begin to turn into heated debate all around her. With the amount of upset she had faced that day, she didn't need brawls taking place within the walls of her home, as well.

Seeing her kinsmen stare at her expectantly, and hearing the muttering of the crowd, Jeanne decided a distraction was needed. She signaled for the food to be served, thick slices of bread studded with currants, and tasty scones, along with pots of tea and a barrel of ale. Whisky, with this lot, volatile as they were, was entirely out of the question the young woman concluded prudently.

Though the simple repast provided by Jeanne would have been spurned in richer households, the impoverished Scottish villagers considered it a feast. Within a short time, shouts had become no more than murmured conversation as the people of Linclachan munched contentedly, filling their all-too-often empty stomachs while discussing their present dilemma with one another and the clan elders.

Looking around her, Jeanne found it good to have quiet once more, though she knew from experience that some of her kinsmen were only taking a short respite until they regained their stamina. Still, a few moments' peace was better than none at all. She had even been able to avoid Andrew, escaping his attentions by engaging herself in conversations with some of the tenants, and then with Malcolm and Duncan.

"Leslie, do you have something in that herbal pouch of yours that will dispel the headache?" she asked when she was finally able to tear herself away from the others and approach her friend and Maggie.

"Certainly," the tiny blonde replied, beginning to rummage in the small bag suspended from her belt. "But do have a seat here with us where you can ignore your troubles for a few moments and relax."

"That's right, have a nice sit-down. A friendly chat will do you good, help you forget today's turmoil," Maggie encouraged, patting Jeanne's hand and then pulling the girl down to join her on the faded settee. "Though of course I must tell you I don't ken how you could manage your grandfather's lands for the last eight years and not discover how his fortune, wee enough to begin with, was diminishing."

"Because I stayed within the budget Grandfather allowed me without ever being privy to his overall financial situation," Jeanne replied, suppressing an indulgent smile at the direction in which the crafty old woman was steering this supposedly soothing conversation. "Unfortunately, he hid that all too well. I had no idea how disastrous things were until after he died."

"And how did you come to find out?" the spry, white-haired seamstress asked, oblivious to the gentle look of remonstrance Leslie was sending her way.

"Andrew Robertson told me, of course."

"Of course," Maggie echoed dryly, "though he's not a man you should trust. Why Fergus used his services is beyond me, and many is the time I told the laird just that."

"Because he approved of Andrew's sly cunning when it could be used to the manor's benefit," the dark-haired young woman answered with a disapproving grimace.

"And sly Andrew is, Jeanne," Leslie interrupted with a delicate shudder as a frown creased her pretty brow. "Why, when he read that bit about your marriage, his eyes just about devoured you. I thought he would get down on bended knee right there and then to ask for your hand!"

"He can ask all he wants for the good it will do him," Jeanne assured her friends, her mouth drawn tight with determination when she saw Andrew approach the council table and call for the villagers' attention.

"I am certain," the solicitor began, addressing the elders and then turning to include all who were in the hall, "that when

Fergus suggested finding a husband for Jeanne or, if she refused to marry, searching for a new laird, he did not mean the terms, 'strong and brave,' to be taken in a strictly physical sense. Surely he expected you to realize that they also referred to wisdom and education. For that reason, I can, with clear conscience, propose that I—''

"Thank you, Andrew, but there is no need for you to suggest anyone at this particular time . . . for either position,'' Jeanne interrupted, arriving at the table and expertly dismissing her unwanted beau.

"The council and I have yet to come to any hard-and-fast conclusion,'' she continued. "You, on the other hand, have completed the task my grandfather set you, and done it most admirably, I might add. It is up to others to decide what is to be done now.''

"But . . . I feel I must . . . I want to . . .'' sputtered the thwarted solicitor.

"Now, now, Andrew, you've already done more than I wanted you to do,'' Jeanne said prettily, though her meaning was not lost upon her rejected suitor. "You deserve a good rest. Why not return to the comfort of your hearth and home while we spend the rest of this long night dealing with the questions at hand?''

"I might remind you that I am part of this clan,'' Andrew protested loudly, "and I have an interest in its future.''

"Aye, we all do,'' Geordie said, "but right now it falls to those most immediately involved to determine what our course of action will be. Listen to Jeanne and go home, man. The others will be following soon enough.''

"And if you can't find your way, we can always send you with an escort,'' Jamie said with a nod of his head, the motion bringing forward a handful of the brawniest men at the assembly.

Andrew Robertson blanched at the intimation and then reluctantly spun on his heel and stalked from the room, pledging a silent oath that these ignorant plowmen would pay for their treatment of him one day soon.

"And now that only those most closely concerned are left,'' Jeanne said to loud guffaws as a wide sweep of her hand indicated all those present, "it is time to get down to the crux of the matter."

"Well, one thing is apparent. It is bound to be an endless evening, lassie," Jamie said from his spot at the table. "Already I feel the cold creeping into these old bones."

"I can take care of that," replied Jeanne, moving gracefully to a corner of the room and returning with the stack of old newspaper Fergus had frugally saved for starting fires in the hearth. "There's a bit of coal put by," she said, beginning to crumple the yellowing sheets.

"Nay, that's not what I had in mind," Jamie said, staying her hand with his own. "A man needs to build a fire from within."

A jerk of his head toward the door sent a man scrambling outside to return with a keg of Jamie's best whisky. Soon the villagers were being warmed by the smoothness of its liquid fire, and even their anxiety seemed to lose its edge, as they continued to ponder their future.

"Are you certain you do not want to marry, Jeanne?" asked Geordie, tipping his glass to watch the amber whisky coat its sides. "If there's no one here in Linclachan to catch your fancy, we could look elsewhere. The eastern branch of the clan perhaps?"

"No, I've not seen anyone in our village, nor among the rest of the clan, to make me change my mind," Jeanne said with a small smile.

"Then can you be persuaded to take on the responsibilities of being laird yourself?" inquired Malcolm, and all present awaited the young woman's reply.

"I'd really rather not, if it can be avoided," Jeanne responded softly, busying herself with the newspapers so that the others would not see the regret reflected in her eyes. "Linclachan needs more than I can provide at present. Perhaps there is someone among the other branch of Donnachys and Robertsons who is better qualified."

"There's not a man there who is any wealthier than you. Besides, why would anyone want to take on the problems of a village not his own?" a voice in the back of the room intoned solemnly.

"Perhaps because the title earl of Lindall, laird of both the manor and Linclachan sounds more impressive than it actually is," Jeanne commented, a sad shadow passing across her striking features.

"But any real Scot would know it for what it is," stated Maggie, who, with Leslie, had come to stand beside Jeanne.

"Aye, Maggie. You speak true. What we need is some unsuspecting outsider," said Duncan with a comical wink, continuing to take advantage of his kinsman's largess by pouring another glass of whisky.

"A *rich,* unsuspecting outsider," corrected Jamie to the amusement of the others as he replenished his own drink.

"Someone like this," said Geordie with a grin, holding aloft a tattered piece of the newspaper that still rested on the table. "Here's a wealthy American, an enterprising fellow who has turned honest effort into a fortune worth over a million pounds."

"Who is the man?" asked Malcolm, his usually poor hearing made sharper by Geordie's mention of such a vast sum of money.

"C. Robertson Blake. According to the *Glasgow Tribune,* he has bought a small steel mill in England and was in Glasgow seeking to do business with the shipbuilders."

"Robertson, did you say?" asked Duncan. "Wouldn't it be a grand thing if he were related to us somewhere along the way?"

"Aye, we could make *him* our new laird," joked Jeanne, entering into the playful mood of the others, and disappointed when no laughter greeted her silliness.

"I wonder if we might manage to convince him that he is the rightful laird of Linclachan," Jamie said all too slowly and gravely for Jeanne's liking, as he took the article from Geordie.

"It says here that anything the man touches turns to gold, and everything that's his receives only the best of care," he continued, pointing out the line to the others. "In fact his grandfather was Scots, something the lad was quick enough to point out to the shipbuilders while trying to do business in Clydebank."

"I do not ken," Maggie was saying. "It's not as though he is actually one of us—"

"Give me that paper," Jeanne demanded, almost tearing it from Jamie's grasp when she realized just how serious the others were. "Why, this story is nearly a year old. The man is surely back in America by now."

"All the better," said Duncan, his eyes fired as much by craftiness as they were by the whisky. "Then he could have no idea of how poor the village really is."

"You're being ridiculous, all of you!" Jeanne nearly shouted. "What would a wealthy American want with Linclachan?"

"There is the title," Malcolm replied after considering the question. "And we all know how Americans feel about them."

"That's right!" agreed Geordie. "If we tell him he is the earl of Lindall, laird of the Donnachys and Robertsons alike, it just might entice him."

"He gets the title and we get the money, what could be a better scheme?" yelled one of the manor's tenants.

"But you're giving away our heritage," Leslie protested, finally daring to speak up to these fierce-looking men, old though they were.

"Aye, lass," answered Duncan sadly, "but only to preserve it."

"That's right. Without money in the coffers, this will be the last generation of Donnachys and Robertsons we see in Linclachan, and well we all know it," reproved Malcolm.

"But an American?" Maggie asked with a disapproving shake of her head.

"Desperate times call for desperate measures," Jamie said, shrugging his shoulders philosophically.

"And it's not as if a man of that sort would really settle in a little village such as ours. If we saw him once, likely it would be the end of it," Geordie added in support of his brother.

"In the meantime," interjected Duncan, "we'll have the benefit of his money. Now all we have to do is have Andrew draft a letter informing the American of his good fortune."

"And needless to say, not a one of us will tell the solicitor that Blake is not entitled to what we offer him," Malcolm enjoined shrewdly. "After all, we do not want to deal with Andrew's efforts to be appointed laird if he thinks a chance still exists."

"Agreed," yelled Linclachan's blacksmith. "'Twill be a conspiracy of silence."

"Easy enough to keep," shouted another, "when there's the possibility of so much money involved."

Jeanne could see from the growing excitement of the crowd that they were more intoxicated by hope than by the whisky they were consuming, and it took all of her strength not to fall prey to their enthusiasm. It was, after all, a foolish dream, an absurd idea.

"What about Jeanne?" demanded Leslie anxiously. "It's her home you're ready to give away. With the title goes Lindall Manor."

Suddenly silence fell upon the room, and all eyes were fixed on the tall, comely woman who stood with the council.

As she regarded them, Jeanne was put in mind of a group of small children who desperately yearned for some prohibitively expensive treat with very little hope of ever getting it. Their wistfulness tore at the pretty Scot's heart, and she found herself longing to make their wishes come true.

What harm would it do, after all, to say that she didn't mind if they offered C. Robertson Blake the title of laird? Let them write their letter. The rich American wouldn't likely be interested in such a poor little village in Scotland anyway. And until they received his reply, if he even bothered to send one, the people of Linclachan would have some dream to clutch at for the next few months, while she herself tried to come up with a solution to their dilemma.

There was an added incentive. Such a ruse would keep Andrew Robertson from her doorstep to be sure. If he supposed another man was to become the earl of Lindall, he'd have no further use for her. No, she mused with a thoughtful gleam in her dark green eyes, it wouldn't hurt to agree to this preposterous plan . . . at least for the time being.

"The good of Linclachan is what is most important. Send your letter and let's pray some good comes of it," Jeanne declared, her voice breathy as the result of her well-intentioned deceit. And while the cheers rose around her and Jamie embraced her in a rough hug, Jeanne smiled tremulously, glad she had allowed her kinsmen to have their fanciful dream, short-lived though it might be.

Chapter Two

Stepping from the oversize bath he'd had installed to accommodate his height more comfortably, Creag Robertson Blake stood straight, grabbed a waiting towel and with a practiced efficiency began to dry his muscular, well-built torso. A few quick swipes of the thirsty cloth over his broad shoulders was followed by a taut grip on the two ends of it as he whisked the cotton length briskly to and fro over his back and flanks. Though of English and Scottish extraction, Creag's muscular frame and straight blond hair were reminiscent of the invading Norsemen who had plundered Scotland and mingled their bloodlines with those people already living in the Highlands. A successful business tycoon at the young age of thirty, a man who did not believe in wasted time or effort, Creag reviewed the events of his day even as he finished drying off.

The excursion to the South Fork Hunting and Fishing Club in Johnstown had not been without merit, though the idea of membership in such an organization did not appeal to him at all. Unable to relax away from the pulsing excitement of financial negotiations and constant efforts to improve and enlarge his already-successful business, the Philadelphia entrepreneur could not imagine himself whiling away days at a time in a boat on a man-made lake or awaiting the appearance of a buck in the Pennsylvanian countryside, no matter how picturesque it might be. He had far too much to accomplish in life to waste time on mere pleasure.

Still, one did not refuse an invitation from Andrew Carnegie, and the fact that the renowned financier had included him in the day's fishing expedition was a source of considerable satisfaction, Creag acknowledged. Associating with the likes of Fish, Mellon and Carnegie would certainly not hurt his reputation in the financial community. Indeed, even today, two of the members of the club had casually inquired about the availability of his steel for future projects. Yes, the day had gone well but, at the moment, his concern was for the evening ahead, one which could well determine the rest of his life.

Should he shave again? Examining his finely chiseled features in the mirror above the sink, annoyed as ever at the unaccountable cleft in his otherwise well-defined chin, Creag considered the faint growth of whiskers on his lower face and frowned. Well, there was no avoiding it; he'd best shave if he were to impress the Graysons. He'd waited long enough for this invitation to dine at their home; he'd not appear less than immaculately groomed.

In the space of an instant, the tall male had wrapped the towel about his middle, removed his razor from the cabinet, sharpened it on a strop hanging from the wall, and begun lathering the soap while his mind turned to the delightful prospect of seeing Catherine Grayson again. Not only beautiful and pleasant to be with, she seemed attracted to him and, above all, she was socially flawless.

Having made her debut nearly two years ago, the lovely blonde gave every evidence of enjoying the busy whirl of obligations required by one of Philadelphia's finest families. She had been in no hurry to attach herself to a husband, but was often the center of a large crowd of admiring friends, male and female alike. On the few occasions he'd been able to penetrate her circle and capture her interest, Creag remembered, she had been a superlative example of sparkling, fluttering femininity, so much so in fact, that it made him nearly ache to take her in his arms and flaunt proper society as he plied her with improper kisses.

Yes, the man who'd so recently come to question his single state reflected, as he carefully held the skin of his left cheek and swiped at the sudsy whiskers awaiting his attention, life with Catherine could prove quite amusing. She would be an asset to his existence, capable of giving him not only the home and family he was ready for, but a more acceptable image among the main-liners of Philadelphia, as well. Not that he was ashamed of his immigrant grandparents, he told himself, splashing cool water on his face to remove the lingering traces of soap. The Blakes of England and the Robertsons of Scotland had been hardworking and well-respected people, but they didn't lend the aura of power and importance that a liaison with the Graysons would provide. For her part, were such a union to transpire, Catherine would enjoy anything that his fortune could offer her, a prospect that would most probably delight her material nature.

In fact, Creag acknowledged as he entered his bedroom and began to don the finely fashioned male underclothes already laid out, he suspected all that was necessary to make her his were the formalities with her family. Tonight's ordeal should be the final foray into her world as an outsider; soon, he'd be able to publicly admit his assault on her heart. Then, with her parents' acquiescence to his courtship, Catherine would be able to see him alone regularly and consider his overtures without reservation, setting the stage for their engagement and marriage. His fortune was made, his business secure, now, his personal life deserved the same measure of success.

Though the lovely young woman had unofficially encouraged his attentions for nearly a month, dancing with him three or four times in an evening, riding alone with him in a carriage by the river—once even changing seats to sit beside him at the theater—Catherine had been reluctant for him to approach her parents. Threading the ivory stays into his shirt collar, Creag wondered anew if she could be ashamed of his lack of family connections. It hadn't seemed to matter when she glided so gracefully in his arms under the stars at the Wilsons' gala or when she'd chosen him over Jonathan Enright IV as a tennis partner. Yet the green-eyed vixen had not only postponed this meeting with her parents time and again, she had allowed Philip Danforth to escort her home from church last week. Well, mused the financier, inserting his gold studs through his shirtfront, tonight would tell. Surely this private dinner with her parents was meant to be an evening that belonged to Catherine and him.

"Creag?" came a voice from the hall.

"Come in, Michael, come in."

"Henderson said you wanted to see me before you left," said the tall dark-haired young man, removing his glasses and rubbing the bridge of his nose as he entered and settled himself in a chair by the fireplace. "Sorry I'm late, but I wanted to clear up the paperwork on the Porter deal. Everything is transcribed and on your desk at the office. All that's needed now are the signatures tomorrow."

"Excellent, Michael. Porter will be by around ten. Not that I ever doubted you'd sort out the details. In fact, that's the only reason I dared take the day off today," admitted Creag as his good friend and private secretary poured a whisky from the waiting decanter. "Get me one of those, will you? I must admit, I'm a bit nervous about meeting the Graysons."

"But you worked with him on the Lincoln Bridge project, didn't you?" asked Michael in surprise, taking a second glass and obliging his friend. Creag Robertson Blake was not a man to be anxious about anything, from buying unproven small business firms to making enormous financial commitments on the strength of a handshake. He often said he could tell a man's character by the way he greeted a stranger, and Michael had never known him to be wrong. "What's so different about tonight?"

"First, I'll be in his mansion, not a business office where I know my way around. Second, he'll be the one with the upper hand—he's not after anything. I am. Unless I pass muster with the Graysons, I won't be able to win their approval of my courtship of Catherine."

"Surely the sight of your bankbooks will do that! Just let one or two of them accidentally fall out of your pocket."

"If only it were that easy, Michael," Creag said with a chuckle and a sad shake of his head, accepting his drink and taking a sip before he continued. "Unfortunately, snobbery runs rampant through this town, and since my ancestors didn't arrive with William Penn, I fear that I'm bucking tradition by daring to even dream of courting Catherine Grayson. From what I hear, some of these old Philadelphia families would prefer a son-in-law who was a well-connected pauper to a wealthy man who didn't possess a recognized lineage."

"Surely you're overstating the issue. With your education and business successes, how can anything else make a hoot of difference? Besides, if Catherine is everything you say she is, won't she just tell her parents she wants you and settle the whole matter?''

"I'm not sure. As much as I think she cares for me, sometimes there's this calculating, almost cold side to her that makes me wonder."

"Nonsense, Creag! She more than cares for you. Take my word for it. Why else would she let you know her plans each week so we could get you the right invitations in time for you to be wherever she is?''

"Well, we can only hope you're right and the Graysons are more concerned with their daughter's happiness than my pedigree. Give me a hand with this tie, would you?'' asked the financier, after fussing unsuccessfully with the formal attire's most aggravating accessory. "By the way, I still owe you for all that social finagling you had to do, but you know I appreciate it.''

"So, name the first child after me." Michael laughed.

"You may joke, but I know that invitation to the Dennison affair was especially prized."

"Listen, after ten years of doing the impossible for you, what I can't do can't be done,'' Michael boasted with a chuckle, working his magic on the recalcitrant tie. "What was it you wanted to see me about anyway?''

"I've been thinking it over and I've decided we should go to Scotland next month. After all, there's nothing like face-to-face negotiations. Anyway, I need you to contact the shipping line and make sure we have the best accommodations they offer. Something midships above the promenade deck, preferably,'' said the blond, blue-eyed businessman. "Now, tell me, do I look like a man the Graysons would accept into the family?''

"Only if they want a handsome, intelligent, eligible, eminently respectable and rich son-in-law. Seriously, except for your foolish nerves, you are the best possible candidate Catherine could hope for.''

"Thanks, Michael. I always knew I kept you around for something other than your organizational skills. You lie convincingly, which is a real asset in business,'' explained Creag, straightening the already-perfect tie once more. "Well, good night, then.''

"Oh, while I'm thinking of it, there was an odd piece of mail that came in the afternoon post from Scotland. It was marked personal, so I brought it home and left it on the desk in the library," the secretary announced. "If you're in a hurry, I'm certain it can wait until tomorrow. Enjoy yourself."

"Personal? I don't know anyone in Scotland, other than the men at the shipyards, but that's all business. Besides, friends have my home address for personal mail," mused the financier, impatient now to be on his way.

Despite the qualms he'd voiced to his secretary, Creag Robertson Blake was actually a man of extreme confidence. He decided on a course of action and embarked on it without second-guessing himself, treating his private life much as he did his business enterprises. Such behavior had allowed him to become well-known and respected in financial circles by the tender age of thirty. This fact made it highly unusual that his normal assurance had deserted him now that he had decided to undertake a romantic venture, leaving him peculiarly anxious to begin the trial ahead and thus dispense with his growing apprehension.

Reminding himself, as he descended the stairs from his bedroom, that he usually got what he wanted, Creag acknowledged that at least he already knew Bartholomew Grayson. Actually, the man had been quite reasonable, indeed cooperative, in their business associations. Still, sitting across from the fellow in a corporate boardroom negotiating land access was far different than seeing him across a dinner table when the main item on the agenda was an opening bid for his daughter's hand in marriage.

However, Creag shrugged with a glance at his pocket watch while crossing the main hall, if he wanted Miss Grayson, there wasn't much chance of avoiding tonight's awkward confrontation, but at least there was time for another drink before he faced the inquisition.

Entering the library to pour himself a short whisky, the businessman thought a moment, added a healthy splash of water and noticed the foreign envelope on his desk with sudden interest. Maybe the letter Michael had brought home would occupy his mind until it was time to leave for the Graysons', he mused, as he took his drink to the desk and settled himself behind its massive bulk.

With an eye on the library clock to assure himself he wouldn't be late, Creag slit open the missive and began to read with interest.

My dear Mr. Blake:

As solicitor for the estate of the late Fergus Donnachy, earl of Lindall, I find it my considered duty to inform you that by means of a relationship through your mother's paternal grandfather, Charles Robertson, you appear to be the laird's closest living male relative, and, therefore, his heir.

Although Lord Lindall left no will, and it has taken considerable time and effort on my part to trace the lineage of the clan, I can assure you that the villagers of Linclachan, Donnachys and Robertsons alike, stand ready to welcome you to their fold as the sixth earl and laird.

I have taken the liberty of enclosing a listing of the properties and holdings of the laird and trust I will hear from you in short order.

Yours,
Andrew Robertson, Esquire

Earl of Lindall? Laird? Was it possible, wondered Creag, rereading the odd letter a second time before turning to the other pages: lists of tenants, subtenants and the acreage each held, as well as the names of the crofters and cotters of Linclachan, a map of the Highlands with the Donnachy lands carefully noted, some distance north of Glasgow, and a small map of the village itself. Could he, who'd just moments before been concerned with heritage, actually be a Scottish nobleman?

For several idle moments, Creag Robertson Blake found himself considering life in the old Scotland, an existence in which he was lord of the manor, responsible for the welfare of pensioners and farmers, dairy maids and shepherds, whisky makers and Highland warriors. He'd managed companies with more employees than this little piece of Scotland appeared to support. Surely the job couldn't be that difficult, and if the title had once belonged to his maternal ancestors, it would be disloyal not to pursue the matter....

But then reality emerged and he laughed aloud, picturing himself in an isolated Scottish castle with no running water or electricity, no telegraph—hardly the place from which to run a successful steel business, and certainly not the ideal spot from which to court a fashionable Philadelphia debutante! Besides, the lawyer seemed to be looking for recompense for his time and effort already. The very idea of it was preposterous. Still, it would bear some thought, he imagined, and perhaps a bit of investigation, his mood greatly lightened by the unexpected letter—until he turned once more to the clock.

Oh, damn! The time had apparently escaped him, he realized, as the chimes for the half hour sounded. He had barely thirty minutes to get across town before he disgraced himself by being late. What a foul way to begin the evening, he brooded, calling anxiously for his carriage, a suddenly harried, nervous suitor replacing the calm, assured businessman of only minutes before.

Catherine examined her image in the mirror as her lady's maid waited nearby to dress her hair.

"You don't suppose the décolletage is too daring, do you, Martha? I want to entice Mr. Blake, not scandalize him."

"I'd worry less about Mr. Blake's reaction and more about your father's, Miss Catherine, if I were you. You know he isn't too happy with your little party this evening as it is," warned the servant as she began to brush her mistress's hair and pin it up in a fashionable mass of curls.

"Oh, but it isn't a little party anymore, is it?" reminded the socialite. "I can't imagine why Mother thought a dinner for twelve was too intimate. She and Daddy were going to be here, for heaven's sake."

"How many are coming now?"

"Thirty or forty, I think. I'm afraid Creag is going to be awfully upset. I just know he was going to broach Daddy about courting me." Catherine frowned. "Now, heaven knows when he'll commit himself."

"Ah, the problems of young love," said the maid with a sigh, affixing small bows of ivory lace to the stylishly coiffed hair.

"Love? I don't know about that, but Creag is awfully handsome and ever so much more wealthy than any of the others who want to be my beau. Besides, from what Mother says, love only comes along after the marriage, so it's just as easy to marry a rich man and love him as a poor one. And Creag is terribly nice to be with. He spoils me wonderfully with compliments and little gifts."

"He makes you happy?"

"Oh, yes, except when he tries to steal kisses," confided Catherine. "But then I suppose he can't help himself. He's so much more a man than Jonathan or Philip. It comes from his common bloodlines, to be sure. Still, I trust I shall have no trouble controlling that aspect of his nature once we are wed."

"Well, there you are, miss," the maid said, biting her lip to forestall a comment as she completed her final touches. "You're all set to be the belle of the ball."

"With only a dozen other women invited, that won't be difficult." Catherine laughed as she pinched her cheeks and headed for the door. "Indeed, it shall be great fun."

Fun, however, was not the way Creag Robertson Blake would have described his predicament in the slow-moving traffic along the streets of fashionable Philadelphia.

"Why is it taking so long?" he demanded irritably, poking his head through the window to question his driver when the carriage had barely moved fifty feet in ten minutes. "I'm very nearly late, and it's not as if I could arrive at the Grayson Mansion on foot."

"I'm sorry, Mr. Blake, but it seems these other vehicles are all going to the Graysons', as well."

"What?" Catherine had specifically told him that her parents had invited him to dinner to get better acquainted. Why would others be attending? "Are you certain?"

"Theirs is the only house with a hedged entryway, sir, and that's where everyone is turning. Don't worry, if you're late, so are all the fellows behind us, too," consoled his longtime driver. "You won't be last, not by a far cry."

"Well, do the best you can," said Creag, looking out the back of the carriage in astonishment at the line of crawling conveyances behind him. It appeared this wasn't to be the quiet evening he had envisioned.

* * *

Inside the front door of the elegant mansion, the receiving line was mercifully short: Catherine and her parents. Dressed in a soft lavender silk gown, its enticingly sculpted bodice edged with pale ivory lace, which was echoed in the panels of her skirt and at the edges of her snug-fitting sleeves, the young woman appeared more bewitching than usual, Creag reflected, unless it was the growing possibility of winning her that made it seem so.

"Mother, Daddy, this is C. Robertson Blake. Creag to his friends," the delicate blonde said softly, directing a bright smile in his direction as she placed a small hand on his arm to guide him forward. A brief squeeze of her long fingers suggested pleasure at seeing him, but the touch was gone before he could acknowledge its occurrence. "Creag, I'd like you to meet my parents, Alma and Bartholomew Grayson. I've told them all about you, though of course, you've met Daddy."

"Mrs. Grayson, sir, it is my pleasure. I thank you for having me, though I didn't realize tonight would be such a large gathering," Creag offered tentatively, as he bent low over Mrs. Grayson's hand. "I had hoped to spend some time with Catherine."

"Well, of course, that's why everyone is here," agreed Alma Grayson with a quick nod of her head. "All her friends enjoy my daughter's company."

"All her friends?"

"Of course, there's Roderick Cooke IV, James Hutcheson, Philip Danforth, and ever so many more," announced Catherine's mother, her voice giving clear evidence of her delight at the many male guests in attendance. "My daughter is ever so popular with everyone, you know."

"Yes, she is quite a special young woman," agreed the successful steel magnate, quickly revising his plan for the evening. Turning to Mr. Grayson, Creag addressed his next remark to him. "Catherine's wonderful spirit and enthusiasm for life are among the qualities I value most, and part of the reason I intended to speak with you alone tonight, sir."

For a long moment, Bartholomew Grayson held Creag's eyes, as if taking his measure before abruptly nodding.

"I imagined you might, which is why I encouraged Alma to invite some of the young gentlemen Catherine has known since childhood, sons of old Philly families. I've found that before one takes a risk on a new venture, it never hurts to compare the untried newcomer with old reliable stock."

"Sir, I hardly think—" But before Creag could question his host's turn of phrase, the man was speaking again.

"Sorry if my choice of words isn't to your liking, Blake, but don't despair, I shall give you a fair hearing later on. My daughter is too important to me to do otherwise," promised the Philadelphian main-liner. "For now though, Catherine, you are holding up the receiving line with all this attention to one guest. Isn't that Jonathan Enright IV behind Mr. Blake? His father and I are on the board of First Federal Bank, you know."

Finding himself so curtly dismissed, Creag had no choice but to move forward into the crush of other guests, though his eyes lingered on Catherine as she allowed Enright to take her hand and kiss it. While part of him longed to reclaim his coat and depart, that would be what the elder Graysons were hoping, and he'd be damned if he gave them the satisfaction. Tonight might not be what he'd planned, but Creag Robertson Blake was a man who made the best of bad circumstances, more often than not turning a tidy profit in the process. Indeed, he decided to view this evening as the start of a difficult business acquisition and handle himself accordingly.

Thus, with a polite nod of thanks, the handsomely attired man accepted a glass of champagne from a passing waiter and smiled politely, masking the disappointment he felt. He'd best Grayson at his own game, demonstrating clearly who among the guests was truly better bred. With a fierce effort of determination, Creag donned his social graces and began to greet the gentlemen he knew, and make the acquaintance of those he didn't, clearly at ease in the heady company of Philadelphia's finest families.

Circulating smoothly through the crowded room, the financier laid the foundation for future deals, acknowledged the best wishes of several businessmen whose notes he held, and others who wished his support in their enterprises, while doing his utmost to avoid the avid stares of the few single women present.

All the while, however, he pointedly took frequent opportunities to glance in Catherine's direction and nod or send a sympathetic look, leaving no one any doubt where his attention was centered.

Batholomew Grayson watched the young man's progress around the room, noting with surprise the ready welcome he was given by the vast majority of guests. Speaking mechanically to the men and women streaming by as his daughter introduced them, Grayson found his attention irresistibly drawn to Blake, totally unacceptable though the man was. Damn, but the fellow had a certain flair and considerable worth, if money were the only measure. It was just too bad the match would have to be thwarted. Grayson frowned; Catherine might be awfully disappointed for a while. Still, as a concerned parent, he had no other choice. It simply would not do for her to marry beneath her. The sooner she realized how unsuitable Blake was, the better it would be for all concerned.

"Alma," he said abruptly, as the arrival of guests finally ceased so they could speak to each other. "Have one of the maids see to the seating arrangements. I want Blake on my left."

"But I have him at the other end of the table next to me, paired with the Locke girl," murmured Mrs. Grayson, nodding as Catherine excused herself to circulate gracefully among her friends though she seemed to be moving pointedly in that unfortunate man's direction. "I thought you said you wanted him as far from Catherine as possible."

"I do, ultimately, which is why I want him near me at dinner tonight. Purely temporary, I assure you. Arrange it," Batholomew Grayson decreed. And Alma went to obey.

Catherine allowed herself a small sigh of gratitude as she left her parents and studied the large room, seeking Creag's tall, broad-shouldered form. With his rugged good looks and debonair manner, not to mention his fabled wealth, he was, as usual, at the center of a curious crowd, nodding politely at those who held his ear even as he met her eyes and smiled. Suddenly the chiseled planes of his face disappeared as genuine pleasure registered when Creag realized she was finally coming to join him. Quickly he excused himself from his companions and moved toward her to shorten her journey. She rewarded him with a smile of her own, her expression acknowledging for all to see that he held her interest.

"Join me on the balcony for a few minutes before dinner is announced," she said softly, standing on tiptoe to whisper her invitation to him. "We can talk."

"So will a lot of other people should we do so," Creag murmured, as he noticed just how many of the guests were watching them. Though he would have liked nothing better than to follow her suggestion, such an action would do neither her reputation nor his cause any good. "Don't worry. I know tonight's change in plans wasn't your doing."

"No, really, until this afternoon, I thought it was only a small dinner—"

"My dear Miss Grayson," he interrupted, for the benefit of those pressing closer to eavesdrop, "though I am certainly not the first to tell you so this evening, I must compliment you on how lovely you look. You're absolutely radiant in that gown."

"I think it's the company rather than the gown that causes the effect, but thank you," flirted the young woman.

"I can only hope I have the honor of being your dinner partner, though I fear every other man present has the same desire," continued Creag gallantly.

"I—I'm not certain. Mother made up the seating—"

"Of course you and Blake are paired for dinner, Catherine," interrupted her father, coming to stand between the handsome couple. "In fact, the two of you are seated on either side of me so I can get to know more about this gentleman friend of yours. Having no knowledge of his family leaves me at a disadvantage."

Hearing the unmistakable challenge in his host's words, Creag nodded pleasantly nonetheless, determined to maintain his composure despite the man's rudeness. Heaven only knows what Grayson had in mind, though he feared it did not presage well for his courtship of Catherine.

Not at all to Creag's surprise, the meal was as uncomfortable an ordeal as any he had ever suffered; time and again his character and reputation were indirectly skewed by his host while he could but sit politely, pretending to ignore the pointed insinuations. Bartholomew Grayson took every opportunity to applaud the accomplishments, no matter how minor, of each of the other young men at the table, deliberately dismissing the phenomenal successes C. Robertson Blake had achieved. Indeed, when Hutcheson actually complimented the young financier on his growing association with Andrew Carnegie, Catherine's father reviled even that Scotsman.

"Carnegie? Bah, nothing but another upstart immigrant trying to prove himself better than the good people born and bred on these shores," snorted Grayson. "If you don't like the Biddles or the Dukes, what about Milton? Now, there's an American of good stock and reputation."

"I believe he's much too old for me, Father, and married besides," intervened Catherine with a laugh.

"Perhaps," drawled her father, his eyes narrowing as he tried to calculate his daughter's current interest in Blake. Surely she understood by now just how unsuitable the man was. Unable to decide, Grayson turned back to those candidates at the table he considered eligible. "Danforth, I understand congratulations are in order. You've enlarged your grandfather's company to the point of breaking ground for new offices?"

"Actually that's been postponed, sir, thanks to Blake, here. His title company found a problem that would have hindered clear ownership of the property for years. I don't mind telling you his expertise has saved the Danforths a good bit of trouble."

"Humph." Grayson was obviously displeased to hear words of praise for the man he considered an adversary in the matter of his daughter's happiness. "Well then, shall we adjourn to the library for brandy and cigars, gentlemen?"

It was not until they rejoined the ladies and Catherine was again within hearing distance that Grayson intensified his attack. Obviously his praise of others was too subtle a rejection of Blake for Catherine to take to heart and he couldn't very well forbid her to see him or she'd be all the more determined to do so. No, to embarrass him so completely that he'd not be welcomed in polite company was the only remaining tactic determined the father of the would-be bride.

Following the last of his guests into the drawing room, the gray-haired patriarch cleared his throat and sent his sharp-edged tones cutting through the lesser conversations about the room, effectively calling his guests to silent attention.

"Blake, I said earlier that I know little of your family, yet you've done nothing to alleviate that shortcoming. I should think you would want to do so—unless, of course, you're ashamed of your heritage?"

For a long moment, Creag stood stock-still, answering the audacious charge with only an icy stare, severely tempted to turn on his heel and leave the assembly rather than reply to such a blatant insult. Still, the youthful businessman decided, as Catherine met his glance, perhaps it was better to grasp the viper by the head when it first threatened and immobilize it rather than wait for a lethal sting.

"Not at all, sir, though I fail to see what impact my ancestors could possibly have on my relationship with Catherine, nor what interest such a matter could be for your guests."

"Then there is something in the Blake pedigree you'd prefer to keep behind closed doors?" ventured Grayson, his face beginning to flush in anticipation of what he perceived as victory.

"You are sadly mistaken, Mr. Grayson. Without exception, my family led good Christian lives and have passed on to their eternal reward, leaving me as the sole repository of their name and reputation."

"I'll tell you something, Blake," sputtered Catherine's father in annoyance. "Unless a man's roots are deeply planted in healthy soil, he is likely to be unstable, easily thwarted by the ill winds of life, perhaps even capricious in his affairs, in short, a man I couldn't trust with my horse, let alone my daughter."

"There's not a person in this room who can do anything other than attest to the reliability of the Blake name in business and commerce, sir," said Creag sharply, his face coloring at the import of the man's remarks. "Besides, I find those people overly concerned with other's roots are themselves too often root bound, stodgy and conservative to the point that their very lives wither and rot for lack of any activity and their descendants suffer the same ailment."

"Why, I never—"

"You know full well I can easily support your daughter and care for her. However, if I cannot court Catherine on my own merits without depending on my family pedigree for your approval, I question whether or not I want to do so," challenged the blue-eyed financier, his glance cold and determined.

"Oh, Creag, you can't mean that?" Catherine cried anxiously, hurrying to his side as she envisioned the wealthy bachelor abandoning his suit. Even if she decided to reject him later, being courted by the wealthiest man in Philadelphia would make her the center of social attention. She was determined not to be deprived of such a distinction. "Father, please, be reasonable."

"If Blake is unwilling to acquit himself honorably in the matter of his lineage, my dear, there is nothing more to say. I will not give you over to a man without a background."

"Creag," the young woman pleaded, a small hand pressing urgently on his arm. As she blinked her large green eyes, they began to fill with tears and Creag found himself weakening at her sadness. Maybe it wouldn't hurt to appease her father, a little bit, anyway.

"My family ties are English and Scottish, sir, not as grand as some perhaps, but I've no cause to be ashamed of my people, nor would Catherine," he said quietly, patting the delicate fingers that still clutched at his coat.

"But is there any cause for pride, son?" demanded Bartholomew Grayson. "After all, an absence of scandal is no cause for celebration and a far cry from a good reason to allow my daughter to take your name. After all, your people have not been here very long. You are not like us. What value can your name have?"

"Aside from the wealth attached to it, I'll have you know that my family is just as impressive as yours," Creag retorted, his patience with his host's public condescension at an end.

"Really?" Grayson queried, his tone and expression blatantly patronizing.

"Yes, really. I have a small estate in the Highlands of Scotland. In fact, I've just received word that the old laird has died and I am the new earl of Lindall," continued an infuriated Creag, the fateful words escaping before he could stop them, setting off a sudden murmur in the room.

"Earl? Why, that means you're a lord, darling, how positively wonderful," bubbled Catherine in excitement. "Then I would be a lady! Daddy, you must accept Creag's suit now. Oh, darling, you should have told us sooner."

"Or perhaps I shouldn't have mentioned it at all," murmured the steel magnate, already regretting his premature announcement. He knew nothing of Linclachan, or the validity of his claim. He hadn't even set in motion an investigation of the matter yet. What if the solicitor had been mistaken?

"What? Oh, don't be ridiculous, son," scolded a changed Grayson, slapping him on the shoulder and leading him toward a secluded corner of the drawing room. "You know, this is nothing to hide. A title can be a marvelous aid in society, one I'm certain I can help you use to your advantage."

"Then I am welcome to call on your daughter?" asked Creag coolly, though he struggled to be polite in the face of his fury at the man's sudden reversal of tone and his own careless adoption of a Scottish inheritance he had no knowledge of before today.

"Why, yes. At any time."

"Good, I thank you for a most interesting evening. I'm sorry, but I must take my leave since I've pressing business early tomorrow. Catherine, may I have a word with you?"

"Of course, Creag, dear," the young woman agreed, her eyes still aglitter at the thought of being nobility. "I knew you were the man for me," she confided at the door. "It just took a little while longer to convince Daddy."

"Aye," said her suitor, his mind ajumble at the faux pas he'd committed. But then, the woman he had decided upon was in his arms, her lips searching for and finding his, offering tenderness and sweet reward for the evening, and Creag forgot all else.

Chapter Three

After totaling the column of figures for the third time and arriving at the same discouraging sum, Jeanne laid down her pen and shook her weary head in dismay. No matter how carefully she managed the estate, safeguarding every pence, questioning every expenditure, avoiding all nonessential costs, she did not see how she could possibly gather the funds needed to repay the bank. How could old Fergus have been so foolhardy as to risk Linclachan's existence on a loan from a Lowland bank? And, more urgently, what in blazes had he done with the money?

To be sure, she could account for some of it in the purchase of seed and tools, new livestock to replace what they'd lost in the unusually rugged winter, even the vestments he'd ordered for the church, but what had happened to the rest? Despite her careful perusal of her grandfather's books and papers, begrudgingly turned over to her by Andrew Robertson, Jeanne couldn't make sense of his ledger entries. Yet when she'd questioned the solicitor who'd handled the manor's transactions, he claimed to know nothing, only that Fergus had given the books into his keeping shortly before the laird died. Damn, but if she'd found even some of the money her grandfather had borrowed and returned it to the bank, she might have been able to buy time, she mused, still determined to do all she could to prevent Linclachan's becoming extinct.

In the meantime, the council's great scheme of a rescue by the wealthy American had come to naught. Jeanne frowned. Not that she had expected anything different, but the old men continued to fret over their pints at Blake's lack of a reply. Well, it had been a wild ruse from the start, she reflected, regretting the way she'd encouraged their hopes of a miracle. Yet, tireless as she'd been over the past two months, her own efforts to secure Linclachan's future hadn't done any better. She, too, had met with no success, even in the matter of allaying Andrew Robertson's interest in her.

Thoughts of the obnoxiously persistent solicitor sent an unwelcome shiver down her spine, making Jeanne rise and start for the open window, intent on closing out the late-afternoon chill. Frugal to the point of restricting fires in all but the main hall and the kitchen, she couldn't very well light the kindling in the laird's old study when closing a window and donning a heavier shawl would achieve the same warmth.

Suddenly a loud commotion in the courtyard below distracted her and made the dark-haired beauty hesitate to pull the open shutters toward her. The study was at the back of the house, overlooking the open yard formed by the two wings of the U-shaped building. At the moment, an unfamiliar wagon had pulled in and its driver was arguing with Ewan, the laird's longtime estate hand. Surely it was nothing he couldn't handle, she thought, not wanting to interfere, yet reluctant to miss the excitement.

"Without proper authority I can't admit you to Lindall Manor, no matter how willing you are to work," Ewan was shouting, only to be ignored by the large man he addressed.

"And I'm telling you the laird himself sent me here! How much higher an authority do you need?" exploded the angry giant of a man, an Englishman by the sound of him, as he jumped down from the front seat of the wagon. He easily stood more than six feet, solid muscle and brawn, obviously used to physical labor—and being in charge. "We're here, men, stretch yourselves before we begin unloading."

At his word the others with him swarmed off their heavily laden wagon and stood around their leader, a few lighting pipes, others clearly ready to join in whatever brawl was to come.

"Now look here, I said we weren't expecting you and can't put you up," repeated Ewan, his weathered face growing red in exasperation at the other's disregard of his orders.

The newcomers in the meantime began to mutter among themselves, clearly as disgruntled at the welcome they found as their foreman. Whatever their purpose in coming to Lindall Manor, Jeanne considered from her vantage point above the fray, they hadn't expected to meet resistance.

"The laird sent us and stay we will, little man," bellowed the leader of the group.

"Be gone with your nonsense. The laird is in the ground nigh on three months and we've neither the means nor reason to house a troop of vagabonds," snarled Ewan. "I'll not be having you upset Mistress Jeanne. Get back on your wagon and be off with the lot of you or I'll call out the dogs to speed you on your way now."

Debating whether or not to interfere at the risk of challenging Ewan's ability to deal with the situation, Jeanne couldn't help but chuckle in amusement at his threat. The dogs he referred to were a trio of old hunters, half-blind, who dozed by the kitchen hearth when not eating or relieving themselves. They didn't even scare the manor cats anymore. Still, the strangers wouldn't know that.

"What of that mythical Highlands hospitality the Scottish are always touting?" demanded the man holding the reins of the now skittish horses, reacting to the angry mutterings of the crowd. "Aren't you supposed to make newcomers welcome?"

"Consider it your welcome that I haven't set the master's hounds on you already. Now, be off!"

"The new laird will not be taking kindly to your manners, sir. I wouldn't doubt you'll soon be seeking a new position," said the group's large spokesman in an overly casual tone.

"*The new laird?*" questioned Jeanne from the open window. Her voice drew the attention of the men below as they suddenly doffed their caps and grinned broadly, well pleased at the sight of the slender, fetching lass above them. Her curls, caught by the wind, swirled merrily away from her face, emphasizing the high cheekbones, soft mouth and large eyes.

"Aye, mistress, C. Robertson Blake."

Oh, Lord! Unable to speak for her amazement, Jeanne felt herself growing unaccountably warm as she realized the import of the man's words. The bloody American had taken the bait after all! But . . . was the hook set deeply enough for them to reel him in all the way? Could a foreigner truly be Linc-lachan's salvation?

"Tell me then, sir, is Blake with you?" she called.

"Blimey, no, mistress. He's sent us on to survey the place and see what needs doing, and from what I see down here, that's plenty. I'm his foreman, George Clinton, and I do plasterwork and ceilings while Johnson here is an ace at roofing, shingle and thatch, as needed..." He hadn't expected to have to justify his arrival, George thought, but when the woman asking was as pleasant a sight as this one, he had no objections to detailing every last man's duties. "Over there is Weaver and he's our carpenter while Potter—"

"Fine, fine, I'm certain you are all experts at your jobs," Jeanne interrupted, "but it's getting on toward evening. Ewan, show the men to the kitchen and have Mary rustle up some ale and oatcakes. I'll be down as soon as I've sent word to the council."

"Aye, mistress."

Closing the window and looking back to the statements awaiting payment on the laird's scarred desk, Jeanne felt a momentary stab of panic at the course on which they'd embarked. Yet, Blake was apparently spending money already, sending craftsmen to tend the old manor house and make it ready for his arrival. If he was so enthusiastic and foolish as to invest in Linclachan without first exploring it, what would a few more overdue notes be to a man like that? And, more importantly, who was Jeanne Donnachy to worry about the justice of it all?

Four nights later the elders of the clan sat alone in Jamie's cottage, delighting in the taste of his private stock, whisky he'd aged nearly twenty years for special occasions and, in their minds, this certainly qualified.

"Ah, Malcolm, I never thought it would work, a wild scheme like that one," mused Duncan, holding his glass to the light and admiring its ruddy hue before enjoying a hefty swallow.

"Don't forget who saw the paper and suggested Blake for our laird," said Geordie. "We'd not be here celebrating were it not for me. None of you saw the man's name in that newspaper."

"Right, man, and we thank you for it," agreed Malcolm, well accustomed to humoring the brewer of ale. "But, better we thank the laird when he arrives. Could anyone have expected things to turn out so well?"

"Nay. Lindall Manor is being spruced up like a bride for her wedding night." Jamie chortled, his eyes sparkling at the far-off memory of his own bride. "Jeanne says the men are stripping out the old wood in the back staircases and rebuilding them as though Blake might actually have a staff to fill the servants' quarters."

"I can't imagine Jeanne Donnachy living below stairs," sputtered Duncan, the very idea making him spill some of his precious drink.

"Maybe not, but Blake has already done miracles for Linclachan," reminded Jamie. "For five years MacRae's tavern has stood almost deserted, now in the space of four days, Tammas and Leish have set it to rights and it's busy every night. Why, Tammas tells me Blake's lads drink like they've hollow legs. He has Jock busy carting supplies to keep up with them."

"Is it any wonder?" asked Geordie. "Those Englishmen have never tasted real whisky like yours nor a hardy brew like mine."

"Geordie's right," agreed Malcolm. "Why, before the man himself has even arrived, he's brought more life to the village than we've seen in years. A toast to C. Robertson Blake—long may he live and breathe as laird of Lindall."

"Does anyone know what the *C* stands for?" asked Jamie absently as he hoisted his glass.

"Aye, cold hard currency," muttered Malcolm solemnly, before he broke into a grin, joining in the gleeful laughter of the others.

"Actually I think his name is Creag," said Duncan when the amusement of his companions had died down.

"At least that marks him as a true son of Scotland," said Jamie with approbation. "I think that calls for another drink in the unsuspecting devil's honor."

"Here, here," echoed the others, rising slowly on legs made unsteady by liquor, yet determined to salute their newfound laird and their own devious cleverness, as well.

* * *

"I tell you, Leslie, you must have seen it for yourself since you've moved in to keep me company. Blake has to be an absolute tyrant," fussed Jeanne, her usual composure more unsettled by each day's dealings with the workmen. It was time for afternoon tea, but they were alone in the large kitchen, enjoying relative privacy since the men refused to stop their chores. "His crew work like slaves, barely taking time to eat, from sunrise to sunset, as though death might be the penalty if everything is not to their master's liking."

"Jeanne, you exaggerate so," chided her companion with a shake of her head. "They'd just rather spend their free time at the tavern with Geordie's brew in hand than here with a cup of tea and us for company. Besides, look at all they've done."

"Aside from poking and snooping in every nook and cranny of the manor house?"

"You must admit Fergus's old suite of rooms has never looked more regal or better outfitted," pressed Leslie as she helped herself to another cup of tea, surprised at her friend's attitude.

"Why not, when they filched pieces from all over the manor to accommodate one man? The cherry-wood cabinet I'd used for my clothes had been my mother's, but now it goes to the laird's room. Blake will probably need it to store his long trousers. Heaven knows how much room such outfits take up."

"I know," giggled the small blonde across the table. "Isn't it strange not to be able to see their legs? I'd never thought about it, but a man's calves tell you so much."

"About what's above, you mean?" smiled the dark-haired steward. "Fergus used to say any fellow afraid to show his legs was no man at all. You know, he swore Andrew used padding to fill out his hose and display a good line."

"As if any woman in her right mind would look twice at Andrew," said Leslie with a grimace. "No matter how hefty his calf, his mind is too empty to offer much in the way of satisfaction."

"I don't know. I wager that in bed, muscular legs and what sits nestled between them could certainly prove more satisfying than the most intelligent of minds," offered Jeanne with a wicked grin. Just as she began to giggle at her own foolishness, a strange voice interrupted.

"Excuse me, but I'm looking for Jeanne Donnachy. Clinton said she was in the kitchen," said the tall, dark-haired man standing in the doorway.

"Oh...oh, we were, I mean, she is Jeanne Donnachy," breathed Leslie, a sudden blush overtaking her features. Had they been caught gossiping by the new laird? Wearing glasses and a dark blue suit of worsted wool and carrying a leather case, he looked quite businesslike, though the hint of a smile hovered about very full, promising lips. He certainly didn't look like the tyrant Jeanne expected, but he did have that strange American cadence to his voice.

"Miss Donnachy, I am Michael Winslow, C. Robertson Blake's assistant," explained the newcomer, stepping forward to offer Jeanne his hand, his dark eyes carefully studying the smaller female at her side.

"A pleasure, Mr. Winslow, and this is my cousin, Leslie," answered Fergus Donnachy's granddaughter, nodding in Leslie's direction as the young woman executed a graceful curtsy. Blake's *assistant*, Jeanne's mind echoed, even as she wondered what role if any would be left for her in this rapidly changing household. Why, oh, why had she ever agreed to this foolish scheme in the first place? Casting aside her doubts, she made conversation with the newcomer. "I must tell you, we are all quite anxious to meet the new earl of Lindall, though, naturally, you are quite welcome."

"He'll be along in a week or so, Miss Donnachy. There was pressing business in Clydebank, but he has sent me on to oversee the men and to begin reviewing the Donnachy finances. I must say I was surprised to learn from Clinton that it was you who had served as your grandfather's steward."

"We Scots feel that positions of that sort are best kept in the family," Jeanne answered truthfully, as she apprehensively rued the deceit practiced on C. Robertson Blake.

"That might be true, but, for now, the new earl wishes me to inspect his finances. I understand you have taken possession of your grandfather's ledgers?"

"Aye, for most things, though some accounts are held by the clan elders, the husbandry fees for example. They did not believe I, as an impressionable female, should be privy to the amounts paid for stud fees," she explained, with perhaps more detail than was proper, wanting to shock this stranger as his appearance had unsettled her.

"The older generation often thinks us unworthy of its secrets," Michael agreed, with a small cough meant to disguise the chuckle her words had evoked. "Were that not so, this inheritance would not have come as such a surprise to Creag."

"Aye, and Scots are more closemouthed than most," said Leslie, rising and coming to stand beside Blake's man. "Jeanne, if you'll tell me where to put Mr. Winslow, I'll see that he's settled before supper."

"You might as well give him the chamber next to the laird's. If Blake needs him at night, he'll be handy," said Jeanne. Then a devilish gleam appeared in her eyes as she observed how assiduously Leslie and the stranger were attempting to ignore an apparent attraction each felt for the other. "Although I could assign him a room down the hall from yours, so you'll have no trouble finding it in this maze."

"What?" asked Michael, uncertain he'd heard correctly.

"Oh, the workmen have opened up so many corridors and rooms that were never used that it's somewhat confusing if you're not used to it. I'm certain my cousin is merely concerned you might not be able to find your way around." Leslie smiled, even as she glared at her kinswoman. "We'll see you at supper, Jeanne."

Left alone in the large kitchen, the dark-haired young woman found no joy in her good-natured mischief. Instead she felt the sudden urge to weep. The way the American was sending in people to revamp Lindall Manor and Linclachan, she worried again as to the outcome. When all was said and done, would they be paying too high a price for survival...or could any price be too high if it meant the Donnachy and Robertson lines would continue? Sipping her now-cooled tea, Jeanne shrugged dispiritedly and said a fervent prayer, hoping the new earl would allow her to remain at Lindall Manor. Surely he'd realize her knowledge of the accounts would be invaluable? But then, why had he sent his own assistant along, knowing Fergus already had a steward? Only time would tell.

* * *

As moonlight filtered in through spotless glass panes, Creag Robertson Blake tossed aside the Glasgow newspapers, their front pages still dedicated to the repercussions of the scandalous Johnstown Flood. Well over two thousand lives had been snuffed out when the dam, holding back the waters of the artificial lake constructed for the South Fork Hunting and Fishing Club, had given way. Glad he had chosen not to join the sportsmen's organization, Creag nevertheless felt remorse for so many people killed. But there was nothing he could do about it beyond sending another contribution to the relief fund.

Not willing to devote more time to useless worry, he put the matter from his mind and eased his long, muscular frame onto the ornately carved cherry-wood bed. Pulling the fine linen sheets and rich velvet covering up about his chest, Creag nevertheless felt restless so that he did not attempt to sleep right away. Instead, he reached out to snatch the crystal decanter and waiting goblet from the conveniently positioned nightstand, and poured himself a full measure of Scottish whisky. Taking a sip, he allowed the tasty liquor to linger in his mouth for a moment before swallowing it. Then he heaved a sigh much louder than the hiss of the gaslights gracing the paneled walls of the private railroad car that would be his home for the night.

With a lurch and the shrill tooting of its whistle, the train began to move forward, leaving Creag to hope that the sight of Linclachan would be a less jolting experience than the inconveniences he had to endure in order to get to the small Highland village. In point of fact, the railroad did not stop, did not even run near his new lands. But that was something that could be remedied if he found tomorrow's carriage ride from the nearest station tiring.

Linclachan—it was an odd name, he mused, as the clacking sound of the train wheels gained speed to become an almost steady hum, and the crystal drops hanging from the gaslights began a delicate jingle in response. Odder still, from all reports, was the village itself and the circumstances that had made it his. But then, life was unpredictable. After all, what could be stranger than his being here, surrounded by luxury he had never even dreamed of as a lad? And a ridiculous image he must present, too, he acknowledged with a wry grin of self-deprecation, a man as large and rugged looking as he was, surrounded by such delicately wrought finery. If his increasingly expanding social position didn't demand such indulgence, he would be content to exist in a simpler, more masculine setting.

Tossing down the rest of the whisky, Creag pushed his own preferences aside and leaned his head back against plump down pillows to consider his newly acquired responsibilities while he studied the absurd gilded carvings running along the perimeter of the private car's ceiling.

The results of the investigation he had commissioned had not surprised him. However, having received the final report only yesterday, Creag was still debating the merits of sharing its contents with Michael. Of course, the industrialist had learned nothing he hadn't already guessed, yet even he hadn't expected the degree of poverty that had been reported to him.

But at the moment, Creag Robertson Blake wasted no time worrying about it. Michael had been sent ahead with unlimited funds to see to it that things were up to his employer's standards, and judging from his secretary's performances in the past, the man should be called Saint Michael for all the miracles he had performed.

No, the village's penury didn't disturb him. It could be overcome and Linclachan would be transformed into all he wanted it to be. Though it would take a great deal of money to make the village and manor respectable, in the end it would be worth it, he thought with satisfaction, memories of Catherine Grayson's lovely face flitting through his mind.

After all, offsetting the debts and projected expenditures was a title. The rank of earl was an honorable one, having been established in Scotland during the eleventh century by King Malcolm, the monarch who had delivered the nation from the villainous Macbeth. By all accounts, Linclachan itself had been founded much later, but for Creag, the history of the place was not a pressing issue. All that counted was that his newfound status should bring acceptance by Catherine's parents. And if that were not the case, his earldom might prompt the girl to marry him anyway, he shrugged, settling muscular shoulders more comfortably into the softness of the pillows. Then the Graysons would be forced to see to it that he received society's welcome. His sons would never know the pain of being outcasts, as he had.

Apart from the present vibrations of the railroad car and the clinking of the crystals suspended from the lamp, C. Robertson Blake was suffused with contentment. No matter how he viewed the situation, being laird of Lindall was bound to make things easier for him.

Just after dawn, the coach swayed and bumped constantly as it traveled over a dirt road embedded with stones. As Creag poked his golden head out of the dark interior of the carriage, he observed that someone had attempted to level the confounded lane and eliminate most of the ruts—Michael's doing in all probability. It was only too bad something couldn't have been done about the railroad tracks, as well. Then he might have been able to close his eyes last night, the exhausted American thought with an ornery frown.

Perhaps this business of being the earl of Lindall was not going to be quite as enjoyable as he had imagined, he thought glumly when the coach vibrated ominously upon hitting yet another rock. Narrowing his vibrant blue eyes, Creag momentarily considered cutting his losses and departing the area before he ever arrived at his destination, but the stubborn streak that his mother had deplored in him as a child surfaced to eliminate all ideas of surrendering to such a temptation. After all, he had salvaged countless failing businesses, turning them around to make a handsome profit. How difficult could it be to save one small Scottish village?

By the time he actually reached his destination, the torturous journey he had endured made Creag all the more determined to make his weary discomfort worthwhile and to go forward with his plan. What wouldn't he sacrifice to secure the future happiness of his offspring?

From a distance, Linclachan was a picturesque hamlet, but despite the fresh coats of paint on doors and shutters, closer inspection provoked a guttural groan from the new laird as the carriage rode along the main avenue. In fact, the damn thing might be the only roadway in this little corner of hell, Creag muttered, taking off his hat to protect it from being crushed as he bounced up and down to each loud clatter of the carriage wheels. But noisier than his transport was the squawking of chickens and the bleating of sheep, apparently annoyed at the disturbance to their usually sleepy environs.

Creag supposed the livestock was necessary to feed the locals, but their stench and noise made him apprehensive as to Catherine's impression of rural life, city girl that she was. He was wondering about the feasibility of moving the animals to some distant pasture, far from this stretch of dirt that masqueraded as a road, when he noted the velocity of the carriage beginning to slow and assumed correctly that he was coming to the manor house.

The residence was imposing enough from afar, but as with the village, Creag's heart began to sink when he drew nearer. A large U-shaped structure, the manor, at close quarters, appeared little better than ramshackle. Could the place be made presentable, he wondered miserably, and a staff brought up to snuff by the time the Graysons arrived? But then Creag's natural confidence resurfaced, quelling his doubts. Wasn't he a man who always got whatever he desired, he asked himself? If he wanted this wretched area of the Highlands to be habitable in three months' time, then by heaven it would be!

Before the carriage reached the main entrance however, it came to a halt so abruptly that C. Robertson Blake had all he could do to maintain his seat. Hearing the driver scramble down, he looked out the window in time to see the unfortunate fellow shooing a meandering flock of sheep off the drive. Good Lord, Creag reflected, would the Graysons think such a rustic scene charming, or were they more likely to lift their patrician noses in disdain? Perhaps if he had bows tied around the necks of the docile creatures they might appear more appealing . . . but what was he thinking, he chided himself? The animals would simply have to be penned.

A few minutes later the coach rumbled forward again, moving slowly until it finally stopped before the doors of the formerly grand manor. Alighting from the cramped confines of the vehicle, Creag wished he had had the foresight to have instructed that a horse be sent to await him at the train station. Certainly riding through the rugged countryside astride some spirited beast would have been preferable to traveling by coach. In fact, given the raw beauty of the region, it might even have been enjoyable. But never one to look behind him wishing that things had been otherwise, Creag pushed these thoughts aside, a grin illuminating his handsome face when he saw Michael descending the manor's steps to greet him.

"Creag, welcome!" called the secretary, his features afire with an enthusiasm for the place that Creag found unfathomable.

"Thank you, but I'm surprised I don't find myself ankle deep in sheep droppings," Creag commented with a grimace as he surveyed the courtyard.

"I've set someone to cleaning up the drive twice a day," a smiling Michael replied, raising his voice to be heard over the plaintive bleating now coming from behind the overgrown bramble that had once been a formal rose garden. "But still, what do you think, isn't it grand?"

"Actually, that would not be my first choice of words in describing it," Creag commented wryly, his lively blue eyes moving grimly over the weathered exterior of the edifice in question.

"Oh, but it is not as bad as it seems." Michael laughed, the sunlight shining off his spectacles and making his excitement glow all the more brightly. "Structurally the building is quite sound, and wait until you see the interior."

"I shudder with anticipation," Creag muttered, mounting the stairs with long, powerful strides, so that the other man had to hurry to keep pace.

In reality the manor was not as dilapidated as he had feared, Creag conceded a while later, sidestepping some workmen suspended on a scaffold in the second-floor foyer and entering the study with Michael. God only knows, however, what it had looked like before his friend and secretary had arrived and seen to its overhaul.

Moving purposefully to the ancient desk in the center of the room, Creag leafed through the papers Michael had left there for his perusal before spending the better part of an hour listening to the secretary's report on conditions in Linclachan. Then, after once more noting his aide's odd enthusiasm for the place and quickly assimilating the information he provided, Creag was ready to take charge of his new holdings.

"All right, Michael, I think I'd best start with speaking to the steward," he stated decisively, holding a stack of requests for feed, farm implements and livestock. "Send him in, will you?"

"Creag . . . there's a small problem," Michael began hesitantly.

"We still have a steward, don't we?" the wealthy new laird inquired, bringing his head up sharply. "You didn't get rid of him, did you?"

"No, I haven't dismissed the steward," Michael responded, looking decidedly uncomfortable, "but still, there's something I think you should know."

"Whatever it is can wait," Creag said offhandedly, returning to study the papers in his hand. "I would like to deal with this fellow as soon as possible—let him know what I expect and so forth—before I allow myself to relax for a bit and get some rest after a sleepless night. Now send him in."

"But, Creag—" Michael started to protest.

"See here, Michael, I'm exhausted from this journey, and my disposition has not been improved by the vast amount of work which I see has to be done here. It's not that I don't think you haven't already achieved a great deal, but there is still a lot to accomplish before the Graysons arrive. Now simply ask the fellow to come in here. What is the steward's name, anyway?"

"It's Jeanne Donnachy," the secretary answered, trying to inform his employer as to the gender of the person in question.

"Good," Creag stated absently as he returned to his study of the requests Donnachy had submitted. The man had done a remarkable job considering the little capital he had had at his disposal, and he was anxious to keep such a knowledgeable and effective employee at all costs. "Tell Mr. Gene Donnachy that I require him immediately."

"Certainly," Michael replied in exasperation, executing a bow that was just short of sarcastic. He knew all too well that when C. Robertson Blake was in one of his no-nonsense moods he became so stubborn that there was no dealing with him. But then, he *had* tried to tell him, Michael thought on his way out of the room. Now there was nothing more he could do other than let the laird of Lindall be surprised. Besides, the shock would do him good.

A few moments later, the soft opening and closing of the study door alerted the new earl to the fact that he was no longer alone. Looking up, Creag was surprised to find a woman in his presence. Good God, he hadn't known that Scotland spawned such females! Whether she was the housekeeper or a neighbor coming to call, the American didn't know. The only thing of which he was certain was that his guest was exquisite. She was tall, slender and quite beautiful, with a mass of brown hair that sparkled with red flame wherever the sunlight settled upon it.

But her tresses were not the only thing that was afire, Creag saw quickly. The woman stood regarding him with such arrogant defiance that for an instant C. Robertson Blake felt as though he were an interloper, that it was her desk he sat behind and not his. Curse it, he hadn't gone looking to acquire Linclachan. The manor and its village had sought him out! Now that he was here and had already spent huge sums upon it, the place was his. It was best everyone understood that from the beginning, neighbors and staff alike!

"What can I do for you, madam?" he asked, rising from his chair and unfolding his tall, broad-shouldered frame to its full height.

"I heard you wished to see me, sir," Jeanne replied softly, her burr becoming more pronounced at the sight of a villain who was so handsome and virile. Why he all but took her breath away!

He was uncommonly tall, she observed, her green eyes gliding over him unabashedly. A masculine aura of raw energy and power sat like some invisible cloak upon his broad shoulders. And his face, dear Lord, his face with its angular planes, well-defined lips and jutting jaw, was more handsome than it had any right to be. How dare C. Robertson Blake, the usurper of her birthright, be such a fine specimen of a man! Why he was as muscular and blond as any Viking who had ever plundered Scotland's shores. And most likely as ruthless, Jeanne reminded herself, trying to quell the tingle that ran along her spine when she looked at him. Just like the Norsemen of old, this modern golden warrior was taking what was not his to take, and it would be in her best interests to remember it.

"I'm sorry, what did you say?" Creag asked. Her voice had been low and melodious, but it had taken a moment for him to attune his ear to her strange yet wonderful pronunciation. It wasn't until the woman was repeating herself, more slowly and with a definite note of exasperation, that her initial words registered in the laird of Lindall's consciousness. Well, a mistake had been made to be sure. He hadn't sent for anyone but his steward, certainly not for this comely warrior queen who was quite obviously, though inexplicably, ready to do battle with him.

"There has been some misunderstanding," Creag said archly, reacting to her challenging attitude in spite of his vow to remain in possession of the situation. "I am, at present awaiting the arrival of my steward, Gene Donnachy."

"Then I regret to tell you that the mistake is yours," Jeanne said with as much deference as she could manage. "I *am* your steward."

"What!" Creag cried, his voice rumbling in his chest like captured thunder. "What is it you're telling me?"

"It should be simple enough to understand," Jeanne stated calmly, unable, regardless of her struggle, to stem the proud tilt of her head. "I am Jeanne Donnachy."

Chapter Four

Creag's eyes narrowed as he regarded the beautiful woman standing so proudly before him.

"Is this some sort of joke?" he asked finally, his sleepless night on the train making his deep voice sharper and more ominous than usual. If this truly was Jeanne Donnachy, she appeared to be made more for warming a man's bed than tending his estate.

"Not at all," Jeanne answered, lifting her chin defiantly in response until she remembered that this person was now her employer. If she wished to remain in Lindall Manor she would have to learn to be more deferential to the condescending blond brute sitting behind her grandfather's desk.

Gritting her teeth imperceptibly, the pretty Highlander prepared to assume a role she was unaccustomed to playing, that of tractable servant to the laird of Linclachan.

"I hope that all reports of my past work have pleased you, Creag," she said in more submissive a tone than she had ever used before. Yet even while she was making a conscious effort to be docile, Jeanne could not help but find satisfaction in the widening of C. Robertson Blake's bedeviling blue eyes when she addressed him by his Christian name.

"Yes, they did," he replied abstractedly, caught off guard by the downward sweep of Jeanne Donnachy's long lashes and the familiar manner in which she spoke to him. What had her position been in his predecessor's household to excuse conversing with him on such intimate terms? And, he wondered uncomfortably, exactly what was it she envisioned her new duties to entail?

"Shouldn't you call me your lordship, or something similar?" he demanded, his brow knit in a visible sign of his disconcertment.

"Being an American 'tis only to be expected that you be unfamiliar with our ways," Jeanne replied sweetly. The cadence of her voice made it seem as though she sought to soothe this bothersome foreigner, but in reality she would have relished giving him a set-down. "In England it is certainly true that an earl is called his lordship. Those people are so caught up with their pedigrees and fancy ways that they forget the man and revere the title. But here in the Highlands, we do things a wee bit differently. One of our poets has said, 'A man's a man for all that,' and we set no individual so far above the clan that he must be called by something other than his own name, laird or not. You'll find that all of us, both in the manor and the village, will be calling you Creag."

"Delightful," the American murmured dryly, obviously displeased. Suddenly Creag was plagued by visions of being on a first-name basis with every old crone and poppet in Linclachan. It was certainly not the sort of thing likely to impress the Graysons, and he had to suppress a groan at the thought of it.

"All over the civilized world, I am C. Robertson Blake. Yet here in the Highlands, where I am the earl of Lindall and laird of Linclachan, you expect me to be reduced to the simple appellation of my boyhood?" he asked, his generous mouth drawing together in a tight line.

"There's no disrespect meant by it, Creag," Jeanne responded defensively. Who was this man, no matter how handsome or wealthy, she fumed, to criticize their traditions? He had taken up residence in Lindall Manor less than an hour ago and already he was finding fault with them!

The new laird was momentarily placated and so fascinated by the way his name rolled off this lovely woman's tongue that his annoyance disappeared, until his glance shifted from Jeanne Donnachy's lips to her eyes. Then, the barely concealed anger he saw smoldering in their depths prompted him to forget her charming pronunciation and the distinctive lilt that made his name sound almost attractive.

The woman was extraordinarily haughty for a servant, he thought, his own pique burgeoning once more. But even as he condemned her, Creag found himself reluctantly admitting that Jeanne Donnachy presented a fetching sight with the creamy skin of her cheekbones dusted deep pink and her eyes sparking mutinously. His exhaustion must be overcoming his good sense, he reflected suddenly, for him to be distracted from business, no matter how enticing the bait.

"That may be your way, but it's not mine," Creag finally responded evenly. Having mastered his temper and his awareness of the woman's attractions, Creag's only indication of his discomfort was the drumming of his strong, square fingers atop the ancient desk's surface. For some inexplicable reason, he discovered he had to keep them busy, so that they did not reach out to brush back the curls that had escaped from Jeanne Donnachy's glorious hair.

"You can't just come in here and change everything," Jeanne cried. Not realizing the effect she had on Creag, she impulsively abandoned her attempts to appear the biddable steward as she defended her home.

"Oh, can't I?" he asked in a soft voice, his eyes glinting dangerously. "I am the earl of Lindall, am I not?"

"Of course," Jeanne mumbled, unable to meet Blake's searching gaze. Now was the time neither for the truth nor a show of her fiery temper, she reprimanded herself, angry she had given way so easily to the sentiments churning within her. She had to hold her tongue and maintain her pose as a respectful servant to this arrogant American in order to preserve Linclachan. But, she consoled herself, that did not mean she could not detest C. Robertson Blake while she did so.

Fighting for composure and finding it, she looked up at the new laird with what appeared to be a tenuous smile. "'Tis merely that you are one of us now, and calling you by your first name is a sign of our acceptance."

"I see," Creag replied, his half-hooded eyes giving no clue to his feelings. However, as he studied Jeanne Donnachy, his instincts shouted that something about her suddenly softened demeanor did not ring true, and he vowed to uncover exactly what that was. Engaging her in conversation might provide the answer.

"Tell me, Miss Donnachy—or am I to call you Jeanne?" he interrupted himself to inquire in a sardonic tone.

"Jeanne will do," the woman replied, despising the new-comer for his supercilious nature.

"Yes, I think Jeanne will do quite nicely," he muttered as though to himself.

The words were innocent, but something in the way C. Robertson Blake said them caused Jeanne a pang of anxiety. No matter how odious the man was, there was some element about him that was all too male, and Fergus's granddaughter knew that living under the same roof with him would require extreme caution.

Though she recognized that his good looks and command-ing air were enough to steal the hearts of most women, Jeanne swore it would never happen to her. Everyone else might con-sider the swaggering American a savior, but she had learned from this short interview that C. Robertson Blake had the soul of a conqueror. With such knowledge, it wasn't likely she would ever forget that he was an invader, just like the ancient Norse-men he so resembled.

"...now that I have been welcomed as a member of the clan. I assume, Jeanne, you can provide the information I require," Creag was saying in a deep, husky timbre, the last of his words encroaching on her thoughts just as he had intruded upon Lin-dall Manor.

"I'm sorry?" a flustered Jeanne asked. Since when had she lost her ability to concentrate on any matter at hand? And more importantly, what was it the handsome devil wanted to know?

"I was asking the identity of that fellow in the portrait," Creag repeated, nodding his blond head in the direction of the wall to his right. "If I am to be laird, I suppose I should know something about the place and its history."

"Oh, that's one of my...favorite paintings," Jeanne said, catching herself at the last moment. "It's Tammas Donnachy, one of your third cousins twice removed. He was a great chief-tain," she continued with pride, smoothly fabricating the re-lationship between the man in the portrait and the one regarding her so closely.

Creag knew damn well that the clan chief in the oil was no more related to him than every other descendant of Adam and

Eve. However, if she wasn't aware of it, he couldn't tell Jeanne Donnachy that. He was determined to remain earl of Lindall until the Graysons had departed the Highlands. For the time being, however, he would find out nothing about this woman while she hid behind a mask of docility. He decided to end her masquerade.

"Is that so? The man looks like nothing more than a horse thief. But then I suppose one can say things about one's own relatives that would be downright insulting if uttered about someone else's family," Creag commented offhandedly, sifting through the papers littering his desk while unobtrusively gauging Jeanne's reactions.

There it was, the same shade of pink suffusing her cheeks, and her lips quivering with unspoken words of anger. He hadn't imagined it. She was a chameleon: simpering and sweet one moment, a tigress the next. What game was she playing with him? Whatever it was, he was in no mood for it after the sleepless night on the train and this morning's journey. If Jeanne Donnachy was going to retain her position as steward, something the meticulously kept papers in his hand demanded, it was time the girl learned exactly who would be the master of Lindall Manor.

"Well, Jeanne," he began, leaning his muscular frame back against the chair, "we have dealt with the identity of the horse thief, and established my position within this household. Perhaps we should proceed with determining yours."

At his words, Jeanne suddenly looked so vulnerable that Creag instinctively softened his manner. What was Jeanne Donnachy, after all, but a slender slip of a female? Certainly she was no threat to his authority or his plans. He was in command here, just as he was in command of all of his dealings.

Settling down to business and conversing with Jeanne about the running of the estate, Creag soon knew he had been correct in his assessment. The woman loved this land and was good at what she did. But as Jeanne spoke about the estate and Linclachan, she became different somehow, and Creag began to find himself more captivated by her soft smile than whatever it was she had to say.

Immediately, he tried to shrug off his response to the pretty woman sitting on the other side of the desk. As often as he had been able to ignore physical attractions in the past, the beleaguered American found it quite difficult to do at the moment. Attributing this odd turn of events to fatigue, Creag decided it was more than time for this interview to end.

"I've decided, Jeanne, to keep you on as steward. You've done an admirable job for a woman," he said, meaning to compliment her before he sent the beautiful Scot on her way.

"My sex has nothing to do with it, Creag," Jeanne protested, rising from her chair in vexation, before she recovered herself.

Oh, yes, it does, C. Robertson Blake thought morosely. Jeanne Donnachy was a vibrant creature. That alone would have made her sexually attractive to him, because Creag understood the captured energy dwelling beneath her exquisite exterior. Didn't he, too, possess vitality in abundance? But the fact that he felt she was a kindred spirit made the matter worse. How could he keep so beautiful a female within his household and not be tempted to touch her? Even now, his hands would have liked to explore her woman's figure, and his lips craved a taste of her full, lush mouth.

Perhaps this would not work out after all, he mused. Whether it was the gentle curve of her hip or the previously stubborn set of Jeanne's mouth that cautioned him, Creag wasn't clear. All he knew was that Jeanne Donnachy could not remain under his roof.

Besides, what would the very proper Catherine think if she found so lovely a woman residing in his house? No, Jeanne Donnachy had no place here, he thought with a sigh. But the idea of separating so capable an individual from a job she did well went against Creag's convictions. Then, too, he had his own needs. Certainly he required someone familiar with Lindall Manor, a person who could deal easily with the locals and keep them in line so he was not disgraced in front of the Graysons.

Perhaps there was a way for her to keep her position as steward, he concluded, a smile curving itself around his lips at the brilliance of his solution. There must be a cottage on the estate somewhere that could house her until he and Catherine returned to the States. Damnation, but he was too tired to deal with the particulars now. Michael should have warned him!

As he dismissed Jeanne Donnachy and set her about her duties once more, Creag watched her depart with a regal swish of skirts into the crumbling and cluttered hallway. Good God, he asked himself, wasn't *anyone* or *anything* about this place what he had expected them to be?

Gingerly rubbing his fingertips over his drooping eyelids, Creag surrendered to a mighty yawn. When visions of the pert Jeanne Donnachy appeared, Creag told himself that he wanted all dealings with his steward to be strictly business. Yet, he couldn't ignore the fact that he had been much gentler with her than he usually was with those in his employ.

There was something about her that cried out for his protection, though it was most likely a foolish perception on his part. Jeanne Donnachy did not appear the helpless type at all.

Of course, his seeming preoccupation with the girl could be that he merely admired the girl's spirit, the new laird mused. After all, in matters of international finance he had only to frown and grown men quaked. Yet this girl, compliant as she appeared on the surface, had no fear of C. Robertson Blake. Finding no other excuse for his behavior, Creag decided it had to be the young woman's fearlessness that accounted for his own attitude, until forbidden images of Jeanne Donnachy's enticing bosom accused him of being a liar. Good God, Creag wondered in frustration, what was wrong with him? He wasn't the sort to vacillate. Why couldn't he make up his mind about Jeanne Donnachy? Was it his extreme tiredness that confused him, or something else?

"Michael!" Creag bellowed, seeking to banish his unsettled feelings by ignoring them. "Michael, come here, will you?"

"Yes?" Creag's assistant said, poking his head through the doorway.

"Wipe the grin off your face and get in here," Creag ordered with an exasperated grimace. "Why didn't you inform me my steward is a woman?"

"I tried to tell you," Michael pointed out, the amusement dancing in his eyes doing nothing to improve his employer's disposition.

"Well, you didn't do a very good job of it," Creag grumbled, neatly restacking the papers on his desk.

"I didn't mention she was quite pretty, either," Michael said, unwilling to allow the subject to drop.

"Is she? I hadn't noticed," Creag stated, refusing to be baited. "Remember, I intend to be married soon to Catherine."

"Ah, yes, the very proper Miss Grayson," Michael commented so quietly that it was no comment at all.

"What's that supposed to mean?" Creag asked sharply.

"Nothing, only that I'm glad Jeanne is staying on," the secretary replied with monumental satisfaction, images of Leslie's uninterrupted residence in this house causing him to smile.

"She's continuing as steward, yes, but she won't be living at the manor," Creag replied, his half-closed eyes a clue to his drowsiness. At the moment there was nothing he wanted more than a comfortable bed.

"Not staying here!" Michael protested vehemently, his visions of Leslie receding rapidly. "But you can't ask her to leave, Creag!"

"Why not?" the earl of Lindall growled. What nonsense was this now? First the steward's impertinence, then his own trusted friend questioning him. Was it something in the water or food of Linclachan to make people behave so? Didn't the fact that he was wearing a noble title count for anything other than an argument?

"It will upset the villagers," Michael declared, an obstinate expression descending upon his face.

"For God's sake, I'm not turning her out into the cold," Creag responded impatiently. "I simply want to place her in some cozy little cottage."

"That doesn't matter," Michael persisted. "This has always been Jeanne's home. Throw her out now and you appear the villain."

Allow her to stay, and I have no doubts but that I will be the lecher, Creag wanted to reply. Instead, running his fingers distractedly through his thick wheat-colored mane, he raised another question. "Do you mean to say the woman has never resided anywhere other than this manor house?"

"That's it exactly. She's Fergus Donnachy's granddaughter!"

"What?" Creag roared, beginning to understand the chit's prepossessing air. "Good God! Are you trying to tell me I'm stuck with her?"

"It would seem to be the case," Michael responded firmly, not entirely certain the words he spoke were a lie. "She is, after all, a relative. The investigator's report you received in Glasgow must have mentioned her. Turn the girl out and there is no telling how the locals will react. You don't want a rebellion on your hands when the Graysons arrive, do you?"

"Of course not! But if she is Fergus's descendant, what am I doing here?" Creag asked, vowing to thrash the man who had conducted the investigation of Linclachan. There had been no word of a granddaughter, Creag was sure of it.

"It's the usual story. She's a woman. Because she hadn't wed, the title went to the nearest male, which is you."

"These crafty old Scots didn't lure me here to try and marry me off to the wench, did they?" Creag asked suspiciously, his manner distinctly nervous.

"I hadn't considered the possibility until now. Still, I don't think so," Michael said slowly, after pondering the matter.

"Good!" Creag exclaimed, heaving a sigh of relief. "It wouldn't do to fend off one female while wooing another."

"Jeanne gave you an indication that you will be called upon to defend your honor from her, did she?" Michael asked wryly.

"Your attempted wit escapes me," Creag stated flatly. "Besides, this is no cause for humor. Now tell me, are there any other resident relatives I should know about?"

"Well, there is Jeanne's companion, Leslie."

"That's another name that could be either male or female! Don't these people know anything about gender? Out with it Michael, is Jeanne's friend a man or a woman?" Creag demanded to know with a bit more insistence than was called for under the circumstances.

"Leslie is very female, indeed," Michael responded, noting how the scowl that had been darkening the earl's face suddenly disappeared.

"I see," Creag said, experiencing a strange sense of relief until a new thought struck him.

"If this Leslie is anything like Jeanne Donnachy, I can't deal with it now. Imagine living in a household with two such women! I certainly couldn't envision myself surviving such an experience," Lindall Manor's new master all but moaned.

"No, Leslie is quite unique," Michael commented softly, his tone giving Creag a clue as to why the reports from his usually levelheaded secretary showed him to be so captivated by this earthly purgatory called Linclachan.

It appeared to Creag that while he had come to Scotland in order to found his dynasty, Michael had been the one to lose his heart. And though logically the American laird realized his friend was entitled to a personal life, Creag couldn't help but feel bereft, as if somehow Michael had deserted him and gone over to the other side.

But before the wealthy industrialist could pursue the matter, a terrible commotion erupted from below stairs, most likely the workmen engaged in some row. Unwilling to contend with any more problems at present, Creag requested Michael to see to the disturbance while he sought his chamber and some much-needed sleep. It had already been a very long day, and it wasn't yet tea time.

As he retraced his steps to the rooms his assistant had shown him soon after his arrival, Creag shook his head wearily. Though he might find slumber, the new earl was certain that pleasant dreams were entirely out of the question in this Highland nightmare called Lindall Manor.

Leaving Creag to return to the laird's suite of rooms, Michael hurried down the hall, intent on escaping before the financier called him back on one pretext or another. Despite their long and usually close association, sometimes working for C. Robertson Blake required the sort of impossible diplomacy that could convince a lion to eat fish rather than flesh, Michael reflected. Today had been that type of day, and in Linclachan, he couldn't go home to escape his job. Still, he had to admit, he'd done quite well handling his employer thus far.

With a small grin of self-congratulations at having succeeded in keeping both Jeanne and Leslie in residence, the dark-haired secretary decided that once he checked on the noisy workmen, he would have earned a glass of Geordie's superior brew, to be best enjoyed in the kitchen. The fact that he might chance on Leslie there was insignificant, he assured himself, straightening his tie as he passed a mirror on the stairs, totally insignificant. She did, however, owe him a debt of gratitude, he mused, one which he imagined he might enjoy collecting.

As he reached the lower floor, Michael was distracted by the still-raised voices coming from the kitchen and he hesitated. If this was a matter involving the women of the manor, as it sounded to be, it truly wasn't his concern. Rather, it was the steward's responsibility, and besides, he had had enough discordance today to last a lifetime. Moving quietly, thinking to observe without interfering, at least for now, he opened the door to the kitchen and found Jeanne and Leslie arguing vehemently with a small, white-haired woman.

"Maggie, you can't be serious!" Jeanne protested angrily.

"Aunt, we're full-grown, not bairns," declared Leslie.

"All the more reason I am needed here. I warrant babes in arms need less watching over than the pair of you, especially in a house with as romantic an air as this one."

"Romantic?" Jeanne objected in disbelief, thinking of the drop cloths, wood shavings and hordes of workmen cluttering the once-quiet manor house.

"Aye, you heard me," the old woman insisted, though what Maggie could remember of romance Jeanne and Leslie were hard-pressed to imagine. "It's glad I am that I returned today from visiting Cousin Douglas. If I had stayed any longer, God knows what the outcome might have been."

Suddenly realizing they were no longer alone, Jeanne rose, placed a warning hand on the woman's shoulder and turned toward Blake's assistant, a hesitant smile on her flushed face.

"Michael, when did you come in? Did you want something? Whatever it is, I'll try to oblige."

"Whatever it is? Mighty friendly with strange men, Jeanne, aren't you now? And 'Michael' yet?" observed the older woman as she stared openly at the newcomer. "He's only just come to the manor a week and already you treat him like a cousin. I grant you he is a handsome lad, but—"

"Maggie," said Leslie, trying to hush her aunt.

"I did understand that the new laird's name is Creag, though," finished the village seamstress, well aware of Michael's identity but curious as to how he'd conduct himself under fire.

"It is, ma'am. I am Michael Winslow, his assistant."

"*Ma'am?* Why, even his manners are handsome." Maggie chortled as Leslie again attempted to silence the outspoken woman.

"I wasn't certain if it was Mrs. Donnachy or Mrs. Robertson," explained Michael with an engaging smile, surprised to find himself taken with the refreshingly frank stranger. "In Linclachan, I've found, it's always one or the other."

"Aye, though there are a few Gordons and MacRaes about, you're mostly right. My name is Margaret Robertson, but you may call me Maggie, lad."

"Now who's being friendly to strangers," Jeanne muttered.

"Michael, pull up a chair and join us for a cup of tea," suggested the older woman, thinking that overseeing the young ones in this man's company might answer her questions.

"Actually I was looking forward to one of Geordie's ales," he demurred with a nod in Jeanne's direction. "I find I've taken quite a liking to the stuff, but please, I certainly didn't mean to interrupt your chat."

"Nonsense. Sit down while Leslie gets you that brew," ordered Maggie, all at once the mistress of the kitchen. "And get me one, too, dear, if you please."

Rolling her eyes heavenward, the petite blonde fetched the ales, delivering a scathing look to Maggie along with the drink, though Michael was too busy quaffing his own to notice.

"Has the laird settled in?" asked Jeanne, determined to take over control of the conversation before Maggie could announce her foolish intention of moving in to Lindall Manor.

"He's going to his rooms to rest before dinner. I fear the carriage ride and confusion this morning left him a bit under the weather," replied Michael, setting down his glass and looking more relaxed.

"Oh, you're staying here with the laird?" inquired Maggie, her voice totally innocent as she eyed Jeanne and Leslie with a meaningful glance.

"Yes. Generally, wherever you find Creag, I'll not be far behind, though in this case, I arrived first to oversee the start of work on the manor," he answered. "And lucky I was, indeed, enjoying Jeanne and Leslie's generous hospitality."

"Aye, the Highlands are known for being friendly to strangers, sometimes overly so," drawled Maggie, her tone dry though her brow was furrowed.

"Really, we've done nothing," Jeanne protested, already envisioning how Maggie might interpret Michael's words.

"Nonsense, Jeanne. The both of you have been ever so kind, delivering my morning tea to my room, seeing to my meals, arranging for my baths, even showing me the countryside in the evening twilight. Surely, those are not your normal duties," praised Blake's assistant. "I'm certain Creag will be as taken with your kindness and find you as indispensable as I."

"Not if I have any say in the matter," Maggie muttered with a scowl at the American. "There are footmen for such chores, or there will be once I talk to the council. Until then, Ewan can see to such things."

"Maggie, I am steward here," reminded Jeanne. "There's no need for you to concern yourself."

"You are an inexperienced lass who knows nothing of men or their ways."

"She's done an excellent job thus far. What else does she need to know to see to our comfort?" asked Michael in bewilderment.

"That all depends on just how comfortable you aim to be, sir, and from what I've been hearing, you've been too cozy already," intoned the old woman. "But, make no mistake, my satchels are in the entryway. From now on, I'll be here to see that things go as they should."

"What? You mean, she's moving in, too?" demanded the confused secretary with a look of dismay, already dreading the effect such news would have on Creag. "I wouldn't want to have to tell the laird."

"No, she is not going to stay at Lindall Manor," countered Jeanne, high spots of color appearing in her cheeks. "I've told you, there is *no need,* Maggie."

"Aye, but there is. It is altogether too easy for this romantic old house to weave its spell."

"Romantic old house?" repeated Leslie and Jeanne in unison, amazed that anyone could see the decaying Lindall Manor in such a strange light. Why did Maggie persist in calling it that? Maybe she had been nipping Jamie's whisky.

"Aye, when the candles are lit and fire is glowing in the grate, there's a special mood that just invites lovers to..." Suddenly Maggie realized what she was saying and she coughed in confusion. Abruptly she continued, her voice now clipped and formal. "There are always men who seek to mislead young women, especially if there's no chaperon about, and you are my responsibility, lassies. Once I speak to the council—"

"But, you're Malcolm's sister-in-law," objected Leslie. "Whatever you suggest, he'll agree to."

"With all the strangers in residence now, and undoubtedly more to come, I'm certain the council will decide it's time the manor had a proper housekeeper who can also function as a chaperon."

"But Fergus never had one."

"What?" inquired Maggie sharply, wondering if she had been observed during her nocturnal visits to the manor and the old laird's bedchamber.

"A housekeeper, Maggie. Wasn't that what we were just talking about?" asked Jeanne in exasperation.

"Oh, aye," said the old woman in relief. "But then, Fergus never had visitors or a real staff to worry about, either, Jeanne. You cannot expect the new laird to be satisfied with what made old Fergus happy. Besides, with all the work going on, there's a mountain of cleaning that needs doing. Beth and Fiona will come days from the village to help out, but someone has to oversee them. Mary is too busy with the cooking, and it's certainly not your place," explained Maggie.

"How can you expect to take on the responsibilities of a household you know nothing about?" countered Jeanne. "Besides, Leslie and I are well aware it's us you're intending to oversee and not the maids. You only want to play at being housekeeper so you can work at being chaperon."

"Maybe you could live at home with your family," suggested Michael, hoping to forestall the eruption of the argument he had interrupted earlier, and assure himself of some of Leslie's time in the evenings. "You could just come in daily, as well."

"I've none but a cat, lad, so don't fret about me. I'd gladly give up my bed to be sure the laird was well served. Many's the time I did so for Fergus, with nary a complaint. Besides, the lassies need to be watched after.''

''Watched after?''

''Aye, it's not proper, you see, two American men, unmarried and all, though you do appear well mannered on the surface,'' acknowledged the old woman reluctantly. ''Well I know how easy it is for the laird to entice women to his service. Still, that's neither here nor there.''

''Jeanne?'' Shaking his head at Maggie's peculiar remarks, Michael appealed to the steward for help, certain only that Creag didn't need another female relative about, especially one as given to interfering as this one.

''If the council orders it, there's nothing I can say, Michael. Much as I'd like to refuse some of their ideas,'' she confided with a grimace, ''it's not my privilege. Perhaps it would be best if Leslie and I stayed in the village, too. That way, there'd be no cause for anyone's apprehension.''

''No, no,'' he protested quickly. ''You mustn't leave your home. I—I'll simply tell Creag Maggie's always been the housekeeper but was away for a while and I hadn't met her until today. That much at least is true,'' he consoled himself, picking up Maggie's ale and downing the rest of it at the thought of losing his daily visits with Leslie, and the lies he was being forced to tell his friend.

Upstairs, Creag prowled the laird's quarters, discontent marring his normally placid features. He supposed he shouldn't be irritated with Lindall Manor and the work that, in his exhausted state, seemed overwhelming, but somehow he had expected a better heritage than this ruin. From the moment he had left the train this morning, he had encountered nothing but unhappy surprises, from the torturous carriage ride to the wretched condition of the roads, the squalid cottages of the town, the inconveniences caused by free-roaming livestock, the confusion of the manor itself and the amazing discovery that not only was his steward a woman, but one who affected him in the most peculiar manner. Never before had any female set his mind to wandering, his fingers craving to skim the creamy texture of her skin.

That had been the final blow causing him to withdraw to his rooms in search of a respite, mused Creag. When his usually efficient mind became emotionally involved in a situation, things were definitely akilter and retreat was the only course of action. Alone now in the laird's chambers, he realized at once that Jeanne Donnachy had enticed his imagination so readily only because of his weariness; certainly that was the only likely explanation. He had been working too hard on the acquisition of the English foundry and the trip up here... well, it was nothing some sleep wouldn't cure, the financier told himself.

It was, however, completely out of character for him to rest during the day, and Creag found his body didn't respond to the simple act of lying down. Though he tried to relax, he wasn't able to find a comfortable position or quiet his raging thoughts.

Surprisingly, the bed was large enough for a man his height, a massive cherry-wood four-poster with an intricately carved crest of arms on the underside of the wooden canopy, the Donnachys' he presumed, unless it was the Robertsons'. While he was initially amused to study the two rams butting heads, he quickly grew uncomfortable on the mattress, which felt as if it were cut from those craggy rocks he'd passed on the road that morning, and the pillows from slabs of granite. Comfort was not his to find beneath the family crest, a situation he hoped would not be indicative of his future in Linclachan.

Restless, he paced the room, but finding no release, Creag finally yielded to curiosity and opened all the cupboards in the suite. Unfortunately for his boredom, they'd all been empty, save a few musty bolts of cloth, probably that Jeanne Donnachy's work, he surmised. There was nothing to occupy him but his own unsettling thoughts, Creag frowned, not yet ready to face Michael or the Scots downstairs.

Damn it. How could he—how would he ever impress the Graysons with Linclachan the way it was? Here was the real source of his restlessness, the man of business acknowledged, striding to the window and looking out over the courtyard. Even there weeds grew among the cobblestones and chickens prowled untended.

Usually he saw a problem, arrived at a solution, hired a crew and they resolved the matter according to his direction. But this time, the crew had merely uncovered more problems—and many of them dealt with people, not machinery or land, which could be maneuvered without concern for feelings or lives. No, the revitalization of Linclachan could well be the most difficult project of his career, and the most urgent if he were to win Catherine, Creag admitted to himself, all the more resolute to succeed. Lindall Manor and its village would be made to measure up to his, and the Graysons', standards; of that he was determined. And once he relaxed a bit, he was sure things would look better. After all, didn't Queen Victoria take her holidays in the Highlands? Her property certainly wasn't as ill tended as this.

With a deliberate sigh, the American took off his shoes, hung up his trousers, vest and suit jacket and lay down once again on the laird's bed. Maybe if he counted sheep he'd be able to unwind a bit; he must have seen enough of them, with their black faces and tinkling bells that morning, to have no difficulty envisioning the four-legged creatures now.

One, two, three, four...twenty-two...thirty, they seemed to be passing before his closed eyes more slowly now, Creag noticed with appreciation. There's thirty-two, thirty-three—

Suddenly a loud squawking noise resounded throughout the manor, invading his chamber and piercing the tentative calm he'd finally achieved. The American was on his feet in an instant, startled and angry as he tried to discern the source of the unpleasant clamor.

All at once the unearthly screeching reverberated again, a loud cacophony of discordant notes, and it appeared to be getting closer to his room.

"What in blazes can that be?" he cursed, heading for the doorway and intending to poke his head out into the hall. "It's enough to wake the dead."

As he yanked open the bedroom door, intent on calling for an end to the ungodly racket, he was greeted by the ever-louder presence of a bagpiper and a hall seemingly full of kilt-clad Scotsmen.

"Who? What? Michael! Jeanne?" he called, seeing his secretary and his steward at the back of the assembly, trying to inch their way forward.

And then the pipes trilled and once more, the strident sound echoed wretchedly in the upstairs hall, bouncing off the walls and resounding relentlessly within his weary head. Quickly he fell back into the laird's rooms, totally unprepared for the fact that everyone else followed him, negating his escape.

"Tell me, Miss Donnachy, is this how you manage my household, letting anyone who pleases march into my bedroom?" the new laird demanded, his blue eyes piercingly cold as he glared in her direction.

"Och no, sir," said Jeanne, smothering a laugh as she tried to avoid staring at Creag's well-muscled though amazingly pale unclad legs. "You did that yourself, Creag, when you opened the door. Coinneach, the clan piper and storyteller, was merely playing the laird's reel to welcome you to Lindall Manor. It's traditional for him to parade through the village, collecting all the laird's people and then to proceed through the manor proper as part of the ceremony."

"This couldn't have waited until tomorrow?" Creag asked in resignation, hearing his hopes of a quiet evening evaporate before his ears.

"Oh, no, sir. 'Tis said to be a bad sign for the new laird to try to rest his head in Lindall Manor without a fitting initiation. It would not bode well for Linclachan," answered the piper, a gnarled figure of a man with a broad, almost toothless grin. "It might be best though if you were dressed."

"Dressed? What?" said Creag, suddenly looking down at his bare legs and groaning with embarrassment as he retreated and clutched for a sheet to twine around his middle. Here he'd been seen half-naked by most of his people! True, all of them were wearing kilts, but at least they had the hose to go with them. By comparison, his socks, undergarment and garters just did not look very noble. "Oh, very well. Suppose you folks all go downstairs and I'll follow you after I've made myself decent. Jeanne, serve them something."

"No, sir. Not until after you've been greeted properly as the new laird. Then we'll enjoy a feast the likes of which you've never dreamed of," promised his steward, a gleam in her eye as she imagined the American's reaction to the Scottish fare. The evening might prove amusing, after all.

Chapter Five

By the time Michael herded the gossiping villagers from the laird's suite, Creag was buttoning his trousers, critically examining their crease and contemplating a change of attire. As exhausted as he was, the self-made man understood he had no choice but to permit the villagers their ceremony. Successful negotiations had oft required such social concessions in the world of finance and he supposed Linclachan was no different. In fact, he decided, the best way to deal with these unpredictable Scots was to be businesslike and completely impersonal—and, in the future, to keep his bedroom door locked. He'd have no more processions through his boudoir, whether it was tradition or not! While it was true, he irritably conceded, that the Donnachys and Robertsons had presented him with his title, *he* was now the earl of Lindall. And given the amount of money this village was costing him, his wishes should be gospel around here.

"I don't suppose I need change into formal wear," Creag commented, half to himself and half to Michael.

"I don't think it's wise," his friend answered. "From what Leslie has told me, these particular Highlanders have no use for ordinary trousers, preferring to wear the kilt at all times. If you wore evening clothes, they'd think you very peculiar. For that matter, I would forget about the vest and jacket, as well."

"I can't greet them in my shirtsleeves," protested Creag, envisioning the formal dining rooms of London or Philadelphia, "not when they've probably come to pay me allegiance."

"That custom likely died out in the Middle Ages," said his secretary with a chuckle. Since he'd already met most of the villagers, Michael had no illusions about their pragmatic adjustment of history. According to Leslie, what customs were beneficial to the clan were enforced; others, those inconvenient or senseless, no matter how legitimate their historical precedence, had long been abandoned. "Having seen the poor state of Linclachan, Creag, I warrant most of these folks have come here with their hands out, and not to be shaking yours."

"Nonsense. Poverty doesn't preclude loyalty to the laird or their clan. As the new head of the Donnachys—"

"They're faithful to the clan, certainly, but I wager you'll have to work at earning their respect before you can depend on them," disputed Michael, astutely analyzing the Scottish character. "These people haven't survived in this rugged land without some hard lessons, and they're not about to fall on their knees to you just because you came from the States with money. Actually, I'm surprised there's not more resentment of your ready acceptance of the title, especially when your ancestor rejected Linclachan for greener pastures. I wouldn't offend them, Creag, or demand too much."

"Don't be self-righteous, Michael," Creag all but snapped. Such words on the part of his secretary, sympathetic as they were to the villagers, forced the new laird to keep secret, for a while longer, the contents of the report he had read last night. He couldn't chance Michael's announcing the truth; so, pushing aside his feelings of guilt, he went on as though nothing were amiss. "The ordinary laws of economics apply here just as definitively as in Philadelphia. One cannot take without giving, and I don't begrudge the Donnachys their due in exchange for the title of laird. I fully expect to rebuild the village, to give them a home of which to be proud."

"If you think that's all there is to the matter..." His friend grinned, curious to see the American put his notions into practice. Creag might imagine he could run Linclachan as he would one of his small corporations, but having gotten to know Jeanne, Leslie and now the indomitable Maggie, Michael rather doubted such an approach would work.

"Of course, that's all there is. And believe me, the allure of Scottish nobility and a prosperous village of quaint homes and loyal, colorful people will be just the bait to make Catherine Grayson become Lady Lindall, Mrs. C. Robertson Blake. Toward that end, I am willing to endure a great deal in the way of inconvenience.'' The blond gentleman grimaced, running a brush through his hair and checking his reflection in the laird's mirror. Damn, but that cleft seemed more pronounced when he was weary. "Haven't I already proven that by coming to this uncivilized location? Which reminds me, you must see to the condition of the roads before the Graysons arrive.''

"Of course, but isn't it time you were downstairs?''

"Yes,'' Creag agreed, opening the door to the hall. "By the way, what was that ruckus earlier, before the piper I mean?''

"Ruckus?'' Michael didn't recall any outstanding commotion, but then remembered the argument in the kitchen, and Maggie. "Oh, yes, it was the housekeeper, returning from a few weeks away, recovering from her grief at the laird's death, you know. Anyway, the staff was welcoming her home.''

"Strange, but I never imagined the Scots as a demonstrative people, though of course their impromptu parade was also unexpected. Still, whatever this investiture involves, it can't be any worse than having the whole village staring at my legs.''

The fact that he'd appeared at such a disadvantage still irked the efficient businessman and he wondered momentarily if the Scots would think less of him for it. Concern for his reputation was a relatively new element in Creag's life; indeed, it was an issue only because of Catherine and her family, and one he deeply resented caring about. In years past, C. Robertson Blake did as he chose, in business and play, regardless of others' whims; now, he was all too conscious of the judgments passed on him and his activities.

Therefore, as he started down the stairs to the main hall, he wasn't at all happy worrying about the way the villagers might have perceived him. He consoled himself, however, when the crowd below cheered him as he came into view. Here in Linclachan, he was the laird, leader of these people. Surely they would respect that and overlook his sartorial failings.

Reaching the last few steps, the tall American hesitated, wondering how to proceed into the throng in which he recognized no one. As usual, his efficient secretary solved the dilemma, hurrying down the steps and motioning a few men forward.

"Creag," began Michael, "these are the elders of the clan, the laird's council—Malcolm, Geordie, Duncan and Jamie."

"Welcome, laddie," said Malcolm as he extended a heavy hand, not to shake Creag's preferred one, however, but to slap him forcefully on the back. "I see we've a wee bit of work ahead to make you a proper Scot, but you're welcome nonetheless."

"Actually, I believe my mother and her father before her are the ones who made me a Scot," answered Creag wryly. His shoulder smarted from the blow he'd absorbed without flinching, and his patience was sorely tried by the need to be polite to this bear of a man when all he really wanted was a few hours' restful sleep.

"Aye, the lad would be right there," guffawed Duncan above the crowd's laughter, "but what my cousin means is that dressed as you are, Creag, no one would take you for a Scot, despite the truth in your blood."

At his words, Creag's eyes narrowed. *The truth in your blood,* was it? Did Duncan actually believe him to be the rightful laird? Perhaps the people of Linclachan were unaware of the illegitimacy of his inheritance, the American mused, deciding to look into Andrew Robertson's background more thoroughly. If the investigators had neglected to mention the existence of Fergus's granddaughter, what else might they have overlooked? And who knew what the solicitor had to gain by the announcement of his title? It was an issue he hadn't yet resolved.

Suddenly Jeanne Donnachy came forward from the crowd of well-wishers, greeting the council members warmly but giving him only a curt nod. Irritated as he was, it annoyed him further that her green eyes twinkled in amusement as though she knew some grand secret to which he wasn't privy.

"I've seen to the cleaning of Fergus's plaid," she announced formally. "Here it is."

"Wasn't it buried with him?" blurted Creag before he could stop himself. Unwelcome visions of a wizened old man meeting death as naked as when he arrived in the world crossed his mind. Just how "traditional" were these people?

"Of course it was," scoffed Jeanne, her tone mocking in its dismissal, "but this is the ceremonial dress plaid, worn by the laird only for official activities of the clan, not for personal milestones.''

"All right then, laddie, take off those Yank clothes," instructed Malcolm, "and we'll help you don the Donnachy colors.''

"That's all right, but there's no need. I mean, I am quite comfortable in trousers," Creag protested, taken aback at the thought of baring his legs again. He supposed it was his American upbringing, but somehow he didn't feel it was any more proper for a man to exhibit his limbs in public than it was for a woman to do so.

"What's wrong with his legs, then?" called an unseen female from the crowd of villagers.

"I don't know. I was too far back upstairs to see," replied another.

"Is the man bowlegged?" questioned a young lad.

"Maybe he's just shy." Another guffawed. "He is American.''

"You don't suppose he's crippled?" wondered a male voice.

"So what if he is? We've seen many a brave man exhibit a twisted limb beneath a kilt."

"It's all right, laddie. You've naught to be ashamed of," yelled a woman in the back.

"He seems to stand firmly enough."

"My legs are fine!" announced C. Robertson Blake over the babble of voices. "I simply do not choose to display them for all to see."

"That's not your decision as laird," warned Malcolm in a low voice, sending an angry glare in Creag's direction.

"If you don't attempt to get me to wear the plaid, I shall not make you wear trousers," negotiated the man of finance.

"You've no cause to make me do anything," snarled the leader of the council, peeved at the stranger's manner. The American had been given the title of laird; the plaid was part of the honor.

"But no true laird of the clan Donnachy has ever failed to wear the plaid," said Geordie, his eyes studying Creag as he spoke in a thoughtful manner, wondering how much the man could be intimidated. "Could it be there's been a mistake and you're not really a Robertson of the Donnachy line?"

Suddenly Creag saw Catherine, her parents and his acceptance into Philadelphia's society fading from his future. By comparison, what difference did bare knees make?

"No, no, of course I'm laird," he claimed quickly. "And I'll gladly wear the plaid. Give me the blasted thing and I'll go back to my rooms and change."

"No, you don't understand, man," said Jamie patiently. "You have to be vested here, in front of the clan."

"What?" roared Creag in protest, his temper inflamed by Jeanne Donnachy's smug smile.

"It's part of the investiture ceremony," pronounced Malcolm. "Without it, you can't be the laird."

"But I don't relish undressing in front of a crowd of strangers, a good number of them women!"

"Oh, if that's the only problem—" Malcolm smiled, winking at Geordie "—Jeanne will start pouring the drinks, and with us to shield you, no one will notice while we do what must be done. Gentlemen?"

Without hesitation, the four men encircled Creag, not speaking but attending to their task with great deliberation as the villagers moved toward their free drinks. All at once strange hands were helping him off with his shirt and tie. Then off came his shoes and just about everything else.

Was any woman worth this? he wondered silently, yielding after a brief struggle to the determined attention of the council. Concentrating his thoughts firmly on Catherine's teasing smile, blond curls and petite curves, Creag forced himself to relax, envisioning his fiancée's delight at being a member of the nobility, however minor.

And Catherine's gratitude, when she chose to share it, was plentiful indeed, he recalled with a randy grin. Just as intriguing memories of her kisses began to soothe his discomfort at being garbed in a skirt, Creag was startled to find the female image in his mind was no longer Catherine, but that aggravating, independent Jeanne Donnachy. Damn, why would he be wondering about the softness of her lips, especially when the last time he'd seen them they had been set in such a mischievous smirk?

The she-devil's emerald eyes had laughed at him. She knew full well what was to come, but had she warned him? Drat that saucy wench, he should have sent her packing when he had first considered it. Now, with her taking part in his investiture, seeing to the laird's clothes, and who only knew what else, he had the ungodly feeling she'd be around regardless of his complaints—unless, he thought with dawning hope, he could somehow marry her off. She wasn't at all unpleasant to look at, just to deal with. Surely he could find some impoverished farmer who needed a wife. He'd even provide a dowry if need be, he mused, as Malcolm attached a pouch of fur and leather to the belt at his waist and slapped him on the back again. This time though, Creag was pleased to notice, the heavy fabric of the plaid draped over his shoulder took the force of the man's hand.

"There you be, laddie. From head to toe, you look as fine a Scot as any Donnachy or Robertson in Linclachan," he pronounced with satisfaction.

"This is all I'm to wear?"

"Aye, you've a shirt, the plaid, the hose and the sporran. Your own shoes will have to do for the time being. There's nothing else unless you were going into battle," confirmed Duncan, "and then we'd give you a shield and sword."

"It's a bit drafty," murmured Creag.

"Ach, a touch of my whisky will warm you right soon," promised Jamie, a broad grin covering his face as he licked his lips in anticipation. Contrary to common practice, close association with his own product had never dampened his enthusiasm for it, nor the pride he took in his liquor. "Come along, lad, it's time to join your clan."

Seeing no way to avoid it, Creag squared his broad shoulders, raised his chin and led the way to the front of the great hall, trying desperately to forget his relative state of undress. Who would have thought that under his kilt a Scotsman wore... well, there was nothing he could do about the matter tonight anyway.

As he reached the small dais where a lone chair stood waiting, suddenly the din of the pipes sounded and every man, woman and child rose in unison, right fists clamped to their hearts as the ragged tune echoed over Lindall Manor like a weary dirge. When the last note died away, all stood silent until Malcolm cleared his throat and stepped forward, his face somber.

"Fergus was our laird and our friend for thirty-two years. This night we turn from him to our new protector, Creag Robertson, who will guide us in the future." Lifting his right hand from off his chest, Malcolm extended it in Creag's direction while the others followed suit as if giving a benediction. "Long life and blessings to the laird!"

"Long life and blessings," echoed throughout the hall, the simple words oddly touching Creag even as he realized Malcolm had erred in uttering his name.

"Thank you, Malcolm, but it's Creag Robertson *Blake*," the new laird corrected softly under the joyful chatter of the villagers, who were eager now to refill their glasses.

"Not as head of the Donnachys and Robertsons, it's not," decreed the oldest member of the council. "What name you use in America or in your business away from Scotland is your decision, but in Linclachan our laird shall have our name."

Before Creag could reply, Jamie was beside him, pressing a glass of whisky into his hand.

"Here's to you, Creag," the man said as everyone hefted glasses and fell silent. "May the best that you've seen till now be the worst of your life to come."

"May no hungry mouse e'er leave Lindall Manor's pantry with a tear in its eye as long as you are laird," added Duncan.

"May your chimneys keep blithely reeking till you're old enough to die," continued Geordie.

"And may Linclachan and her people make you so happy you'll think you've already passed on," concluded Malcolm. "Welcome, Creag Robertson, here's to your health."

"*Slainte,*" shouted the clan in unison as their laird nodded gravely, wondering as he raised his own cup whether he was expected to reply to their good wishes. The remarkable taste of the drink, however, chased all thoughts of formality from his mind.

"My Lord, Jamie, you made this stuff?" he asked in amazement, a relaxed smile softening his chiseled features, his tongue partially numb.

"Aye, Creag, but go easy. The cask won't run dry and the whisky takes a fair bit of getting used to," warned the distiller as he moved off to talk to some of his men.

"Not with my Scottish blood," Creag disputed, enjoying the liquor's warmth as it reached his stomach. "I must admit, however, no whisky I've ever had has been so smooth as yours."

"Probably none were as carefully watched over as his," said Leslie, approaching to fill Creag's glass. "Jamie won't let anyone sample the casks for twelve years."

"Believe me, the high quality shows, or should I say tastes?" The suddenly amiable laird laughed, his weariness temporarily forgotten as his body welcomed the soothing power of Jamie's whisky. "And, I might add, I've rarely seen a lovelier serving girl. Do you live in the village proper?"

"Oh, no, Creag. I belong to the laird's—"

"I warrant I'll enjoy that," he murmured in surprise, a broad grin splitting his face as he winked in her direction. This, then, was a more approachable lass than Jeanne Donnachy.

"—household. That is, I live with the laird, here at Lindall Manor, I mean," said Leslie, flushing at her poor choice of words. Before she could explain her situation any further, Maggie joined them, eyes sparking though she knew not what the stranger had said to embarrass the girl. From the looks of it, Michael too was concerned as he stood watching from across the room.

"See to the council, lass, they'll be wanting seconds by now," urged the older woman, putting her arm around Leslie and steering her away from apparent danger. As the young woman obeyed, Maggie turned to the laird. "That is Leslie Robertson, the clan healer and my niece, Creag, and any ideas you've got about fancying her, you can just forget them, be you laird or no."

"And just who might you be to give me orders?" he asked, hearty amusement at the woman's protective instinct lessening his annoyance at her manner. While Leslie was attractive, she didn't have the spectacular coloring Jeanne Donnachy did, he reflected, frowning abruptly and shaking his head from left to right to dislodge such absurd thoughts.

"Are you all right, then?" queried Maggie, concerned that her sudden dismissal of Leslie might have upset the man's mind. "I could fetch Leslie back with a potion."

"No, I'm fine," said Creag, sinking into the large wooden chair set on the raised dais, only to be so worried about how he could possibly sit decently in a skirt that he couldn't get comfortable. After shifting about uneasily to adjust the drape of the plaid, moving this way and that, he decided it was more practical to stand. Quickly he regained his feet, noticing that the old woman was watching him strangely. "Well then, tell me who you are, other than Leslie's aunt."

"I'm Maggie, the village seamstress and the old laird's, ah, your housekeeper," she answered, narrowing her eyes at the American's peculiar behavior. Oh, dear, the council wouldn't thank her for making Creag Robertson a madman, she feared, or at least any crazier than he already was for accepting the title they'd offered him.

"Yes, Michael did mention you returned today." He nodded, feeling oddly pleased as he saw Jeanne moving across the room toward them. "I understand you were taken poorly with Fergus's death."

"Ah, well, any man's a loss," agreed Maggie, uncertain what Creag wanted to hear. She had mourned no more than the rest of the village. Though he had been a frisky partner at times, Fergus had been mean tempered more often than not, and their relationship, sometimes sweet as honey, was just as often as bitter as the worst of Leslie's herbs.

"Especially one as loved as the laird," added Jeanne, nudging Maggie sharply with her elbow. It wouldn't hurt to give Creag an exaggerated picture of the old man's generosity in hopes he'd try to do better. "A generous and kindhearted man my grandfather was, may he rest in peace."

"Amen to that," murmured Creag, offering a silent prayer that the old laird wouldn't decide to haunt his illegitimate successor. Tonight of all nights, he craved a peaceful slumber, even one gotten by deceit.

"Generous and kindhearted." Maggie coughed, choking on her whisky. Could the girl have lost her senses? she wondered. Everyone knew hard times had made Fergus Donnachy squeeze every pence till it cried for mercy, and while he provided for

Linclachan as best he could, *kindhearted* was not the first word that sprang to mind in describing him.

"Well, Maggie, I'm pleased to make your acquaintance. Tomorrow I will ask you to show me the laird's housewares so I can see what needs replacing before I entertain," announced Creag, deliberately addressing the older woman though his traitorous body longed to crush the younger one in his arms. Damn, was it the Scottish air or the superb whisky that made Jeanne seem so soft and feminine rather than warlike? Maybe it was the shadowy candlelight in the large hall and the increasing weariness overcoming his body.

"Aye, if Jeanne will show me where it's kept," agreed Maggie, forgetting her role as housekeeper.

"What?" Surely Creag hadn't heard properly. What kind of housekeeper didn't know the inventory of her wares or their whereabouts, for that matter? Unless his ears were now as unreliable as his eyes, which couldn't seem to register anything but the creamy rose texture of Jeanne's cheeks against her brown hair, something was definitely peculiar about the old woman.

"She will be glad to do so," interceded his steward, "but now, Maggie, you had best see to Mary in the kitchen. You know she gets flustered with large crowds and probably needs help."

"Then let Fiona or Beth lend a hand," began Maggie, only to fall silent under Jeanne's pointed glare. Sullenly she moved off toward the kitchen, though clearly not so intimidated by the steward's orders that she neglected to top off her glass.

"I'm sorry for her outburst, Creag, but she's not been quite right since she found Fergus dead in his bed," explained the lovely Scot, brushing a stray curl from off her cheek. Somehow, she felt a pretext might be useful to excuse Maggie's oversights in the days ahead. "It was a terrible shock."

"I imagine so," conceded the American, as he took his glass in both hands and swallowed deeply to stop himself from reaching out to caress her tempting form. Maybe he was going daft to be so affected by her, he thought, trying desperately to remember what color Catherine's eyes were, compared to Jeanne's emerald ones.

"Creag, sir, I'm Andrew Robertson," announced a paunchy fellow, coming forward to join them.

"Yes?"

"We corresponded," he explained, standing much too close to Jeanne for Creag's liking. "I'm Linclachan's solicitor."

"Ah, yes, Andrew. I wondered when you would turn up," admitted the financier, pointedly hesitating before taking the Scot's extended hand. Whatever the man wanted, Creag fumed, suddenly becoming very protective of his household, it couldn't be business, not the way he was leering at Jeanne.

"I've been here all evening, but you were busy. However, you'll find I am quite knowledgeable with regard to the laird's legal dealings, and I would be most happy to handle your work, as well," gushed the balding lawyer, running a damp handkerchief across his head. "Actually, Jeanne here can tell you just how experienced a man I am if you know what I mean."

For a moment, Creag knew only the sudden urge to pound the man into the hall's stone floor for even vaguely suggesting such familiarity with his comely steward. As laird, it was certainly his duty to safeguard the women in his care, he reflected, even if he didn't especially like them.

Then Creag took a deep breath and his emotions righted themselves. He was the newcomer here. He had best not interfere in a situation he was unsure of. He doubted there was any way the brown-haired beauty would ever allow her attentions to be engaged by this middle-aged Don Juan. Therefore, there was no reason to encourage him and plenty to ignore him.

"I'll discuss the matter with Miss Donnachy," Creag said curtly, taking Jeanne's arm and leading her away from the irritating fellow, dismissing the enraged solicitor without so much as a backward glance. "At the moment, however, I am more interested in this portrait. Who was he, Jeanne?"

"Oh, let me think. Yes, that would be the fourth earl, Colum Donnachy, the laird before Fergus. I believe he would have been your grandfather's third cousin on his mother's side," Jeanne explained carefully, hoping she'd be able to recall these relationships she was spinning if he ever asked again.

"No, I don't believe that's possible."

"It's not?" Momentary panic tinged Jeanne's voice as she wondered how Blake could question her identification. Surely she knew more of the Donnachy lineage than he. It had to be his own relationship to Colum that he was questioning.

"No. Grandfather had a portrait of the Robertson branch and I swear this man was in it, though he did have a small scar on his chin that is missing here."

"Oh, that explains it. Your picture shows Colum's twin, Gavin. Their mother was the last of the Robertsons of that generation and for fear the line would die out, they christened one twin a Robertson and one a Donnachy. Gavin was a soldier, wounded in some skirmishes with the English, but Colum ended up as laird of the Donnachys," lied Jeanne nervously, noticing suddenly that Creag had a slight cleft she'd never noticed, just as Colum did. "Actually, I think you have his chin."

"Oh, you're right there, lass," agreed Jamie, reappearing with a full glass of whisky for Creag. "There's a definite similarity in the way they hold their heads, too, sort of aristocratic, you ken?"

Aristocratic? Creag thought. Well, why not if I'm the earl of Lindall? I have every right to look aristocratic, even if Colum is no more my grandfather's third cousin than Lucifer is.

"Here's to Colum," he called loudly, feeling the need to establish his presence in the now-rowdy assembly. When all quieted, he continued. "And to all the lairds who've gone before me. May I do them proud!"

So saying, he lifted his glass high and proceeded to empty it in one swallow, then place it on a table nearby. Suddenly the room began to spin and his body to sway and before he knew what was happening, the very dignified C. Robertson Blake, earl of Lindall and laird of Linclachan, crumpled to the floor as though struck by lightning.

With a startled gasp, Jeanne knelt beside him and loosened his shirt, relieved to hear the heavy rasp of his breathing. So was Malcolm, who feared the new laird had joined the old before he'd settled Linclachan's problems.

Quickly Leslie joined Jeanne and checked Creag's eyes before she rested her hand on his dampened forehead. Then rising to her feet, she whispered briefly to the clan's steward.

"The celebration can continue," announced Jeanne. "Creag is only Jamie's latest victim. Our new laird is unused to fine whisky and is merely *stottin*. There's no sense in ending the party for the sake of a man who's had too much to drink."

"At least not until the rest of us have, too," shouted a hoarse male voice.

The four council members regarded each other silently, their eyes rolled heavenward and their eyebrows arched in consternation.

"It would seem they don't breed them strong in the States," muttered Malcolm, shaking his head.

"Aye, he'll have to learn to keep up with us," agreed Jamie, giving a loud snort as he stepped over the unmoving Creag, "or we'll have to reconsider him as laird of the Clan Donnachy."

"Aye, well you might," murmured Jeanne softly, her eyes softening at the sight of the newly kilted American, passed out on his first night in Lindall Manor. From this sad demonstration, she somehow doubted C. Robertson Blake would be the leader they'd hoped he would be, despite the wealth he'd brought to Linclachan.

Chapter Six

The next morning, the pounding in Creag's temples kept painful time with the plaintive bleating of the infernal sheep that had roused the newly installed laird from his slumber.

In annoyance, Creag cracked open a bleary eye only to discover the dreariness that passed for early daylight in this cursed region of the Highlands. Promptly he snapped his eye shut once more, but the stone disguised as a pillow in his ramshackle manor house refused to cradle his head. Besides, no matter how tightly he drew his lids together, images of Jeanne Donnachy danced before him. Perhaps they were the remnants of last night's dreams, he realized with a frown, but whether they constituted vision or nightmare, he was in no mood to decide.

Heaving a sigh, Creag determined to ignore his headache and begin the day. God only knows what other unpleasant surprises he would be called upon to face that morning, though it would take considerable effort on the part of the inhabitants of Linclachan to come up with something worse than that wretched unclothing ceremony of the night before. It had to have constituted the most embarrassing moment of his life.

In exasperation, he threw back the bedcovers and swung his long, muscular legs over the side of the bed. The coldness of the bare floor and a considerable draft caused him to wince as he got to his feet, his fingertips holding his throbbing head together.

Ambling over to the washstand, Creag scowled when he glanced down to see last night's damnable kilt still wrapped around his waist. Good God, he thought with a start, beginning to rip at its folds and tucks, he couldn't even remember climbing the stairs to return to his chambers when the celebration had concluded. Yet he must have done so, he tried to assure himself. Otherwise, he wouldn't be here in the laird's chambers. Would he?

The last thing he recalled clearly was sipping a glass of whisky. But surely the small amount of spirits he had consumed could not account for his inability to remember how the night had ended. He could drink along with the best of them, these damned Scots included. No, it had to be last night's complete exhaustion that clouded his memory, Creag decided, though the dissipated image glaring at him from the looking glass made the American grimace, and wish he could be certain he had not somehow disgraced himself in front of the villagers.

Not that he should be concerned about the opinion of the locals, Creag asserted, splashing cold water on his face as he considered their poor manners of last night. Still, it would be easier to gain their respect, and more importantly their cooperation, if he had not exhibited behavior unbecoming a laird on his first evening in Lindall Manor.

Yet, in light of what he could recollect of the welcoming festivities, Creag was hard-pressed to imagine any conduct that the Highlanders of Linclachan would deem unacceptable, judging from their raucous conversation and the way they had burst into his bedroom. They were a rough-and-tumble lot, a good deal more independent and proud than he had ever expected them to be. How was he going to turn this miserable, free-spirited bunch into the sort of villagers who would respectfully doff their caps when he and the Graysons rode by in his carriage?

To make matters worse, the members of his own household were no better than the residents of Linclachan, he fumed, fragmented memories of his investiture as laird making the muscles along his jaw grow taut with anger. He could swear he had definitely seen a glint of amused satisfaction lighting Jeanne Donnachy's agate green eyes just before he was stripped of his clothing and wrapped up in that musty length of plaid wool.

Surely the witch must have known what was planned, and she had warned neither Michael nor him. But, he suspected that if he questioned her about the matter, she would only lower those exquisitely long lashes of hers and deny any wrongdoing. Even when she was trying to appear compliant, there was fiery defiance in her, and somehow a resentful Creag doubted he would ever be able to command Jeanne's loyalty. He imagined she was the sort of woman who would either give her cooperation or not, as she chose.

Still, for all the aggravation he felt whenever he thought of Jeanne, and despite the fact that he was accustomed to grown men quaking before him in the most prestigious business offices in the world, Creag had to admit that he admired the girl's magnificent spirit almost as much as he deplored it.

As the problems of Lindall Manor seemed to loom before him, and the pounding in his head became more insistent, Creag decided a bit of food might help. After all, he had eaten practically nothing yesterday, at least nothing he could recall. Certainly a substantial meal would help him regain his optimism.

Deciding to forego the clucking ministrations of a valet, if indeed the staff of the manor even ran to such servants, Creag donned the first clothing he grabbed from the cupboard. Soon he was ready to leave the drafty bedchamber behind, his limbs warmed by a proper and welcome pair of trousers.

Immediately outside his door, Creag almost tripped over the prone body of a snoring Highlander. Fitted out in what must have once been a ceremonial kilt, the man, even in sleep, clutched the handle of a rather rusty sword. From the looks of him, Creag assumed the fellow was likely some sort of guard set by tradition to watch over Linclachan's laird as he slept.

With a weary shake of his aching brow as he stepped over the comatose form, Creag could only be grateful that he had had no actual need of the Scot's services. From the sound of the rumbling emanating from the man's chest, an entire army could have entered his rooms and slain him a hundred times over without this guard ever having been aware of a thing.

Descending the stairs, Creag saw no sign of Michael. Assuming the secretary was awaiting him at the breakfast table, he skirted the artisans and laborers setting up to begin their day. In the process of searching for the dining room, the new earl of Lindall discovered a few more of *his people* tucked away in corners and under staircases, apparently sleeping away last night's excesses. Though he was appalled at the thought of the Graysons encountering such a sight during their sojourn, Creag had to admit that finding them brought him some solace. Certainly, no matter what he had done last night, it could have been no worse than the behavior of these men.

A relieved smile settled about his lips as the tall, blond American made his way into the dining room, his mouth beginning to water at the thought of eggs and bacon, toast, ham, pastries and plenty of strong black coffee.

But when he entered the dining area, Creag saw that something was terribly wrong. No tempting aromas assailed him, no heaping platters sat on the sideboard, and no Michael sat waiting his arrival. In fact, there was not even a fire laid in the hearth. The place was almost as cold and dark as a mine shaft.

Was everyone still abed? he wondered. Or was this horrific lack of service simply an oversight on the part of that doddering, poor excuse of a housekeeper who had been so intent on warning him away from her niece the night before?

Determined to set things running smoothly, quickly as possible, Creag bore down on the kitchen with a purposeful tread. His mood was made all the more belligerent when the manor began to ring with the sounds of the workmen hammering and the pain in his head responded to the din.

After a few false starts and wrong turns, the nettled laird found the staircase that led below stairs to the cook's domain. To his mind it was growing increasingly absurd that a man couldn't have a decent meal in his own home, especially when he was in such dire need of sustenance.

Reaching the lower floor and rounding a corner, Creag stopped suddenly when he heard, beyond a partially opened door, the sound of feminine laughter following the mention of his name. One of the voices, he was certain, belonged to Jeanne Donnachy. The other, lower pitched and more raspy, like as not was that of the addled housekeeper.

Cross and needlessly hungry as he was, it took a mighty effort for Creag to resist barging into the kitchen and demanding to know why his meal was not ready to be served as it should have been. But some lilting quality in Jeanne Donnachy's laughter caused him to stay where he was. The vibrant joy of her took him by surprise, and he experienced an irrational satisfaction at the sound of his pretty steward's gaiety. In fact, he found his own traitorous mouth turning up until he became aware of exactly what it was Jeanne was saying.

"Can you imagine, Maggie, C. Robertson Blake being sent into oblivion by little more than a dram of Jamie's best?" Jeanne said with a giggle that Creag might have considered seductive under other circumstances. "I don't know how we managed to get him up the stairs."

"You can't blame the new laird just because he is unused to good Scotch whisky," Maggie stated with more charity than Jeanne would have ordinarily expected from her.

"Oh, Maggie, don't make excuses for him. What kind of a man is that, to be laid low by such a wee drop?"

"Believe me, to my eyes he seems strapping and manly enough," the older woman commented dryly. "Someone should talk to the lad about how to sit when he's wearing a kilt."

"Why, Maggie! You wicked soul!" Jeanne chided, laughter bubbling over to mingle with her words.

By now, Creag's increasingly darkening face was as ominous and black as the most threatening thundercloud. Before old Maggie could say another word, he stormed into the kitchen, his eyes flashing and his deep voice booming like some crazed creature fashioned by Thor.

"Where, might I ask, is my breakfast?" he demanded, his arms crossed in a lordly manner over his broad chest as he strode to the middle of the room and took up an arrogant stance. "I have a headache that would kill an average man, and all due to a lack of nourishment."

"Perhaps if you lowered your voice, the headache wouldn't be quite so bad," Jeanne snapped impulsively, uncowed by the murderous expression on the American's face. How dare this outlander think to intimidate her within the walls of her own home?

C. Robertson Blake stared at his chastising steward with such outrage that he didn't trust himself to reply, the logic of her words adding to his silent fury.

He moved closer, towering over the woman, seeking to put her in her place. But Jeanne Donnachy didn't cower. Nor did she take a step back. Instead, she lifted her face to his, raised a nicely arched brow and smiled, wordlessly daring Creag to do his worst.

Her blasé attitude in the face of his foul mood infuriated him all the more, so that his fingers curled tightly into frustrated fists as his hands hung helplessly at his sides. Still, the willowy Scot never flinched, but persisted in regarding him with detached curiosity and amusement, as though he were one of P. T. Barnum's oddities put on display. Creag could only continue to glare blackly in return.

How long this contest of wills would have continued, Jeanne could not have said, though she did notice herself weakening, becoming vaguely distracted from her anger as she studied Blake's commanding features.

Annoyed with herself, she would have redoubled her efforts at defiance, but suddenly Maggie caught Jeanne's eye, and a silent warning was sent. This man was the new laird. False as his title might be, in truth he was the only one who could save Linclachan. He could not be taunted.

For an instant, Jeanne fervently wished there was no such thing as clan loyalty. But then she berated herself for her selfishness. Hadn't dealing with her crochety grandfather taught her how to cope with obstinate and haughty men? Demurely Jeanne dropped her eyes before addressing Creag in a voice laced with honeyed sweetness.

"I'm sorry for the misunderstanding, Creag. I can assure you, this will happen no more. Needless to say, we thought you would not be rising so early after your... your... weariness yesterday evening."

Damn it! She was doing it again, Creag thought. Though it appeared she was smothering her natural fiery inclinations under layers of false docility, her spirit was shining through. And so, too, was her implied insult, beneath its sugar coating.

His pride seriously stung, Creag was astonished to find that he could not exhibit as much control as she. No matter how he struggled to do so, he was unable to respond to this woman on a civilized level. But the whole idea of such raging passions was ridiculous! After all, he was C. Robertson Blake, a man who had learned to control his feelings in order to attain whatever goals he had set for himself. He had surrendered his life to cool, logical thinking, reacting in all his business dealings with a level head instead of his heart. And yet he could not bring that same attitude to bear with this willowy slip of a woman. Within the space of twenty-four hours, Miss Jeanne Donnachy had been able to delve beneath the detachment with which he had cloaked himself for so many years, and release the emotions still simmering beneath his reserved facade. Damn the woman! And damn the fact that he couldn't find it within himself to simply ignore her!

"Now that you have made your apologies, do you think it possible that I might be served some breakfast in my own house?" he snapped, annoyed as much at himself as he was at Jeanne.

"But, of course, laddie. We'll see to it ourselves. It's just that Mary was out of sorts this morning," Maggie soothed, coming forward to place herself between this snarling, offended male and the young woman whose temper was only too ready to flare once more. "And while we are at it," she continued in a crooning voice as she placed her hand on Creag's arm and gently steered him toward the door, "why don't you find Leslie and ask her for a headache powder? I'm certain she has something that will have you feeling fine in no time at all."

"Ah, yes, Leslie," Creag murmured. A soft smile highlighted his face as he recalled the gentle, feminine woman he had met the night before. She was so different in temperament from Fergus's nettlesome granddaughter that the mere thought of the amiable blonde brought him a needed respite from his roiling emotions. Casting Jeanne a disparaging glance, he added, "Surely such a tender soul as she will know how to sympathize with an ailing man."

"I thought it was treatment for your head that you wanted," Jeanne stated, a scowl settling upon her mouth.

"Hmm? Oh, yes, that, too," Creag responded, pretending to be distracted by thoughts of Leslie before he turned on his heel and left the room.

The minute he disappeared, Jeanne began a whirlwind of activity, clanging pots and pans and making numerous trips to the pantry, her lovely features overcome with pique.

"What's gotten into you, lass?" a mystified Maggie inquired. "You're not a wee bit jealous, are you, that the laird seems to be more tolerant of my grandniece than yourself?"

"Jealous? Are you daft, Maggie?" Jeanne snorted with derision.

"And is that why you're acting like an inmate in an asylum?" the old woman asked knowingly. "Besides, surely you ken that Leslie has quietly set her sights elsewhere?"

"What Leslie does is her own affair, my only concern is that I wouldn't want to see my best friend involved with such a beastly and vile man as C. Robertson Blake," the younger woman protested, spooning oatmeal into a bowl and sprinkling it liberally, perhaps too liberally, with salt, in the Scottish manner. Then she turned and began readying the delicacy one of the villagers had brought to the manor for the previous day's celebrations.

"You're giving him haggis for breakfast?" Maggie asked incredulously. "If the laddie is feeling poorly, that might not sit well on his stomach, him not being used to our food and all."

"Oh? Do you really think that might be the case?" Jeanne asked much too innocently, a vengeful gleam in her emerald eyes. "I simply thought the new laird might like to sample the native foods. And now that it's dished out, I certainly can't waste it."

"You're playing with fire, lass," Maggie warned. "A man like Creag is not about to put up with your games."

"A man like Creag? You're talking then, of a male given to rudeness, arrogance and unbearable crossness?" Jeanne asked blithely as she unwrapped some smoked fish, hacked off a chunk and tossed it upon a plate, without bothering to remove the bones.

"Och, Jeanne! Even the best of men can act that way at times, especially when they feel a woman doesn't appreciate them. Why I can remember instances when your grandfather—"

"My grandfather?" Jeanne asked in surprise, looking up quickly to note the sudden red flush coloring Maggie's withered cheeks. "What about my grandfather?"

"'Tis nothing, nothing at all," the old woman demurred, turning her back and fussing with the kettle on the hearth so that Jeanne wouldn't notice the soft look in her eyes as memories of Fergus carried her back to other times.

Though Jeanne's suspicions had been aroused, she held her tongue. Everyone deserved to hold on to their secrets, she decided. Besides, she was too busy with *his lordship*'s breakfast to worry about what might have once been between her grandfather and old Maggie Robertson, absurd though such a notion was.

Creag, more irritated than he had been before going to the kitchen, had searched along a half-dozen corridors for Leslie before he finally spied the missing Michael emerging from a room filled with workmen. Though the man was obviously seeing to his duties, he, too, looked much the worse for last night's wear. But then breakfast would soon be forthcoming, Creag thought with smug anticipation, and a good meal would see them both feeling better. First, however, he wanted to find Leslie, and rid himself of this insufferable pounding in his head.

"Michael," Creag called to his secretary before he disappeared into the labyrinth of the manor house once more. "Have you seen Leslie?"

"Leslie?" Michael inquired sharply, remembering clearly the attention Creag had paid her the night before. "Whatever can you want with her?"

"What do you mean what do I want with her?" Creag barked, taking offense at his friend's defensive attitude over such a simple question. Michael was acting as though the laird of the manor had decided to whisk the woman off to his suite of rooms to sample her favors. Good God! What had come over his usually reliable and intelligent aide? Did everyone but he who spent some time in this accursed part of Scotland lose his senses along with his heart?

"Exactly that! Why do you wish to see the girl?" Michael rejoined, surliness tinging his voice as he considered how the rugged, blond looks of his employer might appeal to a woman. And Creag, he well knew, had never been one to ignore a pretty face.

"Damnation, man, I simply need one of her headache powders, though why I should have to explain to you is beyond me," Creag exploded. "What is going on in this house? I send you up here to straighten things out, and you become as bad as the rest of them. Just see if you can find Leslie and get what I require, then meet me in the dining room for breakfast."

"Right away," Michael replied, his lips drawn together in a grim line. Perhaps he should have asked Leslie for something to cure his own sour stomach and throbbing head before he had left her that morning. Last night had been quite a celebration, and the drinking had definitely left its toll.

Creag wandered around the manor, his broad-shouldered frame filling many a doorway as he inspected the renovations. Finally he decided that enough time had passed to give Jeanne the chance to see to his breakfast.

For the second time that morning, he approached the dining room expectantly, anticipating a hearty meal and, hopefully, Michael's normally good-natured company.

As he neared the door, Creag was pleased to note a definite aroma of food coming from within. Though he could not distinguish, by the smells alone, the dishes that had been prepared, he congratulated himself on taking a firm stand with Jeanne and the old housekeeper that morning. After all, women did have to be told what to do if a man expected his wishes to be carried out. Now there could be no doubt as to exactly what he wanted.

Entering the room to find a packet of powder on his plate but no Michael, Creag shrugged his shoulders and made ready to enjoy his meal. He was not about to allow his secretary's strange behavior to diminish the sweetness of his own victory over the recalcitrant women of his household. Nor would he be put off by the portrait of some ancient, gnarled Scot glaring down at him in a menacing manner. Instead, he would savor every mouthful of this breakfast, Creag told himself, as he had relished no other.

A superior smile on his face, the handsome American laird reached a well-muscled arm forward to uncover a serving dish. Fish! One of the others had to be the eggs, he assumed, his mouth already tasting their delicate flavor. Porridge! A third lid was removed, clanging to the tabletop as a result of Creag's haste. Boiled mutton! Still another cover went flying, only to expose an indescribable pudding or meat substance, he couldn't tell which. Pouring the contents of the pot beside him into his cup, Creag was incensed to find tea instead of coffee. It was open mutiny, that's what it was, and his rage vented itself in a mighty roar.

Almost immediately, the door opened and Jeanne Donnachy came into view.

"Is aught the matter, Creag?" she asked, her silken voice soft and soothing while a triumphant smile graced her fine face.

"What do you call this?" Creag asked, his tone dangerously soft.

"We call it breakfast. Why? Do you have another name for it in America?" Jeanne inquired, her green eyes widening a bit too guilelessly for Creag's tastes.

"We would label this slop," Creag replied, pointing to the haggis and biting out each word slowly as he fought to keep some composure.

"Well, here it is called haggis," Jeanne commented glibly. "It's ground meat, spice and oats wrapped in sheep's intestines."

Sheep! When he had first come here, Creag had hated the damned creatures on sight. Now he knew why. For the love of God, he silently raged, his fingers wrapping around his cutlery, everywhere else in the civilized world, he had only to utter a word and businessmen and bankers rushed to do his bidding. But here, in this wretched house, no matter how he bellowed, he couldn't get a decent breakfast. He found the situation incomprehensible.

"Where," he began, his voice so low and indistinct as it wended its way through his gritted teeth that Jeanne had to come closer to hear him, "are the eggs? The ham? The bacon? Where's the *damned coffee?*" he finished, his deep voice moving to a magnificent crescendo.

"As laird of Linclachan you should be eating Scottish food," Jeanne replied, tempted to back away from this furious male, but holding her ground. "It's good, hearty fare. We exist on it, and so did your ancestors."

"This type of thing is probably what prompted my ancestors to leave Scotland. As for me, as laird of Linclachan, I'll eat what I damned well please, and that means eggs—two of them—bacon or sausage or ham, toast and coffee. Every morning! And while we're at it, allow me to inform you, just so there are no further misunderstandings, that I expect luncheon served at one and dinner sharply at eight each night. Do I make myself clear, Miss Donnachy?"

"Perfectly, Creag," Jeanne answered, tilting her head truculently, "though I don't ken why you're being so insufferable about it."

"Oh, you don't?" Creag asked, drumming his long, lean fingers on the tabletop in a staccato rhythm. "Then permit me to enlighten you. I didn't come seeking this title. You people came to me. I agreed to become the laird, and the laird I will be. That means my wishes are the ones to be carried out...not yours, not Maggie's nor Leslie's, and not those of the bloody shepherds. Mine, do you understand? Mine!"

"Being laird doesn't give you the right to become some tyrant," Jeanne blurted, impressed in spite of herself at the depth of passion lurking in this good-looking man's soul. "There is very little power in being laird of Linclachan, but much responsibility."

"I am only too aware of my obligations to this village and its people. Yet I stand ready to undertake them," Creag said, shaking his head wearily, having no wish to ignore the welfare of this place as men he knew personally had subjugated Johnstown to their own interests. "But as long as I am laird, whether I am here alone or with friends, I expect you to comply with my wishes and obey me."

"Friends?" Jeanne repeated numbly. Somehow it was difficult to envision anyone getting close to this complex male. What man would suffer his arrogant nature? As for women, Creag's good looks and muscular frame might be enough to attract their notice, but any female in her right mind would bolt from this overpowering bullying the moment C. Robertson Blake opened his mouth and began his intolerable roar.

"I do have friends, you know," Creag responded, intruding upon Jeanne's thoughts. The corners of his brilliant blue eyes crinkled in amusement as he watched a crimson wave creeping up his rebellious steward's delicate cheeks. So he had read her thoughts correctly, he thought with satisfaction. Still, for some odd reason he was not vexed with her at the moment. Blushing became her and made her appear all the more attractive. In fact, standing as she was, the sunlight turning the topmost layer of her brown hair to flame, Jeanne Donnachy was loveliness itself.

In that instant, responding on a much more primitive level than he could have ever admitted, Creag felt a sudden rush of sympathy for the girl. In his childhood, he had been nurtured by the stories of knights and fair ladies that his mother had told him. But until this moment, he had never given any thought to the feelings of the princess when the victor had laid claim to her castle. Now, however, looking into Jeanne Donnachy's eyes, he knew exactly what it was the princess had felt. And though Lindall Manor, decrepit and in dire need of repair, was far from the many-towered citadel depicted in fairy tales, it couldn't be easy for this young woman to see someone else assume ownership of her grandfather's house.

Perhaps he had handled her all wrong. She was a person, after all, not some business competitor. It could be that a simple gesture of friendship would solve his problems with his pretty but wayward steward.

"You know, Jeanne," he began softly, "I don't thrive on arguments. If you allow it, I could be your friend, too."

"I would never be that desperate," Jeanne quickly protested with vehemence, completely misconstruing Creag's intentions. "I've no desire to share the laird's bed regardless of the name you give such a relationship."

Creag's strong jaw tightened as Jeanne's stinging remark found its target. Damn the girl! Did she believe he was the sort of man to try to compromise a country innocent? How could she really think he would have to resort to the seduction of unwilling females in order to get a woman to warm his bed? Though he had only himself to blame for trying to tame such a wild little hellcat with kindness, it was time to settle things with Jeanne Donnachy once and for all.

"You mistook my meaning entirely, Miss Donnachy. I have no designs on you," Creag said coldly, relying upon self-righteousness to help him ignore his illogical anger that she would have rejected him so hotly and fiercely if he *had* been trying to compromise her. "However many local swains you may have gathered to your side, I have no desire to be one of them. And if you disbelieve me, it might help to know that I have already inquired about the possibility of asking you to leave the manor house."

"What?" Jeanne interrupted.

"Nevertheless," Creag continued, forcing himself to ignore the red streaks of anger and embarrassment coloring the girl's otherwise lovely face, "I have been informed that I cannot do so without causing hard feelings on the part of the people of Linclachan. That is the only reason why you remain in this household. But, just because you happen to be Fergus Donnachy's granddaughter, it does not give you the right to disparage me. Continue to do so and I swear I will get rid of you. I don't care if I have to marry you off to the first eligible man who crosses the manor's threshold."

"You wouldn't dare! You have no right!" Jeanne cried.

"Try me. It's either that, or else I stick you in some isolated convent. It makes no difference to me. Do you understand what I'm telling you, Jeanne?"

"Only too well," the pretty Scot replied, unshed moisture glistening in her eyes at the thought of this ignorant imposter speaking to her so rudely, threatening her in the home that had belonged to her family for centuries.

Good Lord, there were tears in the woman's eyes. Tears! And he had put them there, Creag thought miserably, wanting to pound the table in frustration. Was nothing simple in this god-forsaken place? His dealings with Jeanne had made him think that nothing could compel her to weep, yet here she was, valiantly trying to hide the fact that she was doing just that. Where the hell was Michael? Why wasn't he here to help him deal with this?

"Look," Creag said awkwardly, reaching out to pat Jeanne's hand and then thinking better of it, "I'm not asking you to like me, or even accept me. But I must insist on some sort of respect. Here, do you want a handkerchief?"

"Whatever would I need that for?" Jeanne asked proudly before lapsing into a pathetic little sniff so quick and quiet that Creag wondered if he had imagined it.

"For no reason whatsoever," he said, reaching out with the crisp white cloth to gently wipe the crystal droplet hanging from Jeanne's long, seductive lashes. "Now why don't you return to your duties, and send Maggie to me. I want to talk with her."

Watching Jeanne leave the room, her head held high despite her evident upset, C. Robertson Blake wondered what he was going to do with the woman. She drove him to madness! He wanted to shake her, he wanted to throttle her, he wanted to... good God! Did he want to kiss her, to explore the possibility that the fire that ignited whenever they were together might be rooted in something other than anger?

But what was he thinking? he asked himself with a groan as he buried his still-throbbing head in his hands. Surely the impulse had been spurred by Jeanne's reaction to his overture of friendship. He would never have thought of such a thing on his own. After all, he was going to marry Catherine Grayson. It was a goal he had set, and he never veered from an objective, no matter what the distraction. Wedding his society miss was what all this effort was about. It was the reason for tying himself to the problems of Lindall Manor and Linclachan.

Yet, when he had reached out to Jeanne, the simple touch of her skin beneath his fingers had driven all thoughts of Catherine from his mind. Damnation, he swore, would he never be himself again, and just as important, would the throbbing at his temples never cease?

He picked up the package of headache powder to empty it into his water glass and then thought better of it. No one had actually told him this was a cure for headaches. For all he knew, it was a dose of rat poison Jeanne had deposited on the table.

With a scrape of his chair, he rose from his place and began to pace the room. The manor house was a physical disaster, and the locals were disrespectful. Even Michael was not himself and out of sorts. The noise made by the workmen made the ache in his head unbearable, and he was certain there wasn't an acceptable meal to be had in all of Scotland. Yet what did he, a captain of industry, find himself doing in the middle of such chaos? Waiting for the appearance of a feebleminded housekeeper, that's what! Never had he envisioned the simple little village of Linclachan changing his life, damn it, his world, so drastically!

Shuffling footsteps pulled Creag from his thoughts and alerted him to Maggie's arrival. The old woman entered the room and looked at him with a steady gaze, as though she could see what was going on here, even if he couldn't. It was an absurd notion, he told himself, to think that such an addled soul would know more than he did. Then, recalling her prattle in the kitchen, an uncomfortable Creag wondered if he really did hold any secrets from the old woman. The very idea of her judging his manhood made his voice gruff when he addressed her.

"Maggie, have a seat," Creag ordered.

"You've had words with Jeanne, haven't you?" Maggie reproved in a grandmotherly fashion as she settled herself in the chair Creag held out for her.

"Now that's nothing to concern yourself about," he said, wanting to forget the entire incident but continuing to be haunted by the tears he had placed in Jeanne's eyes.

"What affects one of us, affects us all," Maggie murmured. "You'll soon learn that's what it means to be part of a clan."

"I promise I will do my best to do so," Creag replied, astounded to discover that he had actually meant it, and was not merely placating the elderly servant.

"Good. As for Jeanne, she's a fetching lass, is she not?"

"Whatever you're suggesting, I want no part of it," the new laird objected heatedly, wondering if the girl had accused him of dastardly behavior. But the smile the housekeeper gave him was that of a matchmaker not an outraged matron, and Creag found himself breathing a deep sigh of relief.

"Say what you want, but I see what I see," the old woman replied.

"Enough of this nonsense," Creag said with a false laugh, experiencing discomfort at the images Maggie's suggestive notions had evoked. How could his traitorous body react so? He found himself fervently wishing Catherine was due to arrive on the morrow so that her presence would distract him from any notice of Jeanne Donnachy. He didn't desire the beautiful Scot, and the girl herself had made it plain that she wanted no part of him. Shoving troublesome thoughts aside, he rapidly changed the subject, addressing Maggie once more. "I sent for you in order to discuss something other than Jeanne."

"What might that be?" Maggie asked skeptically.

"The contents of the household," Creag replied quickly, before the woman could return to the topic of Fergus's granddaughter. "I'll be having some important guests in the not-too-distant future, and I must be certain that they are duly impressed with the manor. This morning I would like to inspect the linens, to see if any new must be ordered."

"But surely a grand man like you shouldn't concern himself with such mundane trifles," Maggie protested, her mind working feverishly to try to think where the manor linen could be stored. This business of posing as a housekeeper in order to keep an eye on Leslie and Jeanne was difficult enough without the new laird demanding that she actually know anything about the job. A simple seamstress, she possessed very little knowledge about running so large an establishment as the manor house. And from the smile Leslie had been wearing that morning, Maggie worried that even her abilities as chaperon could be called into question. What in blazes had the girl been up to?

"That's the secret to being successful," Creag confided, "attention to details. Now shall we be off to see the linens?"

"Why not allow Jeanne to tend to it, so that you don't have to be bothered, a man as busy as you must be?" Maggie suggested, attempting once more to escape her predicament.

"At this point, I fear Jeanne might resent anything I ask her to do. I wouldn't put it past her to insert nettles between the folds of the sheets," Creag murmured, as if to himself.

"Our Jeanne would never do such a thing," Maggie protested, while Creag helped her to her feet.

"She's definitely not my Jeanne. She's yours. And that's the way it's going to stay! Now I would appreciate seeing the linens," Creag said. His voice, ringing with authority, effectively put an end to the subject of the manor's peppery steward. "We'll begin with the table coverings. Where are they kept?"

"Near the kitchen, I suppose," the old woman muttered.

"I beg your pardon?"

"Near the kitchen, stacked in rows," Maggie said, hoping as she led the way from the dining room, that they would encounter Jeanne and get some clue as to where the bloody things were actually stored.

"Maggie, this isn't the way I took to the kitchen," Creag said curiously, following the old woman down a gloomy hall.

"No, of course not. This will be quicker and the passage ends nearer the cupboard holding the table linens," the anxious Scot asserted, praying that she was fortunate enough to have guessed correctly.

But luck was not with Maggie that day. An hour and a half later, she had yet to uncover one tablecloth, runner or napkin. Starting out from the laird's bedroom, she could find just about anything in the manor. But beginning a quest anywhere else left the old woman totally baffled.

After an unexpected tour of the wine cellars, a vault containing ancient, rusty weapons, a root cellar, and numerous storage areas, Creag seriously doubted he would ever complete his simple objective. Having moved among the wealthy, he knew that they despised the new and cherished the old, and had thought he might be fortunate enough to find some elegant and outdated cloths that could be used during the Graysons' visit. But now, he was despairing of finding any linens at all, and he was fast losing patience with Maggie . . . despite the fact she had defended his manhood that morning.

"All right, that's enough," Creag growled, when their last turn had landed them in a cinder-strewn area beneath a hearth. "I'll simply purchase new."

"Now, now, laddie, it's right this way, around this curve, I'm sure of it," Maggie lied, aware of Creag's growing intolerance for her ineptitude, and unsure of how to handle such a bristling male. Then a smile curved itself around the crafty old Scot's mouth. He considered her feebleminded anyway. Why not keep him thinking it rather than learn she did not belong in his household at all?

"Are you certain?" Creag demanded, his massive shoulders heaving with exasperation.

"Aye, I am," Maggie replied with a smile. "Now what was it again you said we were searching for, Creag?"

"What is it we're looking for?" Creag all but exploded. "Nothing, Maggie, absolutely nothing. Come on, we're going back upstairs. And this time you're following me!"

Suddenly the old woman wondered whether she had played the American incorrectly. Though he had exhibited a fair amount of tolerance toward her, the man suffered from no such charity at the moment. What if he decided to rid the manor of its ineffective housekeeper? Who would stand guard over Leslie and Jeanne, then? Maggie fretted. No, before she took another step, it would be best to make amends.

"You know, Creag," she said as they entered a hallway that brought them back to the sooty area beneath the hearth, "I am fair good with a loom, as well as a needle and thread. Allow me to fashion a kilt for you, one made to your measurements and befitting the laird."

"Thank you, but I'll have one made in Glasgow," Creag replied crisply. After witnessing this woman's senseless meanderings in the bowels of the manor house, the laird of Linclachan was not about to allow her near his person. God only knows where her snipping shears might inadvertently wander.

Chapter Seven

Jeanne Donnachy was not a woman to shirk her duties—those spoken or merely understood. As unpleasant as some had been over the years, she had stood her ground and obeyed. Yet today this aspect of her character gave her no comfort. Indeed, hours later, still smarting from Blake's remarks, she strongly resented having done what she had originally perceived as her duty at that fateful council meeting when she'd tacitly approved the ridiculous scheme to invite him to be Linclachan's laird. Of course, she hadn't really anticipated his acceptance....

Now, little more than twenty-four hours after he'd set foot in Lindall Manor, the man had turned her world topsy-turvy with his whims and wishes, and she had a dreadful feeling that this was only the beginning.

"No porridge? He wants eggs every morning. Many the Scot who is thankful to have a single egg to call dinner and the American requires two to begin his day," grumbled the restless brunette. "And dinner at eight sharp. God knows what he'll expect then . . . probably an entire side of beef! The man's a barbarian treating others the way he does!"

Realizing her mood, rather than improving during the course of the day, had actually darkened as she brooded overlong, Jeanne paced the corridors of what was now *his* home, abruptly deciding to air her fiery temper outdoors. Maybe the brisk air of the early June afternoon would tame the anger eating at her heart and flashing in her eyes. Before any of the servants or workmen could call her back, she grabbed a shawl, smoothed her brown woolen skirt and headed for the door behind the kitchen.

Outside, the tall Scotswoman inhaled the sweet scent of the green fields and moved past the rough cobblestones of the old courtyard, intending to climb the footpath to the waterfall. She had barely gone thirty yards, however, when the sight of two ewes heavy with young caught her eye and she stopped to watch as they foraged the grass, taking in nutrients to feed their own. Looking up the cliff side that backed Lindall Manor, she could see the rest of the laird's flock grazing the richer, if less accessible, turf.

"I guess sometimes even you have to live with situations you'd rather not," Jeanne murmured, feeling oddly connected to the four-legged creatures kept apart from their kind by nature's limitations. "To protect your lambs, you've given up frolicking to do your proper duty instead of doing what you please—"

"Does that mean you wish you were off frolicking, or merely doing what you please?" asked a sympathetic voice.

"Pardon?" For a moment, Jeanne couldn't find the source of the impertinent question. Then she spotted Leslie kneeling in the overgrown herb garden, almost invisible among the brambles in her heather gray cloak. "What are you doing out here?"

"If I'm to convince Creag that I'm truly a legitimate member of his household, I thought I'd best find the old garden and clear it of the worst weeds," the small blonde explained, happily abandoning her efforts to join her friend on the path up the hill. "All things considered, there are some surprisingly healthy plants under those briars."

"I suppose they were sheltered from the weather," said Jeanne, without any real interest. At the moment, anything being done for C. Robertson Blake held no significance as far as she was concerned. He already thought himself too important. "Did Creag ever find you? This morning he was complaining—"

"No, but Michael did. I saw to the poor man's headache."

"Can you imagine any Scot passing out after only two drinks, even if they were Jamie's best? It's a wonder Malcolm and the others aren't still laughing, especially after the way he went on about undressing.''

"I truly expected him to waken when they carried him up to his rooms, the way they were howling about the indignity of it,'' admitted Leslie. "They made enough noise to rouse the dead.''

"The dead, maybe, but not our laird.'' Jeanne grinned. "He's apparently got quite a thick head, if not a strong stomach.''

"Well, when you choose a new laird from a newspaper listing, I suppose you shouldn't be surprised at his inadequacies.'' Leslie laughed, her good humor and the growing distance from the manor brightening Jeanne's mood.

"And I warrant the man has quite a few, considering those we've already discovered,'' said his steward, entering into the spirit of the discussion. "Let's see now, aside from his intolerance of good whisky, there's his insistence that his chores be seen to immediately, his reluctance to eat Scottish foods, his absurd modesty and his aversion to wearing a kilt—''

"Yes, I heard he was back in his trousers today, but his legs really are quite good, well muscled though pale—''

"I hadn't noticed,'' Jeanne lied.

"Judging from Michael's account of his incessant grumbling while I mixed the headache powders, I'd say the laird's temper is awfully fierce,'' said Leslie, abandoning her discussion of Creag's physique since Jeanne clearly had nothing to add. "That's certainly a fault.''

"Absolutely, as well as his demands to learn everything about the running of the manor and his ancestors all at once.'' Jeanne stopped as they reached an outcrop of rocks on the cliff. "Every time he passes a portrait in the halls, I have to invent another story and then there's the worry of forgetting what I've told him already. Who would imagine he'd care about little Linclachan with all his businesses and the fortune he has in America?''

"Isn't his wealth and reputation for getting things done what attracted our notice in the first place?'' asked Leslie.

For a long moment the women were silent, contemplating the small village below them and the changes C. Robertson Blake had already wrought, introducing strangers and repairs to their home.

"I suppose I never really expected him to arrive. In my mind, he either laughed at the notion of being a Scottish laird or said thank you from afar and sent a blank check. Certainly I didn't believe he would decide to live here."

"Oh, I don't think it's permanent," consoled the clan healer. "From what Michael says, Creag has too many concerns in the States to remain in Linclachan very long."

"Well, I pray he'll be off soon then or I won't be responsible for controlling my temper. Do you know that, among other outrageous acts, after I personally served his breakfast, Blake turned up his nose at good Scottish cooking and announced he'd only eat eggs in the morning?"

"That's not a crime, Jeanne, nor is it particularly outrageous," Leslie said, and smiled. "His men have done a lot to clean up Lindall Manor—the roof is almost completely repaired, and most of the dry rot in the old wing has been replaced. Surely the hens can accommodate him."

"More easily than we can, I imagine," snorted the comely brunette. "Leslie, I know it's wrong to resent Blake when it was the council's decision to invite him—"

"One with which you concurred."

"Aye, but—"

"But, you're only human, lass, and he's not Fergus though he's taken over as if he were." Leslie squeezed her friend's hand in understanding. "I know it's going to be difficult for you, Jeanne, so if it's any consolation, I've done my part to make him less troublesome—"

"Oh, no! Leslie, what did you give him?" demanded the Donnachy steward, memories of the healer's various potions suddenly worrying her.

"Nothing special, just a wee touch of verbena in his headache powders—"

"You didn't!"

"Oh, now, just the tiniest dab in with the usual mint and melissa. You know, it is recommended for soothing the head."

"And heightening the heart—" laughed Jeanne as she started down the path "—if Blake even has one."

"I don't think there's any doubt of that."

"Remember when you gave Annie pure tincture of verbena and told her it was good for fatigue?"

"Well, it was, wasn't it? She suddenly had enough energy to chase old Jock and catch him, didn't she?" Leslie giggled, relieved that her friend wasn't angry. It had been only the merest touch of the herb after all.

"Their match was the talk of the village for months," recalled Fergus's granddaughter, "but it still doesn't give you leave to start matchmaking."

"Jeanne, I swear I gave Creag just a hint of verbena, enough to put a smile in his heart instead of a frown, nothing to set his blood to boiling. Though I warrant with his temper, he's already too fired up. It's too bad he's not more like Michael, less driven."

"They are different, aren't they?" agreed Jeanne. "Michael's easy to talk to, almost like a brother, whereas Blake seems too authoritative to see any need to be human."

"Maybe his being in charge is the reason. When all is said and done, Creag is the man responsible for Lindall Manor and the village of Linclachan. He's probably preoccupied with making the right decisions."

"I'd rather him be more aware of the people around here and not so worried about the buildings and the look of the place," confessed the laird's steward. "I swear I wouldn't mind his constant demands if I believed he really cared about the Donnachys and Robertsons."

"Give the man a chance, lass. He's barely here a day," soothed Leslie, surprised at Jeanne's strange lack of sympathy for the American. Usually she was the most compassionate of creatures, yet clearly that was not the case in this instance.

"Jeanne, Jeanne," came a far-off call.

"Here, on the hill," she answered, hurrying down the path toward the manor as Ewan came into view.

"The laird's been calling for you," he announced solemnly. "He says there's work to be done and time's passing while he sits idle waiting on you. Indeed, he's in a right fierce humor."

"Thank you, Ewan, I'll go right to him," she said with a grimace. "Well, Leslie, it doesn't sound as though he's any calmer, does it? I told you he hadn't a heart!"

Michael looked up from the papers he was sorting and mentally counted to twenty. He knew from experience that ten would not suffice, not when Creag was in such a foul mood and there was such a distance between them.

"Creag, you have searched through all those records and journals and I've looked, as well, nearly a half-dozen times. There's nothing more to examine until the servants find Jeanne—"

"You think I'm incompetent without her services?"

"Not at all, but I do think you could put your energy to better use than tearing apart drawers and prowling the cupboards. Can't we attend to some of this mail? You've received four different inquiries about your proposed foundry outside Glasgow."

"And I've told you that they can all just wait for my response. They are trying to sell, Michael, I am buying. How many times must I explain to you that I am the one in the stronger position?" demanded the financier, his annoyance clearly evident as he paced the laird's study.

"Well, then, what about your American correspondence? Surely Mr. Frick's query deserves a timely answer," ventured his secretary, risking another outburst but knowing full well that if he could channel Creag's impatience into productive work, the man would thank him later.

"Why don't you draft a reply to that and anything else you believe so desperately urgent, Michael?" suggested Creag with a dismissive wave of his hand. "I'll look at them after a while."

"Very well," agreed the secretary, realizing he'd lost the battle. Quickly he collected his papers and headed for the smaller room next door where he could concentrate in peace.

As the door closed behind his assistant, Creag frowned at his loss of temper, but he never had been a patient man, even in the best of times, and he didn't enjoy waiting for a woman. Anxious to begin the plumbing renovations for the manor, a necessity for Catherine and her parents, he'd searched all the paperwork in the place and found not a single floor plan or architect's rendering, and his steward was nowhere to be found.

Damn it, his employees in America never left their positions during working hours, he fumed, stopping to look out the window. They knew better. And if little Miss Jeanne Donnachy didn't learn quickly, well then, Fergus's granddaughter or not, she would be dismissed. C. Robertson Blake, earl of Lindall, would not tolerate slackers on his payroll.

Suddenly he caught sight of her crossing the courtyard below, her brown curls tousled by the spring breeze as she hurried toward the house. Watching her progress, Creag suddenly realized with a mounting sense of irritation that he was waiting for her to glance upward, see him and smile. She did that too infrequently, he decided, recalling the high spots of color in her cheeks and the flashing anger in her eyes when she had confronted him, even if her words were civil. Well, today the anger would be his, and rightfully so, the brooding male decided.

When Jeanne entered the study a few minutes later, he was still at the window, and he remained purposefully unmoving until she cleared her throat uncomfortably and spoke first.

"You wanted me?"

"No, I would never be that desperate," he replied coldly, echoing her words from that morning, "but I've needed your assistance for the past hour. Where were you?"

"Out on the grounds. I did not think you'd be looking for me," Jeanne answered quietly, determined to keep her temper in check despite his insult and this dressing-down. "The last time we spoke, you were under the weather."

"That does not give you leave to disappear, Miss Donnachy. As my steward, you are to be readily available at all times should I have questions about the estate."

"With Fergus, I had set hours to assist him, and otherwise I saw to my duties as I chose, without his interference," she informed the American, unwilling to promise ready obedience.

"I am not your grandfather," Creag said sharply, irritated that he had to state the obvious, and then even more annoyed with himself as her cheeks colored in response to his words. "What I mean to say, Jeanne, is that as my employee rather than my relative, you shall be paid for your services, but said sum shall require you to perform efficiently, not wander off without leaving word as to where you'll be. Is that clear?"

Oh, it was very clear, fumed the brunette, her eyes snapping with fury she was hard put to contain. C. Robertson Blake considered himself to be lord and master while she was but his slave. Still, she reminded herself, if she wished to remain at

Lindall Manor, she had no choice in the matter. She would, however, make him pay to keep her.

"Yes, Creag, very clear, all but the amount of my earnings. What shall I be paid?"

The rugged blonde eyed her slowly, measuring the defiant tilt to her chin, the fire in her eyes and the proud stiffness in her spine. Damn, but he should have realized talk of money would land him in quicksand faster than he could blink. If he undervalued her worth, she would be even more angry, yet if he named too high a figure, she'd undoubtedly believe he was trying to buy her loyalty. Such a woman as she could easily be head of a clan, so strong and absolute did she stand before him, he mused, wondering at the fate that put him in the laird's chair instead of her. Well, let her make the decision then, he decided.

"I'm unfamiliar with Scottish practices," he admitted softly, moving to the laird's desk and settling himself behind it. "Tell me what you believe your stewardship is worth."

Startled by the American's invitation, Jeanne hesitated.

"I know the staff and the village. I've overseen Lindall Manor for nearly seven years. I believe I deserve four guineas monthly," she announced finally, naming a generous price.

"I'm paying the foreman of my repair crew that and he's not familiar with Linclachan, nor can he do figures," Creag replied, making a note on the pad before him. "Say six guineas, but you'll oversee Maggie and Ewan, as well."

A quick nod and a surprisingly sincere smile greeted him when he glanced in Jeanne's direction, making him wish he'd been even more generous in his decision. When the lass smiled, she made the sun pale by comparison, he thought, temporarily distracted.

"Thank you, Creag, that is quite fair. Now, what was it you wanted so urgently?" she asked, seating herself in a chair across from him, prepared to earn her wages.

"I wanted a floor plan for Lindall Manor, but I couldn't seem to find one."

"No, probably not."

"What?"

"I doubt one was ever drawn up," she explained. "Most of the house was built nearly two hundred years ago, but the south wing, the buttery and other sections were added more recently. If you wish, I could draw you a rough map to keep you from getting lost. I know the place can be confusing.''

''I have not been getting lost,'' Creag snapped indignantly, preferring to forget the morning's excursion with Maggie. ''And a map won't suffice. I want you to choose a few men to help you, and have them take careful measurements of all the rooms so that you can prepare a proper rendering of the manor, starting with the second floor since that's where the bedrooms are.''

''Certainly, but may I ask why? Many of the rooms aren't even furnished. They haven't been used in years.''

''Now that the roof is no longer leaking in the hallways during a heavy rain, I wish to install other, more conventional sources of indoor water supply.''

''There is a pump in the kitchen,'' said Jeanne, puzzled by the laird's words, ''and the servants bring water as needed. Isn't that sufficient?''

''Maybe in the Highlands of Scotland, but in most civilized houses in the States, and in England I might add, indoor plumbing, including toilets, are a common part of the household furnishings,'' the American snapped, somewhat embarrassed at the need to explain this to his steward. ''I intend to see them installed in the manor, but I need floor plans to decide where.''

''Them?'' Jeanne didn't know which was more surprising: that the American missed his usual conveniences or that he apparently needed more than one.

''Yes, them,'' the laird confirmed coldly, effectively ending the untoward topic of conversation. ''Now then, aside from the plumbing, which will require experts, I've made a list of other renovations I believe the staff can handle. You are welcome to hire additional help at five shillings per day should you wish. First, I want all the wall hangings removed—''

''Removed? But most of them are centuries old,'' protested Jeanne, her cheeks flushed with indignity. If the man preferred a toilet to a chamber pot, she'd not interfere, but when he toyed with ancestral trappings she was honor bound to speak up.

"All the more reason then. Their colors are undoubtedly muted by years of soot and dust. They need a thorough cleaning and airing," Creag replied, surprised at the young woman's vehemence. "Once the walls have been whitewashed and the wooden panels and balustrades polished, perhaps I'll have a few rehung, but for now, they all come down."

"And the Donnachy and Robertson portraits?" inquired his steward, her voice clearly disapproving if coldly efficient. "Surely you won't displace your ancestors."

"Temporarily, I will. I noticed this morning that Colum Donnachy's frame has dry rot and Tammas appears to have only four fingers on his left hand, the paint has darkened so much."

"Mayhap you are right about Colum, but Tammas lost a finger at Culloden. He only had four when he returned," stated Jeanne, pleased at Creag's startled look.

"Be that as it may, you will oversee the house survey and inform Maggie of the cleaning to be done. And, before I forget, I want Ewan to build fences to contain the sheep."

"Fences? But why? They've roamed free as long as the Donnachys have held this land," objected the brunette, her fiery temper finally loosening her tongue. "Just because you feel the need to organize the house to your wishes doesn't give you leave to interfere with nature's creatures."

"The matter is not open to discussion. I will not have them wandering in the drive and all over the lands. It's a miracle anyone knows whose animals are whose the way they roam so freely, bleating constantly."

"The sheep are clearly marked with dyes to identify their owners, if you had bothered to look at them. Blue dye signifies the laird's herd, green is Duncan's, red is Malcolm's—"

"I do not need a lesson in colors," he interrupted, determined to set the tone of this meeting, whether Jeanne's eyes sparked angrily or not. After all, he was the laird, and as lovely as she was, Jeanne Donnachy was only his steward, Creag reminded himself. "Now, you will tell Ewan the sheep are to be penned by week's end and then he can begin grading the drive—"

Jeanne counted to ten and then continued on to twenty and thirty, reining in the fury that coursed through her veins at the man's effrontery. C. Robertson Blake was indeed the conquering Norseman she'd first considered him to be, having no care for what once was, only what he wanted to be. Well, she had no choice other than to listen to his nonsensical plan, but later, later, the council would hear from her, that she vowed.

It was early evening and Malcolm had just returned to his home after milking when he found the other members of the council gathered around his fire.

"Trouble, lads?" he asked in surprise, accepting the glass Jamie offered.

"Nay, just the need to share a pipe," answered Duncan, "and some self-congratulations, of course."

"Aye, we did choose a right one, didn't we?" agreed Geordie, leaning back in his chair with a broad grin. There were few pleasures to be compared to sharing good fortune with friends.

"Though he does need some educating with regard to whisky, the lad recovered well this morning," conceded Jamie. "I'd say we did right by the clan."

"Lindall Manor has a new roof, the carpenters are replacing the bad wood, and workmen have been into the village to see to the priest's house and the school," contributed Malcolm. "And now that the man himself is here, I wager, improvements will be all the quicker."

"Even his taking on Maggie as his housekeeper was a generous deed, given her moods sometimes—"

"I think that was Jeanne's idea, but then that wonderful lass is always thinking of others," Geordie praised. "It's only too unfortunate that she couldn't be laird, she has the heart."

"But not the purse," reminded Duncan, thoughtfully sipping at his whisky. "Still, she is a fine-looking woman. Maybe our new laird might fancy a Scottish bride—"

"The laird might fancy many a thing and get most of them," interrupted Jeanne sharply, as she entered the cottage without knocking, "but on the grave of Fergus Donnachy, I swear that'll not be one of them."

"Och, now, lass, there's no need to be so touchy," cautioned Geordie. "You ken we've only your best at heart."

"Then tell Blake there was a mistake and he's not truly laird," she snapped angrily. These men were her grandfather's friends. How could they talk such sacrilege as marrying her off to the American?

"Sit a spell and tell us what's wrong, Jeanne," urged Malcolm as Jamie poured her a drink. "You know full well we can't undo what's been done. The survival of Linclachan depends on the man's goodwill now."

"But that needn't include sacrificing me like so much haggis," the brunette chided.

"Of course not, lass, it was only Jamie's whisky talking about a way to make you happy. We'll not interfere with the two of you, I promise," assured Duncan.

"There is no two of us. He's the laird and I'm his steward, that's all," Jeanne insisted. "And with the notions he has for changing Lindall Manor, I swear the man is deranged."

"My heavens, why?" cried Malcolm.

"What's he proposing, girl?" Duncan demanded.

"He wouldn't level the place, would he?" worried Jamie.

"Maybe you should give him some of my ale," suggested Geordie. "It soothes most men's humors."

"He's insisting on a plan of the house so he can have indoor plumbing installed—" Jeanne began.

"Well, now, I hear from my daughter in Edinburgh that's quite a convenience, nothing very bizarre at all." Duncan chewed anxiously on his pipe stem. "What else?"

"He wants all the wall hangings removed—"

"They are rather old, Jeanne," cautioned Malcolm, unwilling to give up the village's good fortune unless it was absolutely necessary. "I don't think even Fergus's grandfather could remember where they came from."

"He even demanded the portraits of the Donnachys and Robertsons be taken down," announced the brunette to the general consternation of the council.

"Och, now there's trouble," said Jamie. "Ashamed of his Scottish blood, is he then?"

"Well, no," admitted Jeanne. "He said some of the frames need fixing and he wants to whitewash all the walls."

"Sounds to me like the man makes sense." Malcolm was able to breathe with relief once more. "If he cares about the house, he wants it to be in first-class order, and everything in it, as well."

"That newspaper article said he was a go-getter, lass, not the man to sit still on a problem," Duncan reminded her. "I think you're just upset he's making the decisions without consulting you, Jeanne."

"And the sheep?"

"What about them?"

"Blake wants them penned up and not roaming free," argued Jeanne, irritated that the council thought her concern was a matter of misplaced pride. "That's not right."

"It isn't necessarily wrong," countered Geordie. "Down south, a lot of places keep the sheep and cows in separate fields. It doesn't hurt the milk or the wool, girl. Don't be fretting so."

"Aye, Jeanne, you're just weary with the extra work he's causing. Get a good night's sleep and it will seem better tomorrow," advised Malcolm.

"Here, lass, take a bottle of my ale," invited Geordie. "It will make you sleep sweetly."

A bottle of ale, muttered Jeanne as she set off in the twilight to return to Lindall Manor. I tell them how he's trying to change their world and they give me a bottle of ale! Regardless of their age and eyesight, how blind can they be?

Chapter Eight

Creag strode into the sitting room, his blue eyes flashing dangerously and his usually generous mouth set in a purposeful line. Something had been gnawing at him these past few days and he was hard put to ignore it rather than deal with the situation.

Never could he remember being so dissatisfied and frustrated, he fumed, running a hand through his golden-colored hair. In the past, whenever he had run into an obstacle, he had simply applied more effort, easily overcoming any barrier that stood between him and his goal. But somehow that technique had become unworkable now that he was dealing with the people of Linclachan rather than the faceless members of the financial world. There, one only had to worry about a man's business acumen. Here, he had to give attention to the entire man . . . or woman!

Perdition, but Linclachan and Lindall Manor were not at all what he had envisioned. In his innocence, he had seen himself as his lordship, the respected earl of Lindall, affecting a few minor changes in his Highland holdings in order to impress Catherine. He certainly had not expected to be beset by problems greater than the ten plagues visited upon Egypt in the Old Testament. And he most definitely hadn't thought that he, with all of his money, would have to earn the regard of a handful of penniless Scots.

Entering the room and seeing the tea he had ordered laid out on a side table, a smile tugged at Creag's lips. He might not be able to push aside his sudden and inexplicable guilt over coming to Linclachan to accept a title that wasn't his. Nor could he immediately alleviate the problems caused by his ruined house, surly steward, useless housekeeper and still-distant secretary. But he could tend to the issue that had bedeviled him most, the irritant that had had him snarling these past few days when a mere bark would have sufficed. He would gain the esteem of these Scotsmen, and demonstrate once and for all that he was not some weakling to merely be tolerated rather than respected.

Making short work of a fat slab of bread, Creag disdainfully eyed the prim glass of sherry positioned on the tray, bypassing, too, the ornate teapot set alongside it. Instead, he reached for the accompanying jug of milk, a thick layer of cream afloat on its surface. Bringing the container to his lips, he drained its contents in short order, devouring, between gulps, the remainder of the generously apportioned foodstuffs.

Then, with a determined gleam in his eye, C. Robertson Blake set out for the house of Jamie Robertson, distiller. If he accomplished nothing else this day, Creag would prove to the people of Linclachan, Jeanne Donnachy included, that he was as much of a man as anyone could wish to meet.

"He's a nice enough lad," Duncan contended as he sat around the table with the others.

"Well, we could have done worse," Geordie agreed.

"A bit priggish at the investiture ceremony the other night, though, wasn't he?" Jamie commented. "But then I suppose all Americans are puritans at heart."

The words rankled Creag as they drifted through the open window to the spot where he stood, prepared to rap on Jamie's door. However, he merely shrugged his shoulders philosophically. These men hadn't known him when he was just starting out, a raw youth as anxious to experience all life had to offer as he was to work his way up in the world. Ultimately he had done both, Creag thought with satisfaction, and to a much greater extent than most men he knew.

But before he could lapse into reverie, other words came seeping from the house, commanding his attention and forcing him to abandon his fond memories of life gone by, of a time when he had been rough and ready and full of dreams.

"For all that he gets things done right well enough, our Creag is a bit slow-witted, isn't he?" Malcolm asked, joining in the conversation.

"True, how the man ever managed to amass a fortune is beyond me. Imagine him coming here thinking he's the rightful laird all because he received our letter to that effect!"

"Aye, I almost feel pity for him, believing our lies," Duncan declared, "until I remember how sorry I felt for us before the lad came along."

"But even if he is a bit of a dullard, he has his pockets to recommend him," Malcolm declared, his voice tinged with meaningful humor.

The good-natured guffaws that flowed from Jamie's small cottage effectively drowned out Creag's surprised expletive.

"Why, those sly old bastards," he muttered, a reluctant grin emerging in spite of himself. Poor and uneducated they might be, but the elders of Linclachan were a crafty lot! When he had read his investigator's report, he had thought that the Highlanders who claimed him as their laird had either made a mistake or were after some of his wealth. Now he had his answer as to which one it actually was. They had dangled the right bait and landed him as effectively as they did the salmon that swam in the nearby stream.

Because he had arrived in Linclachan practicing his own deception, Creag knew he couldn't be irked by the shrewdness of these aged Scots. Instead, his respect for their enterprising nature did away with the anger he might have felt at being deceived, just as it wiped away the guilt he had been battling concerning his own duplicity.

He had come down to the village to confront one problem, and inadvertently he had managed to solve another. Never again would he feel conscience stricken for having taken Fergus Donnachy's title and home. Besides, he thought, his handsome grin widening and his sense of competition coming alive, he now had the advantage. He had uncovered their plot, and the old foxes had no inkling that he had done so.

Pleased that he had gained the upper hand, Creag was about to announce his presence, when more discourse made its way through the open window, melting his smile and hardening his features.

"'Tis a pity though, for all we've defended him to Jeanne, that we have ourselves a laird who can't hold his whisky. How we are going to keep such a shameful thing from the Campbells and the Menzies is beyond me," one of the elderly Scots maintained. "Look where two drinks left him, dead to the world! What with his great size and brawny build, it's still evident the lad's more weakling than not. Why, ancient though we be, we've more stamina than C. Robertson Blake when it comes to whisky."

"So do most of our women," Jamie boomed, his laughter almost muffling his words.

"I've heard he hasn't had a drop since the other night. Imagine a laird who can't drink? Who would have thought it?"

"Aye, it's worse than his being an American."

The impact of this light banter on Creag was considerable. He could live with being called a prig, and scoff at being thought dim-witted. But a weakling? Never! Before he realized what he was doing, he was pounding on the cottage door so sharply that its hinges groaned in protest.

The old men seated around the table eyed each other curiously while Jamie hastened to admit his visitor.

"Why, Creag, how good to see you!" the cottager said nervously. "We were just talking about you, and how lucky we are to have a laird as fine as yourself."

"You flatter me, gentlemen, I'm sure," Creag responded dryly, noting the way the council members shifted in their seats and stared guiltily into their drinks. Their actions told him they were not all that practiced in dishonesty, and for some reason, the handsome blond foreigner found that a comforting thought.

Somewhat mollified, Creag settled his large frame, emphasized all the more by the tiny structure's dimensions, onto the roughly hewn wooden chair offered by his host.

"Have I stumbled upon some celebration?" he asked, nodding to the jug of whisky sitting in the middle of the crude table, its surface grown smooth from the innumerable tankards and glasses that had scraped across it.

"No," Duncan swiftly denied, his stubble-covered cheeks turning to flame while his eyes sent a silent message to the others.

"'Tis no more than friends gathering at the end of a day's labor," Malcolm muttered, unable to meet Creag's piercing eyes.

"But what am I about?" Jamie protested, going to fetch another glass in an endeavor to put an end to the room's burgeoning awkwardness. Placing it in front of Creag, he added, "Surely you'll join us."

"Just a wee drop now, Jamie," Geordie cautioned, imagining the great effort it would take to get this blond giant home should he pass out.

The distiller, already pouring the drink, snapped his wrist back abruptly as he caught his brother's meaning, and handed the barely filled glass to the new laird of Linclachan.

Creag's eyes narrowed as he accepted the golden liquid. How many of these thimbles would he have to drink, he wondered, before they poured him a decent amount?

"Ahh. So it wasn't a dream. This is as wonderful as I remember it being," Creag said, taking a sip before he threw his head back and tossed down the drink in one magnificent and impressive gulp. "I'll have another if you please."

The council members cast their eyes about worriedly while Jamie slowly complied with Creag's request. They did not want to insult their benefactor, but neither did they wish to deal with him when the whisky took its inevitable effect.

Watching four pair of eyes widen, Creag raised the glass to his lips and gave the same performance as before, setting the empty glass in front of the whisky maker yet again.

"Easy now, lad. It's not that I begrudge you the drink, you understand. I simply don't know, after what happened the other night, how much tolerance you have for the stuff."

"You'll find I'm quite tolerant, indeed," Creag said pointedly. "What you witnessed at the manor was the result of going for nearly two days without sleep, not your whisky, man. I'll have you know I can drink along with the best of them."

"Oh, can you now?" Duncan asked with a smile lighting his wrinkled face. If this was a challenge, it was one he would enjoy.

The rest put their cups forward as Jamie refilled Creag's glass with a healthy portion. Perhaps, they thought hopefully, there would be nothing to hide from the Campbells and Menzies, after all.

"Now tell me," Creag began congenially, settling in for a lengthy stay. "I've been admiring the swords over the hearth in the large hall at the manor. Whose were they?"

"Aye, they're beauties, aren't they?" Jamie said. "They belonged to Gordon Donnachy and Donald Robertson, heroes and followers of Robert the Bruce."

"I see," Creag muttered as though duly impressed. "And tell me, just how am I related to such fine men?"

"Why, they be kin on your grandfather's mother's side," Duncan gasped after almost spraying the table with the whisky warming his tongue.

"Aye, cousins," Jamie supplied helpfully.

"Fourth cousins twice removed," Geordie added.

"Is that so?" Creag asked, his innocent expression effectively masking his devilish intent. "Then I'm a fortunate man indeed to have such illustrious ancestors, in addition to kinsmen who are so well-informed. I'm sure I'll be coming to you with many a question about the family history."

"That's right, laddie," Malcolm hastened to assure him. "If there's something you've a mind to know, you ask us. There's no sense in poring over musty records and such when we can save you the trouble."

"Why, thank you," Creag said, hiding his smug smile behind the rim of his glass. Staying in the Highlands, he decided, might prove amusing after all.

The golden hours of the afternoon slipped away into early evening, and then at last into night, the time marked by laughter, tall tales and high humor. As the evening drew to a close, Creag had to hand it to the old Scots. They had built up a remarkable resistance to Jamie's potent liquor. But he was determined to see this through until he was the only one capable of walking away from Jamie's table.

At last Malcolm was dozing in his seat, and Geordie was not too far behind him. Duncan was babbling something that made no sense, and only his host was left to contend with.

"All right, lad, I concede," Jamie slurred finally, after draining his glass and unsteadily setting it in front of him. "I've no stomach for more. You've proven your point. You're a better man than I am."

"Not better, only equal," Creag returned, earning the old Scot's gratitude and his admiration. With a slow scrape of his chair, the laird rose and left the cottage, concentrating mightily upon a departure that exhibited no faltering steps or loss of dignity.

Setting out from the manor, Creag was quite pleased with himself, the twinkle in his eyes brighter than that of any star studding the blackened sky overhead. Whether the council members knew it or not, he was one of them now. He had been accepted. And somehow the experience had proven a damn sight more satisfying than blustering his way into Philadelphia society. The only problem that remained was finding that same approbation within his own Highland home.

"Didn't the dinner go well?" Leslie whispered when Jeanne stormed into the kitchen, her visible aggravation answering the question long before she could give voice to her seething emotions.

"It went as well as could be expected with dried-out mutton and vegetables almost scorched from being kept warming," the willowy steward replied curtly, her anger at C. Robertson Blake making anyone who spoke to her, even her best friend, a target for her ill humor. "Eight o'clock sharp each evening, the man said. Eight o'clock! And we've only just started serving now though it's nearly half past nine."

"Doesn't he like the looks of it, then?" Leslie asked, offering what little comfort she could.

"I wouldn't know," Jeanne snapped. "He's not here. The laird hasn't deigned to grace us with his presence, but Michael was famished, and to keep the food waiting any longer would have made it totally unpalatable."

"Not here?" Leslie echoed. "Where is he?"

"Where the blue-eyed devil is, I've no idea. If I'm fortunate, he has stumbled down some back staircase and broken his neck!"

"Och, now, lass, you do not mean that," Maggie reprimanded softly from her place by the fire. "He's a fine young specimen of a man and you'd do well to notice it. Shoulders that broad and a face as handsome as his are not something we see very often in Linclachan."

"I'd be more pleased if we had never seen him at all," Jeanne retorted stubbornly. "As for his looks, you might think them bonny, but I find them eclipsed by his overbearing manner."

"Surely you know by now that's the way of men," Maggie said wisely, recalling Fergus's gruffness. "But there be ways to gentle them, ways that are as pleasant for a woman as they are for a man."

"I don't want to gentle him, Maggie. I want him gone," Jeanne averred. Yet unbidden images of the pleasures to which the old woman alluded besieged Jeanne's consciousness, making her exceedingly angry, and more than a little uncomfortable.

"But for the good of the village, that is not to be," Maggie stated pragmatically. "You'd best learn to live with him, at least until he decides to return to America."

"Which can't be soon enough for me," Jeanne claimed obstinately, the struggle to push aside visions of coupling with Creag strengthening her existent resolve to detest the insufferable C. Robertson Blake.

To Creag's surprise, the manor house was exceedingly quiet when he finally crossed its threshold. Feeling exhilarated, and very much like a returning conqueror, he was disappointed that there was no one about with whom he could share his good mood.

Thinking that his meal was set out in the dining room as he had ordered, he made his way there, swaying so slightly that he was sure no one would notice.

Upon opening the door, he was surprised to find the room dark and the table bare. Damn the women of Lindall Manor! Hadn't he told them he wanted his dinner served promptly at eight? But as Creag left the room intending to set out for the kitchen, he heard the clock strike eleven. A sheepish grin appeared on his face, boyish now that he had let down his guard. It would seem that he was a little late.

He had never expected the old boys on the council to have lasted that long, and in the course of the evening, he had evidently lost track of time. He grimaced at the thought of the rare temper Jeanne Donnachy must have displayed when he did not materialize in the dining room at the appointed hour. But then he chuckled to himself when the idea struck him that Jeanne couldn't have a rare temper. She was in one most of the time.

Ah, well, he mused, turning toward the stairs and his study, if she wasn't upset about his missing dinner, she would only have found another reason to be annoyed. Lord, but he had never met such a fiery woman!

The study seemed inviting, Creag thought happily, noting the healthy fire that still burned in the grate, and the soft glow of the yet unextinguished lamps. It was a good place for a man to end his day, surrounded by his work and away from the prattle of the manor's women. And the fact that he had made it a practice more often than not, wherever he had been, to spend the latter part of each evening immersed in business matters, only caused this room to look more appealing.

Moving toward the desk, Creag stumbled once or twice, indignantly blaming uneven floorboards. He reached his chair none too soon, emitting a contented sigh. Still congratulating himself on the outcome of his visit to the village, the new laird now anticipated a few moments of peaceful solitude before he retired for the night. It had been a grand day.

Creag had just made himself comfortable when the door flew open and Jeanne Donnachy entered, followed by Mary bearing a tray.

"Put it right down here on the desk," the tall and graceful steward ordered, haphazardly shifting Creag's carefully stacked and sorted papers.

"What's this?" Creag asked, his tongue thicker than usual as he signaled for Mary to leave after she completed her task.

"It's dinner, of course! Seeing as it's so late, I assumed you'd be hungry," Jeanne stated in a superior fashion. Still, her manner was calmer than Creag would have expected, and he couldn't decide whether he was pleased or disappointed.

"How thoughtful. I was a bit tardy in returning," he replied, gratified to note how his blasé attitude perturbed the pretty Scot. When she leaned over him to remove the dish covers, Creag observed something of a far different nature. She had one of the loveliest bosoms he had ever seen.

"I would think this is the housekeeper's job. Why am I so honored as to have you tending to this?" Creag asked absently, his eyes drawn to Jeanne's breasts as she leaned forth once more to arrange the plate before him.

"You can't expect a woman of Maggie's age to dance attendance on you so late at night," Jeanne snapped. "And if you're thinking you can use that as a justification to send her away, you're wrong. What Maggie can't accomplish, I'll see to myself."

"Are you sure you're not just using that as an excuse?" Creag teased, his natural inhibition with this woman vanished along with his sobriety. Bending forward to peer up into Jeanne's face, he continued mischievously. "Could it be that you wished to see me once more before you retired for the evening?"

"The only time I wanted to see you was at eight o'clock," Jeanne replied tartly, though she was startled enough by Creag's playfulness to immediately straighten her posture and retreat a few steps.

"Even when you're out of sorts, you're lovely," Creag said, enjoying the way light from the old lamps penetrated the material of Jeanne's blouse and illuminated the shadows of her curves. "Do you know your eyes have golden sparks when you're angry?"

"If they do, then you have put them there," Jeanne declared.

"I could think of another way to make your eyes flash, Jeanne Donnachy," Creag murmured, leaving his seat and coming to stand before her. He reached out to gently capture her face in his large hands, tilting her chin upward so that she had no choice but to return his stare.

Suddenly Jeanne was aware of Creag's masculine essence as she had never been aware of a man before. She watched in wonder as he began to bend his head toward hers, and though she knew she should turn and run, she didn't have the heart to do so.

"Shall I show you?" he murmured just before his lips brushed hers.

"Why, you're completely drunk!" Jeanne exclaimed, easily pushing away from Creag's broad chest. That was the only reason he had tried to kiss her; he was in his cups! Though her discovery granted relief, it made for disappointment, as well.

Instantly Jeanne Donnachy was incensed. She had almost fallen victim to Creag's considerable charms. And they *were* considerable, she admitted honestly. She liked the way he towered over her, the broad expanse of his back, the muscular quality of his arms that not even a well-tailored suit jacket could hide. She was drawn to his clear blue eyes and rugged good looks. To his blond hair and seductive mouth. And good God, because of her own weakness she had almost succumbed to his kiss, a kiss that would have taunted her for years untold, a kiss he would not have even remembered come morning.

"I may have had a bit of whisky," Creag protested as Jeanne retreated toward the door. "But that doesn't change anything."

"You great fool," she cried, as much in frustration as in self-directed anger. "I want nothing to do with you!"

"Are you lying just to me, Jeanne, or to yourself, as well?" Creag asked, even while his mind, benumbed though it was, told him it was wrong to pursue this woman. Yet the wealthy American couldn't remember why that was, any more than he could help wanting to do so.

"Listen to yourself! It's Jamie's whisky talking and no more than that," Jeanne avowed. "I'll have no drunkard dallying with me that way!"

"Jeanne, don't," Creag all but pleaded, not wanting the glow he had felt when she had been within arm's reach to fade.

"It's not Jeanne anything! It's Creag!" the pretty Scot insisted as she moved to the doorway. "All of this is your fault, not mine."

"Damn it, woman! I want none of your sermons now," Creag grumbled.

"Well, you wouldn't be getting one if you had been here at eight o'clock eating the dinner you demanded instead of out hoisting a glass," Jeanne retorted, flinging her comments over her shoulder as she left the room.

"Just you remember what I told you once," a wounded Creag called out to her retreating back. "Keep up this disrespect and I'll marry you off to the first man who enters this manor. And I swear I'll do it, too, without any thought as to whether the poor bastard deserves to be miserable or not!"

Not long after Jeanne had departed, Michael poked his head through the doorway to find a scowling Creag attempting to study some financial papers and feeling very sorry for himself.

"I thought perhaps you had returned when I heard the din," he said with a tentative smile. When he wasn't thrown from the room in a fit of temper, he added in a more serious vein, "I was worried about you, Creag."

"Somebody should worry about me with reports such as these coming in," Creag fumed, his intoxication obvious to this man who knew him so well. "Whatever made me think I could go away for a few months and leave Brisbane in charge of my businesses? The fellow's an idiot."

"You know very well John is a man who can handle any problems that arise," Michael said with a shrug of his shoulders, wondering just how much whisky Creag had consumed to leave him in such a state, and more importantly what had driven him to it. "If there is a dilemma at present, he'll be able to sort it out. Now stop being so apprehensive. Besides, you were traveling abroad to visit Glasgow and Clydebank for business reasons anyway. The time you spend in Linclachan won't make that much difference. Why not treat this as a well-deserved rest? It can only do you some good."

"Do me...do me some good?" Creag sputtered, his disobedient tongue feeling as though it had a life of its own. "I'm living in a ruin about to fall down around me, stepping over sheep droppings, listening to the pounding of hammers and the wailing of instruments that sound like screeching tomcats on the prowl, coping with a houseful of women who confound me, and a village of rustics who want to poison me with alcohol and you call this an opportunity for relaxation! Somehow I had always thought you brighter than that."

Michael hid his smile from the man sitting across the desk. If he was anything, Creag Robertson Blake had always been a decent employer and a better friend. But the man had driven himself so hard that he no longer knew what it was to enjoy life or the fruits of his labor. For some time, he had not been the Creag to whom Michael was devoted, as their recent cross words and the cool distance that followed had made quite evident.

But seeing C. Robertson Blake as he was now, suit slightly rumpled and looking exceptionally human, Michael was aware that the man who had first employed him had not disappeared forever behind the fastidious social facade he had erected. The thought cheered him immensely and he knew he had Linclachan to thank. With this in mind, there was no way whatsoever that the secretary was going to allow him to leave before Creag rediscovered the person he had once been.

"Creag," Michael said, choosing his words carefully, "this is only a small Scottish village. I never thought to see you bested by such trifling matters."

"I wouldn't let Jeanne hear you say that anything about this place is inconsequential. The woman has a horrific temper," Creag responded with an inebriated chuckle, glad to have Michael help him put things in perspective.

"No worse than yours," the other man remarked wryly. "You're simply not used to having anyone other than me question your decisions and commands. Putting up with Jeanne Donnachy will do you some good, help you to remember what it is to be treated as a normal man rather than as C. Robertson Blake."

"I wouldn't mind playing the man if she would act like a woman," a frustrated Creag mumbled, recalling how close he had been to feeling Jeanne's lips beneath his own before she had pushed him away.

"Mind you, hands off Jeanne," Michael said with mock severity. "You're going to marry Catherine Grayson, remember?"

"Catherine! Now there's a sobering thought if I ever heard one," Creag said, rising and crossing the room with a steadiness he wished to see disappear. He stopped in front of a cabinet and withdrew a decanter of whisky and two glasses. "I need a drink."

"You need your bed," Michael observed.

"No, not until I've had one last drink. I want to toast my bride-to-be," Creag insisted, turning to his chair.

"To Catherine," said Michael, his mouth set in a grim line as he raised the glass Creag had filled just shy of the brim.

"To Catherine," Creag repeated dutifully before disposing of a mouthful of whisky. "I only hope she's worth the trouble this laird business is costing me."

"Come on," his companion jested. "It's not all that bad. And think of all the good you're doing for Linclachan."

"I could have done the same thing with a lot less aggravation if I had simply sent the villagers the money and rejected the title they offered," Creag slurred, placing his elbows on the desk top and resting his suddenly weary head upon his hand.

"That's absurd!" Michael countered. "You've met these people and you've seen how proud they can be. They never would have accepted a handout."

"I still say I should have walked away from it all," Creag maintained, his eyelids beginning to droop.

"How could you? They are family, after all, no matter how distant."

"But that's just it, Michael. They're not family at all."

"The fact that they are strangers doesn't nullify your common blood," the secretary contended, removing his spectacles and wiping their lenses with his handkerchief.

"You're not listening," Creag whispered fiercely. "I'm not the man they were looking for."

"It's not like you to be lacking in confidence. But, rest assured, Creag, I think you'll make a fine laird," Michael replied cheerfully. With Creag's best interests at heart and his own as well, the last thing Michael wanted was for his employer to cut his ties and escape Linclachan.

"That might very well be, but get this through your thick skull," Creag murmured, his head beginning to nod, "I am not the rightful earl. I am no relation to these people."

"All right, Creag," Michael placated, discounting what he had just heard and attributing it to the besotted financier's wishful thinking. "But it makes no difference. These people have established you as their leader and you have accepted. You'll have to remain in the Highlands, for a while at least, no matter what."

"I was afraid you'd see it that way," Creag complained, getting to his feet and heading unsteadily for the door. "The problem is, so do I."

* * *

Creag was surprised at how clear his head was the next morning, especially when his memories of the preceding night were so damnably hazy. He had slept well enough, he supposed, if he didn't count those disturbing dreams about kissing Jeanne Donnachy. Where they came from, he couldn't fathom. After all, so fiery a woman held no attraction for him when he compared her with his sweet-tempered Catherine and entry into Philadelphia society.

Still musing about the inexplicable nature of dreams, he completed his grooming and was on his way to the dining room when Maggie intercepted him to announce a visitor, one Andrew Robertson.

He had barely time to enter the sitting room, shake the man's hand and offer him a seat when Jeanne came barreling through the doorway. From the look on her face he could see he was in for a hard time of it, as though the woman had something troubling her and was determined to have it out once and for all.

But the moment she saw the solicitor sitting there, ogling her intently, she stopped in midstride and scampered from the room, her eyes wide with alarm.

Creag wondered at this odd turn of events. He didn't particularly want to spend time with Andrew Robertson, either, but the man certainly didn't frighten him. And as for Jeanne, he didn't think anyone or anything could daunt her indomitable nature.

Then suddenly he recalled his return home last night, the rejected kiss and his threat to marry Jeanne off if she didn't accord him the deference he demanded. But surely she couldn't think he had meant it, and not to a creature like Andrew Robertson, Creag thought in amazement. Yet by all indications she did. Perhaps he'd know a few days' peace here in the Highlands, after all. Suddenly the earl of Lindall began to laugh, the first real laughter he had known since he had arrived at the manor. The more he thought about the situation the more he relished it, until finally he threw back his head and roared in amusement, leaving the miffed and mystified solicitor to wonder if the new laird was a madman, as well as an outsider.

Chapter Nine

That night, in pitch-darkness, Leslie climbed the last few stairs, listening as she went to be certain no one was behind her. Satisfied, she pushed open the attic door, glad the recently oiled hinges no longer groaned, and stepped inside.

The stars looked close enough to touch, and the place was awash with moonlight filtering through the large open area overhead where a portion of the sagging roof had been removed during the renovations so that it could be replaced rather than merely shored up again.

The open-air effect was delightful, Leslie decided, noting how even the grime built up over the decades had been transformed to silver dust by the moon's gentle illumination. But was it the moon that had converted such a mundane place into a veritable fairy bower, or was it the love in her heart, the pretty blonde wondered, moving forward into the enchanted kingdom.

"Here I am," sounded a beloved voice, quite obviously American, as a shadowy figure stirred in the corner.

Then Leslie was in Michael's arms and his lips were on hers, making their trysting spot all the more beautiful and irresistible.

"When you felt it too difficult to slip out of the house and away to some secluded glen, I promised you starlight anyway, didn't I?" Michael murmured in her ear.

"Yes, you did," Leslie answered shyly. "I thought you would have to be a wizard to keep such a vow, but I believed you all the same."

"I'm glad you did," he said, placing an arm about her waist and drawing her to a spot he had made ready for them, a blanket spread beside a bottle of wine and two goblets. "I don't mind saying, however, I was beginning to worry when you weren't on time."

"I had a problem tonight giving Aunt Maggie the slip," Leslie said with a dainty laugh, as she settled herself comfortably and indicated a place for Michael at her side.

"You don't suppose your aunt suspects about us, do you? I mean, whenever I've lingered outside your door at odd times, she always seems to happen by and send me on my way—"

"Well, some of the clan credit her with second sight, especially since she went to Fergus's bed in the middle of the night and found him dead, claiming she sensed something was wrong. Personally though, I've never seen evidence of anything other than a fanciful imagination."

"Praise the Lord," murmured Creag's secretary, not anxious to explain his extracurricular activities to his employer or to the clan.

"Then again, you'll not believe the absurd notion the woman has about Creag and Jeanne." Leslie laughed and accepted a glass of wine as Michael drew her to him, supporting her slight weight against his powerful chest.

"Oh? What's that?" he asked, feeling very comfortable as he shared the intoxicating liquid with this even more intoxicating girl in his arms.

"Maggie claims the reason they irritate each other so much and are constantly bickering, no matter what the topic, is because they are kindred souls who feel such an overpowering attraction to one another that they're afraid to admit it—"

"Creag's never been afraid of anything in his life," scoffed his assistant, "especially not a woman."

"It's not Jeanne he's afraid of, according to Maggie, but the fact that he wants her and doesn't care to acknowledge it," she clarified. "You have to agree that something's awfully peculiar about the two of them. They're always sparking over the most ridiculous of issues."

"Maybe Jeanne is just too accustomed to having her own way and not answering to any authority. Fergus was on in years, wasn't he, and her grandfather, to boot?"

"Aye, but he was also a stubborn mule of a man who never yielded an argument regardless of how wrong he was or how right Jeanne's ideas. She is accustomed to argumentation, never fear."

"Well, see then? That's the whole issue right there. Your friend misses her grandfather and provokes the squabbling with Creag because it reminds her of how life used to be when Fergus was alive." Michael was pleased he had resolved the issue distracting Leslie from their time together.

"I don't know, maybe," she considered. "But couldn't Maggie be right?"

"Never in a million years," scoffed the American. "Besides, as long as I've known him, it's been Creag's dream to be accepted as a member of Philadelphia's high society. Despite his money, they frown on his lack of family connections, and the only way for him to resolve that problem is to marry a debutante from one of the old, established families. He knows what he has to do, and, believe me, C. Robertson Blake is not going to sacrifice his future in America for Jeanne Donnachy."

"I suppose you're right. You certainly know Creag better than my aunt does, but I just wish they could be civil to one another—"

"Forget about them, Leslie," Michael said, gently urging her face to his, and when the loving man kissed her, that's exactly what Leslie did.

Jeanne was surprised to note that the days fairly flew with Creag in residence at Lindall. With his demanding nature, she had expected each moment to drag endlessly on, especially now that Leslie seemed so preoccupied and Jeanne had less and less of her company. Yet such had not been the case at all. And whenever Jeanne truly considered the situation, she had to acknowledge that when he wasn't arguing with her, Creag's presence was really not all that unbearable.

No such charity was in her heart, however, when she was awakened from a deep sleep one morning by an imperious command issued by the laird himself. It was barely dawn when Creag notified his slumbering steward that her presence was required in the stables immediately. The summons came in the form of a sharp rap upon her door and curt, if muffled, instructions as Creag shouted through the planks of oak comprising the only barrier between her nightdress-clad form and his keen blue eyes. Without waiting for a response, the man had left, assuming his orders would be obeyed, the sound of his arrogant male footsteps receding down the cold stone corridor and echoing in Jeanne's mutinous heart.

Hastily fastening the gray skirt that hugged her waist and skimmed her hips, Jeanne Donnachy wondered what it was the American wanted now. Lately, as he inspected his holdings, it seemed almost as if Creag Robertson Blake couldn't exist without her. No matter what the time of day or night, he was forever ordering her to his side, and often for the most inane reasons, Jeanne mused, her slender fingers working to tuck her matching gray blouse neatly inside her skirt.

Being with Creag so constantly was unsettling, to say the least. She had seen him ebullient with boyish enthusiasm in the morning, deeply engrossed in work at noon, pensive in the fading light of day, and weary in the late hours of the evening when the soft glow of the fire in the hearth turned his hair a deeper gold and played across his rugged features, making him seem more like some ancient Viking marauder than ever before.

And always, the memory of the forsaken kiss lingered in her mind, like some wraith sent to haunt her. But she had no one with whom she could discuss this specter of what might have been. Though usually she and Leslie shared everything, this somehow seemed too personal a matter. Besides, Jeanne decided her friend was likely the recipient of so many caresses lately that the tale of one abandoned kiss wasn't likely to seem very important.

At times the recollection sharpened her tongue as she sought to deny the tingle that ran along her spine each time she thought of how closely Creag's lips had hovered above her own. But there were instances, too, even while *his lordship* was in the midst of proposing the most outrageous changes, when the imagined sensations of his mouth claiming hers made the fiery Jeanne subdued, bewildering her as much as it did the man expecting to be the object of her latest burst of temper.

Braiding her thick hair into a single plait, Jeanne tried to excuse her odd behavior with the notion that life in the manor had suddenly become so chaotic and frustrating. The place was alive with workmen, and more changes had been wrought in Lindall Manor and Linclachan these past few weeks than had taken place in the entire last century. Then, too, there was Creag himself to contend with. He was the most enigmatic male she had ever met. One moment she thought him vile and detestable, and the next, she was grateful for some improvement he had made in the village. With things as they were, of course she was not herself! How could she be?

Still, as Jeanne fumbled with the door latch and recognized a rush of anticipation at the thought of her upcoming encounter with Creag, she marveled at the realization that the biggest changes the new laird had so effortlessly brought about had been not in her home but in her.

Creag stood just inside the stable door, wondering how long Jeanne would keep him waiting. Impatience built irrationally as another moment ticked by, but it was, of course, merely the result of wanting to begin his day's work, the muscular American assured himself. Wasting time was something he abhorred. Why he would be just as anxious to have his steward with him at this moment if Jeanne Donnachy had been the man he had expected her to be instead of the lovely woman she actually was. Or so he silently asserted while he paced up and down, at a slower pace than usual, his feet crushing odd bits of straw and his eyes straining into the gray morning mists for some sign of Jeanne.

The scuffling sound of footsteps that soothed Creag's restlessness only presaged Michael's appearance, however, and the young financier was hard put to rationalize the sense of disappointment he felt when his friend stepped into the gloom of the stables.

"I needed to speak with you about shifting the women's quarters," Michael began, looking around at his surroundings with perplexity. "When Ewan said you had come this way, I thought he must have been mistaken. What the devil are you doing out here so early?"

"Waiting for Miss Donnachy," Creag replied irascibly. "Just how long can it take the blasted woman to make herself presentable and join me?"

"Give Jeanne a few more moments. It would take Catherine much longer to ready herself. She'd keep you cooling your heels at least an hour, and well you know it," Michael placated as Creag began his uneven pacing once more. "By the way, why are you limping?"

"You forget, Michael, that Miss Grayson will be my fiancée. You certainly can't compare Catherine and Jeanne," Creag snapped.

"No, most assuredly not," Michael muttered. "They can't be compared at all."

"As to my limp, I fell over that damned old sot who persists in sleeping outside my doorway each night. I don't think I'll ever get used to him being there. You'd think the fellow would prefer a bed to the cold stone."

"Why not just order him to give up his vigilance?" Michael asked, having his own reasons for wanting to see the man gone.

"I've tried, but the old fool is always dead to the world when I leave my chambers, and when I return, he's nowhere to be seen. Very much like Miss Donnachy at the moment. Blast but where is that woman? I want to talk to her about a few mounts."

"Why all this fuss about some horseflesh?" Michael inquired casually, removing his spectacles and wiping away the dewy moisture that accumulated on them.

"Why to impress the Graysons, of course," Creag replied, his manner preoccupied as he peered through the stable door yet again.

"But you've told me yourself that other than in a carriage, those people don't ride at all. Are you trying to persuade me you are out here just after sunrise in order to win over Catherine and her parents when they can't tell the difference between a jackass and a Thoroughbred? And I mean that in more ways than one."

"Of course that's the reason. What else would it be?" Creag protested, his voice edged with gruffness and his eyes on the pocket watch he had taken from his vest. "All of this effort is for Catherine. She is at the root of everything I do in this miserable corner of Scotland."

"Do you really think so, Creag?" Michael observed, remembering Leslie's words and regarding his friend with an odd expression as he placed his glasses on the bridge of his nose once more. "You've always had a good eye for horses. Surely you don't need to drag Jeanne from her bed to help you make any decisions when it comes to riding stock. Why, you need the girl's assistance no more now than you did late last night when you sent for her to discuss the length of the lambing season. Ewan could have given you that information. Is it for Catherine's sake that you are demanding Jeanne's presence this morning? Is that why you are strutting around like some lame barnyard rooster?"

"There is nothing wrong with wanting my steward with me when I make decisions about my estate. These people are going to have to live here after I am gone back to America. Shouldn't they have a voice in what is done? Actually, I think including Jeanne in the process is rather magnanimous of me," the tall American said with extreme self-satisfaction.

"Oh, do you?" asked Michael dryly.

"Yes! And I can't imagine how you could see it any differently."

"And I can't fathom how I can see things you can't," Michael replied, the fingers of his right hand tapping emphatically at the gold rims of his spectacles.

"Are you implying something?" Creag asked ominously. What was it about this place that made everyone think he was the logical target for their impertinence? Just because he hadn't fallen under Linclachan's spell as Michael had was no reason for his friend to behave like no friend at all.

"I'm not implying anything," Michael said with an exasperated shake of his head, his natural affection for Creag outweighing the frustration he felt. "But I tell you, Catherine can't get here soon enough to suit me."

"Good, then we agree. I have never been so anxious as I am for her arrival," Creag said without as much conviction as he might have wished. "Now why don't you go see to the consolidation of the laborers' quarters? And just put the women where I want them."

"I don't know if it's a good idea," Michael protested, thinking not only of Jeanne's reaction to the plan, but his own, as well. "They might not like it much."

"It can't be helped. Now tend to it, will you? And if you happen to encounter Jeanne, hurry her along," Creag ordered in those stubborn tones his friend had come to abhor.

After Michael's wordless departure, a sure sign of his disagreement, Creag continued walking back and forth, trying to work the stiffness from the muscles of his leg. As he did so, he cursed the fact that he was already in a bad mood, and Jeanne had not even as yet appeared.

It seemed that since that fateful night in his study, there was more strain than usual between them whenever they were together. It was the result, he supposed, of his attempt to kiss the striking wench. When they were in each other's presence, the tension thickened until they could stand it no more. Oh, they would start out well enough, he trying to be pleasant and she civil. But no matter what they said, no matter what they did, sooner or later one of them would erupt, and the snapping would begin, their tempers the only release they allowed themselves.

But a kiss, and a forsaken one at that, should not have been the cause of so much trouble, Creag fumed. He had certainly never mentioned the incident, preferring that Jeanne think he had been so drunk that he didn't recall it. Yet still, it loomed betwixt them, like some huge bonfire that singed and tormented them no matter how they sought to escape its flames.

Surely, Creag thought with a start, he wasn't losing his heart to some Highland miss. Love, at least the love touted by the poets, didn't exist. It couldn't, or else he would have felt its pangs before now, he assured himself.

Besides, he desired Catherine, or at least the place in society she could offer him. He wanted to give his sons a world far different than the one he had endured as a boy. And that did not mean the ramshackle village of Linclachan with its crumbling manor! No, he would furnish them with a world of wealth and power where they were welcomed and respected. With his fortune, Creag did not have to worry about his children knowing hunger and poverty as he had, but even his money could not buy acceptance. And he swore that they would have a mother who would lift them above the contempt he had suffered as the child of struggling laborers.

Suddenly, lost in swirling thoughts of the past, Creag recalled being sent on his way, a string of curses following him when he had sought employment in order to buy bread. He remembered his patched clothing and his resentment when those who were better off snickered as they passed him on the road, a young boy gathering manure to sell to the gardeners of the wealthy. But most of all, he recollected how, except among his own kind, he had been shunned. No, he vowed, pounding a fist into an open palm, his sons would never know what it was to have a door shut in their faces. And the alluring Jeanne Donnachy was nothing more than another obstacle he had to overcome in order to ensure his offspring a happy future.

Suddenly Creag was pulled from his troubled musings by the light fall of footsteps approaching the stables through the mists. He looked out to see a vision of Jeanne's lovely face, still soft with the remnants of sleep, drifting toward him like some enticement sent to lure him from his goal. But it was a temptation he would conquer, Creag determined, his lips drawn together in a grim line so that he looked as forbidding as Thor. He was not about to give his sons Linclachan when he could give them an entire world, he reminded himself as Jeanne stepped into the building, a swirl of mist clinging to her plain gray clothing.

Standing there patiently, Jeanne looked like some beautiful nymph, part of nature yet set above it. The mystical effect caused Creag to struggle anew, and he responded the only way he knew how.

"You're none too early," he muttered disapprovingly.

"You didn't give me much time, Creag. I had to dress, or did you want me out here in my nightgown?" Jeanne retorted, until the impropriety of her question made her blush so that her face was the same pink as the early sun fighting to break through the gray shroud encircling the manor.

Neither the pretty picture of her embarrassment nor her words were lost upon Creag. His traitorous mind immediately conjured up images of Jeanne in her nightdress, and how he would react to such a situation, alone as they were in the stables. Finally, with reluctance, he squared his shoulders and drove such bedeviling thoughts away.

"Actually, having you about fully clothed is more than enough," he murmured. Realizing with a start that he had spoken his words aloud, he rushed on. "But now that you mention your garb, I must tell you that the sort of things you wear are unsuitable for your position. I want you to get rid of your clothing and order new."

"What's wrong with what I have?" Jeanne objected. Despite the plainness of her gray skirt and blouse, she had always thought they showed off her figure rather nicely. How dare this man insinuate that he didn't approve of the way she dressed? Why, she would never say such a thing to him, though in truth she liked how his loose white shirt encased his broad shoulders, and the manner in which his tight riding breeches stretched tautly across his seat and clung to his muscular thighs. But even if she didn't, she wouldn't apprise him of that fact any more than she would tell him she appreciated the cut of his garments.

"For one thing," Creag said, his deep, calm voice masking the effect of the tempting vision Jeanne had presented when she had stepped out of the mist, the effect she was still having upon him even now in the muted light of the stables, "they're too drab. Get something with a bit more color. And while you're at it, have them made looser so that you can be more comfortable while you work," he added, though it was in reality his own comfort that he had in mind. What fiendish demon, he wondered, what demented Celtic deity had seen fit to grace him with a woman as lovely as Jeanne Donnachy for his steward? By all rights, he should be standing here talking with some old man, not this striking female.

"And where am I to get the money to dress in order to please you?" Jeanne asked, her lips pursed together in a way Creag found most seductive.

"I'll pay for it, of course," he replied, taken aback, a shadow of hurt crossing his handsome features.

"Relishing the role of laird of the manor again, are we? And so early in the morning, too," Jeanne bit out. "Well, Lord Lindall, you can take your new clothes and stuff them in trunks. You didn't call me out here to speak of fashion. What was it you wanted?"

"Mind your tongue, Jeanne," Creag instructed while he cast about hurriedly for an excuse that would explain his demand for her presence that morning. Certainly a discussion about breeding the horses was not an idea to be considered, not when the two of them were alone in the deserted stables, Jeanne looking uncommonly beautiful and he feeling inordinately randy.

"I'm a busy man, Jeanne," he hedged uncomfortably. "I've already tended to the chore that needed doing, and without your help, I might add. You may as well return to the house, have your breakfast and get on with measuring the rooms. And by the way, it might be a good idea for you to work below stairs today."

"Below stairs, is it? I take it that's another of your orders," Jeanne stated, annoyed that she had hurried out here for nothing. If the man had been able to handle whatever it was, why had he called for her assistance in the first place?

"Look here, Jeanne, please do as I ask. I have my own work to do and very little time to spend explaining myself to you," Creag replied, uneasy and ridden with guilt about his attempt to keep her out of the way while her things, along with those of the other women, were being moved from their wing to his.

Of course she would be infuriated, but what was he to do? the laird asked himself. Renovations were beginning in her part of the manor, and he couldn't leave her there along with Leslie and Maggie. Yet as he regarded Jeanne, standing so impudently with hands on her hips, Creag suddenly regretted dismissing Michael's protests. He should never have failed to notify the women about the matter. However, there was nothing to be done about it, not with the fiery fit of temper she was in now. He'd deal with Jeanne's tantrums later, Creag decided, preferably after a bracing drink of Jamie's whisky.

For her part, Jeanne was disappointed at being dismissed so casually. Yet it was a truth she could admit to no one, least of all herself. Instead, her anger began to flare anew, directed as usual at the new laird of Linclachan.

"I don't know what all this talk of your work is, Creag Robertson Blake. You're a man who pays others to labor for him. Why, since you've been here, I haven't seen you lift one finger to join in the toil. Granted, with your fortune, you don't have to do otherwise, but still, a true laird wouldn't ask others to do what he wouldn't.''

"You forget yourself, Jeanne!"

"Maybe so, but I think it is you who has forgotten even more, Creag. This is a village, a clan, a family. It's not a mere business venture. We're supposed to work together.''

"Most of the work is being done by outsiders," Creag protested, as Jeanne headed for the open door of the stable.

"Aye, but the Robertsons and Donnachys labor right alongside them," Jeanne called back over her shoulder as she slipped back into the gray morning. "Why, as old as Ewan is, I've never failed to see him engaged in some task or other. In the entire area, you're the only man I know who can't recall what it's like to undertake good hard physical toil.''

Creag stood there helplessly gnashing his teeth, wishing it wasn't against his principles to lay a hand on a woman. He found the idea of Jeanne's shapely rump upended over his knee particularly appealing until he realized that he did not visualize himself spanking her, but running his fingertips over her curves in the softest of caresses. God in heaven, the wench was right. It would be a good idea for him to become involved in some sort of physical work. Perhaps then he would find an acceptable release for his rampant energy and its accompanying urges.

Jeanne was in the cellars of the main wing, instructing the men in the measurements they were about to take, when suddenly Leslie flew down the stairs, panting and out of breath.

"Jeanne, I've been looking all over for you," she said, gasping for air.

"What's the matter?" her friend asked anxiously. "Is something wrong with Maggie, Michael or... or... Creag?''

"No, no, everyone's healthy," Leslie hastened to inform her, "though Creag might not remain so when you and Maggie find out what he has done now.''

"And what is that?" asked Jeanne, her ire beginning to seethe before she even learned what it was that constituted her latest cause for upset.

"I saw a workman in the main wing of the house toting a trunk filled with your things!''

"What!" exclaimed Jeanne. Had this morning's encounter with Creag prompted him into casting her from the manor?

"Yes! And when I asked him what he was doing, the fellow said he was moving your things to a room in the laird's wing . . . to a room right next to Creag's own chambers! Nothing I said could stop the man. He told me, politely mind, those were his orders, and that was the way things were going to be."

"Oh, really?" asked an enraged Jeanne, forgetting the laborers under her direction and heading for the stairs. "Well, we'll just see about that!"

It had been a long time since he had felt this satisfied, Creag thought with a smile. Standing in shirtsleeves and trousers covered by flakes of ancient plaster, his hair more closely resembling an out-of-date powdered wig than his own thick blond locks, the laird of Lindall surveyed his surroundings. All around him, the ceiling in the sitting room lay at the base of his ladder, and though his muscles were sore and he was beginning to tire, Creag was the happiest he had been since coming to Linclachan.

There, he thought smugly, now let Jeanne Donnachy intimate that he was some soft, spoiled rich man. He could work along with the best of them. How else could he have ever scratched and clawed his way to the top of his chosen profession, a profession where he had begun by putting in grueling eighteen-hour days while he hoarded his salary to make his first investment?

When he had entered this room with the intention of venting his pent-up frustration and anger on the sagging ceiling, Creag had sent Clinton and his crew scurrying. And now, not only had he removed the crumbling surface overhead, he had also dealt with the sinfully ugly molding—a travesty of stags, acorns and thistles crudely carved in a wood too dark and pitted to be attractive. As difficult as the task had first appeared, finally it had been dismantled, along with his temper and his lust, so that the weariness Creag felt was a welcome one indeed. Nothing, he thought, could detract from his present contentment.

"Where are you?" Jeanne raged as she stepped into the debris-strewn room in the middle of Creag's self-congratulations.

Suddenly she took a shocked look around her and fell silent for a second, leaving Creag to think that this evidence of his physical strength was enough to impress even her.

"Why, you great lout, what have you done?" Jeanne began, gathering up the pieces of discarded molding to see if they could be reassembled and embarking on a new tirade before Creag could ready himself for this unexpected attack. "Don't you realize how old and valuable such carving is, you jackass?"

Creag's mouth dropped open. Even Jeanne had never gone this far with him before. Didn't the woman know he had been trying to pitch in, to exhibit his manliness, to help in the actual renovations of the manor though his money made it plain he never had to involve himself physically at all? Didn't she realize she was talking to a man who could buy her miserable village and manor a thousand times over? And damn it, when all was said and done, didn't she know that it was his molding, to do with as he pleased?

No one had spoken to Creag in such a manner in years. But as he stood on the ladder above her, the handsome American found that he was too spent to be anything but amused at this supreme display of his steward's fiery nature. Besides, he discovered with a chuckle that caused Jeanne to send him a withering look, it was refreshing to have someone speak to him unguardedly, spilling out what was on her mind instead of mouthing banal social niceties. Still, he knew he had best try to soothe this ruffled Highland dove.

"I was extremely careful when I removed the molding. It can easily be reassembled, but not in here."

"Why not?" Jeanne demanded to know.

"Because, quite simply put, my dear Miss Donnachy, it is hideous," Creag responded in his most charming manner as he descended the ladder, his boyish smile causing Jeanne's heart to skip a beat until she remembered the reason she had come searching for C. Robertson Blake.

"Be that as it may, it belongs in this room," Jeanne said hotly. "You had no right to touch it."

"I have every right," Creag reminded her, his smile growing into a grin as he came to the conclusion that Jeanne's temper, when it wasn't infuriating, was actually quite attractive, speaking as it did of emotions strongly felt and passions that ran deeply. It certainly made her green eyes glint in the most provocative way.

"I'll tell you something you don't have a right to do," Jeanne persisted obstinately, switching the subject rather than agree with him. "And that's what brought me in here in the first place."

"And that is?" Creag drawled lazily, his continued fine humor infuriating Jeanne all the more.

"Moving my room next to your own," Jeanne nearly exploded. "Tell me you have the right to do that!"

"Yes, I do, and the obligation, as well. The men have started work in your wing, and many of them will be housed there. How could I leave you and the others living among them and the chaos they create? You were moved for your own protection. Now you can go running to the council if you wish, but I think they will quite agree with me," Creag said calmly, exhibiting such a patent male reliance upon logic that Jeanne was hard put not to scream outright. "It is, I assure you, but a temporary thing after all."

"No matter how temporary, it will seem like eternity to me," Jeanne retorted. "Don't I see enough of you without knowing you are sleeping each night on the other side of my wall?"

The reference to the proximity of their beds caught Creag by surprise. He fought back against the unsettlement Jeanne caused by trying to recapture the amusement he had felt when she had first burst in upon him. If only he could maintain that playful diversionary distance, he knew he could handle living in the same house with Jeanne Donnachy. But unfortunately, he didn't always feel like laughing when she was around. In fact, he felt like doing something entirely different, he thought. Self-condemnation drew the corners of his generous mouth down into a frown as Jeanne stormed from the room, plaster dust rising in the wake of her skirts like mocking, mischievous phantoms sent to plague him for playing at being what he was not.

"Thank you, Father," Andrew Robertson intoned perfunctorily as the priest in the small village of Dunheath showed him into the tiny office of the parsonage.

"Not at all, Mr. Robertson," the priest assured him, handing him the well-worn book that contained the parish records. "It's not every day that some poor Scot comes into an inheritance. I only hope you find what you are looking for so the man gets what he deserves."

He'll get what he deserves all right, the solicitor thought angrily. When the door clanged shut behind the departing cleric, Andrew Robertson began the task that had brought him to Dunheath, situated on the lands of the other branch of the Donnachy clan.

Opening the fragile book that went back generations, he began to pore over its pages as he had the records in his own parish. What he was searching for, he hoped he would not find. Yet before he could hatch any retaliatory plots, he had to ascertain, for his own safety, that there was no relationship between C. Robertson Blake and the people of Linclachan.

Ever since the council had approached him and browbeaten him into sending that damnable letter to the States, he had suspected that the wealthy American was in no way connected with his clan. After all, it was just too convenient for this rich relative to materialize out of nowhere when Linclachan had been faced with the fact that its own solicitor desired the title of laird.

Still Andrew had done as he had been told, drafting the letter and never imagining that the foreigner would actually appear. He had continued building a case for his own succession to the title, touting his qualifications and attempting to court Jeanne. Slowly he had inched forward, grasping greedily at his goal until the day he looked out his window to find the villagers rejoicing, and learned that all of his efforts had been in vain.

If he had been a braver man, he would have lain in wait for Blake's carriage as it traveled the road from Kilneath. But courage had never been his strongest point, not when slyness and deceit could get him what he wanted without putting him in danger.

Each day that Blake was in residence, Andrew Robertson grew more and more desperate. Initially he had tried to salvage the situation, thinking that if he served as the man's solicitor, he could siphon off a fortune during the prolonged absences Blake's international business concerns would demand, marry Jeanne in order to live in the manor, and enjoy a style of life befitting a laird, even if he didn't have the title.

Yet those plans, too, had come to naught, the paunchy man of law thought wrathfully. Blake had refused to retain him, in fact had hardly spoken to him, no matter how much Andrew had tried to fawn upon him. And Jeanne wanted less to do with him than ever before. Worst of all, the new laird was staying on longer than Andrew had supposed. It was only a matter of time until the American noticed the discrepancy in the books and laid the blame for the missing money at Andrew Robertson's door.

No, something had to be done to stop the man, to get rid of him before it was too late. And every day, the situation grew worse. Though Jeanne seemed to have little tolerance for the usurper, the people of Linclachan loved him, or at least they loved what he did for them: painting their homes, rethatching their roofs, supplying them with implements needed for farming, and accounting for the surge of trade taking place in the usually forgotten and near-deserted village.

Andrew Robertson was astute enough to know that if he hoped to rid Linclachan of the American invader, he would need to establish a reason for doing so. Desperately he had begun his search through the parish records, hoping to find no trace of Blake's maternal grandfather. To date he had not been disappointed.

Studying the births, marriages and deaths recorded in several neat hands before him, Andrew wished fervently his luck would hold. He did not relish the idea of permanently disposing of Blake by means of an unfortunate accident of some kind. He would much rather satisfy himself that there was no link between the American and Fergus Donnachy. That would put him in a position of power, though whether he would threaten Blake with exposure or simply make his case to the council, he had yet to decide.

Two hours later, Andrew Robertson concluded his search and snapped the book shut, a grim smile illuminating his face and making him appear more unattractive than ever.

At the end of the afternoon, as soon as she could put aside her duties for a few moments, Jeanne set out for the village, intent upon speaking to the council about C. Robertson Blake yet again. This time, she vowed, still in an enraged state, those old men were going to listen to her! She'd make sure of it.

"Why, come in," Jamie said hospitably as he looked up from his conversation with Geordie to find Jeanne and the other two council members standing in his doorway. He smiled warmly at Fergus's granddaughter though from the looks of the lass he knew it would be much easier to send her on her way and allow Blake to deal with her unhappiness. Being younger, the foreigner was better equipped to deal with the woman Jeanne had become of late. Besides, it was a small enough price for the American to pay in order to be earl of Lindall and laird of Linclachan, the distiller told himself.

Yet, despite the thoughts crossing his mind, Jamie's fondness for the lass made such a scheme unthinkable. If Jeanne was aggravated enough to collect Duncan and Malcolm before she came calling, he and the others had to try to soothe her. After all, it had been she who had sacrificed most to assure Linclachan's good fortune. They could not desert her now if she was unhappy or in need.

"What's the matter, lass? You've the look of upset all about you," Geordie commented as the young woman entered his brother's house and stood facing the council members, Malcolm and Duncan already having taken their seats.

"Is it the laird making things difficult for you again?" asked Malcolm, hoping against hope that such was not the case. Though he sympathized with Jeanne's plight, there was little he or the others could do under the circumstances to alleviate her distress. And for that reason, they all felt guilty each time they simply placated the lass and sent her on her way.

"He's making things difficult for all of us," Jeanne announced peevishly. "This is not a personal feud, and it would help if you would recognize that fact."

"All right now, Jeanne, calm yourself and tell us of the latest troubles," Jamie ordered, assuming the authority he wore when he sat at the council table.

"The man is making life at the manor impossible!" Jeanne burst out. "He's forever issuing commands to one and all."

"We've not heard complaints from anyone else," Duncan stated gently.

"That's because everyone but me is afraid of him," Jeanne declared, questioning the truth of her statement even as she uttered it.

"If that's the case, there is nothing we can do for the others until they speak up for themselves," Malcolm uttered wisely. "But you, Jeanne, tell us what is troubling you."

"Why, the man is constantly calling me to his side, asking me for advice and then doing as he damn well pleases!" Jeanne announced. "He never leaves me in peace."

"It could be he enjoys your company," said Jamie calmly, sending the others a hopeful and meaningful look. If they could marry Jeanne off to Creag, he would be the one who would have to deal with her temper.

"He enjoys tormenting me, that's what it is! Do you know he set me to measuring the entire manor house, room by room, and then had the nerve to question the measurements I recorded!"

"Now you cannot blame a man for being exacting, Jeanne," suggested Duncan, trying to pacify her. "Such a trait is likely the key to Creag's great success."

"All right then, he has torn down the original woodwork in the sitting room," Jeanne went on, her head tilting upward, a silent challenge to the council to tell her that, too, was forgivable.

"Well, ancient as those thistles and stags were, they were also bloody unattractive," Malcolm answered finally, after warring with himself over the importance of the carved wood in question. "It's understandable if the man doesn't want to look at them."

The assenting nods of the other council members all but sent Jeanne into a frenzy. It would seem that no matter what occurred, Creag, an outsider, was always right, and she, with her long line of true Donnachy and Robertson blood, was always wrong. Well, she was not about to stand for this treatment a moment longer. She was going to let the council know just how shabbily the American had been treating her.

"And is it also understandable that this very morning the laird moved my things to a room near his own, an action undertaken without my knowledge or consent?"

Malcolm and Duncan looked to Jamie for guidance, and the four gray heads bent together in quick consultation.

"Aye, Creag sent me word of it just a short while ago," Jamie said, tired of these frequent conferences with Lindall Manor's steward, "and given his reasons for shifting you, along with Leslie and Maggie, to his wing, we find it not only perfectly understandable, but quite commendable."

The council's reaction to her complaint only inflamed Jeanne further, and she became so angry she could barely speak.

"And I suppose it is also commendable that this very morning, the laird told me in no uncertain terms to get rid of my clothes?" Jeanne demanded in a hoarse whisper.

"That bastard!" Geordie exploded, his hand flying to the handle of his dirk.

"Aye, we should have known it would come to this, no matter what precautions we took," Malcolm muttered. "Give a man something that isn't his, and he'll only try to take something else that doesn't belong to him."

"Did he hurt you, lass?" Jamie inquired, a murderous look clouding his usually sunny face so that he appeared fiercer than Jeanne had ever seen him. But even before she had answered him, he and the others stood, ready to go off and defend the honor of their friend's granddaughter, no matter what the cost to the village.

"No, no! You misunderstand," a crimson Jeanne hastened to reassure them, though the image of Creag skewered at the end of a sword wasn't all that unbearable. "He wasn't trying to compromise me. He was ordering me to buy new things and dispose of my old garments. Though the insult is nearly as bad."

"Och! Is that all, lass?" asked Jamie scornfully as he and the others took their seats with relief. "There's nothing wrong with a man wanting to see a bonny woman such as yourself prettily dressed."

"But...but...he's not just a man, and I'm not merely a woman. He's the laird and I'm his steward," Jeanne floundered, disappointed that the rage of the council had abated so quickly.

"You are a woman, Jeanne, and Creag is more a man than you realize. Maybe if you remembered that, there'd be less friction between the pair of you," Jamie said sagely. "Now if that's all that's bothering you, lass, a nice long talk with Maggie and a cup of hot broth will have you feeling better in no time."

"Really? And what's going to help you feel better when you find out how the laird's latest plans, hatched but an hour ago, are going to affect you?" persisted Jeanne, furious at being dismissed so summarily.

"And what projects are those?" Duncan asked warily.

"Oh, the ones that call for creating an artificial lake as a backdrop for a small pavilion Creag intends to build."

"I see nothing wrong with that, let him do what he wants," Geordie said, still angry he had jumped to conclusions a few moments before.

"Even if it means constructing a dam across your favorite salmon stream? What will the poor beasties do when they can't swim upstream to spawn?" asked Jeanne with a superior arch of her brow?

"What!" an incited Duncan roared.

"Aye, that's the way of things. Of course, forced to give up fishing, you might turn all your spare time to golfing, that is if the golf course wasn't destined to be fenced off and used as pastures for the sheep and cattle."

Instantly the four gray heads fell together once more, the intense buzzing of their muffled conversation brightening Jeanne's mood. It was time the old men learned what it was when Creag's penchant for changing things touched their lives adversely.

Finally they had finished conferring and debating.

"Well, lassie, this is serious business indeed," began Malcolm solemnly, "and correct you were to bring the matter to our attention. But the council feels we've no right to make a fuss. These days, everyone has to be willing to make sacrifices. We can't ask you to do what we wouldn't do ourselves."

"Oh," said Jeanne forlornly. If this latest bit of information didn't prod the council into ridding Linclachan of its spurious laird, nothing would. Her hopes in the matter had just been completely shattered. Bidding the clan elders goodbye, she set out for the manor, trying to adjust to the realization that

C. Robertson Blake would be earl of Lindall for as long as he wanted to be.

The council members watched Jeanne depart, weary of the frequent hearings she demanded. Could they help it if the forfeit she assumed them to be making was greater than the one they intended? After all, Blake would be gone soon enough, and dams could be dismantled and fences knocked down. Besides, doing without the stream and their ancient, beloved golf course for even a few months was truly penance enough for their dishonesty with the girl. At least that is what the elders told themselves, as they slapped one another on the back and poured a round of ale, congratulating themselves on their handling of Jeanne Donnachy.

Chapter Ten

A few days later, Leslie rose from kneeling among the moss-covered crags on the hillside and stretched, relieving the muscles stiffened by the awkward position she'd held all morning. The gentle warmth of the June sun and the far-off bleating of the laird's sheep made the scene almost mystically tranquil, a peaceful world removed from the impossible chaos that was now Lindall Manor, she thought.

With one contingent of workmen concentrating its feverish efforts on repairing years of decay while another crew introduced the wonders of modern plumbing to the old house and, all the while, Jeanne and Creag civil to each other one moment and warring the next, it appeared to Leslie that there was no nook or cranny in the place safe from confusion and disarray.

This morning, her head echoing with pain from the unceasing noise of the past weeks, she eschewed her own potions and escaped instead to the bucolic hills to replenish her dwindling stock of moss and lichens, so much in demand of late. The temporary respite was a balm to her soul, Leslie decided, strolling among the green fields, feeling freer and less harried than she had in days. She was only sorry that she had not been able to persuade Jeanne to accompany her.

The once imperturbable steward had become so tense and irritable since C. Robertson Blake had arrived that she almost seemed a different person. Where she always used to have a smile and words of encouragement no matter how bleak the outlook for Linclachan, now Jeanne would grumble like a thundercloud at the least provocation, real or imagined, especially if its source was the laird. Leslie frowned as she worried about her friend.

And Creag seemed to be everywhere, with a hand in every renovation and refurbishment, often as not demanding the presence of his assistant and steward for commentary. It wasn't that he accepted their advice, Michael said, more that he wanted a sounding board for his own notions, a fact that infuriated Jeanne even more. Given her volatile temper and what she saw as her duty to the clan, she undoubtedly would rather not have been consulted than have her opinion invited and then blandly discarded. Still, C. Robertson Blake *was* the laird, a medicine apparently more bitter for Jeanne to accept with each passing day and each change the American suggested.

Indeed, it was a wonder Creag had not sent her packing for all Jeanne's fiery insolence; more than once Leslie would have sworn he'd been about to, yet he seemed to have greater control than anyone would have guessed. Oh, occasionally he stormed off in a rare humor, but he'd reappear a bit later with no hint of his former fury, no drawn-out rehashing of the conflict. Maybe that was why he was a successful businessman, Leslie reflected, he didn't let emotion color his decisions.

Idly watching the manor for some sign of Michael, she noticed a pair of riders leaving the gate, heading toward town, Creag and Jeanne from the look of them. Even when they were on horseback, one couldn't help but notice the continuous struggle for dominance that existed between them as they fought to keep pace with each other. It was almost as if they were each afraid the other would take control if they slackened their tight hold on the reins for an instant.

Watching the riders until they were out of sight, Leslie fretted more than ever. Surely some disaster was bound to occur if Jeanne and Creag continued to go on the way they were. If only her friend could find the joy and tranquility she had discovered, Leslie mused with a sigh as she saw Michael leaving the manor and making his way up the path to join her.

"Do you have to be in such an awful hurry? Linclachan has been there for nearly two hundred years, it's not going anywhere," Jeanne complained, urging her horse forward to stay abreast of Creag's. "It is a beautiful, sunny day, a rarity for the Highlands, but rushing the way you are, you'll not enjoy it."

"My dear Miss Donnachy, may I remind you that you are the one who insisted, no, make that demanded, to accompany me on this outing, and you who first set out from the stable yard as if the hounds of hell were behind you. If you are now tired and wish to take a leisurely jaunt in the countryside, I suggest you go off on your own then. I, however, have too many chores to waste my time lollygagging at green fields or sheep in the glen," drawled Creag, determined to provoke this woman, just as she never missed the opportunity to try to change his behavior or opinion, regardless of the matter at hand.

It was only too bad he couldn't remain angry with her. It would certainly make life easier, but for some reason, no matter how hard he tried to do so, he couldn't. Granted, it could be because her looks were so spectacular, especially this afternoon as the sun's rays caught the reddish tones in her brown curls, making it appear as though she wore a fiery helmet. Abruptly he caught himself and snorted; it was appropriate for him to picture her in warrior's garb. At times such as these, her personality grated on his as if she were a conquering general. If she weren't so damnably efficient, and Fergus's granddaughter, he would have dispensed with her position weeks ago. At least that was what he told himself, trying to forget the way she often set his blood afire. Then he realized she was speaking again and for once he was grateful for her peevishness, knowing it would distract him from the dangerous and unsettling direction his thoughts had been taking.

"I'll do my duty as your steward, Creag," said the brunette, her voice making her displeasure quite clear. "Besides, you admitted you know nothing about cloth."

"I am knowledgeable enough to decide what I want draped around my bed," he disputed in annoyance. "And you had better take my word on it, Jeanne. In this matter, I will tolerate no interference from you, none of your silly notions of what is best. Besides, what possible difference could it make to you how my bed is decorated?"

"Giving advice is one of the functions of steward," she said archly, "but, come on, if you are in such a hurry, I'll race you to the village." Spurring her horse forward, Jeanne didn't wait for the laird's reply, fully accustomed to his inability to refuse a challenge. Despite her annoyance at his high-handness, she would have to admit that the man knew what he liked and disliked. However, when it came to bed hangings, he'd certainly not know the style or type of fabric that would be appropriate. And she would not have the laird's suite looking like a brothel, she fumed, regardless of his insinuations or his instructions to hold her tongue. Maybe if she reached the village first, she could choose a few respectable patterns and have Mairi show him only those. It was worth a try, she decided.

Galloping over the familiar road the villagers had tried so valiantly, if unsuccessfully, to smooth to Creag's satisfaction, Jeanne noticed Robbie and Hugh tilling their soil and Malcolm herding his cows, but she didn't take the time to stop. Her lord and master, she muttered to herself, was in too much of a hurry to permit her to socialize, but the men would understand.

Arriving in Linclachan well before Creag, Jeanne was warmly greeted by the villagers, and when she explained the situation to Mairi, Maggie's sister-in-law, she quickly found a half-dozen appropriate patterns that wouldn't be out of place in the laird's bedroom, dignified but not proud, sedate but not dull. It was only when the kettle boiled and tea was ready that Jeanne felt the faint stirring of distress.

Creag should have been along ten or fifteen minutes ago. Where was he? A few steps took her out of Mairi's house to the road but brought no reassurance. There was no dust or activity of any kind to be seen. Suddenly panic gripped her as Jeanne considered the frightful possibility that he'd fallen from his horse and hit his head along the rock-strewn path. Wasn't it true C. Robertson Blake was really a city man, unaccustomed to riding? Anything might have befallen him, anything at all.

Hastily the pretty brunette bid Mairi farewell, mounted her horse and hurried back the way she'd come, scanning the horizon for some sign of the earl of Lindall. Without hesitation, she rode back to where she'd issued her foolish challenge, dreading the sight of his motionless body prone on the stony ground, yet telling herself not to really expect such a tragedy. After all, many a time in the course of their arguments she'd wished him struck dumb, but she certainly hadn't meant it. He was much too vital a man, too energetic and opinionated to be still about anything, especially issues that even remotely concerned him.

When she reached the clearing where they'd last spoken, she halted and scanned the empty ground, anxious for some indication of what had happened, but he wasn't there, and there was no sign of him. Now the steward set forth at a slower pace, keeping watch for another rider to be sure but training her eyes more carefully on the irregular ground and the small ditches and gullies that bordered it. Thoughts of the arrogant American lying bloodied and bruised upset her more than she would have expected, given the offhand way he treated her. Yet, Creag was laird of the Clan Donnachy and it was her responsibility to see to his welfare, no matter what her feelings, Jeanne castigated herself, her anxiety mounting with each passing moment of her lonely search.

A tall, well-muscled man like Creag, of course, he was all right, she tried to tell herself. With a head as thick as his, it would take more than a little fall from a horse to knock him out. It would take Jamie's whisky, she thought, remembering the first night he'd sampled the stuff and the effect it had on him. From all reports of late, however, and from her own observations the night he had tried to kiss her in his study, it would seem that Creag's tolerance had improved markedly. Even Malcolm complimented the laird's staying power the last time she'd seen him. Malcolm? Maybe he would know what happened to Creag. He'd been moving his herd to a different pasture when she'd passed.

In an instant, Jeanne was riding up the lane toward the crofter's cottage, but before she had even dismounted, the old man was beside her.

"Och, now, lassie, what's your hurry? 'Tis too lovely a day to be rushing this poor animal like that."

"Malcolm, have you seen Creag? Today, I mean?"

"Aye, and didn't we just share a pint of Geordie's finest?"

"He was here, and he's all right?" Jeanne wasn't certain whether she should be pleased or furious. While she'd been scouring the countryside for him, apparently C. Robertson Blake had been playing lord of the manor and visiting his tenants.

"The lad's come a long way since he arrived, girl. To be sure he's all right. One cup never hurt any man," scoffed Malcolm.

"Did he say where he was going?"

"Into the village to invite the others to tonight's doings, I imagine, though he didn't rightly say."

"Tonight's doings?" repeated Jeanne. She knew of nothing special planned for this evening.

"Aye, the laird said his grandfather's birthday was today and we should come to dinner at the manor and lift a glass or two in memory of the good man who spawned his line. After all, 'twas his blood that made him laird, or so Creag said," guffawed the clan elder. "And who am I to dispute the laird's beliefs?"

"No one he would listen to," acknowledged Jeanne, heading back down the lane, "though I doubt Creag heeds anyone's word."

Damn him, she fumed, all afternoon she had been beside herself with worry for tempting Blake to race, and not only had he never competed with her, but he'd announced a dinner party for the council without consulting her. Well, she'd give him a piece of her mind all right, just as soon as she found him.

"Good day to you, Jeanne," Jamie called from his door as she passed. "See you this evening."

"Aye, that you will," answered the Donnachy steward, gritting her teeth behind her gracious smile. Blast C. Robertson Blake and his notions of hospitality, she thought sulkily.

"Creag asked Tammas if I would bring along one of my Dundee cakes tonight," announced Leish from the tavern steps. "Tell him I'd be happy to."

"You're coming, too?" asked the brunette in surprise, her cheeks growing rapidly pinker by the moment. "What about your customers?"

"Oh, there'll be no one here tonight, lass. Everyone is coming to the laird's feast, from his English workmen to Coinneach with his pipes. Creag said even the wee bairns are welcome. His grandfather loved babes, you ken?"

"No, I didn't know," said Jeanne, struggling not to scream aloud as she continued to Mairi's shop, cursing the American with every step. Was there anyone in the village C. Robertson Blake had overlooked, she wondered, any mouth that wouldn't be at his table looking to eat its fill? And did he worry about what she'd serve them? Did that ever cross his mind?

Knowing him, he'd say blithely that that was her concern, Jeanne seethed, her temper flaring as hot as any glowing ember. Wait, just wait until she saw that arrogant lout, letting her fear for his safety while he planned a party, had he? Well, she'd not permit him to get away with it, that she wouldn't.

"Ah, Jeanne, there you are," called the man in question as he exited Mairi's small holding and mounted his horse. "I know I told you to have a ride, but I was beginning to worry about you. Then I realized how foolish that was. You're probably the most adored woman in Linclachan from what the villagers have to say. Why, everyone sings your praises to the sky."

And, much as it galled him to hear the clan's compliments about his prickly steward, each telling him what a wonder she was, each urging him to value her highly as there were no others like Jeanne Donnachy, Creag had been warmed by their concern for one of their own. If only they would look on him with the same attitude, he was certain Catherine would be enchanted. Not that they hadn't thawed toward him recently, but a laird had to do more than be able to hold his liquor, which was why the idea of the party had seemed so perfect. If he started entertaining the locals regularly at the manor house, then they'd surely be pleased to welcome the Graysons when they arrived. It had been a stroke of genius on his part, he decided, noticing suddenly that Jeanne seemed a bit put out. The high spots of pink in her cheeks were a clear warning sign. Well, whatever the trouble, he'd soothe her ruffled feathers and then broach the subject of tonight's dinner.

"Mairi showed me the fabrics you recommended, and I agree with your choices. I've bought them all. The blue with the touch of green for my room, and the soft peach for the guest quarters," he began. "You have a marvelous sense of color—"

"Creag," his steward interrupted hesitantly, uncertain she could contain her temper properly to hold this discussion in the middle of Linclachan, but well aware she could not restrain her tongue much longer. "I wasn't off for a ride. I was looking for you, and when you didn't follow me . . ."

"Oh, I decided you were right, but, about the cloth. It's truly excellent, and a week ago I had the most wonderful idea—"

"What? About my being right, I mean."

"It was much too nice a day to hurry anywhere," he explained, a sheepish grin making him look like an errant schoolboy as he abandoned his efforts to talk about the woman's handiwork. "I saw Malcolm and Robbie and stopped to chat—"

"While I was waiting at Mairi's, and then fearing something had happened to you?" Jeanne couldn't believe her ears; the man was totally irresponsible.

"We had an ale and got to talking about the clan and those who have gone on and—"

"And you decided to invite the entire clan to dinner?" she finished, her voice soft but furious. "Well, hear this, Creag Robertson Blake, your little dinner cannot happen."

"It can and it will," he replied quietly, his blue eyes turning hard at her defiant attitude. For God's sake, hadn't he just taken pains to be inordinately nice to her? What was she so put out about? Maybe it was time he reminded her who was running Lindall Manor. "I've told them eight o'clock and you will have everything ready."

"No."

"Since I am laird, Miss Donnachy, my wishes, orders if you prefer, take precedence over your whims. I said there will be a dinner and it will happen," Creag declared, reaching over to grab her horse's reins. Why, he wondered as he crushed the leather beneath his strong fingers, did he always want to bend this woman's will to his, even in the most inconsequential of matters?

"You might be laird, but I am the one who has to worry about the household stores," Jeanne retorted, calling him back to the subject at hand.

"Money is not an issue. I'll increase your allowance and you can replenish the stores, buy extra if it will please you, but I will entertain when I wish," stated the earl of Lindall.

"It is impossible."

"It is my grandfather's birthday and we will remember him."

"There's not enough time or help or—"

"Send to the village for extra hands if need be or use Ewan and Michael."

"Men in the kitchen? Never, aside from the fact that—"

"You will do whatever is necessary, Jeanne," he announced in firm tones that prohibited further argument.

"But—"

"I tell you I want no more excuses. Whatever it takes, to-night you will serve a feast fit for kings, or in their absence, the Clan Donnachy. Is that understood?"

"Aye," she murmured, her eyes flashing furiously as the need to explain the problem warred with the desire to see the mighty C. Robertson Blake humbled. The latter urge won. Let him have his way tonight, she decided, he would rue it tomorrow. Finally Jeanne nodded agreeably. "I'll do my best, Creag."

"That's more like it," he said, releasing her horse's lead.

"I've work to do then." Without apology, the brunette galloped off, giving no evidence of her surrender to his will.

Watching her disappear, Creag shook his head sadly. She was really such a beautiful woman. If only she would learn her place, she would make some man a fine wife, but that would never happen in his lifetime, he feared. She was much too intractable.

Well, she'd done the best she possibly could with the short time the laird had allowed her, the uninspired stores in the larder and the unskilled help pressed into service, Jeanne reflected. The great hall had been given a hurried cleaning to dislodge the dust of the renovations. Flowers had been gathered and arranged in the old vases about the hall, and place settings had been laid the length and breadth of the laird's table.

In the kitchen, huge baskets of bread, scones and bannocks were warming, waiting to be served to the guests, as were the large pots of cock-a-leekie soup and the platters of cold salmon, haddock and trout for the fish course. Following, there would be the side of beef and two dozen fresh-killed chickens, accompanied by haggis, bashed neeps, stovies and fennel, not to mention countless kegs of Jamie's whisky and Geordie's ale, which would hopefully dull the appetites of anyone seeking seconds.

"I must commend you, Jeanne. After all your protestations earlier, I almost expected a disaster, bread and water, perhaps. This all looks wonderful," Creag marveled, entering the busy kitchen in search of his steward. Dressed as the occasion demanded in the laird's plaid, he stopped in amazement at the sight of the groaning tables.

"I am glad you're pleased, Creag," she said softly, unwilling to meet his eye, afraid her expression would betray her. "If you will excuse me now, I would like to go to my room for the evening."

"And miss the dinner? Surely not," he argued.

"I've not been invited and, before you remedy that problem, I will tell you that I fear I am too exhausted to be able to enjoy myself," she explained, pushing her bedraggled hair off her forehead. "Organizing this feast in barely five hours amid the confusion of all the construction has totally spent my energy."

"Won't you join us for a little while at least? You deserve to hear people's praise of your efforts," the laird declared, feeling oddly disappointed by her refusal to attend his celebration. Why should he care whether she came or not? Though he often felt an attraction toward her, at least when she was quiet, it was nothing more than physical desire. He must have told himself that a hundred times since his arrival. Why then did he have doubts about the matter?

"It is your party, Creag, not mine. You enjoy it," Jeanne persisted, her patience drawing to an end. All afternoon she had berated Mary and the others from the village to pluck the chickens, make the stuffing, poach the salmon, but above all, hurry, get it finished, make it perfect for the laird. And it was; that should have been enough to satisfy C. Robertson Blake. There was absolutely no need for her to dance attendance on him, as well, especially when it meant joining in festivities to celebrate a blatant untruth. Creag's grandfather had no more made him laird than Queen Victoria had made Grover Cleveland president of the United States. If the council and the villagers could stand there and salute the memory of a stranger, let them. The thought of such hypocrisy sickened her stomach.

"Please, Jeanne, come as my guest, not my steward," the American asked gently, regretting the harsh words he'd used earlier. "I know I behaved badly this afternoon, and I may do so again in the future, but I'm dreadfully used to getting my way."

"I've noticed that," she admitted, the ghost of a smile teasing her lips upward.

"Well, tonight, my way would be to see you having a good time along with the rest of us Donnachys and Robertsons. Do come," he urged, "though I won't order you to do so."

For a long moment Jeanne hesitated. Standing in the old stone kitchen, he seemed so innocent and earnest, she felt her heart quicken in sympathy, her feet anxious to dance with such a handsome man.... But, no, the die had been cast; it was out of her hands. She could no more tell Creag the truth about his lairdship than she could fly. However, she did not have to be so hypocritical as to watch him delighting in a relationship that never existed. She would rather go to bed.

"I'm sorry," she said simply, "although your wearing the plaid almost convinced me."

"I thought it only fitting, for my grandfather's memory, the idea, not the plaid, which is a bit cumbersome," Creag confessed, still uncomfortable in his adopted Scottish garb.

"Well, good night then and enjoy your feast," said Jeanne, slipping from the room before he could protest further. With any luck, and a glass of Jamie's brew, she'd forget her guilt concerning her plans for the morrow. Then maybe she could dream of Creag's powerful legs rather than the wistful expression that had followed her departure so sadly.

The next morning, tired though he was after the previous night's banquet, Creag was pleased to find Michael waiting, sheaf of papers in his hand, as he exited the laird's rooms.

"Your guardian wouldn't let me pass," the secretary explained, nodding at the aged Scot leaving his post across the threshold to Creag's rooms.

"I know. I have tried again to discourage his efforts, but apparently he would lose honor if I dismiss him."

"And his presence would prevent you from compromising Catherine's." Michael chuckled while his employer scowled.

"Catherine is not that sort of woman."

"I suppose not," agreed the secretary, shaking his head sadly as he compared the socially prominent but personally cold debutante to his own warm and loving Leslie. "And, ordinarily, you're not that type of man, but the urge might strike—"

"I'll see to the fellow if the need arises, my friend. But never mind him now, what about the replies to my telegrams?"

"As you expected, everyone is quite enthusiastic at the prospect of superior Scottish woolens. Bradford is anxious to handle the full consignment, presuming the cloth is of the quality you described, but other importers are also interested."

"Excellent. Wool that soft with fibers that strong will find a ready market in the States, I've no doubt of it," said the laird, a broad grin softening the angular planes of his face as he enjoyed the prospect of such an open market. "I'll see Linclachan prosperous in its own right yet. Now, let's go to the study and I'll show you which lengths of wool to pack for shipping. If they make the afternoon train, they can be in New York within ten days. Remind the buyers I expect their bids within three weeks and I know the value of the product, so there's no purpose in underestimating their cost."

"Very good, Creag." Michael was pleased to see his employer actively involved in business again. This was the efficient financier who had made Philadelphia sit up and take notice. With C. Robertson Blake at the helm, Linclachan could well become the wool capital of the British Isles, he reflected.

"What do you mean he wants to buy all the plaids the women can produce, as quickly as possible?" Jeanne demanded as she sat at the kitchen table, not certain she had heard Maggie correctly.

"Creag said that, in all his travels, he's never seen wool so fine and yet sturdy. He told Mairi and Beth he could easily get twenty guineas for a blanket, six for a length to use for a man's vest, and it's not just the plaids he'll be wanting, either," gushed Leslie's aunt. "Why, I'm even thinking of dusting off my old loom, but with these ancient fingers—"

"For pity's sake, Maggie," exploded the steward, her exasperation at the American's audacity stretched beyond bounds. First, there was his extemporaneous entertaining, and now this. He was simply too quick to rearrange people's lives, she fumed. "Just because *he* can sell the wool for such outrageous prices, if indeed he can, how much are you thinking he'll pass on to the weavers? As little as possible I wager."

"Now, lass, don't be judging our laird so hard. He told the council last night."

"Last night?" Apparently a lot more went on at the party held in Creag's grandfather's memory than just drinking, Jeanne realized. She should have known better than to leave him alone with the villagers; his smooth tongue would have them selling their mothers before he got through.

"Aye, last night. He explained three-quarters of the price would go to the women and the rest for expenses, shipping and the like," explained Leslie, wanting to be certain Jeanne understood Maggie's version of the story.

"Young girls who never cared for working at the looms are suddenly seeing their dowries earned with a shuttle and cock, and mighty pleased they are, too."

"Then they're fools for buying his empty promises without any fact," muttered Jeanne, color rising in her cheeks as she envisioned her carefree friends dominated by the awkward machines, their lives controlled by the demands of a foreign cloth market. What was wrong with the village the way it was? she fussed. Why did C. Robertson Blake have to tamper with everything he encountered? He was supposed to be choosing draperies for his own personal use, not selecting them for sale overseas. "And how many of the women are willing to weave ten hours a day, six days a week for the laird's scheme?"

"Creag told us the women could set their own pace, and he'd even build a large shed to hold a dozen or so looms so the women can all work together," contributed Mary. "Mind you, it's not for me, but my daughter Blair is mighty interested in earning some extra money and not being so dependent on the farm."

"Who'll see to the children?"

"Jock is near eight, he can tend the others," said the cook defensively, sensing Jeanne's disapproval.

"And what of his schooling?"

"It's summer so that's not a bother. He can see to them."

"And the cooking and the washing, too?" demanded Jeanne, fears for too rapid a change in Linclachan making her cross. If the business was to be successful, children might not return to their classrooms at all. From what she'd heard of some of the midland villages where factories took over the towns, it wasn't long before everyone in the family worked and had good money, but no life to enjoy it.

A furious ringing of the servants' bell exploded in the emotionally charged kitchen, making the women jump and preventing Jeanne from voicing her fears.

"That will be the laird wanting his eggs," Mary said worriedly. "Whatever shall I tell him?"

"That he served the hens at his fancy dinner last night and he'll have to make do with porridge like the rest of us," snapped Jeanne, a wicked smile gracing her delicate features as the plan she'd hatched yesterday began to bear fruit. "But you don't have to bother, it would be my pleasure to bear the news to *his lordship.*"

"Jeanne, where is my breakfast? I thought we had resolved this issue last month." Creag frowned, irritated that his pleasant morning should be so quickly soured by the steward's inefficiency.

"Aye, and you've not missed a morning's eggs and ham since, until you demanded we entertain the entire village last night."

"And the dinner you arranged was truly superb, I told you so. I fail to see, however, what that has to do with the tardiness of my morning eggs."

"When you decided on your party, we did not have sufficient meat in the smokehouse to serve all of Linclachan," Jeanne announced, her chin high, her green eyes surprisingly clear and angry, "but you would tolerate no excuses."

"So?" asked Creag, a sense of misgiving overcoming his hunger.

"The only way I could feed everyone was to serve chicken last night. Your guests ate them all, and without chickens, there are no eggs. Sorry, but you wouldn't listen to me when I tried to explain the difficulty.''

She looked as repentant as a fox in a henhouse. Creag snorted at a tiny smile curling the edges of her mouth so slightly he might have imagined it, but he couldn't imagine the haughty gesture with which the steward uncovered the wretched bowl of porridge on the serving tray she carried.

"If you're hungry, I fear this will have to do."

"No bread?"

"Only the crumbs on the floor left from last night, and Mary is out of yeast. She used every bit in baking for your guests."

"Fruit?"

"The last of the berries were eaten with the pudding."

"And my coffee?" Creag's voice was soft, but the fury in his eyes would have frightened many a man as he demanded answers.

"Most of the villagers never saw the value of the stuff, but I hear Jamie added his whisky and topped it with cream and Mary said they were calling for it all night. She made a half-dozen pots of coffee and not a drop is left."

Silently the American took the measure of the green-eyed beauty who stood before him so fearlessly, fully expecting his fury yet apparently delighting in it. The fact that she had made no effort to forestall this morning's shortages infuriated him. What kind of game was she playing, or was this what accounted for her sudden acquiescence to his demands yesterday?

"It never occurred to you to save some food for today? A lone egg and a single cup of coffee for the laird, perhaps?"

"Your orders were quite specific, Creag," Jeanne reminded him blandly. "The meal was to be fit for kings, we were to spare no effort. Nothing was said about today. However, I have sent Ewan and Beth for flour, oats, coffee and a half-dozen hens, though they'll probably have to go to Kilneath. Don't worry, you'll have a proper dinner."

"Only if you keep your hands off it," roared Creag, his anger at Jeanne's sly maneuver enraging him. Never before had a woman outsmarted him while doing exactly as he instructed, and he did not take kindly to the sensation of being bested. "Ever since I arrived, you have delighted in making me appear the fool, from your being a woman to not warning me about the kilt ceremony, to trying to poison me with haggis at six in the morning. You've challenged my plans for refurbishing the manor, for penning the sheep, and every other innovation. Damn it, woman, I have no idea what you want from me."

"To care about the people."

"And you believe I don't? What of the expansion of their woolen trade? It will provide a sound livelihood for the women of Linclachan."

"They've survived well enough till now."

"Survived, yes, in tiny hovels that only whitewash held together in a dilapidated village crumbling about their ears with nary a dream or a possession to take pride in."

"Whose pride are you worrying about, Creag? The villagers or your own?" Hands on her hips, Jeanne was long past guarding the words that escaped her mouth. "You don't really care about us. You just want to perfect your little Scottish hideaway, the reformed Linclachan you brought into the nineteenth century."

"Despite your efforts to undermine every move I make," challenged the laird, rising from the table to stand over his steward, his blue eyes claiming hers in a defiant glare. "Well, Miss Jeanne Donnachy, I have had enough of your calculated inefficiency."

"Inefficiency?" If there was anything she wasn't, it was inefficient, Jeanne reflected. Spiteful and calculated, yes, but not inefficient.

"To what else would you credit the fact that there is still a tapestry hanging in the great hall despite my orders that they be removed last month? You failed to have the workmen do as I directed," rebuked the irate man, his emotions overriding his common sense. "However, it shouldn't concern you any longer for I've finished with your quiet rebellion. I'm removing you from your position as steward. You may reside here in some other capacity, but your new role will be one that keeps you out of my sight!"

"What? You can't expect me to relinquish my duties and still remain here."

"Fine, I'll not order that. If someone is foolish enough to offer you lodging in the village, I'll not dispute it, but you are no longer Lindall's steward. Finally I am doing what I should have done weeks ago. I'm taking control of *my* home and you no longer have a say in anything that goes on here."

With that said, C. Robertson Blake turned on his heel and left the dining hall, determined to put the angry scene behind him. Deciding to take a long, hard ride, he headed for the stables without a backward glance. At some point he'd undoubtedly have to confront the council, but he *was* laird. That should count for something when it came to choosing his help.

Jeanne stood where she was, shaking with anger, not yet believing his dismissal of her.

Who did he think he was? she fumed, moving blindly toward the offending tapestry on the wall of the great hall. Telling her that she was inefficient and not able to follow his dictates? Damn him to hell. She'd go, all right, but first that bloody wall hanging would come down. She wouldn't allow it to be said that she had left her position as steward with any of her orders not carried out.

Her strength enhanced by her fury, Jeanne shoved the heavy laird's chair over to one of the oversized sideboards and used the leather seat as a step up to the top of the ornately carved serving cabinet. From there she hoped to just grab the tapestry and pull it down, but she was still too short to reach the pole that supported its weight against the stones. Standing on tiptoe, she tried unsuccessfully to stretch the extra distance, but suddenly she had a better idea.

Certainly if she simply took hold of the bottom of the wall covering and flipped it upward with sufficient effort, the pole would be dislodged long before her precariously balanced body suffered any ill effects. For a brief moment, Jeanne had second thoughts, glancing down at the grimy stone surface four feet below, still filthy from last night's festivities. Then she reconsidered her hesitance. The hangings were to be cleaned anyway; what difference would a bit more dirt make?

Firmly Jeanne gripped the lower edge of the heavy woven cloth and jerked it upward, releasing great clouds of dust, and setting herself to sneezing, but otherwise having no effect on its age-old placement. Again she tried, this time using her whole body to yank at the tapestry, feeling it let go with a triumphant cry.

She was wickedly pleased with her success, until in the next instant she realized that she had not anticipated the sudden weight of the newly loosened wall hanging as it toppled her from her dangerous perch.

"No—"

But before the word escaped her lips, Jeanne lay crumpled on the cold floor, her arms and legs entangled in the musty weight of the tapestry, her brunette curls uncushioned against the hard stone.

Chapter Eleven

It was nearly noon by the time Creag returned to Lindall Manor, his ire and foolish pride spent, ready now to acknowledge his faults and seek Jeanne's pardon. In retrospect, the financier had to admit his steward had been accurate in her denunciation of his renovations in Linclachan as being more for the sake of his reputation than for its people. Still, with a bit of care, couldn't he manage to better the look of the village, as well as improve his tenants' lives? If she'd not rage at him like an unleashed banshee, Jeanne might even have some worthwhile suggestions, provided they could discuss the issue rationally without screaming at each other.

Entering the stable yard and calling for one of the servants to see to his horse, the laird intended to hurry to the house and make his amends as quickly as possible. Surprised when no one answered him, he took no offense, merely altered his plans.

Perhaps they are at luncheon, he allowed, presuming Ewan has returned with the supplies. Actually he found that a bit of food would taste good now; however, he was not one to stand around waiting for anyone else to do a job he could easily manage. Therefore, Creag led his mount into its stall, removed its saddle and found a cloth. It was a long time since he'd tended his own animal, he mused, but one didn't forget the routine. Enjoying the rhythm of the easy strokes as he wiped down the coarse coat, he rubbed the horse's back and flanks, dislodging the briars and signs of their heavy ride. Finally finished, he had just filled the water trough when Ewan hailed him.

"Creag, where have you been? No one could find you and everybody is worried sick."

"About me?"

"No, it's Jeanne—"

"Jeanne?" With a heavy heart, Creag realized the steward must have already recounted their argument to the staff. Well, he imagined it served him right for being so cavalier. "I must tell her I'm sorry. It's my fault, a simple misunderstanding."

"You're to blame?" cried the estate laborer, clearly surprised at the laird's admission.

"Well, of course Jeanne has a fair temper, too, but I never meant to dismiss her," began the American, startled at the tears that filled Ewan's eyes.

"Dismiss her? Lord, Creag, we'll be damned lucky if she doesn't leave this earth altogether with the kind of fall she took. That serving cupboard is at least four feet tall."

"Fall? From a cupboard?" Suddenly Creag found himself impatient for answers Ewan didn't seem to have. Without hesitation, he turned and headed for the house at a fast clip, Ewan falling into step beside him, and explaining the situation.

"She must have been pulling down the last of those old tapestries, by herself of all foolish things. The lass had moved the laird's chair and climbed up on the cupboard to get a better grip on the hanging, I suppose," muttered the servant. "Maggie found her, not an hour ago, on the floor in the great hall, but she's not come around since—"

"Ride to Glenmeath at once for the doctor, Ewan," Creag ordered sharply, reaching into his pocket and tossing a gold coin in the man's direction. "Tell him that's for his time and there's another one waiting here if he arrives before sundown."

"But Leslie is seeing to Jeanne."

"Leslie will do for the moment, but a licensed medical man will know more about what needs to be done if Jeanne remains unconscious for long," argued Creag, irritated by Ewan's reluctance to obey. "I said go, man! You'll do Jeanne more good with your feet in the stirrups of a horse than standing about wringing your hands and fretting. Maybe by the time you return with the doctor she'll be serving you dinner."

"Aye, please God it be so," said the Scot as he headed back toward the stable to do the laird's bidding, pondering how odd it was, Creag's thinking Jeanne's fall was his fault.

Once in the house, the American moved quickly through the throng of anxious servants and workmen and started up the stairs before he thought to reassure them.

"You know Jeanne is in good hands. Your Leslie is looking after her now and I've just sent Ewan for a doctor."

"No doctor knows more than Leslie," muttered Fiona.

"That may be, but if Jeanne hasn't awakened by the time he appears, the doctor might have some suggestions that would help," he counseled. "Now, until we know more, why don't you go about your chores as best you can? Jeanne would want you to keep busy, and there's much to be done after last night's festivities. I promise to tell you of any change."

"You do that now, Creag, and, the rest of you, say a proper prayer as you work," instructed Mary as she herded the maids toward the kitchen and urged the others back to their duties. "Maggie is up there with Leslie, in Jeanne's room."

"Good, thanks."

Taking the stairs three at a time, Creag tried to deepen his breathing in order to lessen the heaviness that lay on his heart, but, instinctively, he knew nothing would help until he saw his steward smile again. Damn it, as independent and waspish as Jeanne Donnachy might be at times, she was a veritable treasure. Unreasonable it might well be after their last confrontation that morning, but he could not begin to contemplate life in the Highlands without her. It wasn't that she was more important than any of the others employed by C. Robertson Blake, he told himself, opening the door to her room, but Lindall Manor would lose its vitality if Jeanne weren't in residence.

For a moment the gloom within unnerved him until he realized the draperies were drawn against the light. Quickly he crossed the room and opened the curtains, hushing Maggie's protest.

"I'll not have Jeanne resting in a dungeon, dark and dim," he chided irritably. "She is too full of life and sunshine to heal in such a shadowy world. I wager she even keeps her drapes open to the moon, does she not?''

"Aye, though I've warned her many the time moonlight can weaken a woman's mind," confessed the housekeeper. "She'd not change her ways though."

"Then we shan't change them for her. This room shall not be darkened. Sunshine or candles shall burn constantly."

"I suppose it will do no harm," Leslie agreed, looking up from her position by the head of the bed.

"Why haven't you gotten her out of that confining dress and into a looser gown? Surely it would be better for her—" started the American, anxious to see Jeanne as comfortable as possible. If only he hadn't reminded her about the damned tapestry...

"We were about to change her clothes when you burst in, giving uninvited advice," retorted the Donnachy healer. While she could understand the laird's concern for his steward, there was no reason for him to give the orders in a sickroom. "Now, sir, if you will allow us some privacy..."

"I will wait in the hall. Then maybe you can make Jeanne one or another of your powders to revive her," suggested Creag, oblivious to Leslie's pursed lips.

"Maybe," she said noncommittally as she closed the door behind him.

Pacing the hall outside the door, Creag tried once more to quell his anxiety about the woman lying so still in the next room. Jeanne Donnachy was one of hundreds of people on the Blake payrolls, the businessman reminded himself, a valued member of his staff in Linclachan, but not the only one that he should be so overly concerned with her welfare.

However, she thought she was part of his family, he realized with a start, stopping before the portrait of his supposed great-great-uncle Bruce and remembering Jeanne's pretty blush as Maggie had confessed the scandalous tale of the man's being killed by a jealous husband for bedding his wife. The steward had tried to hush Maggie's lurid details, becoming more and more embarrassed, but the simple charm of her ways had struck him then and now as being beautifully provincial, another bit of innocence he couldn't help but associate with the fetching brunette. Yes, Jeanne Donnachy had enlivened his life all right; could he rest till he did the same for her?

When the door opened, he was inside in an instant, stunned at how lifeless Jeanne appeared against the white bedclothes. Except for the purplish bruise at her temple, her skin was a pale milky hue. Never could he recall seeing his steward motionless, let alone totally silent and unresponsive to his presence. With deliberate effort, Creag shook aside his dismay and dispatched Maggie for boiling water and Leslie for a healing powder.

"Are you certain you don't mind my going, Creag?" wondered the housekeeper, a curious gleam in her eye. "One of the maids could easily fetch the water for my niece while I stay here. Most men prefer to avoid sickrooms."

"They do not bother me. Now be off with you," he said sharply, anxious to be alone with the she-witch who affected his thinking so strangely.

The door closed quietly then, but he barely heard it, racked as he was by the pain of seeing Jeanne lying so still, her eyes closed, her cheeks peculiarly ashen. Usually high spots of furious color made them vibrant while her eyes flashed their impatience with him. This dull caricature of the lively Scottish lass was hard to accept.

Bending over, he lifted her soft hand into his and smiled at the sight of the small dainty fingers so overshadowed by his own.

"Jeanne, if you can hear me, please know how very sorry I am for my temper. Though you've triggered it often enough in the past month, you should know my moods come to naught once I've had time to think things through. Come back to us and I promise I'll do better," he muttered, squeezing her hand. But she made no reply, and after standing over her for a bit, Creag noticed her hair, still incongruously styled from earlier that morning.

Piled high on her head in carefully arranged curls, her hair had escaped a few of the restraining pins, but he wouldn't imagine its arrangement was particularly comfortable. Without conscious thought about the propriety of his actions, he sat behind her on the bed, carefully raised her shoulders and supported her against his chest, preparing to undress her coiffure.

Slowly, gently, his long fingers roved Jeanne's glorious mane, discovering each pin and removing it as he released the tangled strands from their imprisonment. Her tresses were luxuriously soft and surprisingly long he discovered, relishing their silky feel even as his own body warmed at such close contact with hers.

She was such a feisty creature, he mused, how could she be so still while his own heart was suddenly dancing so rapid a beat?

Refusing to concede that anything but worry could perturb his businesslike efficiency, even as he resisted the temptation to kiss those silent lips, Creag found a hairbrush on the ancient bedside table and slowly began to tame her brunette waves. The rhythmic motion seemed to soothe his patient and she sighed, a deep sound that cut his heart, quickening the hope that she would awaken soon. Yet, when he had finished his task and reluctantly placed her unresisting form back against the pillows, Jeanne remained unconscious and unresponsive.

Again cursing his damnably sharp tongue and quick temper, Creag strode across the room to the fireplace and began to light the fire. Perhaps the extra warmth would rouse her.

"Here we are," called Maggie loudly as she opened the door wide for Leslie to follow her. "We've brewed a nice tea and Mary has sent up a warm broth, guaranteed to put roses back in her cheeks and a bit of life in her step."

"Good, I'll support her while you spoon the tea into her mouth," volunteered the laird. Before the women could protest, he had seated himself at the head of the bed as though he belonged there and had Jeanne resting tenderly across his breast.

Exchanging surprised looks, the women voiced no objection, but readily proffered the tea, praying it would work its magic.

But none of the various teas, the soup or the wet cloths woke Jeanne from her untoward slumber, and by the time the doctor arrived that evening, even Leslie welcomed his expertise.

"Well, sir?" Creag prodded after the man had peered into Jeanne's eyes, felt her forehead, examined her wound and listened to her heart, muttering to himself all the while.

"Clearly her body needs rest, your lordship, and we shouldn't interfere with nature's own healing ways," said the tall, spare figure. Not used to sudden demands to travel twenty miles to a patient he'd never seen before, he readily welcomed the gold pieces the journey paid, but he couldn't understand the high level of concern in the sickroom. This was but a servant.

"But hers is not a natural sleep," argued Leslie, uneasy with the doctor's pat explanation. "She cannot be awakened."

"The young woman is not down with a fever, nor is she showing any visible signs of distress—"

"Then why can't we rouse her?" demanded Creag, wondering at the wisdom of this so-called medical practitioner. Perhaps Leslie knew more than he, after all.

"In all likelihood, the swelling of the right temple there has interfered with her usual behavior, I grant you, but I really find no cause for alarm," continued the doctor in a defensive tone of voice. "Keep her warm, give her as many liquids as she'll take, and in a few hours, a day or two, at most, she'll revive. If not, send for me and I'll try bleeding her."

"No!" cried Leslie and Creag in unison, each somewhat surprised at the other's vehemence.

"There'd be no good served by bloodletting in this case," complained the clan healer.

"I thank you for your visit, sir, and Maggie will see you have a meal before you turn back, but we'll have no further need of your services," said the laird, carelessly dismissing the doctor whose advice he'd sought. "We'll manage from here."

"Oh, well, very good then. She should recover in time, I assure you, no matter what anyone does, though then again she may not," he announced calmly, heading for the door and his dinner. "Now, missus, show me the kitchen."

"I apologize, Leslie. I really thought he would help," said Creag softly. "Not that you couldn't, but—"

"That's all right, I understand. You're not familiar with our ways, but you know I care about Jeanne."

"As I—we—all do."

"Naturally, but why don't you go downstairs and have something to eat, as well? If it's going to be some time yet till Jeanne awakens, there's nothing more you can do here," she advised. "After all, you haven't left her side since early afternoon and it's nearly eight."

"Nor have you."

"Aye, but then I'm expected to nurse the sick. However, by the laird's staying so close, you're suggesting to the village that you fear for Jeanne's life," she cautioned. "When Ewan brought the doctor up, he said everyone is gathering downstairs, and the mood is near panic."

The American considered Leslie's words for a long while, ran a hand over his weary face and nodded slowly. As laird, he could not deny that his duty was not only to Jeanne, but to all the Donnachys and Robertsons alike. Despite his own wish to keep a bedside vigil, he had best reassure the others by his appearance for dinner.

"All right, I'll go eat, especially since my steward gets so upset when I'm not at the table by eight sharp," he said with a tight smile. "However, once I calm the villagers, I'll come relieve you. There's no point in both of us sitting up all night and as laird, I will be doing so. Jeanne *is* my responsibility."

"Don't blame yourself for her fall, Creag. Since she was the smallest bairn, Jeanne did as she wanted. She's never been one to act only to please others and I doubt she started today."

"Perhaps," conceded the American, "though if I had not complained about the remaining tapestry, I doubt she would have thought to climb onto the cupboard."

"Well, that's something you can ask her about when she comes around," said Leslie, urging him toward the door.

"Aye, I'll do that," Creag agreed reluctantly, glancing back once more toward the silent figure in the bed and longing to remain by her side. Then he squared his shoulders, lifted his chin, assumed the role of laird and left the sickroom.

Ten minutes later, having washed and changed, C. Robertson Blake, sixth earl of Lindall, descended the stairs to the great hall, determined to assuage the villagers' fears quickly so he could return to Jeanne's side. Surveying the people in the room, he was amazed to realize that though half the population of Linclachan was present, everyone was empty-handed. Not a single glass was in sight; no wonder Ewan had been perturbed.

"Creag, how is Jeanne?" asked Malcolm nervously as he spotted the laird. Any other time he would have climbed the stairs and visited Jeanne's room himself, but somehow it didn't seem proper with an American in residence. Besides, bad news traveled fast enough and at his age, he'd rather it be delayed.

"That lass is the dearest flower Linclachan's ever grown," bemoaned Coinneach. "We'll not be the same without her."

"Oh, there's no chance—" started Creag, only to be interrupted by a half-dozen voices.

"Tell us she's fine, lad," invited Duncan, a somber face adding urgency to his fervent pleas.

"Will she be downstairs then?"

"Why did you send the doctor away?"

"Is she not dying?" demanded Andrew Robertson, hoping the American would answer in the affirmative so that the woman could be blamed if Blake ever discovered the money missing from the manor's accounts. "We've been expecting the worst."

"No, no, Leslie and the doctor both believe there's no cause for alarm," Creag explained, at a loss as to how to comfort Jeanne's friends and neighbors. "It may take a few more hours until she awakens, but there's no doubt she will."

"Have you tried giving her a wee dram of my whisky?" asked Jamie. "'Tis not called the water of life without cause, you ken. Many a man it's restored to health."

"And many more it's put under the table," returned Creag with a broad grin, "but I wager we could all use a cup about now. Mary, will you see everyone is served? Ewan and Michael will help with the kegs."

"Nay, but we couldn't, lad," protested Malcolm, "not with Jeanne so ill. It would be disrespectful."

"Nonsense, Malcolm. If we toast to her quick recovery, the whole exercise could be construed as prayer," argued the distiller, his throat parched from all the dry chatter. "Even Father Menzies wouldn't begrudge us a drink for such a fine intention as Jeanne's health."

"Aye, it's mightily called for as a statement of faith that Jeanne will rally shortly," concurred the laird, a sudden inspiration striking him. "Where's Maggie?"

"Here, Creag," the old woman replied, coming forward.

"Didn't you tell me you were handy with needle and thread?"

"Oh, aye, quite practiced," she admitted, relieved to be able to tell the truth for a change. "Will you be wanting me to make you that kilt then?"

"No, no, a soft, comfortable dressing gown, actually—"

A murmur of disapproval began in the large room as the Scots worried about their laird's personal habits.

"A dressing gown?" echoed Maggie. "For you?"

"Of course not," snorted Creag, amazed at the density of the woman. "Something pretty for Jeanne, silky soft and feminine for her recuperation."

"There's a length of emerald green silk in the supplies you had shipped from London, Creag," volunteered Michael, recalling the half-dozen bolts of colorful silks Creag had purchased as a gift for Catherine Grayson. Surely he'd not object to giving one to Jeanne instead. "I imagine it would be an excellent choice for Jeanne, if Maggie doesn't mind using English goods."

"Of course not, laddie, why don't we fetch it now and the women and I can work out a pattern," suggested the housekeeper enthusiastically, taking the laird's directive as a sign that Jeanne really would be all right.

"And while you see to that, Mary can set out a light supper for everyone. I'm afraid the larder is pretty barren after last night's feast, but I warrant there's bread, cheese and a bit of meat," declared the financier, trying to recall what supplies Ewan had been sent to fetch.

"Now, don't you be worrying about that," chided Mary, leading him toward an overflowing table at the front of the hall. Hams, breads, crocks of soup and pies covered the entire surface, and other wrapped parcels sat nearby. "Everyone in the village brought some dish or other with them when they heard about poor Jeanne. You have a bite yourself and they'll all follow."

"What a nice gesture," said Creag, unaccustomed to the unselfish camaraderie of Linclachan where the families all shared or suffered together. He had known his tenants adored his steward, but there was easily an amount of food there equal to what he'd served the night before, and all contributed willingly, without complaint. "I'm certain that such thoughtful kindness will have Jeanne back with us in no time."

* * *

A short while later, however, when he finally returned upstairs to send Leslie off to her bed, there had been no change in Jeanne's condition. Her joyful essence remained in a world separated from her body and, he knew of no way to call her back. For that matter, he considered wryly, if she knew it was he wishing her to awaken, she might choose to remain unconscious.

His earlier instructions had kept the room lighted, and as he studied the brunette's serene silhouette in the flickering glow of the burning candles, he found it hard to avoid remembering his grandmother's wake, her body surrounded by light, and lifeless all the same, in the cramped parlor of the Robertson house. Almost without acknowledging his fear, Creag rose, approached the bed and leaned close, listening for the gentle sound of Jeanne's breathing, only releasing his own strained lungs when he was satisfied that she was still with him.

Gently he brushed the wayward curls from her forehead, marveling at the smooth texture of her ivory skin and the silky quality of her tresses. Never tranquil in the course of her day, Jeanne apparently was so completely relaxed now that she wasn't even aware of the tentative strokes of his hand on her cheek, willing her to awaken. Instinctively obeying an unspoken need, he permitted his finger to trace the outline of her pale mouth, wondering how it would feel to caress it with his own lips, only to catch himself in such an overly familiar gesture and retreat hurriedly to his chair again.

It was asinine to worry about this damnably independent slip of a steward, about a woman he suspected would sooner send him and his money to the devil than admit she was in need of assistance, he told himself. What a far cry from American females, he marveled, remembering the many debutantes who used any feeble excuse imaginable to secure his attentions, albeit temporarily. Yet, here he was, well after midnight, sitting by the bedside of the only woman in the world who had ever treated him with such scorn. What a wonder!

Removing his shoes and pulling a plaid rug over his legs, Creag settled in to work on some of the letters and papers Michael had foisted off on him, insisting they needed attention. For a while he worked dutifully, initialing memos, commenting on proposals, making notations on letters, signing checks and approving invoices as appropriate. But his eyes strayed frequently to the quiet presence across the room until, without realizing it, he began to read some of the correspondence aloud and discuss it with his silent steward, sounding out his ideas. Somehow the night passed more easily as he worked this way, and it was only when he heard the clock chime five that he closed his portfolio, rubbed his eyes and checked his patient yet again.

Her high forehead was cool to his touch and her breathing easy, though she stirred restlessly when he changed the moistened cloth protecting the angry bruise on her temple. With a surprisingly strong movement, she tried to push his hand away as if to avoid more pain.

"Maybe the doctor was right," murmured Creag in surprise, hoping for an end to the purgatory of waiting that he'd assigned himself. Yet, to his immense disappointment, without any further sign of life, Jeanne settled down once again, apparently sleeping without fear even while he struggled to shoulder the heavy mantle of guilt for her accident.

It wasn't that he had ordered her to climb the furniture and remove the wall hanging, he told himself for the hundredth time; but C. Robertson Blake should have been familiar with the way his employees jumped into action when he demanded that anything be done. That was the real problem, however: Jeanne Donnachy was *not* his usual employee; she was an infuriatingly capable Scot with miraculous green eyes that tempted him to foolishly irrational thoughts, he acknowledged, shaking his head at the idle notion of kissing her back to consciousness, like the prince in the fairy tales. Instead, he sank back into his chair and closed his weary eyes.

Catherine, Catherine Grayson was the woman he wanted, he tried to tell himself. Blond, buxom, a stunning female who would look magnificent on his arm as he stalked the drawing rooms of financial power, not only in Philadelphia, but New York and London, as well. Creag and Catherine Blake, Lord and Lady Lindall, the butlers would announce, he thought, envisioning the stir such proclamations would cause in society's salons. Entry into such rooms was a dream he'd fought long to achieve, and by dint of the foxy council of the clan Donnachy, success was in sight. But why then was he so disturbed by this willowy bit of an intractable female who more often than not irritated him, a burr under his saddle of authority?

Dozing uneasily, the laird saw Catherine, garbed in a woolen cloak, moving rapidly ahead of him down the sheet-draped halls of Lindall Manor, walking away from all he offered her, fleeing his urgent cries as he hurried down the main stairs in pursuit. Quickly he rushed after her, ducking under scaffolding, dodging paint buckets and workmen; yet, no matter how he tried, he couldn't catch the elusive female. It was only when Catherine reached the oaken front door and had difficulty opening it that he gained her side, pulled her into his arms, brushed back her cloak—and discovered the woman he had chased through endless miles of ancient corridors was no longer Catherine, after all. She had miraculously become Jeanne, alive and well . . . and running away from him.

With a start, he jumped up from the shadows and hurried to the bed, desperately afraid that like Catherine, she might have fled. But no, his steward hadn't left this life as he had feared, even if she wasn't yet ready to embrace its wonder.

A short while later Leslie returned, and together they spooned a cup of Mary's broth between Jeanne's slackened lips, Creag supporting her slight weight as Leslie fed her friend. Otherwise there was little change in the sickroom all day, Creag refusing to leave, Maggie, Mary, Michael, Ewan and the members of the council stopping by to shake their heads and mutter. Even the priest paid a call, offering last rites, but the laird vehemently opposed such a notion.

"She's not close to death, Father, she's near to life," he argued. "Jeanne Donnachy has more fire and spirit in her than half a dozen men I could name. And I'll not see that spirit dampened with the expectation that she's about to die."

"Very well, I'll stop back tomorrow," promised the cleric, shaking his head in disapproval, "and I will pray for her."

"Thank you," said Maggie as she ushered the man out before the laird could offend him further.

Creag had become a veritable bear this past day and a half, fighting off anything or anyone he saw as a threat to his steward. Hours on end he spent by her bed, straightening her covers, brushing her hair, changing the wet cloths on her brow, even calling a halt to the construction that could be heard in the room. He was amenable to any task Leslie set for him, protesting only when she sent him from the room and then, arriving back in half the time anyone else might have taken. Indeed, he hadn't even bothered to shave, Maggie noted with interest as she entered the room late on the second night with the finished dressing gown and found Crag reading to a still-unresponsive patient.

"Do you suppose she even hears you?" the housekeeper asked softly, not wanting to upset him but seeing little point in such an exercise.

"For heaven's sake, Maggie, don't whisper. We want to wake her, not encourage her napping," he chided impatiently, laying down the leather volume. "I don't know if she hears any of us, but I must try. The longer she is unconscious the more likely she'll stay that way, and Leslie said she liked the Brontës. I thought maybe *Jane Eyre* would interest her, but it seems like an awfully depressing tale—"

"Not for a woman, Creag. 'Tis good you care so much, but you ought not neglect yourself. You've barely left this room since the accident. It's not healthy."

"I'm fine, Maggie. Besides, Michael and Ewan can handle any problems that arise. They know where to find me."

"It's not your fault, you know."

"I know," he admitted quietly, "but I can't help but think—"

"Ah, laddie, too much thought isn't wise, not when it can't change what is," advised the housekeeper, patting his shoulder in comfort. "Have you eaten all day?"

"I've no appetite, but don't natter at me all night, woman," Creag said in a surprisingly friendly tone. He knew Maggie worried about Jeanne and apparently all the tenants of Lindall Manor, including himself. "Haven't you a bed calling your name? It's near midnight."

"Soon, but I wanted to bring up the dressing gown. If I say so myself, it turned out right nicely. I warrant its color will match her eyes when they're open again."

"Aye, they're a smiling green just like this, aren't they?" he murmured, taking the silky fabric and running his hand across it, envisioning Jeanne wrapped in its fine design. "Thank you,

Maggie. It really is lovely and I promise you, Jeanne will be awake and wearing it anytime now. What woman could resist a new dress, even one so contrary as my steward?''

The housekeeper laughed and started to leave the room, wondering at the American's concern for Jeanne, when they heard a small whisper.

The voice was weak and very soft but unmistakably Jeanne's, and with a cry of relief, Creag whirled about to hurry to the bed and stand looking anxiously down at the pale brunette before him. When he saw her eyes half-opened, he reacted instinctively, obeying the dictates of his heart. C. Robertson Blake leaned forward and gently kissed the woman who'd claimed his attention so thoroughly these past days.

"Welcome back, Jeanne," he murmured hoarsely, hard-pressed to find his voice. "We've missed you."

"But, Creag, why are you in my bedroom?" she asked in amazement.

"You're right, I shouldn't be," the laird agreed, placing the dressing gown on the bed and turning for the door without another word. A half-dozen lengthy strides later, he had just entered the hall when the tears he'd been fighting began to fall.

Damn it all, she was all right, he marveled, giving in to the utter relief that washed over him, alleviating the guilt and fear of these past two days. Jeanne Donnachy was awake and carping at him once again. Could life get any sweeter?

"Now then, child, why did you chase the poor man like that? Didn't he have this gown specially made for you and sit by your bed night and day since your fall?" admonished Maggie, patting Jeanne's hand and displaying the new dressing gown simultaneously. "Isn't it grand though that you're back to us?"

"I've not been away," complained the patient querulously. "Why do you keep saying that? I merely overslept—"

"It's only natural to forget what's happened," Leslie explained when she entered a few minutes later. A jubilant Creag had rooted her out of bed and sent her to Jeanne with a tray of broth and bread. "I'll tell you all that's happened as you eat something, but most amazing is Creag's total devotion—"

"To me? Don't be ridiculous. The man couldn't wait to leave the room when I spoke to him," objected the brunette, preferring to forget the kiss with which he'd greeted her. That particular gesture would take more careful analysis than she felt able to give it right now.

"Maybe he was just embarrassed to show he cares," ventured Maggie. "Some men are like that, your grandfather, for one."

"Maggie, you've been nipping Jamie's best again." The steward laughed, feeling more like herself every minute, surrounded as she was by such amusing friends. Willingly she sipped the warm soup Leslie handed her, resting back against the pillows once more and listening to the events of the manor she'd missed.

It was the next afternoon before she saw Creag again, and then she wasn't entirely certain if her pleasure at his arrival was because she was glad to see him or because he interrupted a very strange visit by Andrew Robertson.

The solicitor had been trying to press a bottle of elixir on her, guaranteed to have her up and around in no time, but he'd abandoned his insistence at the laird's appearance.

"Jeanne, you know you had my every prayer and good thought," swore the solicitor, mopping his brow and slipping the elixir into his pocket. "Indeed, I've lost a half stone for worrying."

"Then some good has come of such an ill event as this," said Creag with a grin, pleased to hear Jeanne's small laugh even as Andrew colored. "Nice of you to visit, Robertson, but we don't want to tire my steward now, do we?"

"Well, I—"

"Thank you for coming, Andrew, and please tell the others I'll be up and around by tomorrow and will see them in the village," added Jeanne.

"Just tell them she's doing well," corrected the laird as he escorted the tiresome guest to the door and closed it behind the man. "We don't want you overdoing too fast, Jeanne. You need some time to recuperate."

"Really, Creag, I'm feeling fine," she protested, swinging her slender legs over the side of the bed with all intentions of walking to where he stood. However, the floor suddenly seemed further away than she recalled, and then, just as she felt the world spinning, quite inexplicably she was in Creag's arms.

"I—"

"You little idiot," he chided softly, carrying his delicate burden toward the plush chair by the fire. "You're not strong enough to go walking about unassisted. Don't you know I'm here to help? All you have to do is ask."

"I really thought I could stand," she murmured, her voice apologetic even as she relished being in his embrace. There was a secure feeling to having him hold her that she couldn't quite explain but didn't want to question, either. "I didn't feel weak until I tried—"

Setting Jeanne down gently on the cushion and placing a throw rug over her lap, he knelt before her and looked seriously at the woman who had such a claim on his conscience.

"You gave me quite a scare the other day, young lady, and while I suppose I must apologize for complaining about the tapestry, *you* were very reckless climbing onto that cupboard," he began, scolding her gently until he noticed how her very large emerald eyes were quickly filling with water at his words.

"I was so angry at you," she confessed, "that I never thought of how dangerous it was."

"And I was so furious at myself for being pompous about breakfast that I rode for hours, finally coming home with all intentions of asking your forgiveness, only to find you unconscious and badly hurt."

"I'm sorry," Jeanne said, taking Creag's large hands in her smaller ones and squeezing them tightly. "Leslie tells me that you've been very good to me, spending hours at my bedside, neglecting your business affairs, consoling the council, even arranging for Maggie to make this lovely gown—"

"And what about getting rid of Andrew for you just now?" he teased, enjoying the sparkle of appreciation in the brunette's emerald eyes. Now that she wasn't condemning one or another of his recommendations for the manor, he found himself fully delighting in their conversation.

"Oh, definitely, that was a special act of bravery." She laughed. "And I want to thank you for it."

"Then here's how you can do just that," he said, bending forward and impulsively pressing his lips against hers, tasting the sweet innocence of her smile. The gentle pressure she returned thrilled him so much he was hard put to call a halt to what had started as a simple gesture of the heart. But stop it he did, though it cost him dearly to do so.

"Now you're no longer in my debt," he said with a laugh, his voice more hoarse than usual. He wanted more, but he knew it would be wrong to take advantage of her. One sweet kiss between *friends,* he told himself, that was all it was; that was all it could be, with Catherine on the way.

"Fine," Jeanne said with a laugh. "And since we're friends, we shall listen to one another before we yell."

"That will be a refreshing change of pace. For now, however, shall I read to you until Leslie brings your tea?"

"That would be nice," acknowledged the patient, releasing his hands and watching him take a seat in the chair opposite her.

The strong timbre of his voice filled the room as he continued Jane Eyre's story, but Jeanne could only think about how wonderful it was that he had kissed her. Hoping he wouldn't notice, she ran her tongue gently over her lips, welcoming the lingering taste of the laird. Maybe the council's notion of marriage to him wasn't as outrageous an idea as she'd first thought, she mused, turning her attention contentedly to the man before her.

Chapter Twelve

Following Jeanne's accident, Creag became reluctant to allow her out of his sight for very long, as if he feared that without his protection some other harm would befall her. But tonight, two days after she had awakened, he was content knowing he had only to look up from his dinner to see his pretty steward's profile.

Under the guise of attending to his main course, Creag watched as the candlelight flickered over Jeanne Donnachy's animated features on this, the first night of her compliance with his wishes that she, Leslie and Maggie join Michael and him for meals. He suffered no remorse over issuing such an order, despite the knowledge that Catherine would be arriving at Lindall in the space of a few weeks. After all they had been through, it simply felt quite natural to have Jeanne at his side, sharing his dinner and his unusually high spirits.

Selecting the choicest slice of beef from Fiona's serving tray and placing it on his steward's plate, Creag felt he had never been so fortunate, especially when he chanced another look at Jeanne and realized anew how easily they might have lost her. Shuddering inwardly, he pushed the unbearable thoughts aside and directed Beth to refill his steward's wineglass, wishing as he did so that he was free to employ other methods to put roses in Jeanne Donnachy's cheeks.

As the thought crossed his mind, Jeanne's eyes sought his and a tension grew between them, becoming a hungry, animate thing, distracting them so completely the pair forgot for an instant there were others present.

Then an unnaturally timid Jeanne retreated and hid her gaze beneath her long lashes as she played with the food on her plate, seeking refuge from a temptation that could only cost her soul.

"Come on now, you must finish it all if you hope to regain your strength," Creag prodded gently, very much at a loss for anything else to say. Certainly he couldn't confess what was in his heart each time he saw Jeanne, each time he merely thought of her, each time he drew a breath.

"But I've told you, I'm quite hale enough to return to my duties," Jeanne protested with a laugh.

"And I have told you, Miss Donnachy, that you will not be ready to resume your position until I say you are," Creag replied, the tender concern in his voice extirpating the arrogance of his words.

To her surprise, Jeanne had no desire to fight against Creag's domineering proclamation. Instead, she gave him only a sidelong glance and a smile in reply, admitting to herself that she relished the way Creag took charge when seeing to her wellbeing. And if he sometimes acted the bully out of his concern for her, why he was an endearing one, pampering her so that Jeanne had trouble reconciling this man with the one who had originally come to Linclachan.

But then she realized with a soft sigh, neither was she the same woman she had been upon Creag's arrival six weeks ago. His presence in the manor had marked her, changing her irrevocably. What the outcome of such a transformation would eventually be, Jeanne was too frightened to contemplate.

Soon, however, she became aware once more of the conversation being held by the others. Reluctantly she abandoned her romantic ruminations and forced herself to join in, laughing when it was expected of her and asking a question as the occasion demanded. But all the while, she was aware of nothing so much as she was the exceedingly virile man by her side.

A few days later, Jeanne half reclined on the settee in the morning room, an open book upon her lap. Never one to have had much leisure, she discovered herself reveling in it, but only because of Creag's constant attention.

While the others were about their duties, he gave her a great deal of his time, and his considerate thoughtfulness almost took her breath away whenever he hovered about.

The hours they were apart saw Jeanne either remembering what had occurred when last they were together or daydreaming about what would happen when next they enjoyed each other's company. Sometimes, however, those fanciful imaginings prohibited any hope of rest. Rather, they made Jeanne altogether restless, filling her with a sweet yearning that was as pleasurable as it was torturous. Such was the case now, when her book held very little interest for her. Sighing, she closed its cover.

Studying her surroundings with a critical eye, Jeanne had to confess she admired the alterations Creag had wrought. Drop cloths and workmen were gone from this wing now, and the morning room, like all the rest, was quite attractive. There was not a sag in the ceiling, which was as white as fresh-fallen snow, while the walls were resplendent with a new coat of pale yellow setting off the room's dark wainscoting. Even the furniture, old as it was, looked better once it had been cleaned and its original aqua color restored. And the carpet, dragged from some attic chamber and scrubbed before being placed on the newly polished floor, reflected the colors abounding throughout the room in muted tones of blue, green and gold.

Remembering the run-down condition of the manor only a few weeks before and seeing how it glistened now, Jeanne knew she had a lot to be thankful for. And she owed her gratitude to one C. Robertson Blake.

Suddenly that thought spawned another, and the splendor of the room rapidly receded from mind as Jeanne recalled how Creag had behaved when last she had expressed her thanks. Hadn't he claimed a kiss in return? In the early-morning stillness, Jeanne closed her eyes and once more felt Creag's lips upon hers. Had it really been so chaste a kiss after all, or had she actually felt him struggle to tear himself away before that kiss had deepened into something much different? Sighing in bewilderment, Jeanne speculated about what might happen if she were to thank Creag for something else. The possibilities of what could occur should she do so turned her blood to fire.

Hearing a now-familiar voice, husky and deep, calling to her from the doorway, Jeanne smiled and opened her eyes, imagination giving way to precious reality.

"Ah, there you are, Jeanne!" Creag said, his tongue caressing her name ever so seductively despite his best efforts to appear casual.

When he crossed the threshold, the richly adorned room was reduced to a pale reflection of his own magnificent coloring. The gold of his hair was more vibrant than that of the walls, and his blue eyes much more intense and attractive than the pale aqua brocade of the furniture. Jeanne swore that no other man could be so handsome as she luxuriated in the warmth of Creag's brilliant smile.

"It's not even eight, and already you're dressed," he scolded. "That's not what I would call pampering yourself as I have ordered you to do."

"But, Creag," Jeanne replied, laughing at the mock severity of his tones, "lovely though it is, I can't go traipsing all through the house in my dressing gown."

"You'd get no complaints from me if you did," Creag proclaimed softly, his dark blue eyes turning darker as he fell victim to the sultry vision Jeanne presented.

"Yes, but I would from Maggie," the pretty Scot retorted.

"Then that's another reason for pensioning her off," Creag bantered lightly as he reached forward with the intention of retrieving the book from Jeanne's lap so he could read to her while they awaited the summons to breakfast. Yet his hand, unable to resist, brushed ever so lightly across the top of her thigh, lingering for a searing second too long.

"Creag, I've been meaning to tell you what a fine job you have done with the manor house," Jeanne said impulsively, wondering, as she reached out to place her hand atop his, if her haunting daydream was about to come true. "It would be remiss of me not to thank you."

The air of the morning room became hushed and strained for a moment, and Creag seemed to hesitate, his eyes narrowing as he studied the alluring brunette gazing so intently and provocatively at him in return. Then, without warning, he took a rapid and determined step backward, settling himself in a nearby chair.

"Yes, well, there is no need to be grateful. And that's an end to any talk about what I have done . . . or would like to do," he said, his voice unusually raspy. "I thought I'd read to you for a bit before breakfast. Shall I?"

"You spoil me so," Jeanne replied, hiding her tremendous disappointment behind a small laugh and a hint of a smile. "Even with that bump to the head I took, I can read for myself."

"But not as well as I can," Creag stated, his own mouth giving way to a wistful curve that was meant to be an answering grin. "Now where did we leave off?"

Soon Creag had submerged himself in a lively reading of Jeanne's book, though his insistent desires proved to be quite difficult to contain. Still, he kept his eyes only on the printed matter before him, not daring to allow them another glimpse of Jeanne's enticing loveliness. And though he had never before delivered the lines of Jeanne's novel with such verve, the lovely Scot heard not one word he uttered, so lost was she in watching the movement of her laird's sensuous lips.

Creag left the morning room an hour later, just before the call to breakfast, and went directly to his study, his hurry so great that he totally ignored a workman who hailed him.

Relieved to find Michael was not present, Creag shut his door and locked it. Then, he went straight to his stash of Jamie's whisky and poured himself a stiff drink, despite the early hour.

Good God, each time he was with Jeanne, he wanted her more and more, his urges becoming so strong that he was hard-pressed to ignore them. While he looked forward to seeing her, it had actually reached the point that he dreaded it, as well. And yet, when he tried to stay away, he found he could not.

Why, today he had almost given in to the desire to seduce Jeanne on that damned morning room settee! Only an ultimate exercise of self-control had saved him, that and fading memories of the future he had planned with Catherine Grayson.

"Catherine!" Creag muttered, setting the glass of whisky down and resting his head in his hands like some contrite schoolboy. She would be there soon, and then he could accomplish what he had set out to do, leaving Linclachan behind forever. Ironically, however, the prospect seemed neither all that important nor attractive.

With this admission a question loomed, covering the normally cheerful study with a pall. Would he have the ability, the strength, to resist Jeanne the next time they were alone together? Somehow, no matter how he promised himself, Creag doubted he would. Not if she was going to drive him to the brink of control by merely placing her hand on his, or smiling at him so alluringly. Hell, he had only to glance in her direction and his primitive urges became so demanding that he tended to forget Catherine, to forget Philadelphia society, damn it, to forget civilized behavior entirely. And the normally reliable Michael, caught up in affairs of the heart himself, wasn't likely to help him regain his perspective. Merciful God, what was he going to do? He had to keep his distance from Jeanne Donnachy. He had to!

Catherine Grayson, too, was thinking about her intended as she sat bundled in a deck chair under Alma's supervision, watching the dull, lead-colored Atlantic go by.

At the thought of her future fiancé, Catherine's rosebud mouth puckered and then turned into a frown before she remembered that such surrender to emotion could cause unsightly lines. Quickly she remedied the situation.

Still this proposed trip to Scotland was enough to make any girl grimace, she consoled herself. And her feelings had only deepened after learning yesterday from Daddy, who had encountered a banker friend aboard ship, that Creag was apparently involved in establishing a woolen business, of all things, in the Highlands. It seemed the banker had been approached for a loan by a man named Bradford so that the fellow could distribute the goods in the States. The entire thing seemed too dreary and boring for words. Now, more than ever, Catherine had no wish to inspect Creag's isolated Scottish holdings. But, unfortunately, her parents would never rest until they had assured themselves that this intruder into Philadelphia society was truly a titled nobleman.

Snuggling further into her deck blanket, Catherine tried to recall Creag's smile, or his eyes, or even the slope of his chin, but all to no avail. She knew she had thought him incredibly handsome; however, after a few weeks' separation, it was difficult to remember exactly what it was that had made her think so.

It could be that her silly mind was cluttered with images of a different man, Catherine excused herself with a giggle. Cyril Simpson, fourth baronet of Ashby had been extremely attentive to her during the crossing.

Since he was the only unmarried member of the nobility aboard ship, Catherine had encouraged him in order to relish the envy of the other young ladies traveling to England. And in truth, the man had alleviated some of the boredom of the trip.

Yet, her mother and father had spoiled her fun, pointing out that an earl outranked a baronet, and reminding their daughter that the expense of this trip had been an investment to see her married to the more prestigious title. With thoughts of gowns, jewels, town houses and carriages in mind, Catherine supposed she would wind up settling for Creag Blake. But that did not mean she could not continue her flirtation with Cyril, especially since he had invited her to a house party on his family estate.

After all, it would be a few weeks until she had to start considering Creag again. Before the tiresome business of courtship and marriage, there would be a few pleasant weeks of mingling with society and shopping in London. She was certainly not about to allow thoughts of C. Robertson Blake and the dreaded trip to Scotland to infringe upon her enjoyment of such delightful preoccupations.

Happy with her determination, Catherine smiled. Cyril Simpson, walking nearby on deck, tipped his hat in reply, thinking the sweet curve of the girl's mouth was meant for him. Catherine lowered her lashes and allowed the Englishman his false assumption. She might have decided against Cyril, but she was certainly not goose enough to allow any other girl to have his attentions before the ship docked in Southampton.

As the days passed, and her prolonged inactivity produced tremendous boredom, Jeanne found herself growing more cross and out of sorts. Though the others made time to visit and engage her in conversation, their efforts were not enough to make her happy. Nothing could lighten her mood because, since that incident in the morning room more than a week before, Creag had not spent a single moment with her unless they were in the company of someone else.

Oh, when she did see him, he continued to exhibit gallant solicitude, but only in a very proper manner. And though Jeanne was often conscious of Creag's eyes lingering upon her whenever he thought no one was watching, he talked to the others as much as he did with her. For all of his polite consideration, the laird of Linclachan had quite definitely placed a barrier between them, constructed as deftly and sturdily as the dam now restricting the salmon stream. And like the land deprived of its invigorating waters, Jeanne, too, felt as though she were withering, thirsting for the closeness she and Creag had so recently enjoyed, the closeness he currently withheld.

The situation was becoming increasingly maddening, Jeanne mused forlornly as she sat in the now refurbished library after luncheon. How could Creag Robertson Blake, the man who had been constantly at her side since her accident, become so suddenly absorbed in everything else but her? Why, she almost longed for the arguments they used to have. Even those would have been preferable to this polite coolness she was being made to suffer.

However, Jeanne Donnachy had never been one to meekly accept what life had offered her. Looking out the library windows at the sunny afternoon and contrasting it to the gloom settled over her heart, she decided that if Creag wasn't going to do something about the existent situation between them, she would! She'd demonstrate to that stubborn American male that he couldn't force her to sit both idle and alone.

Soon the determined Scot was climbing the stairs to Creag's study, feeling none of the dizziness and weakness he had said she would experience if she attempted such an undertaking alone.

Chiding herself for a slight hesitation outside his door, Jeanne knocked resolutely.

"Come in," the laird called in a distracted, businesslike tone.

Suddenly shy, Jeanne nevertheless swung the door wide and entered the room. When the handsome earl looked up and saw her, unguarded delight illuminated his chiseled features, followed by a flicker of consternation, and, finally, sincere concern.

Rising quickly and offering Jeanne a chair, Creag forgot the ledgers he had been perusing, and the baffling ten-thousand-pound discrepancy he had just uncovered. Instead, all of his thoughts were focused on the willowy brunette looking up at him so charmingly.

"Did you come up here all by yourself?" he reproved in a tone much gentler than the one he had planned to use.

"Yes," she answered with a laugh, "and no harm came to me."

"Then you're very fortunate that you have overtaxed neither your strength nor my patience with your foolishness," Creag replied, the hard planes of his face softening enough to negate his harsh words as he feasted on the sight of her.

Noting the way the American looked at her, Jeanne knew it was not anger that had come between them. Perhaps his tendency to ignore her was merely the result of his preoccupation with business. After all, in addition to his usual work, Creag had assumed the bulk of her duties.

But that would be remedied quickly. She would return to her tasks as soon as possible, anticipation of the hours she would spend working beside Creag washing over her and leaving the most delicious sensation. First, however, she had to convince him she was well enough to do so.

"As you can see, I'm quite fit," Jeanne stated, giving him her most winning smile.

Indeed you are…fit for a man's arms, his lips, his bed, Creag thought, losing himself in imagined possibilities until he observed the gleam in her eye and knew the vixen was up to something. He had seen that look too often in the past, and had suffered its consequences, to ignore it now.

"At any rate," Jeanne went on, planning to demonstrate just how well she was actually feeling, "I have come to tell you that I am on my way out for a walk."

Creag breathed a sigh of relief. He had feared his fiery steward had been about to demand that she resume her duties. That was something he could not allow…not when he knew that he could not trust himself to be so constantly alone with her. And certainly not when he also knew that under such tempting circumstances, nothing, not even Catherine's newly arrived letter advising him of her arrival in London, could stop him from making this provocative female his own.

"All right, Jeanne," he said, smiling indulgently. "We'll get one of the others to accompany you."

"But there is no one. Michael has taken Leslie to the village and Maggie insisted on going along."

"Then I'm afraid it's quite out of the question," Creag declared, his protective instincts making him unwilling to let her go off alone. "Perhaps tomorrow."

"Creag, it's a warm, lovely day and I'm quite up to it," Jeanne insisted. "If I tire, I'll sit down and rest."

"The answer is no," he said, hating to deny her anything, but memories of the anxious hours he had spent at her bedside prompting him to be firm.

"It's been far too long since I've felt the sun on my face," Jeanne declared, her voice both rebellious and wistful. "I don't care if I have to go by myself, I am going to spend some time outside this afternoon."

"You'll do no such thing," Creag commanded, his features forbidding as he ran his hand through his thick blond hair in frustration. Though he vowed he should insist upon her obedience, the forlorn expression on his steward's lovely face caused him to weaken and then finally to relent. "Oh, all right, Jeanne. If you must have your walk, I suppose I can spare a few moments to go with you."

"Thank you!" she cried, her demeanor so happy that Creag found his own good humor restored, as well. After all, he told himself before he could question the wisdom of his decision, there was no reason to be apprehensive. It was merely a stroll. Surely he could handle that.

"Just how far do you plan on taking me?" Creag asked good-naturedly a short while later when Jeanne led him even farther from the manor house.

"Just a wee bit more," his pretty companion promised, entering a stand of trees and reveling as much in Creag's company as she did in the afternoon's warm caress. "But you won't be disappointed when we get there. Listen!"

"Oh, it's a secret place, is it?" Creag teased, hearing the melodic flow of a waterfall nearby. Caught up in the explorations of the wild beauty of the Highlands, and the bloom of health upon Jeanne's cheeks, he all but forgot his anxiety at being alone with her. The result was that for the first time in over a week, he was very much himself.

"A special spot, anyway," Jeanne said, enjoying the handsome American's light mood and exceedingly glad there no longer seemed to be a wall between them. "'Tis the one that gives our village its name, and the manor, as well."

With an engaging smile, she ignored Creag's curious glance until they had trudged through the trees and emerged beside a small cascade.

"This is our *lin*," she said, her voice filled with affection for a thing dear to her. "Linclachan, you see, means village of the waterfall, while Lindall, is the meadow near the fall."

It was an arresting sight, Creag agreed, the crystal-clear water flowing lazily over rough gray stone and then into a pool that seemed to have no bottom. But beautiful as the area was, edged in its velvety green moss, it couldn't compare to the loveliness of the woman standing beside him.

"Is this an enchanted locale?" Creag asked in mock seriousness, trying to keep their mood light as he and Jeanne skirted the pool. "Perhaps a home to fairies and the like?"

"It's not wise to jeer at Highland spirits, Yankee. Why 'tis said this entire area is filled with *shian* or fairy dwellings," Jeanne warned, mimicking Creag's playfulness.

The exercise and fresh air made Jeanne's skin glow, as if she were some charmed being, when she lifted her hand to indicate the rugged countryside with its rough, irregular precipices and broken caverns. In fact, she was so bewitching that Creag ached to reach out to her, and for the life of him, he couldn't seem to think of a reason why he shouldn't do just that.

"You see," Jeanne said as the young laird took her hand to help her climb over a rock at the pool's edge, "according to legend, the fairy folk disguise their turrets to look like just another crag. And their doors, windows and smoke vents are so artfully constructed that by daylight they are invisible to the human eye. Come nighttime, however, for those who look carefully, their lights can be seen glistening through their casements, the cracks and crevices in the rocks."

"You appear a mischievous fairy yourself," Creag commented, still holding Jeanne's hand though the rock was behind them.

"Oh, but that couldn't be," Jeanne replied, gracefully lowering herself onto the soft moss blanketing the ground. "The fairy folk are said to be angels cast out of heaven after the rebellion."

"You've proven my point, Jeanne Donnachy. Or do you deny you've a devilish side to your nature?"

"Aye, that I do, but I'm afraid there's nothing at all angelic about me," Jeanne protested with a giggle.

"I think you're wrong," Creag said, sitting down beside her. To him, Jeanne Donnachy was angel enough for any man.

"Anyway," Jeanne said, becoming flustered by the dangerously unfamiliar look glinting in Creag's eyes, "the part these poor fallen creatures played in Lucifer's plot was not serious enough to see them hurled as far as Hades. Instead, they landed here in the Highlands."

"Not much of a punishment, was it?" Creag whispered, moving a bit closer to Jeanne's side. "From where I sit, this part of Scotland is paradise enough for anyone."

"Aye, 'tis beautiful country," Jeanne murmured, excitement racing through her as Creag's arm gently captured her waist and drew her to him so that there was no hint of a space at all between them as they sat.

"And are there fairies that live in the pool?" Creag asked, his lips burying themselves in Jeanne's hair so that she felt his breath, hot and sweet, tickling her temple and the tip of her ear.

"No," she said in a tiny voice, "most likely water kelpies."

"And what exactly do water kelpies do?" the virile American inquired, his voice muffled as his lips traveled slowly across Jeanne's brow.

"Why, they're wicked creatures," Jeanne said raggedly, trying to recall the tales she had heard as a child. "In order to lure human beings to destruction, they change their shapes to resemble whatever it is a person desires most."

"Oh? And what would a kelpie have to resemble in order to get your attention?" Creag demanded, his mouth moving now down the bridge of Jeanne's nose.

"You, Creag!" she cried, unable to withstand his tender assault any longer. "He'd have to resemble you!"

"Oh, Jeanne," he groaned, his lips falling atop hers. No matter how he had denied it or tried to resist, Creag had always known in his heart that this moment would come. Now that it was here, he wanted to cherish it, to savor it, to give Jeanne all he was capable of giving, to make it the treasured memory for her it would always be for him.

Gently nudging her shoulder with his own, Creag laid Jeanne down on the mossy bank, her head cradled in the crook of his arm.

Reverently he traced the features of her face with the slightest touch of his fingertips. His darkened blue eyes, smoky with desire, urgently searched her green ones in silent supplication. Always a man to take what he wanted, what Creag needed now was to be given the gift of Jeanne's love.

Reading unconditional acquiescence in her gentle smile, Creag's moan of joy was smothered by the pressure of Jeanne's lips rising to meet his own. Entwining her arms around his neck, her body pressed against his, telling him without words how eager she was.

Inhibitions vanished as Creag's tongue sought Jeanne's, exploring her mouth and teaching her what it meant for a man to kiss a woman.

Excited by the knowledge he brought her, Jeanne began to move beneath Creag's muscular frame, her artless responses exhorting him to increase the tempo of their passion, to carry her along with him on a rapid road to ecstasy.

Struggling to hold on to restraint until he knew Jeanne was ready to receive him, Creag began to unbutton her blouse. His movements were so slow and tantalizing that the pretty Highlander had no thought of anything save the anticipation of baring her bosom for this virile male. She wanted him to glory in her femininity, to see, to touch, to taste what she was offering him with such shameless abandon.

Though he untied the ribbons of her chemise, pushed back its edges and gently kissed the tip of each nipple, sending shiv-

ers into the very core of Jeanne's being, Creag did not stop
methodically undressing her. Instead, his hands traveled to her
waist, undoing her skirts and her petticoats until finally he un-
loosened her drawers. Then he snaked his large hand beneath
her hem and along her limbs, urging each stocking downward
with seductive strokes. When these had been removed, his
gentle tugging soon had the rest of her garments gone, as well.

Completely naked, Jeanne suffered no humiliation, but lay
there motionless beneath Creag's hot gaze, boldly demanding
his approval. When she began to writhe with impatience, she
tore a groan from his throat that originated in the depths of his
soul, and he came to her, his hand exploring the gentle swell of
one breast while his lips captured the straining nipple of the
other.

Now it was Jeanne's turn to give voice to wordless pleasure
as she lost herself in the rapture Creag offered. While his hot,
moist mouth tugged gently at the tip of her breast, his fingers
descended to caress her belly, traveling ever downward until his
probing fingertips found the source of her femininity. Then he
coaxed her until she blossomed for him as readily as any Highland wildflower under the nurturing caress of the sun.

The strangled sounds issuing deep in her throat turned rapidly to hoarse, irregular whimpers that alternately urged
Jeanne's beloved outlander on and then begged him to cease.
But Creag determined to continue his sweet torture, his ardor
increasing each time she cried out in pleasure. Finally Jeanne
began to greedily demand more than he was giving.

Reaching toward Creag, she started to unbutton his shirt
until his huge hands around her slender wrists forced her to
stop.

"There'll be no turning back, Jeanne," he whispered
hoarsely.

"No, no turning back," she agreed.

"Then tell me you want me," he commanded.

"I want you Creag, *mo cridhe,* my heart, more than I have
ever longed for anything in my life," she whispered, complet-
ing her task and rubbing her outspread palms in broad sweeps
across Creag's now-bare chest.

"God help me, woman, but I want you, too," Creag gasped. Then he was fumbling with his trousers, cursing his clumsiness and muttering about the advantages of kilts.

At last he stood before Jeanne, his proud wild bearing putting her in mind of the Viking she had first supposed him to be. And then he was beside her once more, kissing her tenderly and murmuring assurances as he made ready to love her.

The touch of Jeanne's silken skin next to his own soon had Creag beyond rational thought. Primitive urgings took control of him and imbued him with a male magnificence that set his lover's blood afire.

Capturing Jeanne's soul with a deep kiss, he nudged her long legs apart with his knee. Then with one swift thrust, he entered her, seizing the prize that had both taunted and lured him since the first day he had arrived in Lindall Manor.

A startled cry of pain escaped Jeanne when the barrier of her virginity gave way before her majestic, commanding invader. Attuned to her needs, Creag remained motionless for a time, simply stroking Jeanne's hair while he assured her with murmured words of endearment and encouragement that the worst was past.

When the fear in her eyes subsided, Creag began a dance of love, wooing Jeanne with his hardened masculine body, the gentle pace he set pleasing and then teasing her beyond endurance. In response, she started a rocking motion of her own, answering him thrust for thrust and then instinctively quickening their rhythm. Then it was she who was in control, and the intensity of their coupling increased, inaugurating a craving that drove them to abandon.

As Jeanne called Creag's name, his triumphant roar rent the air, drowning out the splash of the waterfall, beckoning her to follow him into paradise. Without hesitation, she hastened to him, giving herself up completely to the love of her American laird.

In the sweet aftermath of their union, the lovers lay wrapped in each other's embrace. The dulcet sound of the waterfall echoed their heartbeats and supplied a harmonious background to their whispered endearments. For both of them, at that moment, the glen by the waterfall was truly a magical place.

"Perhaps the *lin* is a charmed spot after all," Jeanne said with a sigh, running an idle finger along Creag's firm jaw. "What else would explain the spell that binds me to you?"

Raising himself up on one elbow to peer down into Jeanne's passion-glazed eyes, Creag was content with the look of love she wore.

"*Mo cridhe,*" he said softly with a tender smile, echoing the words she had used in the throes of ardor, "if I have left you uncertain as to exactly what it is, I suggest we surrender ourselves to enchantment once more."

Delighted by Jeanne's shy nod of assent, Creag slowly and expertly conjured up yet again the sort of magic that exists in the hearts of those who have given themselves to love.

That night, the laird of Linclachan lay abed wishing Jeanne was in his arms rather than in her own room on the other side of his bedchamber wall.

Though their lovemaking had been impulsive, an illogical surrender to the yearning that had haunted them for weeks, Creag had no remorse for what had occurred that day. Hadn't he really known for some time that he could never take any other bride but his captivating Highlander?

Oh, he might have thought he had wanted Catherine because of the social position she could give him, but his desire for Jeanne Donnachy held no such demands. He no longer needed the world to accept him as long as she did. And the open doors of Philadelphia's best houses he had sought for his sons were nothing compared to the unconditional love and sense of belonging they would know in Linclachan.

Only one problem remained for the handsome American laird. He could not lie with Jeanne again without giving her more than a physical sign of the love in his heart.

And yet, what more could he proffer until the matter with Catherine Grayson was resolved? Anxious to make Jeanne his own for all time, Creag decided to leave Linclachan the next morning and travel to London. There, he would settle things with Catherine, which should be easy enough to do. He had no delusions about the place he held in that young woman's heart. The promise to provide an extended stay in London and a new wardrobe at his expense would no doubt soothe any regrets she might have. Then he could return home, free to offer Jeanne his love and his name.

Satisfied with his plan, Creag wondered if he should inform his bewitching little Scot about the reason for his trip. After much deliberation, he decided against it. Their relationship was too new and fragile, and Jeanne too proud and feisty to ask her to accept his past mistakes. Besides, she might not understand that Catherine had never possessed a piece of his heart, that the understanding between them had been no more than a business arrangement. Since there had been no official engagement, it was prudent to keep Jeanne in ignorance and save her needless upset, Creag thought practically. After all, with a word to Michael upon his return, what likelihood was there she would ever find out?

Chapter Thirteen

Late the next morning, Jeanne seated herself behind Creag's desk in the study, intent on reclaiming her duties in his absence. Though she'd nodded at his tender instructions to rest and think of nothing but herself and her full recovery to health while he was away on business, such a notion was absurd. Even as she had happily returned his hungry farewell kisses, the brunette had been anticipating going over the household accounts. It was not that his kisses failed to excite her; indeed, furious memories of the day before had made her blush so outrageously that she'd remained a bright pink when waving farewell five minutes later. Still, it would not do for C. Robertson Blake to believe he had her completely under control; she'd need to maintain some semblance of independence in their relationship and the sooner he understood that, the better.

Shrugging off the desire to sit and dream about the handsome American who had taught her so much about loving in one long afternoon, or to wonder what had called him so urgently to London, Jeanne resolutely opened the ledgers and found traces of Creag there, too. No matter where she looked in the manor, some change or improvement of his made her smile, but perhaps it was just being loved, she mused, idly studying the new page of figures. Creag had added columns detailing the cost of renovating Lindall Manor, as well as a page for expenses in the village. For a moment, the huge sums stunned the pretty Scot until she decided Creag must have miscalculated. Quickly she redid the totals, only to find his figures were completely accurate; he'd spent over twenty thousand pounds!

Well, she thought with a wistful smile, Creag Robertson Blake is not one to begrudge the best, no matter what the price, four separate water closets, after all. He is apparently accustomed to having only the finest of goods about.

Examining her well-worn dress of gold-hued wool, Jeanne recalled his belittling her wardrobe that morning in the stable and the recent appreciation in his eyes when he'd seen her in the green dressing gown. Perhaps the laird had been right, she mused; his steward should not be dressed in old rags. The books had waited this long. Surely they could wait a few more hours while she spoke to Maggie about a new gown or two. The deep purple bolt of wool Mairi had delivered last night would be attractive, and perhaps the rosy heather one, as well.

"A new outfit? Of course, dear, you know you've only to ask," agreed Maggie readily. "Stay a minute while I get my tape and check your measurements."

"I didn't want to bother you, but I so enjoyed the dressing gown and with Creag away—"

"Aye." The housekeeper smiled. "Our laird is quite the man, with or without his trousers."

"Without his trousers?" echoed Jeanne, high spots of color invading her cheeks as Maggie pretended not to notice. "When would I have seen him without his trousers?"

"Why, when we all did, the first night he arrived when Malcolm got him into a kilt," the old woman explained, an innocent expression on her face. "Unless of course there's some other time I don't know about—"

"No, of course not," declared Jeanne a bit too hurriedly.

"You needn't feel awkward or ashamed, lass. Love sets its own rules. I'll not tell you to ignore its call. Just be sure."

"Love? Do you really think Creag—"

"If you'd seen him at your bed night and day, mooning like a sick calf, you'd have no doubt. I haven't," confided Maggie, patting the steward's hand. "The man lost his heart to you—"

"And I've given him mine," admitted the brunette, her green eyes dancing with the joy. "But you mustn't say anything—"

"Aye, well I know the fairy folk delight in tripping our cherished dreams, so I'll do naught but have you looking like a princess in your new gown when he returns. You'll be so pretty you'll take his breath away, and if you don't, we'll get one of Leslie's potions for him.''

"Heaven forbid! Neither the laird nor I need any assistance, I assure you." Jeanne laughed, warmed as much by Maggie's gentle affection as the certainty of Creag's devotion.

Though they had left him to cool his heels for nearly two days before they would receive him, Creag finally found himself face-to-face with the entire Grayson family. Judging from the bits of conversation he had heard let slip, Catherine, clearly not pining for him in his absence, had not even been in London when he had arrived, but off at a house party in the country in the company of some English nobleman. And now that she was here, Catherine was nothing but annoyed that her fun had been interrupted by her parents' urgent missive to return to England's capital city.

The blonde's attitude had made his mission much easier, he thought, wondering how he could have ever considered spending a lifetime in her spoiled company. Still, he had felt a twinge of guilt as he had quietly, and gently as possible, made it known that he would not be offering Catherine marriage. Now, as he shifted about in his chair, awaiting their response, he was pleased to note that the ensuing silence was not entirely hostile.

The girl's parents looked at each other a long while, communicating silently before turning back to face their visitor, each wearing a small, tight smile. As for Catherine, herself, she appeared more bored with the proceedings than heartbroken, Creag noted with relief as he held himself in readiness for the family's reaction.

"I expect it is all for the best," conceded Bartholomew, clearly not distraught by the news, and happy that Catherine wasn't proving to be petulant about the matter. Blake's Scottish title might have made him barely acceptable, but there were other, better, available men about for his daughter to consider.

"I must say at some level, I am comforted, young man," confessed Alma, nervously crumpling a linen handkerchief in one hand and then smoothing it with the other. "The very idea of my daughter living in the wilds of Scotland, even for a few months a year, was quite perturbing. It is so far from the comforts of home.''

Creag noted with a wry smile, the young woman's subtle, confirming nod. It would appear that for Catherine, any time spent residing in Scotland was too dear a price to pay for his title and his company.

"I appreciate your concern, Mrs. Grayson, and that was one of the reasons for reconsidering my intentions. Your daughter is too fragile a blossom to be transported so far north,'' lied Creag, determined to avoid any mention of Jeanne Donnachy, the only consideration in his heart. "However, my obligations make such a sojourn there inevitable.''

"That's all very noble of you, Creag,'' Bartholomew Grayson said gruffly, "but I want you to realize that we are going to put it about in society that it was Catherine who rejected you. I hope you will be a gentleman in the matter.''

"Of course,'' the American financier agreed, more than willing to permit the untruth as the price of his freedom. "If you had come to Linclachan, I'm certain that would have been the case, anyway. It's a rather primitive place.''

"That may be so, but it's unfortunate you didn't think to inform us of your change of heart before we traveled across the Atlantic,'' Bartholomew Grayson stated indignantly, the cost of the trip and his daughter's spending in London suddenly coming to mind.

"Since that was not possible,'' Creag replied smoothly, reaching into his pocket and extracting an envelope, "allow me to make amends by underwriting the cost of your journey. You'll find enough there to also pay for an extended visit in London, with plenty left over to cover the cost of any new wardrobe Catherine might wish to purchase while she is here. Though it's highly unusual, I would like to present her with a necklace, as well, as a token of the good terms on which we part. I hope you accept my gesture in the spirit in which it is offered. But what about you, Catherine? I've yet to hear your feelings on the matter.''

"Of course I'll take the necklace, the price of the trip, and that of the new wardrobe, as well,'' the pretty but superficial blonde said, reaching greedily for the box and the envelope.

"Good," Creag said, rising and making ready to depart. With all feelings of guilt behind him, he was ready to return to Scotland and Jeanne. As it was, he had been in London too long. "I leave you then with good wishes for your future."

The moment the door shut behind their visitor, Catherine opened the jewelry case and was amazed at the expensive emerald-and-diamond necklace Creag had given her as a parting gift. She could see that her father's eyes widened, too, at the estimated cost of such a handsome piece. But when she tore at the envelope and caught sight of the extravagantly large figure written on the bank draft, she was little less than stunned. Rather than soothe ruffled feelings, Creag's generosity had stirred second thoughts. If he was so magnanimous now, how much more could she have gained by becoming his wife?

Passing the check over to her father for his perusal, Catherine watched his eyebrows rise in surprise.

"You know, Daddy," she said petulantly, "I'm beginning to think I made the wrong decision."

"Perhaps you did," the head of the Grayson family announced, slowly stroking his mustache with forefinger and thumb as he continued to gaze at the amount of money Blake had been willing to part with. "But there's little we can do about it now."

"Oh, but I beg to differ with you, Daddy, there's plenty that can be done," Catherine murmured with a pert tilt of her curly, blond head.

"I don't know how you can say that. I, for one, feel like one of those poor bastards in Johnstown, swept away by the whims of the nouveaux riches," the girl's father stated glumly.

"Creag visited the club at Johnstown once," Catherine mused as she thoughtfully tapped the check against her open palm. Suddenly a speculative gleam transformed her face into a portrait of ambitious greed.

"Was he a member?" Bartholomew asked hopefully. "We could easily hold disclosure of such information over his head."

"No, Creag didn't belong to the club, but if we said he did, who would question us? After all, there is no one who is admitting to membership," Catherine said, her determined mouth and steely expression distorting her otherwise flawless features.

"Catherine! Such a thing is dishonest," her mother protested.

"Now, now, Alma. All is fair in love and war," reproved her husband, his tone effectively silencing his spouse's participation in the conversation.

"That's right, Mama," a petulant Catherine added, running a fingertip reverently along the edge of Creag's check. "And can I help it if I've only just discovered there's so very much to love about Creag Blake?"

Well, that was thankfully over and well-handled, Creag reflected a few minutes later as he entered Russell Square and decided he could do with a drink in celebration.

Entering a nearby pub, he hailed the pub's proprietor and ordered a whisky.

"Here on holiday, sir?" the man inquired as he placed the amber-colored liquid before his customer. "Most of my patrons prefer ale or gin."

"I'm down for a few days from the Highlands where I've acquired quite a taste for their whisky," Creag explained companionably, picking up the glass and tossing it back, only to find it coarse and burning. When he tried to speak, his voice was a rasping croak. "Wa-water!"

"Certainly, there you go, sir. A wee bit stronger than you expected, was it?"

Quickly Creag grasped the glass and drank thirstily, trying to quench the angry flames searing his throat. After two glasses of cooling liquid, he felt better able to complain.

"Whatever that fluid was, it bears more resemblance to a lethal poison than a fine liquor."

"It's whisky just like you wanted," defended the pub's owner, displaying the bottle in question.

"Aged Scottish whisky?"

"No, the regular kind. The old stuff is a might dear, most folks won't pay its price. But I tell you what, me not knowing you wanted that, have a shot on me for your trouble," offered the barman as he poured a generous portion from a dusty bottle.

"I'll gladly pay for the pleasure of drinking good Highland whisky," declared the American, though he eyed the new liquor a bit suspiciously. "In Linclachan the liquor has a smooth, smoky taste that could make a man weep for the experience as it tickles his taste buds. I've never found anything half as good elsewhere."

Taking the glass to his lips, Creag sipped more cautiously this time, not really surprised at the disappointment that greeted his palate. Sadly he shook his head and replaced the whisky on the bar.

"It's an improvement over the first to be sure, but it can't compare to the magnificence of Jamie's finest," he confided, putting a guinea on the bar and preparing to leave.

"Well, that may be, of course, but I've never had any better than this. It's aged seven years," disputed the barman, displaying the label attesting to the whisky's reputation. "And it's hard to come by at that."

"Jamie's whisky is aged twelve years and is so mellow a babe could swallow it without a whimper," praised the earl of Lindall, licking his lips in memory of the splendid flavor. "When I come back this way, I'll bring you a bottle."

"And glad I'll be to give you the cost of it, though liquid gold like that would be hard to keep in stock, no matter what the price, I wager."

"It does make a man stop and appreciate his blessings," murmured Creag, his blue eyes sparkling with sudden inspiration. He'd wanted a way to make Linclachan prosperous in its own right . . . this could well be better than the woolen trade.

"As a matter of fact, let me take those bottles, would you?"

"The bottles? But—"

"Will ten guineas cover it?" the American asked, already reaching over the bar to take the poor-quality whisky.

"Yes, of course, though I thought you didn't like either."

"I don't, but the men I have to convince are awfully thick skulled. They'll never believe what passes for an aged Scottish whisky unless they taste it themselves," explained Creag, heading for the door. "And I mean to see that they not only believe me, but do something about this sad state of affairs that makes the finest Scottish liquor only available in Scotland."

Then he was on his way to the hotel before catching his train home to Scotland and bonny Jeanne.

* * *

"Michael?" Jeanne called hesitantly as she knocked on the door of the small room he'd made his office.

"Yes, Jeanne, come in," invited Creag's assistant, rising to his feet and ushering her to a chair. "Is there a problem?"

"No, no, nothing like that," she demurred, already regretting her decision to ask Michael about Creag's delayed return. She had expected him yesterday, but there'd been no sign of him nor any word that she knew of. "Mary wanted to know if she should include Creag in her plans for tonight's dinner and I didn't know what to tell her."

"I'm afraid I can't help you there. He said the earliest he'd be back was Tuesday, but since it's already Wednesday, obviously he miscalculated the time his negotiations might take," hedged the secretary. Nervously removing his spectacles and polishing them, he wondered if it was Catherine or business that had taken Creag to London. "And the trains tend to be rather unreliable, as well. Was there something I could help you with?"

"No, really, it was just a question of planning for dinner," claimed Jeanne, quickly exiting the room. The last thing on earth she wanted to be was a nagging shrew, but concern for Creag's well-being had overcome her qualms of impropriety. If business was as unpredictable as Michael seemed to indicate, she'd worry no longer. C. Robertson Blake was probably the most astute negotiator in all the United States if his behavior at the *lin* were any indication, she reflected with a soft chuckle, still delighting in the memories of that special afternoon.

"And just what has you so very happy in my absence?" demanded the laird, appearing suddenly to draw her into a tender embrace, leaving her no doubt that he'd missed her as much as she had missed him.

"Thoughts of your lordship, if truth be told," the brunette answered, her smile and the excitement flashing in her eyes testifying to the truth of her words.

"Aye, then, were you daydreaming of my doing this?" pried Creag, stealing a lengthy kiss where they stood in the upstairs hall. "Or was it the thought of my sweeping you off your feet with my devoted attention that had you smiling?"

In the merest fraction of an instant, Jeanne found herself in the air, safely ensconced in Creag's muscular arms, being gently carried in the direction of her bedroom.

"Creag, believe me, I'm perfectly healthy," she protested, not realizing his intent.

"I'm counting on that," he chuckled, delighted to be holding the lovely brunette, knowing he was free to court her openly.

"Don't send me to my room like a naughty child," she teased.

"You, Jeanne Donnachy, are anything but a child," he murmured, his lips tracing a fiery trail down her neck toward the scoop of her bodice.

"I suppose Maggie told you I've resumed my duties about the manor, but you mustn't be angry. It was only because I—"

"Had nothing worthwhile to occupy your time, such as the laird himself," finished Creag, opening her bedroom door, stepping across the threshold and then locking it, his steward still in his arms. "That's all changed now, Jeanne, I'm home."

"You're not only home, you're in my bedroom," she observed hoarsely a few moments later, finding speech difficult after enjoying Creag's increasingly amorous kisses.

"Actually, it is mine, since you're in it," he said offhandedly, setting Jeanne on her feet. He started to speak, only to look into her deep eyes and enfold her in his arms, once again caressing her lips with his.

Relaxing in his embrace, Jeanne relished the heat coursing through her body and the short, quick breaths that her lungs demanded as signs of her joy. But most of all, she delighted in the knowledge that Creag evidently wanted her as much as she wanted him. Gone was her earlier hesitation at the *lin;* she met the American now as a willing partner, deepening their kiss and wrapping her arms around his neck, moving her body closer to his, the better to meet his demanding tongue. Welcoming the chance to rekindle the flames they'd ignited nearly a week ago, they thrust and parried, feinted and teased, each of them forgetting all but the other.

Then Creag stepped backward, drew a steadying breath and led the beautiful Scot to a settee near the window. Sitting beside her, he began to remove the pins that kept her long curls swept upward, wanting to see her glorious hair loose about her shoulders as if it had been the first time they loved.

"This is my bedroom," he repeated, returning to their previous conversation though Jeanne had forgotten his claim.

"No, it's not," she said and laughed, enjoying this lighthearted side of the laird. "Yours is next door."

"Nonsense, this room and all the others in the manor are mine, so if I choose to sleep here, who could complain?" he asked, a mischievous glimmer brightening his blue eyes.

"Well, forgetting Maggie, who would have a terrible case of temper if you slept here, where would I sleep?" Jeanne inquired innocently, a half smile playing about her tender lips as she realized the path on which he'd embarked.

"With me, of course," Creag murmured, burying his fingers in the silky waves that covered them and lifting the hair up so he could plant a kiss on the nape of her graceful neck.

"You're thinking about sleep now?" Jeanne stalled, wanting to elicit some verbal commitment from the man. True, she wanted him, as well, but something should be said of the future.

"Actually, that is not my primary interest," he confided with a smile, moving so he could look into her eyes, "and I've dreamed of little but enjoying you since I left Lindall Manor six days, five hours, and forty-odd minutes ago."

"Oh, Creag, I lost track of the number of times I cursed your business dealings for taking you from me so abruptly. If they went poorly, it's probably my fault," conceded Jeanne, pleased at his frank admission of his desire. She, too, had dreamed of being caught in his embrace and traveling back to the fields of rapture they'd discovered by the waterfall, but she would never have imagined confessing such a secret. Obviously Creag was more honest than her. "I am very glad that you're back, Creag."

"So? Shall we see if your bed is as comfortable as that mossy bank?" he pressed.

"Now? But, it's daytime."

"So what?" he asked seductively. Then he leaned forward as his long, sensuous fingers unbuttoned the bodice of her rose-colored gown. "We visited the *lin* in the afternoon and the sky didn't fall. Indeed, it was quite wonderful, in case you've forgotten."

"No, of course, I haven't, but everyone will be looking to speak with you since you've returned from London—Ewan, Michael—"

"I saw Ewan briefly in the stable, answered his questions and sent him out to check on the new sheep enclosure. Some of the darn creatures were loose as I came up the drive. But I deliberately avoided meeting anyone else," the rugged male admitted, parting the fabric of Jeanne's dress and slipping his hand inside to fondle her already anxious breasts. "The only one who knows where I am at the moment is you."

"Then, my laird," she teased, half-reclining on the settee and closing her eyes, "I am suddenly *very* weary. Bed seems like an excellent idea."

"You didn't overdo while I was gone?" he questioned, a look of worry briefly crossing his face until he caught sight of her twitching lips and she began to giggle. This was paradise, he thought, to love and be loved in the freedom of his own home, without a care in the world.

Kneeling at his steward's feet, the financier removed her shoes and stockings and then rose to extend his hand to her.

"Come with me, Jeanne, to glory we've never imagined possible."

Blushing furiously, Jeanne accepted his invitation, stepping out of her dress as she stood up and spoke softly.

"In truth, Creag, since you left, I've thought of little but the wonders we shared."

That was all the encouragement the man needed, those simple heartfelt words demanding that he make her his own. Suddenly Creag remembered the ring he'd purchased in London when he'd bought the necklace for Catherine, and considered fetching it now, but it was with his baggage in the stable and to mention it to Jeanne without giving it to her would be crass. The ring could wait, he decided, knowing they could not.

His lips once again sought to possess the lovely Scot's even as her hands began to unfasten his shirt. Her slender fingers swiftly completed her task and then she was splaying their softness across his chest, her touch imprinting him with an ache that swelled with her every motion, urging him onward, necessitating satisfaction. Groaning with desire, he opened the ties of her chemise and allowed the lovely breasts he recalled so well to spring free. In a selfless act, he stilled her roving hands, choosing to concentrate on her pleasure first, willing to postpone his own.

Standing before Jeanne, Creag lowered his head until it hovered over her creamy bosom, his tongue licking at one nipple while his practiced fingers rewarded the other for its patience. With little effort, Jeanne's body responded. When her breath caught and her sighs echoed in Creag's ears, he swept her up into his arms and carried her to the bed, laying her gently on the snowy covering before he removed the rest of her undergarments and his own clothes and joined her.

As nomads lusting for an oasis before escaping the treacherous desert, the laird and his lady clung together, yearning to experience every sweet morsel of pleasure, to taste every inch of honeyed flesh. Without discussion, they took turns, indulging each other's passions, inflaming their hearts, wearying their bodies as kiss after kiss, tender caress after tender caress had them feverish and short of breath.

She smelled of heather, Creag noted as he kissed her neck and shoulders, slowly moving toward her breasts, finding an erotic satisfaction in considering her needs first.

When Jeanne finally thought her body could know no further excitement, her heart pumping as if it were a locomotive, her breath shallow and rasping, she discovered Creag had only begun to teach her the arts of being loved. Without warning, his evocative mouth abandoned her cresting nipples, but before she could summon the energy to protest the suddenly cooling skin, she felt his warm breath and teasing mouth tracing a path down the smooth, flat plane of her stomach, circling slowly as he kissed his way downward to the warm center of her being.

With quick, darting movements, a hummingbird after its nectar, his tongue's touch was so light she almost thought she imagined it but for the sudden lurch of her heart, the fiery jolt of lightning that arched her back and made her cry aloud for the joy of it.

"Creag, oh, Creag," she whimpered, at once energized and exhausted by the loving he expended on her body. How could one man be so powerfully generous?

Then he was beside her again, drawing her into his arms as he rose over her, supporting his weight on his elbows as they joined together for their journey to the heavens. A rhythm as old as the stars took over as the international language of passion ignited their souls, sending them scaling heights beyond reality till they hovered in communion with the gods, existing for nothing but the moment.

"Jeanne—" For Creag, one word said it all. His release was so intense that he could manage no more.

"I know," she answered as the world about her exploded into a million sparkling fragments of light and breathing became an overwhelming effort. She clung fiercely to Creag, overwhelmed by the majesty of their coupling and wanting the ecstasy they shared to go on and on.

Later, replete with joy as she lay beside him, Jeanne reached out her hand and caressed the odd cleft in Creag's chin, the unusual indentation somehow making him seen more masculine, more rugged.

"I hate that dent," he murmured, snatching her fingers from it and bringing them to his mouth.

"You shouldn't. It makes you different from everyone else. Most men have such boring jaws."

"Except for Colum Donnachy," reminded Creag, regretting the words even as they escaped his mouth. This time with Jeanne was so precious he would have done anything to call back the ugly reminder of his deception, but it was too late. His claim to the title of laird might be counterfeit, he reflected, but his love for Jeanne Donnachy was completely genuine.

"Aye, except for Colum," agreed the brunette, a shadow falling over her soul at the thought of Linclachan's deceit. Creag Robertson Blake was a good man. How could they—and she—continue to take advantage of that?

"Forget about the family," commanded the laird, urgently reclaiming Jeanne's lips as a certain means to ending the discussion at hand and she made no protest, enthusiastically mirroring his growing ardor.

"I think I'm hungry," he observed a while later as Jeanne lay dozing, her head resting on his shoulder, her lovely brown curls cascading down his arm.

"You can't be serious." She giggled, amused at the male's easy shift of moods. She herself was filled with such languid contentment that even conversation was an effort, let alone independent thought that might require action. "I would have thought I satisfied your appetite."

"Well, my carnal ones, of course, and masterfully so," he praised, "but when it comes to food and drink—drink! I almost forgot. Jeanne, you'll never believe the luck I had in London. We will make Linclachan known through the British Isles—"

"I thought the wool trade was going to do that," she murmured sleepily.

"No, no, this is much better. We could have a worldwide market! Of course, it will take some initial outlay of capital naturally, but that's no problem. The organization of personnel and staffing will be your department, but you've had plenty of experience at such details—"

"Now, you see here, Mr. C. Robertson Blake," she cried, abruptly sitting up and placing a warning finger across his lips. "You are a world-renowned financier and businessman and I realize that, but in my bed, you are only Creag and I will *not* have you making plans or even proposing them when we are naked. Do you understand me?"

"Yes, Jeanne, I'm sorry," he admitted sheepishly, pulling her into his arms and kissing away her frown. "I'll save the details for later, but I think the council will be well pleased."

"They seem to be thrilled with everything you do, though your activities this afternoon might dull their enthusiasm," the brunette teased, running her fingers across his chest.

"Then let's not tell them," he whispered softly, rising from the bed and reaching for his trousers. "Though if I don't escape your amorous clutches soon, the whole village will know."

"*My* amorous clutches?" Jeanne repeated, taking aim at the American's head with a pillow and sending it sailing at her target. "I recall being clutched pretty fiercely myself, sir. In fact, I thought this a mutual exercise in passion."

Easily deflecting the pillow, Creag finished buttoning his trousers before he sat down on Jeanne's side of the bed, his expression gentle.

"Of course it was, but I don't imagine you're ready to announce it to all of Linclachan quite yet—"

"No, oh, no," agreed Jeanne, envisioning Andrew Robertson's face as he heard the news. The man was enough of a nuisance now without his deciding to challenge Creag directly for her affections. "For the time being anyway, let's keep our—"

"Personal relationship?"

"Our personal relationship quiet. I'll try to steal away tomorrow after breakfast and meet you in the study."

"All right," said Creag, "though dinner will be awfully difficult, seeing you right across the table and not being able to touch you."

"I could always take my meals in the kitchen again," the steward offered with a smile.

"No!" her laird protested quickly. "I promise I'll be circumspect in the dining room. I can tell you all about the whisky then. That will keep my mind busy and Michael might even have some useful suggestions."

Jeanne had been right, Creag reflected the next morning, as he carried his carefully wrapped parcel out to the stable. There would have been no point in having the elders of the clan sample the inferior whisky last night. With the flavor of Jamie's splendid vintage coating their palates, they would not have appreciated the vast difference between it and what he'd brought back from London. No, catching them this morning when they perhaps needed the hair of the dog to remedy their night's indulgence was a much better idea. Smiling in appreciation of the clever young woman who had just bid him such a fond farewell, Creag promised himself that he'd give her the ring as soon as he returned from Linclachan and the council. He'd take no chances of anyone else interfering in his plan to take Jeanne to wife.

"Ah, Creag," said Malcolm as he opened the door to his cottage and tried to hide his dismay at the laird's early call, especially when he realized the other members of the council had accompanied him. "Friends, come in. Whatever the reason for your visit, you ken you are welcome here."

"Don't look so worried," chided Jamie with a grin. "Creag says he has good news and he wants us all to hear it at the same time. He even had me bring a bottle of my finest whisky to celebrate later."

"Then Jeanne won't be following you to complain about your newest scheme the way she usually does?" asked the council's oldest member, feeling too old for the job of keeping the peace between the laird and his steward.

"No, I think I can safely promise you that Jeanne will be quite happily occupied at the manor all afternoon," avowed Creag, grinning as he envisioned the effort he'd made to keep her so. "What I've come to discuss is your whisky, Jamie's actually—"

"My whisky?" echoed Jamie, looking nervously at the other Scots. "What's wrong with it?"

"Nothing, nothing at all. It's perfect. That's why you can't keep it to yourselves any longer."

"Why can't we?" asked Geordie, seeing Jamie was too perturbed to speak. No man had ever given him instruction or criticism about his liquor.

"London, England, the States, all over the world, people will gladly pay a bloody fortune to drink what you take for granted!" exclaimed Creag, so delighted with his information that he failed to notice the others' lack of enthusiasm. "Here, this is rare Scottish whisky, or what passes for it in England, and this is the common variety, but they're poor imitations of good drink, I swear. Taste them and see what I mean."

"Ah, it's a wee bit early for me, lad," demurred Jamie, his refusal signaling his upset to the friends who knew him so well.

Here, they had encouraged the American to change their village. Indeed, they'd sacrificed their prime fishing stream, the best golfing range, and even pacified the women over his woolen trade, and now the man was about to ruin their existence. No wonder Jamie had no taste for the whisky that might soon be the bane of their existence. Exchanging glances, they considered how they might best deal with the laird.

"Look here, if you don't know how bad this is, how can you really appreciate the superior quality of your own whisky?" pressed the American, producing glasses and pouring four measures. "At least sample the seven-year-old variety. You'll understand in an instant why a factory producing Linclachan's Delight—''

"A factory?" said Jamie, a noticeable tremor in his voice.

"Here?" cried Malcolm, "in addition to the woolen looms?"

"Well, I thought it most suitable to keep the manufacture close to the water you've used for ages. Of course, we'll need a power supply but, when we raise the dam on the river coming off the loch, we'll have no difficulty."

Creag was pleased to see his words had affected the Scots' imagination as the four men reached out for the liquor and downed it in unison, their hands shaking. When Jamie uncorked his bottle and, without comment, began to pour, the laird knew his plans for the future had impressed them. Eagerly he started to explain the ideas he had for marketing and manufacture.

"I know we're twelve or thirteen years away from being able to go wholesale into the industry, but I thought if we managed to sacrifice two or three hundred bottles a year of what you already had put aside, we could slowly build up the market so that when we were in full production, the demand would already be there," he began, warming to the subject as his listeners rested their heads in their hands and absorbed his words.

To be sure their sins had returned to haunt them, Malcolm reflected. Why, oh, why had they ever thought the American their savior?

Chapter Fourteen

Creag had been gone for almost two hours when Jeanne, impatient for his return, happened upon Leslie in the library, where she had been perusing a book on herbals.

"What are you doing? Reading about a powder to chase the doldrums or perhaps searching out a new formula for another one of your love potions?" Lindall's steward asked in greeting as she took a chair opposite her friend.

"Neither appears to be necessary in your case. You're looking cheery this morning," Leslie commented with a knowing grin.

"No more so than you've been these last few weeks," Jeanne rejoined good-naturedly. A wicked arch of her eyebrow sent both women into a fit of schoolgirl giggles, leaving Maggie's grandniece anxious to tell Michael that for all his denials, she had been right. Jeanne and Creag were in love.

"Where is the laird, anyway?" Leslie asked, brimming with happiness for her friend. Although they had shared all the joys and maladies of childhood, this breathless experience of adulthood formed a bond that drew them closer than ever before.

"He's gone into the village to institute another of his endless modifications to life in Linclachan," Jeanne said with an indulgent chuckle. Tracing the pattern of the carpet with the toe of her shoe, she resisted the urge to glance at the clock yet again. The two hours since Creag had kissed her goodbye seemed more like two days, and constantly looking at the time only made it proceed more slowly.

"For the life of me," Leslie mused, putting her book aside and bringing Jeanne's mind back to the moment at hand, "I can't believe how things have changed for the better—in the village, at the manor, in our lives. And to think we owe it all to a counterfeit laird, and an American at that."

"Creag may not be the rightful earl of Lindall, but he's been a better laird than many a true-blooded one we've had. The man is real enough," Jeanne said, the natural sparks in her eyes muted by the dreamy look that settled over them.

The sound of carriage wheels coming to a halt in the courtyard interrupted their conversation before Leslie could comment. Though Jeanne could have sworn Creag had gone into the village on horseback, she ran to the window in joyful expectation nevertheless.

The vehicle, however, was a hired one. As Leslie joined her to peer outside, Jeanne wondered who these visitors might be, when a richly dressed, middle-aged man emerged from the coach. Shrugging her shoulders at her friend's questioning glance, the steward watched the man turn to aid his companions in their descent of the carriage's precarious steps.

A lady not much younger than the gentleman appeared first. Making no effort to hide what she was doing, the matron looked about with a sharp, assessing eye as though she were considering acquiring the place. But it was the other female, the extremely youthful one alighting, who captured Jeanne's interest. The woman's expensive traveling costume and elaborately styled blond curls combined with her fetching features to make her one of the prettiest women Jeanne had ever seen. At least the young stranger would have been beautiful were it not for the look of disdain that settled upon her face as she studied the manor.

"They must be lost," Jeanne murmured, watching Ewan come out to greet the trio.

But when the lovely Highlander saw the manor's faithful servant begin to unload baggage, a vague sense of apprehension taunted her, poking at her peace of mind.

"Did you ever see clothing so grand?" Leslie whispered. "I wonder who they could be?"

"I don't know, but we're going to find out," Jeanne said determinedly as she turned and hurried from the room, leaving Leslie to follow in her wake.

The strangers and Ewan had just entered the manor when Jeanne intercepted them in the vestibule, a nearly breathless Leslie right behind her.

"Can I help you?" Jeanne asked the man curiously.

"Yes, you can inform his lordship that the Graysons are here, and then see to it that our things are placed in our rooms," he ordered. His pronunciation proclaimed Grayson to be an American, but his supercilious tones, eating at Jeanne's pride like acid on metal, informed her that he was also an overbearing swaggerer.

"I am sorry, but the laird is not here right now. I'm afraid you'll have to deal with me," Jeanne responded with surface calm, her very formal manner alerting Leslie to possible trouble.

"And exactly who are you?" the youngest member of the party asked haughtily. With a speculative stare that swept Jeanne from crown to toe, Catherine couldn't help but consider that this woman, raw though her beauty was, might be the reason for Creag's change of heart.

"I am Jeanne Donnachy, steward of these lands and granddaughter to the old laird," the proud Scot answered, mindless of Leslie dancing daintily from foot to foot in rising anxiety as the two women took each other's measure.

"Oh, a servant," the young American said, dismissing Jeanne's presence in the household with a superior air. Satisfied, Catherine patted her hair with confidence, chiding herself for her foolishness. How could she have considered for a moment that Creag, improper though his breeding was, would ever desert her for a woman so unfashionably dressed? "In that case, kindly see to it that we are shown to our rooms. It has been a long and arduous journey, and my parents and I are tired. Also, I'll require a hot bath. Bring up the water as soon as possible."

"I'm sorry, Miss Grayson, but I've no knowledge of expected guests," Jeanne said, refusing to play the serving wench to this American chit's grand lady.

"I fail to see why an earl would take someone in service into his confidence concerning our sojourn here," Bartholomew Grayson said, balking indignantly.

"That's right. I am certain Creag didn't feel he had to consult with his staff over the matter. After all, what business is it of yours that his intended and her parents have come to call?" Catherine asked with a self-satisfied smile, enjoying the impact, subtle though it was, that her words had on the lithesome brunette.

"You are the laird's fiancée?" asked Leslie, unable to restrain herself.

"My daughter and his lordship have an understanding, yes," the girl's mother interjected, having determined to push the situation by announcing this falsehood to as many people as she could. It would make it that much harder for Creag to dismiss Catherine, after all. "Wasn't he just down to London to see her, and didn't he recently present her with a beautiful necklace? Their engagement will become official after her father and I have inspected the earl's Scottish holdings and satisfied ourselves that things meet our standards."

"And it seems, Mama, as if the dear boy has been working very hard to impress you and Daddy. Didn't you notice how everything is freshly painted both here and in the village, doubtless for our benefit?" Catherine asked sweetly, her tone belying the smug, victorious gleam in her eyes. He was obviously as generous with his tenants as he'd been with her, she mused. But that, of course, would change.

Jeanne stood in silent outrage, trying to stifle any physical manifestation of her turbulent emotions. First there was the shock of this person's appearance, and then the knowledge that it had been affairs of the heart rather than those of business that had prompted Creag's trip from the manor. Now she was being told that everything Creag had done in Linclachan had been for the express purpose of winning the woman's hand. Fiery though she had always been, Jeanne Donnachy had never been so furious as she was at that moment.

Yet even as her rage burned hotter than a Beltaine bonfire, Jeanne questioned the veracity of what these outlanders told her. How could the man who had stayed by her bedside for countless hours, the man who had taken her love so tenderly beside the *lin*, and upon his return yesterday, be filled with such deceit?

The thoughts tumbling around in Jeanne's head were painful and confusing ones. She wanted to escape the odious company of these Americans, to forget they had ever appeared. In frustration, she decided that it might be best to banish them to some far-removed bedchambers so she could consider her dilemma in peace, away from their distracting and loathsome company.

"Ewan, please see the Graysons comfortably settled in the north wing and have their trunks taken up, as well."

"Good! It's about time we were treated like honored guests," Mr. Grayson muttered. "Inform the earl of our arrival as soon as he returns."

"Have no worry. It's the first thing I'll discuss with Creag when he gets back," Jeanne said coldly.

"Creag! Young woman, you forget yourself," Mrs. Grayson exclaimed. "You will refer to his lordship with proper respect."

"That's right!" Catherine's father dictated. "Your behavior has been nothing but unseemly. Though my daughter is so softhearted that I doubt she will insist his lordship dismiss you for your rudeness, I caution you, I suffer from no such charity. A word to the wise."

"And don't forget that bathwater," Catherine called peevishly when the Graysons followed Ewan up the stairs.

"Leslie, get Michael," Jeanne whispered through gritted teeth, watching the Americans retreat from view. "Creag may not be here to explain himself, but God help him if his friend isn't able to do it for him."

"Jeanne, I'm sorry," Michael said with ominous sympathy as he entered the morning room at Leslie's side.

"So it's true then? Creag plans to marry this Grayson woman?"

"I'm afraid so. He has intended it for some time now," the secretary said, removing his spectacles and polishing them nervously. It was obvious that he felt deep dismay at being the one to tell Jeanne, especially now when Leslie had just informed him that Creag had behaved dishonorably with the girl.

Damn him! Michael thought, watching Jeanne fight to maintain some degree of dignity and composure. Why the hell couldn't his friend have acted like a gentleman instead of a brash villain, taking what he had wanted at the moment?

"You should have said something about it, Michael!" Leslie cried, her usually tranquil and demure manner disappearing in her current upset.

"I did mention it...once," he said, misery and anger at one C. Robertson Blake growing more intense with each tick of the clock. "You didn't believe me. I suppose I could have been more insistent, but with the way those two fought, I never thought there was a need to say anything else. Besides, I had other matters on my mind at that moment."

"Michael! How could you say such things in front of Jeanne? Especially now when—"

"It's all right, Leslie," Jeanne interrupted. Her voice was icy calm despite the tears spilling over her cheeks, and it thoroughly frightened her friend. "Certainly you can't fault Michael for what has happened. I was a fool, and if there is any man to blame, there is only one."

"Creag is the fool," cried Leslie bitterly, feeling Jeanne's pain now as she had shared everything else during their lives.

"No, actually the bastard was quite sly," Jeanne remarked, her voice sounding as hollow as an echo on a starless night. "But there's no reason for you to worry about me. Now that I know what the truth is, he'll never be able to hurt me again."

Creag burst through the doors of his house, full of high spirits and impatient to be with his Jeanne. As always when he undertook a project, he was filled with enthusiastic optimism, and he had no doubts but that he would persuade the council to accept his viewpoint concerning the whisky.

Bounding up the stairway to his study in search of the woman who held his heart, he was oblivious to the scathing scowl Maggie sent his way as she scuttled through the vestibule, her arms full of fine clothes in need of pressing. Nor did Creag notice the unnatural silence that hung over the manor. All he thought about was his lovely Highlander and the happiness she had brought him, a happiness that had become as necessary to his life as breath itself.

Peering into his makeshift office through the open door, Creag smiled to see Jeanne there. She was unmindful of his presence, however, as she stood with her back to him, staring out through the parted draperies of the window, lost in deep contemplation. In his euphoria, Creag assumed Jeanne's thoughts reflected his own, full of remembered pleasures and present cravings. The notion was enough to stir his most primitive instincts. And after they made love, he would offer his pretty Scot the ring that would symbolize their betrothal.

He approached his beloved eagerly but quietly so as not to disturb her pensive mood. When he was standing behind her, his arm stole around Jeanne's slender waist and he bent his golden head to kiss the nape of her neck. But rather than melt longingly against him as he had anticipated, Creag felt Jeanne's spine stiffen at his loving touch. With alarm, he wondered what he had done to provoke such aloofness, and when he spoke, his voice was less confident than he would have liked.

"What's this then, bonny Jeanne?" he asked, imitating the lilting speech of the Highlands. "'Tis not how the lady of the manor should greet her adoring laird."

When his playfulness provoked no response, he bent to whisper in her ear, his breath hotly seductive and his tone quite serious. "And I do adore you, you know."

"Is that so? How kind of you to inform me. Otherwise I might never have guessed," Jeanne replied coldly, turning around to confront the man who had stolen her innocence along with her heart.

"I don't understand," Creag said slowly, a sense of foreboding clawing at his peace of mind like some aggressive, wild beast tearing apart its prey.

"That might be, but thank God, I finally do."

"Jeanne, what in heaven's name is wrong with you?" Creag asked, his apprehension bringing him to the brink of impatience.

"Nothing that a search of your conscience won't explain," she retorted hotly, turning to move away.

"Wait! Where are you going?" he asked in rising panic. "We have to talk about this." Had Jeanne learned, he wondered as he saw her waver for an instant, that he had assumed the title of laird knowing it was not rightfully his? Was that what her reproach was all about?

"There's nothing to say," Jeanne stated resolutely. "Besides, you have guests awaiting you."

"Let them wait, whoever they are! This is more important."

"More important than your fiancée?" Jeanne asked casually, the incriminating word hanging heavy in the air between them. "I wouldn't think so."

"Fiancée?" Creag repeated in bewilderment, a sinking feeling filling the pit of his stomach nonetheless.

"Yes. Catherine Grayson arrived a short while ago in the company of her parents," Jeanne informed him. Her vivid green eyes accused and condemned him simultaneously as she took a step backward in an attempt to leave the room.

"Wait, there's been a mistake!" Creag protested. What the hell was Catherine doing here anyway? he thought. But the fault of Jeanne's upset was his, and guilt was imprinted on his handsome features for never having mentioned the troublesome wench to Jeanne.

Seeing his expression, the lithesome Scot misinterpreted its cause and she forced herself to ignore the regret mirrored in Creag's compelling eyes.

"Aye, there's been a mistake, and it's been mine. But it's not one I'll be repeating," Jeanne vowed, her soft burr becoming thicker as her own eyes danced with golden sparks of wounded fury.

"Jeanne," Creag beseeched, "allow me to explain."

"There's no need. I've already learned more than I wanted to know."

"You don't know anything," Creag cried, reaching out to capture her hand in his.

"Don't I?" Jeanne asked. Her whole demeanor was rife with frosty disdain as Creag's strong forefinger lovingly caressed her skin in an attempt to call her back to him.

"No, you don't," he said in an emphatic whisper, bringing his face closer to hers.

"Can you deny that you gave her a necklace? Or that you paid for the woman's trip to Britain, and have but recently purchased her trousseau?" Jeanne asked, turning her head aside as she repeated the things Maggie had learned while unpacking Catherine's trunks. "Are you saying that you didn't visit her in London, or that you never spoke to her father about marriage? Can you tell me that none of these things are true?"

"Jeanne . . . I . . ." Creag began, at a loss as to how to proceed without upsetting her further.

"It's just as I thought. You can't deny any of it," Jeanne said, glaring defiantly at the man she had thought she loved. "And the worst of it is that you've done nothing in this village that wasn't done for her sake. You've used us, all of us in Linclachan, and me most especially."

Creag wanted to tell this fiery woman that he, too, had been used, by the people of Linclachan, but he couldn't bring himself to say it. Accusations constituted a poor defense and would do nothing to alleviate the anguish each of them felt.

"Jeanne, listen to yourself. You're being absurd," Creag retorted instead, his voice dropping to a dangerous growl. "Now it's time to hear what I have to say."

"I've already done that, and believed you, too, much to my shame," Jeanne cried out, trying frantically to disentangle her hand from his larger one. "I actually imagined you cared for me."

"You *imagined?*" Creag demanded, unwilling to believe what he had heard.

"Exactly!" she spat.

Jeanne's sharp tongue sliced through Creag's heart. If she loved him as he had thought, how could she judge him without giving him the chance to explain? And yet, for all her present cruelty, Creag desired her still, knowing it was his well-intentioned deceit that caused Jeanne to lash out at him now. He wanted to teach her to trust him once more. Desperate to keep her, Creag reacted to this situation as he had always reacted in the past when he was in danger of losing something he wanted. He reached out and took her. Pulling his beloved to him tightly, his mouth claimed hers, hoping to end her anger by demonstrating what was in his heart.

It took all of Jeanne's stamina to resist Creag's insistent urgings. But she remained steadfast. Despondent he had evoked no response, Creag finally released her. The moment he did so, Jeanne brought her hand up quickly, a resounding, stinging slap leaving the outline of her fingers on Creag's tightly clenched jaw.

"Save that for Catherine Grayson," she hissed. "No one I know would welcome your attentions."

With that, she hurriedly escaped the study. It was only when she was safely away that Jeanne surrendered to the deluge of tears she had barely managed to hold back.

Behind her she left a man filled with self-recriminations, and a desire to throttle Catherine Grayson. While that would be not only unwise but illegal, Creag decided there was nothing to stop him from seeing Bartholomew Grayson and demanding that he and his family depart immediately.

Having fully expected Creag's imperious summons, Bartholomew Grayson was not at all disposed to scurry off to the study like some repentant sinner. Instead, he told the maid he'd be along shortly and, determined to maintain the upper hand, stopped to enjoy a cigar before condescending to join his host.

"Hello, Blake," Catherine's father said by way of greeting, as though his presence was only to be expected. "Don't concern yourself about not being here to greet us. We made ourselves at home."

"So I've been told," Creag snarled, his temper clearly worsened by Grayson's delayed appearance. "My only concern, however, is why you are here at all. I thought we'd settled the matter in London. I have absolutely no intention of courting your daughter."

"Ah, but Catherine is interested in you, and I've decided that you should have the opportunity to renew your acquaintance with her. I'm certain if you spend some time together, you'll quickly remember all the reasons you were so smitten with her in Philadelphia. Indeed, I haven't spoken to my lawyers, but there might be a breach-of-promise action—"

"Don't be ridiculous." Creag's hard blue eyes reflected his fury as he struggled not to pound some sense into this pompous fool. "I made no promises, nor, might I add, did you or your daughter. Besides, Catherine seemed more than satisfied with the necklace and financial settlement."

"Once you'd gone, she realized how impossible it would be to replace you."

"Me, or my money?" asked Creag with a short laugh.

"Unless you reconsider your position, and welcome Catherine to your home, I will ruin you so badly that you won't have any money. And make no mistake, I can do it."

"Ruin C. Robertson Blake? You haven't one third the assets I have, or the friends and business contacts."

"Maybe not, but then *I'm* not a member of that nouveau riche hunting and fishing club, responsible for the deaths of over two thousand innocent people in Johnstown."

"Neither am I, nor have I ever been."

"Half of those affiliated with the place are busy telling the newspapers exactly the same thing," said Grayson, his voice cold and hard. "But most of them are still being savaged by the press and shunned by decent businessmen everywhere, no matter how much they plead their innocence."

"You'd blackmail me to force me to marry Catherine? Just what kind of a marriage do you think that would be?"

"I want you to spend time together, to give the romance a chance, that's all," corrected the older man.

"And if I refuse? In all probability, I shall spend the rest of my life in Linclachan. Why should I worry about my reputation in the States?"

"Your life here could become very unpleasant, too, Blake. If your plans for the woolen trade suddenly come to naught and your finances are affected adversely at home, you might not be able to afford to play the munificent laird," countered Grayson, pleased at his own contribution to the plan to manipulate this rich upstart.

"The woolen trade?"

"Yes, Bradford's banker told me of his interest in subsidizing the endeavor, but a few words in the right ears about your involvement in Johnstown and the questionable moral issue of underwriting any enterprise even remotely connected to you…" With a practiced eye, Grayson gauged Creag's rising fury, smiled and rose to his feet. "You needn't give me your answer now, son. Take some time to think it over. After all, what's the cost of a few houseguests compared to the future of your Scottish and American holdings and the fate of your newfound Highland relatives?"

Watching the man leave, Creag slowly sank back into his chair. His first impulse had been to throw the Graysons out of Lindall Manor and dare Bartholomew to do his worst, but as quickly as it appeared, the idea vanished. Though he was free to choose his own fate, Creag knew he couldn't gamble with Linclachan's welfare. No, he wouldn't give way to angry inclinations until he had taken steps to safeguard the Highland village.

Why, he was acting almost as if he truly were the laird, bent on protecting his people, the handsome American realized incredulously. It didn't matter what his motivation, Creag thought, frustrated by the decision he had been forced to make. The Graysons would remain at Lindall, at least for the time being. After all, no matter how he chafed at the Philadelphians' intrusion, he needed time to consider how best to assure the future of the Clan Donnachy without destroying his good name.

Once this mess was settled, he wanted something to offer Jeanne, if she'd ever speak to him again. Shaking his head over the injustice of it all, he rose and prowled his study, not trusting himself to leave its confines in his present mood. Finally he poured himself some of Jamie's marvelous whisky and took solace in the smooth comfort it offered.

Following much discussion after Creag had left them, the council members marched into the manor's kitchen, their plaids swinging in unison and their faces solemn.

"We've a grave problem," Jamie announced to Maggie.

"So you've heard, have you?" Maggie asked, her face as unhappy as their own.

"Didn't the man come to us himself and tell us about it?" Malcolm asked in exasperation.

"The important thing is, something has to be done before it's too late," declared Duncan.

"Aye, if we can't come to terms with the laird, he has to go, money or no," Jamie stated, ignoring Malcolm's forlorn frown.

"Aye, that he does," said Geordie grimly, supporting his brother. "Now where's Jeanne?"

"Och, the poor lass is no doubt off somewhere crying her eyes out on Leslie's shoulder," the old woman replied. "She's that upset about it."

"I had no idea young Jeanne felt so strongly about the whisky, but then she's always been a fine lass," Jamie said with pride.

"What whisky, you great dolt?" Maggie asked in derision. "That's not what has her in tears."

"If it isn't, it should," Malcolm snorted indignantly. "Doesn't she know Creag is planning to industrialize our whisky production and sell the stuff abroad?"

"If she knows, she doesn't care. The poor wee mite has other troubles on her mind."

"And what might that mean?" Geordie scowled, mindful now of Jeanne's previous complaints about life in the manor after Creag had been installed as master. "Is the laird making her more miserable than usual?"

"'Tis not Creag himself, but the fine American miss who arrived today with her parents. She claimed to be the laird's intended."

"Three more Americans? It's a bloody invasion!" exclaimed Duncan. "No wonder Jeanne's upset."

"Aye, especially when the young chit, Miss Grayson her name is, regards the manor, Linclachan, and all of Scotland with disdain." Maggie snorted contemptuously. "'Twill not be easy keeping that one happy... although I don't think that's exactly what Jeanne has in mind for her anyway."

"So... the American lass does not like the Highlands," Geordie said slowly, a cunning light gleaming in his eyes. "If she's Creag's betrothed and she comes to actually hate Scotland, it may be that she could sweet-talk the laird into taking her home, the pair of them never to return."

"Who's to say she'll hate it that much?" Maggie protested, love of her homeland overcoming her wish to see the arrogant girl gone.

"Oh, she will, have no doubts about it. Just leave that to us," Jamie said meaningfully, surmising his brother's plan before the brewer had actually explained. "And with Creag back in America, all sorts of impediments might arise to foul his fool plans for my whisky."

"How do you know this whole wild scheme won't blow up in your face?" Maggie asked crossly. "'Twas one of the council's daft schemes got us into this mess to begin with."

"And so we need another one to get us out," a gruff Duncan retorted.

"But who's to say that the American wench's intense dislike for the place won't be the end of her and Creag? Couldn't it be that it might send her packing alone?" the manor's spurious housekeeper asked hopefully.

"Not if we work to promote the match. We'll make things as romantic as possible for the two of them. What man in love can deny his sweetheart anything?"

"Not a one of you can remember anything about romance, to be sure," Maggie scoffed, knowing such a plan was not in Jeanne's best interest. Yet how could she admit as much to the council when the lass would no longer admit it to herself? "You won't find anyone else to take part in your wild enterprise."

"You're wrong, Maggie. I'll do it," called Jeanne from the doorway, her eyes now dry and her face stony.

"But, Jeanne, why should you?" the white-haired woman asked in protest. Wasn't the lass willing to fight for her rightful place at the new laird's side?

"Because there's no one here who wants to see Creag Robertson Blake gone more than I do," she stated bluntly.

"Aye, Jeanne, you're a good lass!" boomed Geordie. "You're always ready to help whenever there's need."

"And there's not a one of us who doesn't love you for it," Malcolm said with a wizened grin.

But as Jeanne listened to the elders put forth their plan, their effulgent praise still ringing in her ears, she thought of one particular person who didn't love her, and she wished to God she had never met him.

Creag sat brooding behind the closed door of his study for the next few hours. Never had he felt so bereft. His companies, his wealth, nothing meant so much to him as Jeanne Donnachy's love. He could have lost all he possessed and still have counted himself the most fortunate of men if only Jeanne were his. But did he have the right to risk Linclachan's future just to satisfy his own desires? He had, after all, taken on the role of laird voluntarily. He couldn't abandon it now just because the responsibility of the title had become inconvenient.

Troubled as he was, his mind kept turning from the plight of the Donnachys and Robertsons to the fiery Scot who had stolen his heart.

Though he resented her lack of trust and the slap she had delivered, Creag bristled at his own idiocy most of all. Damn, but he should have told Jeanne why he was going to London! In fact, it might have been wise to have taken her with him.

"There you are, Creag," came Catherine's voice, following the sound of his door being opened and then shut again. Her speech was couched in low and sultry tones, yet it was the most unwelcome and irritating thing Creag had ever heard.

"One of your servants said you had returned. Mama and Daddy are in their rooms, but that's no reason why you and I can't visit," she continued, as though nothing had changed between them. "I do think, however, I am entitled to a pout. You've been back all this time, you naughty man, and you didn't come to seek me out."

"I thought we had come to an understanding in London," Creag growled. "You took the gifts I gave you rather than insist upon a proposal."

"Oh, that!" Catherine replied with a toss of her pretty blond curls. "I agreed to accept what you offered, but I never said I didn't want to marry you. I knew you were only jealous because I wasn't in London when you arrived, and I've decided to forgive your abominable behavior."

"There's no need for such charity on your part," Creag stated, his voice curt.

"Now, now, don't be so out of sorts," Catherine chided. "I'd be quite upset with you if I wasn't looking forward to that Donnachy woman's suggestion that we go for a romantic stroll by the estate's waterfall this evening."

"What!" Creag roared, stung as he had never been hurt before. "Jeanne intimated that you and I go to the *lin?*"

"Lin?"

"The waterfall," he said impatiently.

"That's right, she did," Catherine answered complacently. In truth she had been surprised when the attractive servant had proven to be an ally instead of a rival. But in all likelihood, the woman was intelligent enough to know that she stood no chance in the race for Creag's fortune now that a true lady was in residence at the manor.

"It's out of the question. I have work to attend," Creag growled gruffly, opening the ledger at random to the page on which the odd ten-thousand-pound discrepancy had first appeared.

"You know I can change your mind. If you're not ready to escort me in an hour, expect me back," Catherine said flirtatiously, though her steely eyes may have held a hidden message. Then, with a flick of her silk skirts, she was gone.

Creag stayed where he was, his breathing fast and furious. Not only was he being forced to endure the Graysons, he was being betrayed by the woman he loved. Though he wanted to dismiss Catherine's allegation about who had proposed the outing to the *lin,* he had a difficult time doing so.

With the columns of financial entries spread before him, Creag did what he always did when he was upset. He attempted to lose himself in his work. But the figures proved more difficult than usual, and he discovered he could not focus on things as his turbulent emotions seethed within him.

Swearing he would never permit Jeanne Donnachy to know how deeply she had injured him, Creag nevertheless found himself standing at the door to his study, bellowing her name.

She appeared a few moments later, her manner more distant than he had ever seen it.

"Come in here," he snapped, pulling her inside and closing the door when she seemed to hesitate.

Jeanne's already rapid pulse beat faster when Creag backed her against a wall. With one hand placed beside her cheek on the newly painted woodwork he bent his head so that he could look into her face. The contained rage evident in Creag's flashing blue eyes made Jeanne fear her heart would stop altogether.

"Let me make one thing clear, Jeanne. I've no intention or desire to give Catherine Grayson a tour of the manor grounds."

"You can't ignore your guests, Creag. As laird of Linclachan you are obligated to preserve the old and noble tradition of Highland hospitality. If you fail to do so, I shall remind you of your responsibilities," Jeanne said, pretending to misunderstand what it was he was saying.

"And perhaps I should remind you of something, as well," Creag threatened, bringing his face closer to hers so that his lips hovered just a few inches away from her own. "How could you suggest I take Catherine to the *lin?*"

"She's your fiancée and some think it is a romantic spot," Jeanne said with a casual shrug of her shoulders. "I assumed you would want to take all of your lovers there."

"Damn it, woman! Catherine is no more my lover than she is my fiancée," Creag thundered. "And though we had an understanding, she was never either."

"I don't believe you," Jeanne said simply.

"You won't accept what I tell you?"

"Accept it? I refuse to even consider it," she retorted, more gratified now than frightened by Creag's building ire.

"How can you do this to me, Jeanne?" he asked, his hoarse voice trembling with unspent emotion, and the ring he had meant to give her burning a hole in his pocket. "How can you consider me so base as to think I could bring another woman to the place where we first knew love?"

"But it wasn't love for either one of us, was it?" Jeanne asked sharply.

"You may doubt me, Jeanne Donnachy, but I have no uncertainties about what it was you felt that day. I saw it in your eyes. I discerned it in the trembling of your body. I heard it as my name tumbled from your lips."

"You were mistaken," Jeanne protested, her eyes beginning to well with tears. When Creag proceeded to gently brush them away with the side of his thumb as they spilled onto her cheeks, panic seized Jeanne's heart. Good God, if she stayed here any longer, if she didn't fight this handsome, seductive male, the little reserve she had left would crumble.

"I was there, if you'll recall," he insisted tenderly, wanting to take her in his arms once more and prove how much he loved her. "I know what happened."

Seeing the longing on Creag's face, Jeanne cast about desperately for a way to turn that expression into loathing before she fell prey to its charm.

"You may have been at the *lin,* but in your preoccupation, the reason why I accepted your advances escaped you entirely," Jeanne replied, her need to put a permanent end to Creag's pursuit so great that she ignored the callousness of the fabrication she was about to tell. "I lay with you not for my own pleasure or out of personal desire. I did so only to keep you contented for the sake of the villagers."

"What!" Creag roared, his fine, strong features a study of enraged disbelief. "You're trying to tell me that you didn't freely and lovingly surrender your innocence because you cared for me? That it was a selfless act on your part to ensure that I continued to pour my money into this miserable little place you call home? I don't believe you. You may fool yourself Jeanne Donnachy, but you don't fool me."

"It's true. I swear it," Jeanne insisted, fear and not revenge the basis for her lie.

"Damn it, if you can sacrifice yourself for Linclachan, I suppose I can do the same for your sacred Highland hospitality," he snapped. He knew she was telling him a monstrous untruth, just as he knew she would never admit it. But it did not safeguard his heart from her piercing words. Finally she had driven him beyond rational thought and his previous feelings of guilt. "See to it that a bottle of wine is packed in a picnic hamper," he directed, realizing that if he was going to get through this outing with Catherine, he would need a drink.

"As you say," Jeanne murmured. Then she hastened from sight, leaving Creag to curse his own stupidity and her false heart.

C. Robertson Blake lifted his head and straightened his broad shoulders, his normally excellent posture becoming rigid as he steeled himself for the coming ordeal with Catherine Grayson.

Descending the stairs at a brisk clip, he regretted having blurted an intention to escort the Philadelphia debutante on this damnable trek. But Jeanne had provoked him so that before he had realized it, he had surrendered himself to complete and utter idiocy, as well as a few hours in Catherine's company, though the outing would buy him time to decide how to deal with Grayson's threats.

Indeed, though Creag found the idea abhorrent, what could he do and still maintain his pride, other than endure some time with the cloying Miss Grayson? And that was as much Jeanne's fault as his, he decided, running a hand haphazardly through his thick golden mane.

Ironically, there had been a period in his life when a few stolen moments with the attractive, cultured American miss would have given him a sense of triumphant joy. But in this instance, elation was absent, and so was his patience, knowing as he did that his unwanted houseguest would view their stroll as an opportunity to inveigle her way back into his pockets if not his heart.

There was no question about it, he no longer wanted Catherine Grayson. In fact, he doubted he ever really had. He desired Jeanne. Merciful God, how he hungered for that proud, fiery woman. But she had made it exceedingly clear the feeling was not reciprocated, and C. Robertson Blake, one of the brightest young men of industry, was at an absolute loss as to what he could do about it.

Meeting Catherine in the vestibule, he almost cringed when she looked up at him with seductive eyes and linked her arm through his. Lord, he didn't know how he was going to get through the next hour or so. The only thing of which he was sure was that he was not going to take the spoiled socialite to the waterfall! Such an expedition might not bother Jeanne Donnachy, but it damn well troubled him, and he refused to go along with such an idea.

Ringing the newly installed service bell, the earl of Lindall signaled that the wine and glasses he had ordered be brought up from the cellars. He might have been more involved in his relationship with Jeanne than she had been with him, Creag fumed as he stood waiting his steward's appearance, but he would rot in hell before he acknowledged that fact to her. Since Jeanne had rejected his love, at least he would have the perverse satisfaction of seeing her face when he took the basket from her hands and casually walked off with Catherine Grayson. That, in itself, might prove adequate compensation for the loathsome task of putting up with the woman's tiresome conversation and flirtation.

But it was Maggie and not Jeanne who arrived in the vestibule, small hamper in hand. The old housekeeper handed the laird what he required with nary a glance, though he could sense her bristling all the same, blaming him as though this whole thing were his fault. Her actions and Jeanne's failure to appear made Creag's ill humor fouler still, so that he was hard-pressed to smile softly at Catherine Grayson despite his hopes that such a tender glance would be reported back to the person responsible for this fiasco.

Dragging his steps, he led Catherine from the manor, his only solace the anticipation of viewing Jeanne's speculative, worried glances across the dinner table when they returned.

After a hurried walk to a small stream and back, stopping only long enough to bolt down one glass of wine and shrug off his companion's subtle advances, Creag retired to his bedchamber to dress for dinner, ignoring Catherine's kittenish suggestion that he escort her to her room.

In spite of his anger and frustration, he dressed carefully, telling himself that his meticulous grooming was merely a part of his nature and not something designed to impress the woman who had captivated his heart. Yet it would be wonderful if Jeanne found him too attractive to resist, he thought, until he realized that he was indulging in useless fantasy, and resolutely returned to the task at hand.

As he inserted his shirt studs with sure fingers, he sternly reminded himself that he had to ignore Jeanne's curiosity about what had occurred that afternoon with Catherine, even as he steeled himself for the possibility that she might not be curious at all. Damn, she drove him to distraction! He never knew what to expect from her, he reflected, leaving his quarters and heading for the dining room.

But when he arrived, Jeanne had indeed managed to surprise him once more. She wasn't at the table, and neither were Leslie, Maggie nor Michael. He had been condemned to dining alone with the three Graysons, and he was miserable. Though he had yearned for such an intimate dinner back in Philadelphia, he spurned it now. What was the good of walking out with Catherine if he couldn't gauge Jeanne's reactions?

His appetite disappeared so that he merely shifted his food around with his fork. How could his life, his plans for the future become unraveled so quickly? In all probability, he could find another buyer for Linclachan's woolens; in fact, he had sent out some letters dealing with that matter today. He could survive Bartholomew Grayson's threats, though the man's allegations would likely cost him some business. Still, no matter what happened, tomorrow looked bleak, a fact that was underscored by Jeanne's failure to appear that night. Though he knew his future was no longer with Catherine, apparently it was not in the Highlands, either.

Chapter Fifteen

Creag rose early the next day, the dreariness of the morning mists reflecting that of his soul. He was still smarting from the absence of his makeshift family at last night's dinner table, knowing their actions denoted censure, and their disapproval weighed more heavily upon his heart than he had dreamed possible. After all, he had lived his life for himself, discounting the opinions of others for so long that he thought he had grown immune to such concerns. But apparently his little household had come to mean more to him than he had realized, so that this place and these people who had given him so much happiness now brought him the greatest misery he had ever known.

True, he had hurt his lovely Jeanne, Creag conceded while he shaved, clumsily nicking himself in the process; but didn't anyone here realize that his sin had been one of ignorance and not outright villainy? Though he could well understand Maggie and Leslie condemning him for his transgression, Michael's traitorous behavior was another matter. Creag had always thought the man was as much his friend as his employee, and his desertion had been both unexpected and deeply felt.

But the greatest of his sorrows most certainly centered around Jeanne, Creag reflected, as he eased his perfectly pressed trousers over powerful thighs. He hadn't seen her at all last evening, and her deliberate absence spoke louder than her tongue—at its sharpest—ever had. She had been the woman who taught him to love, how could she destroy his heart?

However, it seemed his words, his supplications had meant nothing to her, the wealthy industrialist thought with helpless frustration, and he vowed once again to pretend that he cared no more than she. But, despite his intentions to go about his life in as normal a manner as possible, he was not in any mood to submit himself to being snubbed once more by Jeanne and the others at his own table. He was permitting the Graysons to stay at Lindall Manor; surely he did not have to suffer their company at this hour. No, he would forego breakfast and repair directly to his study. If he could not lose himself in the workings of his businesses, at least he would present the illusion of being able to do so.

Donning his jacket, Creag left the room, remembering for a change to step over the body of his prone, snoring guard. But for all his promises of ignoring Jeanne Donnachy, the handsome male found himself restlessly prowling the hallway, considering the notion of pounding on Jeanne's door. He was stopped from doing so, though, by the sight of Michael at the other end of the corridor.

Noticing Creag in return, the secretary frowned deeply and spun on his heel, bent on making an escape before he was forced to deal with the despicable man he had once regarded so highly. But before he could retreat, Creag's deep voice rang out, stopping him where he stood.

"Wait, I want to talk with you. Let's go into my study so we won't be disturbed."

"If you insist," the bespectacled secretary answered, his tone curt, wishing he could avoid the confrontation with this man who had been his friend and was still his employer.

"I was sorry not to see you at dinner last evening," Creag began, carefully keeping his voice free of reproach.

"If we were in Philadelphia, I wouldn't be joining you and the Graysons for meals," the other man replied.

"I want you at my table," Creag said, truly needing a friend for the first time he could remember. Indeed, if Michael had been amenable this morning, Creag had intended confiding in him, though obviously that was not about to happen.

"But I have no desire to be there," Michael asserted. "I don't want to break bread with a man who would use a woman the way you used Jeanne Donnachy."

"Surely you don't believe I did such a thing intentionally!" Creag exclaimed in surprise.

"Did you lie with her while you were engaged to someone else?"

"It wasn't what you think. You know Catherine and I were never officially betrothed. Besides, I wouldn't take advantage of Jeanne. Aren't you well enough acquainted with me to know that?"

"I have recently formed the opinion that I don't know you at all. And right now, it is almost more than I can do not to punch you in that handsome face of yours for the unhappiness you caused Jeanne. But if I ever hear of you bothering the girl again, I'm going to do just that, employer or no," the secretary promised, egged on by the upset the situation had brought Leslie.

"So that's the way of things, is it?" Creag asked, his voice shrouded in ice. "You're not the friend I thought you were."

"And you're not the man I thought you to be," Michael retorted. "You can have my resignation immediately."

"No, that's not what I want at all," Creag said wearily, watching the other man head for the door. "Before you do anything so drastic, take a few days to think about it."

"And while I'm doing that, what will you be pondering," Michael called over his shoulder, "how to seduce the next innocent woman who falls victim to your charms?"

"That's unworthy of you," Creag said in soft but fierce tones. "And anyway, from what she has implied, Jeanne never loved me at all."

"What a fool you are," Michael said, stepping out into the hallway. "It astounds me that a man who understands so little about human nature could have amassed such a fortune."

"It's love, not human nature, that confounds me," Creag whispered to the empty room once the door had closed. "That and the rules of friendship."

"Now, child, you can't go around sulking all the time," chided Mrs. Grayson the next morning when she happened on Catherine scowling over a book in the library. "It's no wonder the earl avoids you if you're always wearing a frown. Given a choice between your mood and a quiet ledger, I would have business that needed my attention, as well.''

"Oh, Mama, it's not me that's the problem, it's this place. Scotland has taken the C. Robertson Blake I knew in Philadelphia, sophisticated, urbane, witty, and turned him into just plain Creag, even to the servants, for heaven's sake! Yesterday on our romantic stroll, all he could talk about was how many acres of grain he'd need to plant to corner the whisky market. The cut of my dress, the color of my eyes, none of that concerned the man, whereas at home, he would have stolen as many kisses as I'd allow him. I tell you, I barely know this Creag.''

"Come now, Catherine, how well did you really know him before we came here? Besides, he did come to London to tell us that he was very preoccupied with renovating his estate. You can't say his attitude comes as a shock,'' reminded Alma. Then, perceiving her daughter's emotional state, she relented and softened what the girl might read as criticism. "If you're patient, dear, he'll come around. No man could resist you. Though nothing gives him leave to ignore his invited guests.''

"I beg your pardon, Mrs. Grayson, but if you will recall, I explained my change of heart in London,'' said Creag, quietly entering the library to find a volume he'd misplaced. "I was under the impression you would not be visiting me at all.''

Mrs. Grayson looked faintly chagrined at being overheard, but Catherine showed no remorse. Of course he wasn't surprised to hear Catherine complaining, but it did irritate him nonetheless to be condemned for the very situation he'd tried to avoid. The Graysons would be gone soon; surely he could tolerate them until then. In truth, he would have to, the laird reminded himself, or Linclachan might suffer. Besides, if he didn't, Jeanne would only be lecturing him again about Scottish hospitality. He'd afford the Grayson women a modicum of graciousness; that was what Jeanne wanted, wasn't it? Deciding to make a more magnanimous effort to be charming, he smiled graciously.

"Though I regret I cannot escape all the paperwork that needs attention, if you would like, ladies, I will steal an hour before luncheon and give you a tour of Lindall Manor. Some of the rooms are quite impressive now that they've been restored.''

"I'm certain they are, Creag, but I'm rather weary from our journey north. I imagine, however, Catherine would enjoy it,'' replied Alma Grayson, as determined in her own way as Jeanne Donnachy to throw the pair together. To her way of thinking, if Catherine wanted C. Robertson Blake, and Bartholomew agreed, there was no earthly reason why the girl shouldn't have him, and his fortune. Besides, knowing her daughter, once they were back in Philadelphia, she would have the man tamed in no time.

"That would be wonderful, Creag,'' simpered the blonde, fluttering her eyelashes at the financier. Her mother had been right as usual, Catherine thought. Creag wouldn't remain indifferent to her for long, not when the only other women he saw were servants who undoubtedly possessed none of the feminine wiles at her disposal. "Shall I meet you in your study?''

"Why don't I stop back here for you about eleven?'' he suggested, quite happy to postpone the activity as long as possible. Suddenly, however, he noticed his steward lingering in the hall, and a desire to irritate her forced him to continue. "Catherine, my dear, I am sorry if you feel I've neglected you. I promise to clear my calendar for tomorrow and we can take a picnic up to the meadow near the loch. It's so peaceful there, it makes you forget the unpleasant obligations of life.'' Unless you carry them with you, he thought to himself, already regretting his impulsive idea.

As Catherine gushed enthusiastically over the prospect of such a romantic afternoon, Creag stole a glance at the door and was rewarded with a glimpse of Jeanne, her cheeks flushed with color.

"Fine, fine, I'll see you later then,'' he interrupted, escaping Catherine's clutches to hurry after the departing brunette.

"Miss Donnachy,'' he called sharply to halt her rapid retreat.

"Yes?'' Jeanne stopped reluctantly and waited for him to join her. She couldn't imagine the reason for her sudden upset at hearing Creag's plans. He was renewing his attraction for Catherine. Wasn't that the whole premise of the council's plan? Why then was she feeling so out of sorts? "You wanted me?''

"Merely to inform you that if you wish the details of my social engagements, you needn't listen at doors," the American
rebuked, hovering over her, his icy blue eyes challenging her to
deny the accusation. "You have only to ask, and I'd be more
than happy to tell you what Catherine said over dinner, how her
head barely reaches my shoulder, or how her kisses compare to
yours—"

"I have absolutely no interest in your affairs, past or present," Jeanne snapped, her heightened color giving lie to her
words. Indeed, with Creag standing so close to her, she had to
struggle not to fall victim to his masculine presence. He had
wronged her, the brunette reminded herself; for the good of
Linclachan she had to remember that.

"Oh, that's right. I'd forgotten. Your interest in me ended
when the repairs on the manor and the village did," said the
laird softly, measuring her reaction.

His mocking accusation wounded Jeanne as no chastise-
ment could have and she had to fight for control, to avoid saying something she'd regret. True, she'd told him that falsehood,
but did he have to accept it so readily? Didn't he know her better than that?

"Unless you'd like to change that story?" Creag pressed,
wanting nothing more than to crush her in his arms and make
her see how good they had been together.

"No," she replied quietly, refusing to meet his eyes.

"All right, then. Prepare a picnic basket for tomorrow, and
make it special," he ordered in exasperation, turning toward his
study and a temporary respite from the exasperating world of
females.

"It will be that, indeed, Creag," Jeanne murmured, wondering how the council would try to make Catherine hate the
countryside they all enjoyed so much. Well, that was their
problem. Hers was merely throwing Catherine and Creag together, and that she'd been doing. The rest was up to Malcolm
and the others.

Again Jeanne had surprised him, Creag thought in bewilderment the next day, as he examined the splendid luncheon she
had organized. While Catherine reclined on the blanket his
steward had suggested he bring along, he unpacked not only a

bouquet of flowers but a bottle of mead and glasses, in addition to the well-appointed menu consisting of everything from cold poached salmon to cheese and crackers and cakes drenched with honey for dessert. And all of it too good for Catherine Grayson.

Could Jeanne sincerely want him to succeed in his supposed quest of the blonde? he wondered, the possibility frightening him. The American socialite was so shallow and self-centered compared to Jeanne . . . couldn't the Scot realize that he still wanted her, not Catherine?

"Creag, I'm getting awfully lonely over here by myself," Catherine said with a pout, patting the plaid next to her. "Won't you join me? The food can wait awhile."

"I thought you might enjoy some crackers and mead—"

"Mead? What pray tell is that?" Catherine asked, eyeing the glasses of pale golden liquid rather suspiciously. "You wouldn't be trying to get me drunk to have your way with me?"

"Heavens, no," he said, handing her a glass, his voice scornful.

"Well, Father always warned me about the dangers of liquor," she said defensively.

"This is a mild honeyed wine, quite pleasant, and harmless to your reputation," asserted Creag as he sat down on the other side of the blanket. "Take a sip."

"Oh, you're right, it is nice. I know, let's drink to us," she demanded, lifting the mead heavenward. "To a love that transcends separation by time, oceans and land."

"Certainly not! Besides, love is such a fickle passion," Creag reflected, thinking of his feisty steward and not realizing he spoke aloud. "It can so easily turn to hatred without warning."

"What?" Catherine cried in surprise, spilling the wine on her pale pink dress. "Do you hate me then?"

"No, though your appearance at Lindall displeased me," the laird said, even more put out by the recollection that this picnic had been his idea. True, he had planned the outing with the intention of irritating Jeanne, but he had not meant to actually hurt Catherine, merely make her go away. He had no proof she was privy to her father's threats. Besides, hadn't he used her enough already, initially agreeing to her trip to Scotland where he had meant to woo her as his wife? Could he really fault her for continuing the journey she had begun, though his mind had changed? Determined to make it up to her, Creag soothed his insult.

"No one could hate you," he said, "but a relationship between us wouldn't work, I fear. Scotland has changed that."

"Then, come home with us. Your manor is pretty, but it's so far from everything. There's no real city, no shops, how could anyone live here?" she asked urgently, not noticing the resentment in his expression.

"The Donnachys and Robertsons seem to do well enough, and have done so for centuries," he defended coldly, looking out over the loch. Though he was not surprised at her dissatisfaction with Linclachan, it pained him to hear anyone disparage it.

"Yes, but they haven't been exposed to the education or culture our class has enjoyed," Catherine said, trusting her inclusion of Creag with the Graysons would ease the tightness about his mouth. "It's fine for them, they don't know any better. But you and I, we could never live here, not happily."

Before Creag could reply, Catherine began to scream, and he turned around in astonishment as bees swarmed over her.

"Creag, oh, help me, oh, for Lord's sake, Creag, do something! Get them off me!"

It was the strangest thing he'd ever seen in his entire life, as Creag told Malcolm and the council that evening once Leslie had treated Catherine's stings and administered a potion to calm her nerves.

"From out of nowhere, a huge swarm of honeybees approached and headed straight for her as though she were the sweetest flower in all the meadow. All at once, she was a sobbing mass of swirling insects, their hum warring with her cries of fright."

"*You* weren't stung, were you?" questioned the council elder, pleased the plan had worked so well. Between Maggie's rubbing clover all over the girl's clothes and preparing the sweet menu to attract the bees from Fergus's old hives, while Leslie had contributed an extremely saccharine perfume, they had hoped to leave nothing to chance, but one never knew.

"No, maybe because she had spilled the mead on her gown, the bees went after her first. I can't explain it." Creag shook his head.

"Well, it was quick thinking of you to get her in the loch so fast or she might really have been stung to pieces," praised Duncan. "I mean, a few stings about her mouth, that's not a tragedy. She'll recover."

"She wouldn't put her head underwater," explained the laird with a rueful chuckle. The image of the bees swarming about Catherine's blond head as she refused to follow his advice and duck her head beneath the water was one that would remain with him long beyond the swelling on her face, but one she'd never find half as amusing as he, Creag mused. For an instant, he longed to share the memory with Jeanne, but then he shook his head, erasing the notion, and rose from the table.

"I'd best go look in on Catherine, excuse me," he said, leaving the council members to their drinks.

"Good work, Malcolm," complimented Geordie, raising a glass in his direction once Creag had left them alone.

"Aye, who would have thought my beekeeping talents would help our cause?"

"The cause of right can never be lost, and Creag, good as he's been to us, must take that girl and go back to the States," reminded Duncan solemnly. "Whatever the bees did to help, all the better. We can't let him interfere with our lives."

"Don't forget it was my whisky keg that we used to transport the hive," warned Jamie. "I had to bottle its whisky almost six months early, and I don't want any complaints that the vintage isn't up to par."

"It's a wonder the bees weren't too drunk to attack." Geordie chortled. "But now, don't *you* forget to retrieve that keg before Creag gets it in his head to look over the scene again tomorrow. It wouldn't do for him to suspect the bees didn't happen to the meadow by themselves."

"Aye, he might blame Jeanne, and she seems unhappy enough of late," agreed Duncan. "Come along, Jamie, let's see to it now while Malcolm arranges our next surprise for Miss Grayson."

* * *

Catherine woke with a start, cursing whatever had drawn her out of Creag's affectionate embrace and back into the empty bedroom. In her dream, Creag had been unceasingly solicitous, nearly out of his head with concern that his picnic might have marred her beauty, even temporarily. Though she knew that wasn't the case, she'd felt it wouldn't hurt the man to feel a little guilty for a while. Indeed, the laird of her imagination sat beside her faithfully, entertaining her, and most important, he was more interested in her welfare than any business affairs! When she had assured him that she was fine and there'd be no scars, his smile could have lit the world. In her dream, she'd closed her eyes as he had leaned forward to kiss her, but then nothing happened, and when she'd opened her eyes to learn why, she was back in bed alone in the dim light of early dawn.

Sighing in disappointment at the phantom laird's fickle nature, so like the real one, Catherine snuggled deeper into the reassuring warmth of the bedclothes and concentrated on Creag's attentiveness, rare though it was. She had expected him to kiss her yesterday in the meadow's summer sunshine, but first the mead and then the bees had interfered. Surely that was the reason he had resisted her.

Suddenly she heard a noise in the room. Oh, he is here, she thought with a sudden shiver of delight as she sensed warm breath on her face. She would play possum and let him steal a kiss, Catherine decided impishly, hard-put not to giggle and alert him to her wakefulness. Dying to open her eyes, she resisted the temptation and waited for the sweet embrace she anticipated, intending to return it quite warmly. Suddenly, however, she felt a wet slobbering on her cheek.

Opening her eyes wide, Catherine greeted the sight of a large black-faced ram looming over her, one of her favorite bonnets resting lopsidedly over one horn. With her typical aplomb, she screamed loudly.

"Help! Help! Somebody get this animal out of here before it eats me alive," she yelled, inching up toward the head of the bed and cursing the bed draperies she'd refused to have closed. "Someone, please help me!"

Her door was ajar, they should have no trouble hearing her, Catherine thought, anxiously watching her woolly visitor for signs of an impending attack. The sheep, however, seemed unaffected by her shrill cries and stood placidly, staring fixedly at her, its dark eyes unblinking and intense.

"Shoo—go home now. You don't belong here, go home," she shouted, absurdly trying to reason with the creature. Grabbing one of the feather pillows, she took aim and lobbed it at the animal. "Scat!"

But the ram merely watched docilely as the airborne missile approached, turning its head just once, to catch the edge of the pillow on its horn, deflecting it and sending hundreds of feathers spilling from the ticking. Instantly Catherine began to sneeze uncontrollably as bits of down settled in her hair and all over the bed.

"Help—achoo—somebody, anybody, help me! Mother!" she called, her voice cracking between sneezes as she contemplated her sad fate if the vicious intruder turned its horns on her. "Please, somebody, save me!"

At last the door opened fully as several servants entered and surveyed the scene, each struggling to contain his laughter as Catherine grew more and more indignant.

"Do something, for heaven's sake! Don't just stand there and snicker! Hasn't the earl taught you better than that? The wretched wool bag over there is nesting in my best silk dressing gown and wearing my favorite hat. Achoo. Take care of it!"

"I'll rescue your hat," promised Ewan, fighting his own amusement, "but I don't hold much hope for the gown. The ram has—"

"Just get that thing out of here," Catherine demanded, on her knees at the head of the bed, her back pressed firmly against the bed frame. That was the moment when Jeanne entered.

"Randy, come out of there," the steward ordered firmly. The sheep, however, looked at her blandly and sat down on the soiled robe. "Oh, come on, don't be stubborn. You're not a mule. You're a soft, cuddly, overgrown lamb. But Fergus is dead and you can't just wander around the manor the way you used to. Back downstairs and outside, now!"

As Jeanne approached it, the ram watched curiously and then stretched its neck to be nuzzled, but the brunette was having none of its games. Quickly she smacked its rump and simultaneously pushed the creature forward. In an instant, complaining loudly, it was nonetheless moving toward the door, still attired in Catherine's bonnet and dragging her dressing gown on one hoof.

"I'm sorry, Miss Grayson," said Jeanne, shooing Lindall's servants from the room, as well. "My grandfather treated that old thing as a pet and let it roam the manor. Creag doesn't, of course, but it takes time for everyone, animals included, to learn new patterns of behavior. I'll see to replacing your hat and bonnet."

"Don't bother," replied Catherine haughtily. "I doubt there would be anything of similar quality in your little town. Creag will buy me something new in London."

"Very well," agreed the brunette, her cheeks flaming at the woman's insolence. How could C. Robertson Blake ever have fallen for such a witch? she wondered, not for the first time. Still, his affection for Catherine was the key the council hoped would remove him from Linclachan, and it was her duty to try to encourage their match.

"Oh, Miss Grayson, if you are up to it, I believe Creag plans to go fishing this afternoon."

"I hate fishing."

"He's built a delightful pavilion at the head of the old salmon stream. You could enjoy the air and keep him company while he fished," suggested Jeanne. "Aren't women supposed to be interested in their men's activities?"

"But the sun—"

"Isn't very strong in the Highlands, and you could always take a parasol."

"I'll give it some thought," conceded Catherine, clearly not thrilled with the idea but weighing the effect it would have on Creag if she did accompany him. It might be the romantic moment she'd been waiting for, but she'd have to be certain all the swelling was gone from her face.

"As you wish then. Good morning," said Jeanne, glad to escape Catherine's company and catch up with Ewan.

* * *

"Randy managed to get into Catherine's bedroom?" Maggie laughed when she heard about it. "Imagine that. Was she very upset?"

"When I arrived, she was shivering in absolute terror," recalled Jeanne with a chuckle, "panicked at what the vicious creature might do next."

"But still worried about her wardrobe," added Ewan, grinning at the memory. "I'd best take Randy back to Malcolm's pasture and give him some extra tender shoots as a reward. He did a fine job for Linclachan, and Malcolm will be pleased."

"Aye, but will Creag when he hears about Catherine's latest adventure?" wondered Jeanne, dreading the explosion if the laird ever suspected these accidents had been arranged by the council.

But it wasn't until late morning that Creag summoned her.

"Catherine informs me that you told her about the summer pavilion?" he asked, his blue eyes dark and unreadable.

"Aye. I thought you would enjoy her company," Jeanne explained. "She could always take a book along and read it if she doesn't want to fish."

"Like *Jane Eyre,* perhaps?" Creag suggested, pleased when Jeanne flushed at the mention of the book he'd spent hours reading to her.

"Whatever she likes." Not willing to be baited, the brunette stood quietly, awaiting his next words. What she didn't expect, however, was an apology of sorts for Catherine.

"I want you to know I realize Catherine can be difficult at times, but she doesn't know any better. Since her parents are only concerned with financial reputations and social position, no one has ever taught her how to love."

"Then you have quite a difficult job ahead of you," she retorted coldly, livid that Creag was so concerned for his fiancée's feelings while he thought so little of his steward's. Damn him, why should she always have to be the understanding one? She had her own life to straighten out and she didn't need him making her feel guilty about it. "If that's all, I have work to do."

"Very well," he said sadly, frowning as she left the room. Damn, but Jeanne Donnachy was a stubborn woman.

Clearly, the fire in her heart had been sparked by Catherine's arrival and announcement that she was his fiancée. While he had hoped her quick temper would cool with time so that he could explain the truth of the matter, it seemed the flames were only growing hotter with each exposure to the woman she thought was her rival. Hadn't Jeanne told him not long after his arrival that the clan slogan was "Fierce When Roused"? That suited his steward perfectly, he mused.

Indeed, by the time he finally succeeded in dispatching the Graysons for home, he wondered if things could ever be the same between him and Jeanne. Idly he reached into his pocket and withdrew the ring he'd purchased in London. Watching it twinkle as he moved it to catch the sun's rays, he vowed not to rest until he'd at least shown it to Jeanne, even if she threw it in his face. As his old grandmother would have said, the Fates will out, there's no point in worrying. A lesson he'd not learned well enough.

The sunny cheerfulness of the early summer afternoon mocked her own desolation, Jeanne thought resentfully, as she sat on a rock at the edge of the pasture, lambs frolicking in the distance. After all, how could the earth breed such unrestricted joy when she knew nothing but utter unhappiness?

These past few days had been the most miserable of her life. Not only was she forced to live with the evidence of Creag's perfidy, she was obligated by her duties to the clan to play matchmaker between the treacherous financier and the condescending debutante from Philadelphia. Worst and most shameful of all, however, was while she did so, she was filled with regret and a longing for Creag so demanding that neither her intellect nor her pride could squelch it.

Throwing back her head and closing her eyes, Linclachan's steward allowed the sun to shine upon her face in the weary hope that the fiery rays could heal her soul as well as warm her body. Escaped for the moment from the agony of watching Catherine Grayson flutter her lashes coquettishly at Creag, Jeanne wanted nothing more than she wanted peace. Concentrating on the smells and sounds around her, she gave herself over to nature, thinking it might quiet the pain in her heart.

The heather was grown tall now, but it would be a while before it was in flower, its rich purple blooms painting the hillsides in splashes of dramatic color. The sight had never failed to stir Jeanne's spirits, and with her eyes closed as they were, she could recall its glory, promising herself that the flowering was not all that distant. But, unfortunately, conjuring up images of the coming heather brought Jeanne more unsettlement than she already knew. Surely by the time the countryside was ablaze with the flowering plants, C. Robertson Blake would be long gone from Lindall Manor and gone, too, from her own life.

The thought was a horrifying one. Yet, Jeanne reminded herself, in the ancient pattern of nature's bounty, didn't life and beauty always arise from the death and harshness of winter? Would her own life then be so very different? Surely it, too, would transcend this barren emptiness she felt so that she could know happiness once more.

While such a thing was hard to accept at that instant, it eased Jeanne's grief a bit to imagine that once this debacle was behind her, the future might still hold grand things. And though she didn't know if she could really believe such platitudes, the feisty Scot tried to pretend that she did. Suddenly her mouth curved slightly upward, and if her smile was an exceedingly sad one, it was a smile all the same.

"I want to speak with you, Jeanne," intruded masculine tones that eradicated the little comfort her solitude had bought her.

Opening her eyes and turning in the direction of the man who addressed her, the striking brunette was disheartened to discover that she had recognized the voice correctly. When would Andrew Robertson accept the fact that she wanted nothing more to do with him other than what the manor's legal dealings demanded?

"Any business you have, Andrew, is to be conducted with the laird," she stated firmly. "At the moment I believe he is in the house."

"Aye, I know well enough where the man is. It's you I want a word with, lass," the intruder persisted, his tone more demanding than Jeanne had ever heard it. Usually his aggressiveness was hidden behind a deferential and fawning facade.

What could have given him the courage he now seemed to possess, Jeanne wondered idly, unless it was an overabundance of Jamie's drink?

"I can't think of anything we have to discuss between us," she said, rising from her rocky perch, ready to return to her home. Her life was unpleasant enough at the moment without having to contend with Linclachan's bothersome solicitor. He was a burden she did not need, and refused to accept.

"Hold on, Jeanne," the arrogant man of law ordered, reaching out to place a restraining hand around her arm. "I said we're going to talk."

Startled, Jeanne found Andrew's touch to be none too gentle, and she looked from his trespassing fingers to the man's determined face. Gone was any pretense of solicitude. In its place was a hardened glare, abetted by a contemptuous sneer.

"Take your hands off me, Andrew," Jeanne ordered with quiet dignity. "You've no cause to touch me."

"You're right," he responded without loosening his hold, as the phrase, *not yet anyway,* danced through his feverish thoughts.

"Then let me go," Jeanne demanded, her eyes glazing with fury. How dare this vile male be so presumptuous!

"I can't do that until you hear me out without scampering away as usual," Andrew pronounced. "What I have to say is too important to be ignored, and this is one time, lassie, you had better realize it."

"That sounds like a threat, and I don't put up with threats from any man," Jeanne said, her voice dangerously soft.

"You'll put up with this one and more unless you want to see the manor and Linclachan destitute once again," the solicitor stated, his fingers tightening so that Jeanne had all she could do not to wince.

"You're a fool, man, and you'll regret treating me with such disrespect," Jeanne spat.

"No, I'm not the idiot others have assumed me to be, and it's you who will be showing me more deference from now on. That is, if you would like your home to survive."

"What have you to do with the manor or the village? Creag is the laird, and it's his whim that will decide what happens here."

"Aye," Andrew replied, "so long as he is laird. But what would happen to this place if he wasn't in control any longer?"

"What do you mean?" Jeanne asked anxiously, the words tumbling out quickly, one upon the other.

"Only that Linclachan and the manor are not his by right," the solicitor answered scornfully. "I know it all, Jeanne. He's no more one of us than that Philadelphian chit who has come to lead him to the altar."

"You're daft!" the willowy steward asserted. "Creag's grandfather shares our bloodlines."

"It's no use, Jeanne. Give it up. I've researched the matter, and I know what I know," Andrew said, taking the liberty of snaking his other arm around his prisoner's waist. "Think of what your *laird*'s reaction would be, to discover he had been taken for a fool by a covey of provincial Scots. He'd leave here in fury, dragging his American bride-to-be, and withdrawing all his support. Then where would your precious Lindall Manor and Linclachan be?"

To Jeanne's mind, Andrew's outrageously intimate gesture supported his confident claim. He knew something to be sure. He was too craven a creature to risk offending her in such a manner if he were not certain of his facts. As it was, the paunchy legal extortionist appeared to feel that there was nothing that was not his for the taking, and Jeanne read such an attitude as an ominous sign, indeed.

"Andrew, I repeat, you are mistaken," Jeanne said through gritted teeth. "Now let me go."

"Och! So you know nothing about it, my bonny Jeanne?" he taunted her. "Then perhaps you would like to accompany me to the manor, and you can learn all as I explain it to the man who has falsely been installed as the earl of Lindall."

"No!" Jeanne cried. "You can't do that!"

"Oh, but I can. And I will, unless you say something that will deter me," he said with a cruel smile.

Silence filled the glen for a moment as Jeanne struggled with her temper, attempting to balance loyalty to her home and clan with her fearsome pride. She was not a woman to be manipulated, and yet, if she didn't listen to what Andrew had to say, and mouth agreement, Linclachan would be doomed once more, and all her sacrifices, all her pain, would have been for naught.

"What is it you want?" she finally asked, her face stony and her voice as hard as granite.

"Not much at all. I'm a reasonable man. Surely you know that," Andrew Robertson stated with a laugh. "I simply want to see that imposter gone back to America, and in his absence to serve as your adviser in administering Lindall Manor and its lands."

"I don't understand."

"Let the clod continue in his delusions. His money makes life here a bit easier, and it is no difference to me who bears the title, as long as I wield the power. But with Blake in residence, there's no chance of that. The man has not even spoken to me about retaining my legal services though I have tried to broach the subject on more than one occasion. Oddly enough, he prefers to have all of his work done by someone in Glasgow. But once the outlander goes home and charges you with maintaining the manor, you can choose me to again be the estate's legal representative.

"That's all I want, Jeanne," Andrew said innocently, though his eyes roving freely over her body told Fergus's granddaughter a different story. "And quite a bargain it is you're getting, considering what I know," he added, watching her intently for a sign of what she was feeling. If he could get the wench to agree to this now, what couldn't he get from her in time to come? As spouse of the steward, he'd live in the manor yet, or else he would see to it that there was no Linclachan Manor and no Linclachan, as well.

"But why talk to me about this?" Jeanne asked, fighting to conceal the revulsion rising in her throat as a result of Robertson's salacious manner. "If you have something to say, why not go to the council?"

"Taking my case to those old fools is not in my best interest. And for that reason, you won't seek them out, either. Do so, and I talk to Blake. It's that simple," he responded with a superior air, as though he had given the matter much thought and could find no flaw in his logic. "Then, we would all be back where we were before he came here, or perhaps a bit worse off. After all, it would be hard for the villagers to give up the wee comforts the American has brought with him.''

"But what have you to gain by going to Creag with this story of yours?'' Jeanne asked, not willing to commit herself to his scheme but yet not daring enough to send Andrew on his way.

"Nothing,'' he replied with a mocking grin. "But then, I've nothing to lose, either. 'Tis said in the village, his country-woman abhors the Highlands. If Blake leaves here with the intention of wedding her, I doubt we will ever be bothered by him again. He won't bring his bride back to a place she detests. But time is running out, and I can't wait forever for the man to make up his mind. I want you to do whatever it takes to get rid of him. Make him leave the manor, and give him no reason to return,'' Andrew said meaningfully.

"I have no influence to make Creag do anything,'' Jeanne protested. "I can't force him to leave.''

"Find some method that will work,'' the solicitor com-manded. "Otherwise, he'll be going anyway, but he'll be tak-ing his money with him.''

"All right. I'll see what I can do,'' Jeanne said reluctantly. All that was required was to humor this man until Creag left Lindall Manor, which by the looks of Catherine's ever-widening smiles would be shortly. Then she'd go to Jamie and the oth-ers, Jeanne vowed, and Andrew Robertson would rue the day he had ever come to her with such a proposition.

She had just come to this decision, and was in the process of prying herself from the varlet's hold, when she heard herself being summoned, the icy quality of the tones calling her coil-ing round her heart and causing it to restrict.

"Jeanne Donnachy! Perhaps you can disentangle yourself from that man's embrace and meet with Michael in my study. He has some figures he wants to review with you,'' intoned the laird of Linclachan, his disapproval all too evident.

With a start, Jeanne slipped from Andrew's suddenly loos-ened grasp and scampered toward the house, her cheeks burn-ing with flame.

Creag stood regarding her as she went, maddeningly curi-ous about just what he had interrupted here, yet loath to ad-mit as much. He had always been under the impression that Jeanne's opinion of Linclachan's solicitor was much the same as his own. Yet there she had stood, wrapped in the man's arms, with nary a struggle in sight.

Was the whole thing a ploy to make him jealous, or was Jeanne perhaps fonder of the solicitor than she had let on? Remembering the way the man had leered at her during the kilting ceremony and then lingered in the sickroom, Creag's anger grew. The thought of an affinity existing between the pair was one he found disturbing in the extreme. Pushing a hand distractedly through his thick golden hair, Creag realized he didn't at all like the idea of Jeanne Donnachy being linked with Andrew Robertson. Especially, when, as near as Creag could tell, the solicitor was most likely behind the disappearance of the missing ten thousand pounds. It needed only a little more proof until Robertson was actually charged with the theft, and that should be forthcoming shortly.

But in the meantime, it didn't speak well for Jeanne to be associated with the man, especially if she had hidden a relationship with him. What would be her purpose in doing so, Creag asked himself, unless she was somehow involved? After all, she had been a virgin when she had come to him. And then he shook his head in disbelief at the direction in which his thoughts had led him. He recalled the shy, gentle, laughing Jeanne of the *lin*, and he knew such a woman could never be less than the open, loving spirit she had been that day. Jeanne and Andrew Robertson involved in a conspiracy? The idea was absurd! It had to be the Highland air affecting him adversely for such a ludicrous thought to form in his head. He could think of nothing else to account for such a phenomenon. Certainly his own befuddled state since the stately brunette had put an end to things between them had nothing to do with it, he assured himself.

Turning to confront Andrew Robertson, and thus find an outlet for the anger he felt, Creag was not at all surprised to discover the man gone. A flash of color in the distance just disappearing behind a small stand of trees attested to the fact that some things never changed. The solicitor was a coward, no matter how he was viewed. It was only too bad, Creag thought as he started on his way back to the manor, that he couldn't correctly gauge Jeanne's nature, as well. Perhaps Michael had been correct, or at least partially so, Creag amended. When it came to the female portion of the world's population, he hadn't the slightest notion of their complicated natures at all.

Chapter Sixteen

Later that same evening, Leslie was startled to find Jeanne in her stillroom, rummaging through the packets of powders, obviously looking for something.

"I...I'm sorry. I shouldn't be here," said the blushing steward, clearly embarrassed at having been discovered. "There used to be a peppermint and chamomile tea I found helpful for sleeping. I wanted to get some without bothering you."

"You know you can help yourself anytime," assured Leslie, distressed at the dark circles below Jeanne's eyes and the timid manner in which she apologized. Jeanne Donnachy was the Lindall Manor steward; she had the right and obligation to go everywhere in the manor. Why was she suddenly so unsure of herself? Hoping to soothe the brunette's mood, Leslie spoke of the day's excitement. "Did you hear about Catherine's latest accident?"

"At the pavilion when one of the railings came loose as she leaned on it and she tumbled forward into the mud and then rolled into the water when she tried to stand in her tight skirt?"

"Aye, there have been no others since dinner that I know of," replied Maggie's niece, handing Jeanne the powders she'd wanted. "That poor woman has the worst luck."

"But she also has Creag," whispered Jeanne, unable to stop her tears from falling as she admitted the cause of her pain. "Oh, Leslie, I honestly thought I could live with his choosing another woman over me, but—"

"You love him," finished her friend, wrapping an arm around Jeanne's shoulder and drawing her close. "It isn't too late, you know. Tell him so. If you explain how you really feel—"

"No, I couldn't," murmured the Donnachy steward, trying to still her futile tears. "He obviously cares for Catherine. Only this morning, he was explaining away her faults, trying to convince me to like the girl, I suppose. Thanks for caring, Leslie, but Creag's made his choice and I'll have to accept it."

Not if I talk to Maggie, and she goes to the council, thought Leslie, determined that Jeanne should find as true a love with Creag as she had with Michael. Perhaps a love potion...

"No. Absolutely not! Woman, you must have lost your mind to think we'd do that," exploded Jamie when Maggie explained the problem. "We cannot allow Creag to remain in Linclachan to marry Jeanne."

"I told you I thought the lass was unhappy," said Duncan. "I say if she wants the laird, we should let her have him."

"But the whisky," protested Jamie, his tone aghast. "What about our whisky? If Creag stays here, he'll not forget about the factories he wants—"

"As good as your whisky may be—" began Maggie.

"It's damned good," snorted Jamie indignantly.

"Aye, there's none better," soothed the old woman, shaking her head at the men's failure to see that Jeanne was more important than any liquor. The devil take their whisky, she fumed, knowing better than to voice such sentiments aloud. "Still, you've often said you love Jeanne like your own granddaughter—"

"Of course. We all do," agreed Jamie.

"Then doesn't her happiness count for more than Creag's far-off schemes of manufacturing? After all, he's talking at least ten or twelve years down the road," Maggie reminded them. "We could all be dead and buried then, and your whisky will have died with you."

"When the time comes, I'll train someone to take over," protested Jamie. "The secret won't die with me."

"If you're going to share it anyway, why not train Creag, or a man of his choosing now?" suggested the white-haired female. When Jamie made no immediate protest, she knew she'd won, for the moment at least. "Now, as I said before, we must—"

"Send that Grayson woman packing," agreed Malcolm. "I wager she already hates Linclachan with all the 'accidents' she's been having. What else can we do?"

"We can make her hate the laird, or at least question spending the rest of her life with him."

"As long as he has money, that may be hard to do," voiced Geordie.

"Not really," said Maggie softly, reaching for the whisky Jamie had poured. "Among other things, we could let her know how much Creag has spent on Linclachan and how much more he's promised to contribute, but, whatever we do, Jeanne can't know anything about it."

"All right, to Jeanne," proposed Jamie, lifting his glass. "May she bring happiness to us all, the laird included."

"And to the man who's stolen her heart," added Malcolm, before swigging a generous portion. "Now, what is it we can do?"

A few hours later, the elders of the council had formulated their plan.

"Now let me see if I ken the situation correctly," Malcolm said for the third time that afternoon as he ran his hand doubtfully through his thinning silver hair. "Before Maggie came to see us, we were trying to make the American wench hate the Highlands but love Creag so that they would leave, get married, and he would never return to the village and interfere with the whisky production. But we still would have had his financial support?"

"Aye," responded Jamie patiently, though in reality he felt no tolerance at all for the herdsman's nonsense. Malcolm was a mere three years older than he. The man had absolutely no excuse for being so addlepated.

"And now..." Duncan prompted.

"Now..." Malcolm continued slowly, "we are still trying to make the foreign female hate the Highlands, but we want her to detest Creag, as well, so she'll leave and he will stay behind to marry Jeanne."

"That's it!" Geordie praised loudly.

"But if the lad remains, what about our whisky?" Malcolm asked stubbornly. "That's the part that evades me."

"It's still open to question," Jamie answered truthfully, a look of consternation adding lines to his already wrinkled face. "But it might be that we could talk the laird into distilling what he wants for market, and allowing us to continue making the stuff for our own consumption as we always have."

"We don't know for certain? Then why are we working so hard on getting the laird to stay?" the eldest councilman asked skeptically.

"For our Jeanne," Duncan said. "Even Jamie agrees that the lassie's happiness is worth the gamble."

"Ah, youngsters! Sometimes they are more trouble than they're worth," Malcolm muttered.

"Now, now, you won't be saying that when you're dangling Jeanne and Creag's bairn on your knee," Geordie offered by way of consolation.

"Aye, I suppose not," the feisty councilman conceded. "But what are we going to do to make Creag unattractive to the Grayson chit? The lad's a brawny one, and personable at that."

"We're going to drink him into oblivion for a start, and deliver him back to the manor well into his cups," Jamie informed him. "If we have to undertake the job of making him appear unsuitable as a future husband, we may as well get some personal enjoyment from it."

"But the laird has already proven he can hold his own against us," Duncan protested even as he silently admitted the scheme definitely had its merits.

"Aye, but it has always been the four of us at one time against him," Jamie replied, a gleam in his eyes. "What if we were to stagger our appearances at the table? Then the man would have to outlast four practiced drinkers. I doubt even Creag could do that!"

"It's worth a try," Malcolm admitted, his mouth already beginning to feel dry. "When is the great event to take place?"

"As soon as I can summon the poor, unsuspecting fellow to my home. If we're all agreed, I'll send the message immediately. The rest of you can leave and show up an hour or two apart. What say you then, for Linclachan and bonny Jeanne?" Jamie asked, raising a glass for practice.

"Aye!"
"Aye!"
"Aye!"

As much as Creag needed a breath of fresh air, he was almost loath to leave the sanctuary of his study and stroll the manor's now pruned and cultivated gardens, afraid Catherine would pounce on him the moment she spied him. He'd done as Grayson had demanded and spent time with Catherine, knowing full well that, as he had anticipated, each moment in her company, rather than reviving his previous interest in her, intensified his dislike of the avaricious American socialite. Surely Catherine's father had to realize his hopes were not bearing fruit. Yet, Creag acknowledged, until he was certain Grayson couldn't endanger his plans for Linclachan's future, he'd have to be prepared to be ambushed by Catherine.

With a mighty sigh of exasperation, he wished Jeanne would present him with the same problem. Initially, when this fiasco began, she had stood her ground whenever he was in her presence, and returned his inquisitive glance with a haughty stare. But since yesterday when he had come upon her in Andrew Robertson's embrace, he had barely seen her, as though she were purposefully staying out of his sight. The only way he knew she was still in residence in the manor was from the stacks of accounts she left on his desk, and Catherine's constant chatter about his disloyal steward's suggestions for romantic outings.

Damn, but it was a curious thing! Although in his heart he was certain of her innocence in the matter of the missing money, he was still at odds over the scene he had interrupted on the hillside. His blood boiled with the thought that his lovely Highlander might have actually turned to the solicitor for comfort after their argument. But what else could explain what he had witnessed? The recollection of the willowy Jeanne in Andrew's arms had eaten at him for the past twenty-odd hours until he was more a bear than not. But still, he could reach no conclusion and he was finding it more and more difficult to bide his time with the Graysons while the instructions he had sent to Glasglow, to counter Bartholomew Grayson's threats, were carried out. Rising from his desk and deciding to chance a bit of time out-of-doors, he thought he would ponder the situation as he walked.

However, there was to be no time for such meditation. Before he reached the door, a sharp rap signaled a visitor. It was one of the village children with a cryptic note from Jamie about some sudden and mysterious problem that needed the laird's attention immediately. With an audible sigh, Creag set out for Linclachan. He might not be the true laird, and he might be beset with troubles of his own, but he couldn't refuse a cry for aid from a member of the clan. He'd do what he could.

"Now, what is it that's so important?" Creag asked, walking into Jamie's small abode to find the man sitting morosely at the table, a bottle of whisky and glasses set before him.

"Och, I'll need a drink or two before I can discuss it, 'tis that bad," Jamie replied, pouring a generous measure of the amber liquid for himself and his guest. "You will bend an elbow with me, won't you?"

"Aye," said Creag, unconsciously picking up the speech of the Highlands in his anxiety. "But what can be so terrible that you can't bring yourself to mention it?"

"After the whisky calms my heart and makes the telling easier, I'll relate it to you in full," the distiller said, fixing his glance on the glass as he upended it and swallowed its contents in one gulp, encouraging Creag to do the same.

"It's not about Jeanne, is it? She hasn't been hurt again, has she?" Creag asked, viewing the glass in his hand with growing uncertainty.

"Nay, it concerns her not at all," the old man responded. "It has to do with the village."

"I see," Creag said, tilting back his head and swallowing the whisky with relief.

"Ah, but you don't, lad. And it is a matter of some grave concern—at least for those of us who inhabit Linclachan. Perhaps after another round, I might be able to start speaking of it," Jamie muttered pitifully, pouring out another liberal amount for each of them.

And so it went, with Creag prodding and Jamie, reluctant and evasive, refusing to delve into the heart of the matter, though more than willing to part with unstinting quantities of his best whisky. And as Creag lifted his glass, he thought it ironic that whatever the old Scot's dilemma, he had no inkling of the trouble actually facing his village.

After a few more drinks, a mellow Creag began to feel that he didn't really give a damn what Jamie's problem was. In all likelihood it was something that could be remedied quickly enough, he told himself, relishing the relaxing atmosphere of the cottage all the more for the tension rampant in his own domicile.

Perhaps, he thought rather happily, raising the glass to his lips yet again after a countless number of like actions, it was fortuitous for the council member to have summoned him, though he still had no reason why the man had done so. Whatever the turmoil might be, it was obvious that Jamie thought it could wait for a bit. Why not linger, then, and allow the potent alcohol to mitigate his own anxious discontent?

An hour or so later, Malcolm came calling, and joined the pair at the table. Though Jamie was forced by his advanced years to slow down his consumption of whisky, Malcolm arrived fresh. With good humor, the eldest member of the council urged the laird to keep pace with him as the bottle was drained of its contents, and another one brought forth.

Just when Creag was starting to find his thinking decidedly befuddled and was getting ready to depart for home, Duncan knocked at the door. It wouldn't do, the American was assured, to leave yet. Refusing to join the newcomer in a cup was akin to insult, and so the laird raised his glass again...and again...and he wasn't entirely sure, but perhaps once more after that, as well.

Time passed and finally Geordie entered his brother's house to see Creag swaying slightly but still in his chair. The old Scot's eyes glimmered with glee. This would be like taking candy from a baby, he thought, rubbing his hands together before reaching for the bottle and pouring himself and the laird a hearty drink.

Though they had thrown him in the back of a cart to transport him to the manor house and thus had saved themselves the worst of the job, the elderly council members found it no easy task to move Creag once the rustic vehicle had stopped before the manor's entrance way.

With great effort, they managed to hoist him upright, and it took their combined strength to keep him so, dragging him slowly up the steps and through Lindall's door. The job was made all the more difficult by the laird's newfound avocation. Suddenly the lad thought he was a singer, and the offended Scots had to suffer through countless repetitions of some sentimental song about a Jeannie with light brown hair. And this sung all the while at the top of the man's considerable lungs with their own ears only inches from his incessantly moving mouth.

"Now if you will come into my stillroom, I'll be able to mix that beauty cream tailored to your individual needs," Leslie was saying to Catherine and Alma Grayson. As planned, the herbalist's suggestion had been issued when she had heard the sound of the cart coming up the drive. Ushering her vain companions into the vestibule in time to see a very drunken earl of Lindall being carried into his home, Leslie had to smother her giggle at the Americans' reaction.

"Good Lord!" Alma gasped with a sidelong glance of warning at her daughter. "I've never seen the like!"

"Does he get this way often?" Catherine asked disdainfully, deploring the wealthy financier's choice of song as much as she did his descent into drunken revelry.

"Och, no!" Leslie hastened to assure them, her voice solemn. "No more than two or three times a week, anyway."

"I have quite reverted to our original position on the matter. I think Catherine's marriage to Blake is a foolish idea," Mrs. Grayson stated at the breakfast table the next morning. "A man who drinks to that extent will soon lose his fortune."

"Or be persuaded to put his money into our daughter's care," Mr. Grayson commented calmly, reaching for his coffee. "That is a possibility that still makes the match worthwhile. Besides, we don't really know that Blake drinks heavily as often as we have been led to believe. After all, we have been here almost a week, and this is the first sign we have seen of such decadent behavior."

"But what about all of the nights the man secluded himself in his study or his chambers, only to miss breakfast the next morning? Surely that suggests something," Alma persisted, more courageous than usual in the face of her husband's mounting irritation.

"It proves nothing. Now do as I tell you, Alma. If Catherine still wants the title and the fortune, I will stand behind her and so shall you. A little motherly advice on feminine wiles would not be amiss," he said emphatically, rising from the table and leaving the dining room.

"Well?" inquired the matron uncertainly, looking at her daughter. "Is this what you really want, my girl?"

"I am certain I can handle Creag once the title is mine. If I can't reform him, he will be easy enough to ignore should he continue to demonstrate a penchant for drinking until he passes out," Catherine said with a tilt of her pretty head. "The possibility of gaining control of his money is intriguing to say the least, but what if that is not the case? How do I know he will continue to be as generous as he was in London?"

"Bear the man an heir and he will shower you in riches. That much I know," Alma whispered, following her husband's directive. "Believe me, it is well worth the inconvenience."

"I suppose I could do that," Catherine said, considering the matter seriously. "And to tell you the truth, he isn't all that bad to look at, though he proves horribly obstinate at times. Yet, when all is said and done, I think I am still willing to accept C. Robertson Blake and his money. I am growing terribly impatient, however, waiting for him to decide once more he wants to wed me."

"There are ways to get around that, too," Alma said, blushing as she lowered her voice so that it was hardly audible, "if you take my meaning."

"Indeed I do," Catherine said practically. "Why, in fact, last night, I toyed with the idea of crawling into the man's bed."

"Catherine!"

"Well, why not?" the girl asked peevishly. "Creag was too drunk to be any real threat, but upon waking and finding me snuggled next to him, he would have had to do the honorable thing. The problem was, though, when I ventured into the hallway, I saw a fearsome Scot stationed outside Creag's door, and I had to abandon the idea. It was quite a pity, actually. Last night, drunk as he was, he would have been forced to believe any claims I made this morning.''

"Perhaps you should remember there are other methods you can try," Alma said brightly, desperate to change the topic. "A pretty smile is irresistible.''

"Oh, Mama, be reasonable. I've already told you it will take more than that and a flutter of lashes to ensnare the earl of Lindall," Catherine insisted, her pronouncement explaining satisfactorily, at least to herself, why she had failed in her efforts thus far. "But I am not giving up hope. With time, I shall think of something.''

"Ah, there you are, miss," Maggie said, shuffling into the room, a length of soft blue wool in her hands. "I found this in my sewing cabinet and it immediately put me in mind of your deep blue eyes. Who else should have it but you if you want it? No one could do it justice.''

"It is rather pretty," Catherine said, running her hands over the soft nap, convinced that the housekeeper had told the truth. "But what would I do with it?''

"Why, I would do all the doing that has to be done, miss. I was thinking perhaps a nice cloak to keep the damp night air off your chest. I'm not boasting when I say that I'm quite a fair hand at a needle and thread if I do say so myself. Why 'tis I who measured the laird for his kilt, stitching and cutting after I draped it over his person," Maggie fabricated, "so that it hugs his hips like a second skin. And a wondrous cloth garment it is, too.''

"This is an admirable piece of cloth," Catherine said, rising and holding it against her, waiting for her mother's approval as to the color. After all, her eyes did occasionally change shade.

At her mother's confirming nod, the girl gave the material back to the housekeeper. "All right. I'll allow you to stitch me a cloak," she said. "It may turn out passably well. And if it doesn't, I don't have to wear it. But I will be able to tell my friends that I have such a garment, woven by my own tenants and fashioned by my own Scottish seamstress.''

"Aye, miss. It would give me great pleasure to fashion something for you," Maggie commented, fighting to keep the true meaning of her words hidden. "Why, it would give me as much pleasure to sew for you, brave sweet lass that you are, as it did to make up the laird's kilt."

"Brave?" echoed Catherine.

"Sweet?" inquired Mrs. Grayson.

"Aye, there's not many a woman who would be willing to overlook the laird shortcomings if you ken what I mean."

"Are you referring to his drinking?" asked Catherine haughtily. "I assure you that after he marries me, the man will have no cause to drink himself to oblivion."

"Nay, it's his physical shortcomings I'm speaking of," Maggie said in a hushed whisper as she lowered her eyes delicately.

"His lordship is a strong, big man," Alma uttered in confusion, trying to make sense of what the woman was saying.

"Strong, aye! But big, no. Not after the accident. I could not help but notice when I fitted him for his kilt."

"What are you saying?" Mrs. Grayson asked, aghast, her face as ashen as her daughter's.

"Why, just that it's not every young girl who would be willing to sacrifice any hope of a family of her own in order to marry the man she truly loved ... in spite of it all. The situation can't help but put me in mind of Abélard and Héloïse. It's so tragically romantic, and you, miss, are as bonny a heroine as ever was."

"No wonder the man drinks! But to have never mentioned his affliction, delicate as it is!" Alma cried, taking her daughter by the hand and pulling her from the room. What would Bartholomew say when she related this conversation?

As for Catherine, she wasn't quite certain she didn't actually like the idea. After all, it would mean that Creag would never bother her in *that way*. There would be no need for any tiresome pregnancy. The man would adore her, thankful that she consented to live with him in spite of his affliction. And if he wanted to keep his secret from the rest of the world, he'd treat her very well, indeed. The situation did have its possibilities.

Maggie watched the pair rush off, her lips trembling in suppressed laughter. This was a memory she would keep for the rest of her life, the old woman thought merrily, though her days might be shortened considerably should the laird ever learn what she had said about him.

Chapter Seventeen

Creag groaned as he opened his eyes later that same morning and found such an exercise to be a painful ordeal. Sweet God, but those old Scots could drink! he thought. And if they had ever told him what their pressing problem was, he couldn't remember it, just as he couldn't recall most of last night.

Fighting off the temptation to stay abed all day, he dragged his body upright and swung his long, well-muscled legs over the edge of his mattress. Hunched forward with his head in his hands, the American laird cursed both Jamie and his whisky. Most of all, however, he cursed his own foolishness.

When he struggled to his feet, he staggered over to the basin and splashed water on his face. Looking up, he could have sworn the portrait of Angus the Bold gazed down upon him in a mocking smile. The painting's only saving grace, however, was that this was one *relative* for whom Jeanne had not manufactured one of her ridiculous genealogies in an attempt to connect the long-dead Scotsman to his own family. Of course, though, the only reason Angus had been lucky enough to escape the fate of all the other Donnachys and Robertsons was because Jeanne hadn't been in his bedchamber since his arrival, and that was her fault, not his own, he thought in irritation.

Groping for a towel, Creag almost knocked over a glass sitting on a tray atop his washstand. Cursing, he caught the goblet just in time, observing an accompanying note as he did so. It said the clear concoction was a remedy sent by Leslie to ease any lingering discomforts yesterday's overindulgence might have caused.

However, Creag was in no mood to put anything in his stomach at the moment. With a grimace, he gingerly picked up the odious-smelling potion and spilled its contents into the washbasin, assured its contents would be gone by the time he returned to his rooms, Leslie's hopes for his imbibing the disguised love potion come to naught.

Then, with great effort he set about getting dressed, praying that no one or nothing crossed his path until he was feeling more himself.

Later that morning, Jeanne found herself in the great hall, overseeing the workmen who were rehanging portraits of the Donnachy and Robertson ancestors. While the task should have fallen to Maggie, the housekeeper had pleaded the necessity of finishing some urgent sewing and Jeanne hadn't objected. Besides, *she* knew exactly where the portraits belonged. Maggie would undoubtedly have had them hopelessly jumbled, regardless of the number of times she'd been in their presence. Poor Robert the Grizzled might have ended up in the kitchen rather than where tradition placed him: at the right of the laird's chair as befitted the first of the Robertson line.

After listening to her initial instructions, however, Clinton's crew worked efficiently, needing no further direction from Jeanne. She sat down, glad of the few moments to relax unobserved and relish the relative peace that allowed her mind to roam. It was bad enough not to have complete control of her heart, as witnessed by those unbidden tears in front of Leslie the other day, but having to hide her pain from everyone was exhausting, she thought, pinning up a straggling curl. To be sure, Michael and Maggie suspected the laird had taken advantage of her, but the shameful truth that, despite everything, she still longed to be in Creag's arms, to hear him explain away Catherine, seemed an absurd weakness on her part, a trap she was determined to avoid.

Still, Leslie's advice haunted her. Was it possible that Creag could make sense of the blonde's appearance and her startling claim to his future? When he'd learned of the Graysons' arrival, his face had paled and he'd seemed shocked; at the time, she'd seen it as guilt, but what if she was wrong? she debated unhappily. Should she reconsider?

No, she'd let Catherine have him and good riddance to them both, the brunette decided for the hundredth time in the past six days, finding it hard to come to terms with what she saw as Creag's deceit. Of course, the village had not been exactly honest with him, but that wasn't personal. That situation was purely financial and it harmed no one, merely lightened Creag's purse, Jeanne argued silently as the laborers looked to her for approval and, getting it, quickly departed.

Creag's deception, however, had been an intimate one, whispered promises made when he had no right to make them. No one but she had been hurt, and it was her own fault for letting her guard down, but that didn't excuse him. She should have known better than to trust a man as attractive and successful as C. Robertson Blake, reflected the unhappy Scot. He must have scattered broken hearts all over the States. What's one Scottish trophy by comparison? she mused, trying to harden her resolve to despise the dastardly scoundrel.

With a good deal of effort on her part, she'd been able to avoid Creag yesterday and today, and even Andrew hadn't been around since she had agreed to his conditions. Catherine, however, had the uncanny knack of turning up at the oddest moments, readily believing Jeanne to be an accomplice in her quest to capture the laird. Even as she thought of her, Jeanne heard the blonde's shrill call echoing in the hall.

"Jeanne? Jeanne, where have you gotten to?" the American cried, spying her and entering the hall in a flurry. "Ah, hiding in here, were you? Well, I won't tell the earl you were shirking your duties, but I've just discovered some clothing accounts that must be paid. I want you to give them to Creag."

"Why don't you do that, Miss Grayson?" demurred the steward, weary of the woman's artless manipulation. If Catherine had overspent the allowance he'd given her, let *her* confront Creag and learn firsthand how his eyes hardened and grew dark when he was angry...or passionate, recalled Jeanne with a pang. "Besides, I only handle the transactions which concern Linclachan or the estate."

"Oh? The way you look at the earl sometimes, I would have imagined that you'd handle anything he suggested, but never mind," said Catherine, happiest when she could flail her sharp tongue and quickly retreat without giving her victim a chance to reply. "Tell me, why is that decrepit old man's portrait hanging where everyone can see it? For heaven's sake, have it removed!"

"I can't do that," said Jeanne, her tone as frosty as her face was flushed. "It represents Robert the Grizzled, the first of the clan Donnachy to use the name Robertson. Knighted for capturing the murderers of James I, he is the most famous of Creag's ancestors."

"So, put him in a back hallway or something, not where everyone can see him," advised Catherine. "He certainly couldn't have been much of a man, all wizened like that. Still, I suppose Creag probably relates to his infirmities, given his own poor attributes in that department."

"What?" asked Jeanne sharply, in spite of everything, unwilling to hear Creag's intended criticize him so harshly.

"Well, I'm sure you wouldn't be aware of it, but your laird isn't much of a man in the real sense of the word."

"I beg to differ. C. Robertson Blake is very much a man and he lacks for nothing in *any* of his chosen activities!"

"I'm not talking of his ability to organize or get things done. I'm speaking of his performance in the bedroom," scoffed Catherine, her eyebrows raised in condescension. "Not that you would have occasion to know."

"Aye, but I do, in the bedroom and by the *lin,*" retorted Jeanne, outrage overcoming her common sense. "I'll have you know Creag is all male, and extremely good at pleasing a woman. But I'm sorry if he hasn't demonstrated his skills for you."

The slap with which Catherine answered her resounded loudly, echoing in the cavernous hall and beyond, alerting a passing Creag to the ugly scene in progress.

"I suppose you would know, you Highland slut, obliging any male who asks you. You're nothing but a filthy bitch," snapped Catherine, so irritated that she failed to notice Creag standing behind her, his face molten with fury. "But what else is there for someone of your questionable breeding to do?"

When Jeanne said nothing, her face clearly displaying the mark of Catherine's hand, the socialite gave a short laugh and continued her harangue.

"I don't blame Creag, you know. He respects me too much to try to bed me before we're married. But as for you, he must have seemed heaven-sent, the ultimate chance for you to make something of yourself. Of course, he would have expected a virgin, but I imagine you found some way around that, women of your kind generally do, I'm told. Now, get out of here," she said, dramatically extending her arm toward the door. "Pack your things and be gone within the hour or you'll be thrown out. I won't tolerate a woman of your morals in my home any longer."

"Funny, that's exactly what I was going to say," announced Creag, his voice hard and distant. For a moment, he glanced at Jeanne and his expression softened, but then he turned back to Catherine. "The only difference, Miss Grayson, is that you were the one to whom I intended to speak."

"What? *Me?*"

"Aye, and your family, as well. I won't have anyone treating Jeanne that way, especially someone as hypocritical as you."

"But, Jeanne is the one—"

"The one who owns my heart and, if she'll have me, the woman I plan to marry," finished the laird, praying the lovely Scot would forgive him. When he looked in her direction, she appeared stunned, but she sent him a small smile. "And you, Catherine, will be packed and gone from Lindall Manor within the hour or I'll know the reason why."

"But, Creag, my parents—"

"Tell them whatever you like, just go," he ordered, moving to stand beside Jeanne and protectively drape his arm around her shoulders. Let Grayson do his worst; he would not risk losing this woman for the sake of a fortune. He, and Linclachan, could survive anything so long as Jeanne was by his side.

With a desperate cry, Catherine turned on her heels and fled the hall, obviously intimidated by the anger C. Robertson Blake displayed toward her even while he showered the fiery Scot with his affection.

After Catherine's departure, neither Jeanne nor Creag moved for a moment, each awaiting the other's words. Then two voices sounded at once.

"Creag, I'm sorry I doubted you—"

"Jeanne, can you ever forgive me?"

Together they laughed and Creag tilted Jeanne's chin upward so he might look into her tear-filled eyes. Gently he stroked her cheek as he opened his heart to her.

"Jeanne, I meant every word I said just now," he murmured softly. "I love you with every ounce of my being and my only regret is that I was too stupid to admit it earlier."

"Oh, Creag," she cried, turning into his chest and burying her head against his shoulder as she relished his warm embrace, comforting her. This was what she'd longed to hear but, after doubting him, did she really deserve such love?

"Now, there's no reason for tears anymore," he said firmly, guiding her to the laird's chair and seating her in it. Still clasping her hand, he knelt before her, determined that she hear the truth from his lips so he could measure her reaction. "Before I came to Linclachan, I believed the only thing that could make me happy was marriage into Philadelphia society. I had approached Mr. Grayson for permission to court Catherine, and he gave it, dependent on their appraisal of my Scottish estate, but that was the extent of our so-called engagement, I swear. I went to London to sever that relationship, because I knew it was over, having fallen in love with you. I never meant to deceive you, Jeanne."

"You don't need—" Jeanne protested, guilt at her own deceit making her tears fall even more quickly. *He'd* done nothing to be ashamed of; *she* had jumped to the wrong conclusions, listening to Catherine's lies when she should have trusted Creag.

"Yes, I do. My heart is so full of love for you, I need you to believe in me, to understand—"

"I do, Creag," she assured him quietly, her voice barely a whisper as she clung to his hand.

"Then you'll be my wife?" he asked, removing the ring from his pocket and starting to slip it onto her finger.

"No, no, I couldn't," the brunette cried, jumping to her feet and running toward the door. "You, you don't know what I've done and you'll only hate me when you find out!"

"Jeanne!" In an instant, Creag had overtaken her, pulling her roughly in his arms and kissing her soundly. "Now hear this, all that matters to me is that you love me. Anything else is nonsense."

"But...but you're not really the laird," she sobbed, the fateful words piercing her heart as she confessed her deepest, most shameful secret. "It was all just a foolish scheme to save Linclachan—"

"So?" The tall blonde smiled down at her, his fingers brushing away her tears. "Even if I'm not the true earl of Lindall, laird of Linclachan, you love me, don't you?"

"Yes, but...wait a minute," she protested, stepping back from his embrace as realization suddenly dawned on her. "You know—you've known all along that you didn't belong to the clan, haven't you?"

"Aye, and I must admit that I found my supposed resemblance to all those spurious relatives quite amusing," Creag said, enjoying Jeanne's astonishment. "And though the cost of being laird was a pretty steep one, I'll not begrudge it. Finding you makes every penny worthwhile."

For a long moment, Jeanne stared at him, unable to decide whether to smack his grinning face for being so damnably superior or to kiss him for being so wonderfully understanding. Curiosity won out though and she did neither.

"But why didn't you let on? Why did you accept the ruse?" she demanded, amazed that he'd fooled them for so long. Then, desiring more than anything to be in his arms again, all the lies forgotten, she reached up and placed a slender finger across his lips. "Never mind. It's not important. What matters is that you came to Linclachan and found me. Why ever you came, I'll not complain if you kiss me."

Happy to oblige the beguiling Scot, Creag drew her into a warm embrace and bent his head, melding his lips to hers, delighted when she returned his passion.

"Jeanne, you never answered me before, at least not the answer I wish to hear. Will you be my bride?" he asked a while later, his deep voice hoarse with the desire to make this woman his in all ways possible.

"Only if you swear never to leave me behind on your business trips," she said, and giggled, envisioning a life with this wondrous male, in the Highlands or wherever he traveled.

"Never," he agreed, removing the ring from his pocket and quickly placing it on her finger. "From this day forward, your place is at my side."

"That's one renovation I'll be happy to live with," she whispered, relishing the way his eyes hardened with passion.

"How very touching," came a mocking voice, its rage barely contained. "But you're forgetting something, Blake."

"I don't think so," Creag said coolly, eyeing Bartholomew Grayson as the man stormed into the dining room.

"Perhaps I should help you remember," the Philadelphian sneered. "I said I would destroy you for this, Blake. I will!"

"Don't threaten me anymore, Grayson. By now, the letters I have sent to the States should have arrived. And before you can get word to Philadelphia, my instructions will, in all likelihood, have been carried out. I'm buying into the institution that handles most of your financial affairs. Ruin me and you will probably ruin yourself. But even if my plans come to naught, it makes no difference. I'll not countenance having you and your family stay here after the way Catherine has treated Jeanne.

"As for Linclachan, I've just finished seeing to it that monies have been put aside to fund the woolen industry I've planned to establish here, and enough to pay for a railroad spur, besides. Even if I should somehow lose my fortune, the village is now protected. There's no doubt but that it will be self-sustaining."

Jeanne looked at Creag, understanding mirrored in her large green eyes and love for this endearing man growing in her heart.

"How dare you try to involve yourself in any way with my finances!" Grayson exclaimed, furious at having been outmaneuvered. "And how dare you treat Catherine as shabbily as you have!"

"As you sow, so shall you reap," Creag replied, daring Catherine's father to contradict him. "I tried to make amends for any transgressions, Grayson, but it wasn't enough for you or your greedy daughter. You came here uninvited, seeking to get more, promising to destroy me, and the village, if I didn't comply. I didn't care what you thought you could do to me. But I had to see to the welfare of Linclachan. It's Jeanne's home. Now it's mine, too. And I take care of my own. Get the hell out of here and take your family with you, or else I'll give you cause to tell the whole world that I'm no gentleman.''

As the infuriated Bartholomew exited the room, Jeanne clasped one of Creag's powerful hands between her own, bringing his fingertips to her mouth so she could brush them with her lips.

"I can't imagine we of Linclachan have ever before been so fortunate in the sort of man we called laird, *mo cridhe*," she said, the sincerity of her words warming Creag's heart as much as her light kiss ignited his passions.

With a smile, he scooped Jeanne up in his powerful arms and carried her from the room, bent on showing her exactly what her words had meant to him.

The mood of Lindall Manor later that afternoon, however, was much more somber, at least from the point of view of the council.

"Have we been successful then?" Malcolm asked in a loud whisper when Maggie met him in the vestibule where the other council members had already gathered.

"I'm not certain," Geordie responded in a soft voice. "We've routed the Graysons from the Highlands, but as for the rest, that's up to Creag and Jeanne. There's not much more we can do."

"Aye, the laird's directive merely said we were to present ourselves at the manor immediately. But whether it is to hear an announcement or to receive a proper dressing-down for our part in this affair, I've no idea," Jamie added.

"You don't think Creag has uncovered our contributions to the Americans' departure, do you?" Maggie asked, pulling a shawl tighter around her thin shoulders and worrying profusely about the last lie she had told the insufferable Catherine. Though the laird had demonstrated God's own patience with her ineptitude in his household, the old woman somehow doubted he would treat her calumny concerning his manhood with quite the same degree of charity.

"I do not know, woman, but standing here is not going to enlighten us," Malcolm stated, his present anxiety making him more crotchety than usual.

"We may as well get this over with," Duncan suggested. "The wondering is driving me daft."

Solemnly the ancient group shuffled their way to the great hall, where the laird was awaiting their arrival, their great plaids fluttering forlornly in their wake.

When they stepped through the doorway, they saw Jeanne dressed in her ceremonial clothes, seated demurely on the settee, her eyes downcast, while C. Robertson Blake, wearing the laird's kilt, paced the room like a prowling wolf. The presence of the rest of the manor's residents and some of the villagers did nothing to alleviate the apprehension Maggie and the old men were experiencing. Surely such a gathering portended an official event of great importance.

"You took your time getting here, gentlemen. Can it be that our drinking bout yesterday has left you as indisposed as I felt this morning?" Creag inquired. When there was no laughing response, he fell silent for a moment, his lips pursed together as if he were considering what he was about to say next.

"In the short time I have been here, I thought I had come to know Linclachan and its people," he began, standing before the huge hearth, his hands clasped behind his back. Then he paused again as though to seek the right words. The council exchanged uneasy glances, at least two of them wishing the laird would simply use one of the swords hanging over the fireplace and put an end to their misery.

"But it wasn't until today that I realized what it means to be part of a clan, to be a member of a family that interferes in your life and plays havoc with your plans, all in the name of concern. In truth, a few months ago I would have resented your involvement in my affairs, but not today. What I am trying to say," Creag continued, going to stand beside Jeanne, "is that despite the differences in our cultures, I have found a home in Linclachan. And more importantly, I have found a wife. Wish me happy, for Jeanne has done me the honor of agreeing to become Mrs. Blake."

"Well done!" boomed Jamie's voice over Maggie's gladsome squeal, while Malcolm received an elbow in his ribs for loudly demanding to know if it was their scheme that had brought about the happy occasion. In an instant, Leslie, Michael and the rest gathered round to proffer their good wishes and admire the ring with which Creag had pledged his troth.

"I'm uncertain what to say first," Michael murmured, extending his hand sheepishly to the laird of Linclachan, while Leslie smiled, smugly thinking it was her love potion sent in the guise of a hangover cure that had done the trick. "Should it be 'congratulations' or 'I'm sorry'? I should have known better than to have doubted you."

"Don't worry about it, Michael," Creag said with a grin, warmly clasping his friend's hand with one of his own, while the other rested lightly at Jeanne's waist. "I'm only too aware that a man in love finds it difficult to think logically. Besides, your anger at me was an outgrowth of your concern for Jeanne. I could never fault you for that."

"Thank you," the spectacled secretary said sincerely, reaching out to cradle the clan's healer in his own embrace. "And tomorrow, after I've had an opportunity to speak with Leslie alone, I hope we'll have an announcement of our own to make."

"I'm sure you will," Jeanne said, sparing her friend a pleased look before turning to gaze once more at the man who had claimed her heart.

"Here, here, Coinneach has his pipes," Geordie called over the joyous din. "Let's have a tune then in honor of the laird and the future Lady Lindall."

"If these two are to be married, that title would be in error, don't you think?" called a rattled voice from the doorway.

"Quiet, man!" warned Duncan, his hand resting on his dirk.

"I've been silent too long already," Andrew Robertson declared in a surly tone as he entered the room.

Furious to hear in the village that Creag had sent the Graysons packing, the solicitor had become further enraged to stumble onto this celebration and find all his plans reduced to ashes. With Jeanne married to Creag, he knew he would never gain control of Lindall Manor. But perhaps, he had thought, as his terrible need for revenge had outweighed his cowardly nature, there needn't be a wedding after all.

At the sight of Andrew Robertson, Jeanne felt the muscular cords of Creag's arm, still settled possessively about her waist, tighten. In fact his whole body had tensed, like that of a warrior about to go into battle. But the solicitor, his face twisted with hatred, was beyond noticing the subtle changes in his adversary's bearing and stance.

"Explain yourself," Creag commanded, his voice no more than a feral growl as he glared at the villain who had taken such liberties with Jeanne but a few days before.

"Have you never wondered, Blake, why you bear no resemblance to any of the many portraits hanging about on the manor's walls?" Andrew asked lightly.

"Why 'tis because Creag's branch of the family gives proof to the Viking invasions of yesteryear," shouted Geordie, trying to forestall a calamity.

"What would you say, *Mr.* Blake," the solicitor continued as though Jamie's brother had never spoken, his eyes still fixed intently on Creag's face, "if I were to tell you that you are not the rightful earl of Lindall and laird of Linclachan? That your blood gives you no claim to the titles whatsoever? That the entire thing was a hoax perpetrated upon you by the clan in order to avail themselves of your fortune?"

Gasps traveled through the room as those assembled waited to see how C. Robertson Blake would react. The elderly council members held their breaths and Maggie despaired of the misfortune that might see Jeanne put aside before she was ever a true and proper wife. Surely the American would be infuriated to find he and his money had been used. He'd wash his hands of the manor, the village, and most likely Jeanne, as well.

"I would say, Robertson, that your information was exceedingly dated," Creag drawled. "Do you think I would actually have traveled here to accept some obscure noble rank without first having an investigation conducted? I knew before I set foot in Linclachan that I was not being given an inheritance, but being offered a business proposition."

At the laird's pronoucement, the room burst into comment.

"Creag!" exclaimed Michael, recalling the night his friend had told him as much only to have his words discounted as drunken nonsense.

"Och! But you're a right crafty lad, aren't you?" Duncan called gleefully, sending Andrew a superior smirk. "Canny enough to be laird for certain."

"Imagine us thinking we were taking advantage of you, and we were being played upon in return. Why it was a stroke of genius!" Malcolm cried in awe, more impressed by Creag than ever before.

"And if you're not one of us by blood, you're enough like us in spirit to be considered one of the clan anyway, even without your marriage to Jeanne," proclaimed Jamie loudly. "'Tis proud of you I am, and prouder still to call you laird."

"I see," Andrew said stiffly. "If the council and the rest of the clan don't care about who is practicing deception upon whom, there is nothing more I can say, except damn you all to hell!"

"But deceit does concern us," Creag said, leaving Jeanne's side and placing a restraining hand on the solicitor's arm when the man turned to depart.

"Oh? From the display I've seen here, I would never surmise as much," Andrew said contemptuously.

"Just as no one here guessed at your own dishonesty?" Creag demanded, bringing his face so close to the solicitor's that the normally pompous man began to quake.

"I—I have no idea what you mean," he stammered, the quavering in his voice denying the truth of his words.

"That's another lie," Creag persisted, more driven by the recollection of Andrew's effrontery with Jeanne than by the ten thousand pounds the man had stolen from his own relatives. "The investigator I use for business concerns in Glasglow sent me proof only today that soon after Fergus's money disappeared, you opened two sizable accounts in a Glasgow bank. Of course, though, it was not the financial institution that held the note on the manor and village, which I only recently repaid."

"That's not true," Andrew protested, his voice rising an octave.

"Yes, it is," Creag contradicted him firmly. "Imagine, stealing the money of a dying man and betraying your own people."

"But the funds you're speaking of were put aside for the clan," the thief alleged, praying as he looked at the surrounding angry faces that the villagers would believe him.

"Then why didn't you tell me about it when I questioned you in the matter?" Jeanne asked indignantly.

"And why did you allow us to believe the place was destitute?" adjured Duncan, his bushy brows drawn together menacingly.

"You don't understand," Andrew objected nervously, trying to take a step toward the door.

"No, it's you who doesn't understand," Creag said, blocking his path. "I can be a generous man, but I protect what's mine. Make no mistake about it. And let me tell you that when you are finally released from prison, if I ever find you coming near Jeanne again, I *will* kill you. The only reason I don't do so right now is that I've no desire to mar my betrothal day. Take him away and confine him until we can get him before a magistrate," Creag ordered.

The four members of the council banded together. Plaids swinging, the elder Donnachys and Robertsons appeared ominous when they moved forward and descended upon Andrew Robertson. The solicitor had no hope of escape as the men restrained him and Duncan, along with Geordie and Ewan, led him from the room.

"Well, that's taken care of," Creag said, smiling down into Jeanne's face once more. "Now let's forget him and concentrate on our happiness."

"A glass or two of whisky?" asked Jamie hopefully.

"After yesterday's excess, I think ale and wine are more in order," the laird said with a laugh that rumbled through his chest like thunder and reminded Jeanne yet again of the mighty Thor.

"Aye, you may be right," Jamie conceded good-naturedly. "But don't tell Geordie I said so."

Soon the people of Linclachan and Lindall Manor were making merry once more, and the plans for the wedding were being debated.

"Didn't I always tell you the manor was a romantic place?" Maggie inquired of Jeanne as she sidled up to the happy couple.

"So you did, Maggie," Jeanne agreed, her emerald eyes brimming with happiness.

"And as for you, Creag, 'tis glad I am everything is out in the open," Maggie murmured, "I've grown right fond of you, lad, and now there's no cause to feel guilty for our deception."

"If you really want to ease your conscience, Maggie Robertson, perhaps you could give me the kilt I understand you've fashioned for me," Creag replied wryly, the corners of his bright blue eyes wrinkling in mirth. "As you can see, this one is really too large for a man of my proportions."

With a squawk, Maggie shot Jeanne a look that asked her assistance. But as the old woman tried to explain her part in the council's scheme, the laughter of the newly engaged couple drowned out her attempts, until finally all she could do was shrug her shoulders abashedly and laugh along with them.

"If you're wedding our Jeanne, what will you do about all of your business concerns?" interrupted Malcolm, ever mindful of money. "Will you return to the States and take our lass with you?"

"No. I'll retain a few interests there, but I've already begun negotiations to sell the majority of them to a friend of mine—another Scot named Carnegie. I'll concentrate on my steel mill in England and shipbuilding in Clydebank. And of course there are the industries I want to set up in Linclachan."

"Ah, yes," said Jamie, taking Creag firmly by the arm and drawing him into a corner. "About the whisky, lad . . ."

It was hours later before the celebration was done and Creag entered his bedchamber for the night. Aching to hold Jeanne in his arms, the room, for all of its new luxury, appeared a cold and lonely place. But in a house where little went unnoticed, he would not dishonor her by blatantly installing his beloved in his bed before they had gone in front of the priest.

Discarding his shirt, shoes and hose, Creag paced about restlessly, the portrait of Angus the Bold hanging in the corner seeming to mock his discomfort. In truth, the handsome American had come to view his strange little household with affection: sweet Leslie with her penchant for mixing healing balms, as well as charms, Mary forever bustling about, Ewan who worked harder than any man he knew, and of course Maggie, who, he had come to note, could find anything in the manor if she started her quest in front of the laird's bedroom. It had taken him a while to deduce why, Creag thought with a deep chuckle. But as endearing as these odd bits of humanity were, tonight was an occasion where Creag wished them gone from his home.

Knowing Jeanne was but on the other side of his wall, he desired her with an intensity that made him mindless of all else. Running a hand through his thick golden mane, the laird of Linclachan imagined his willowy Scot doffing her dress and letting down her hair, brushing it for the night so that it shone like the richest mahogany. The visions increased the fire in his loins until they burned more hotly than they ever had before. Just when he thought he would go mad with wanting his Highland beauty, the door behind him opened softly, and he spun around to see the woman he craved standing just inside his room, her billowing white nightgown diaphanous enough to hide little from his view.

"Jeanne!" he cried, rushing to her side, his mouth descending hungrily upon hers. "I wanted you here tonight more than you will ever know."

"No more than I wanted to be here," she whispered, running her hand lightly along Creag's strong, lean jaw.

"But how did you get into my room without trouble?" he asked in perplexity, his lips pressing blazing kisses against the delicate skin of her long, graceful neck.

"What do you mean?" she asked in confusion, suddenly finding she had trouble concentrating.

"The guard!"

"Gregory?" Jeanne murmured, depositing a few teasing kisses of her own. "I simply sent him away."

"I always knew he wasn't a very good watchman," Creag muttered distractedly, his voice ragged as Jeanne's open palms swept across his bare chest.

"Oh, but Gregory did his job very well indeed!" Jeanne argued playfully.

"Why, not at all. Look how just anyone can come walking in here in the middle of the night," Creag quipped with a tender smile as he began to undo the bows holding her nightdress closed.

"You misunderstand," Jeanne said with a giggle. "The man was never there to protect you by keeping people out. His job was to protect me, by keeping you in!"

"You canny Scots!" Creag cried with a delighted laugh as he pulled Jeanne closer. "Is it any wonder I want to marry into your clan?"

"Well, you'll have to prove yourself before you wear the kilt again," Jeanne stated matter-of-factly, her small hands working to loosen the garment Creag still wore, until it fell to the ground unceremoniously. "You'll have to establish yourself as a true Donnachy or, in your case, Robertson."

"And how do you suggest I do that?" Creag asked, his eyes dark with desire.

"You'll have to demonstrate that you adhere to the clan's motto, Fierce When Roused . . ." Jeanne whispered seductively, leading her American laird to bed.

*   *   *   *   *

Harlequin® Historical

From *New York Times* bestselling author

The powerful story of two people as brave and free as
the elusive wild mustang which both had sworn to
capture.

A Harlequin Historicals Release
December 1993

HHRLOVE

**Relive the romance...
Harlequin and Silhouette
are proud to present**

A program of collections of three complete novels by the most requested
authors with the most requested themes. Be sure to look for one volume each
month with three complete novels by top name authors.

In January:	**WESTERN LOVING**	Susan Fox
		JoAnn Ross
		Barbara Kaye

Loving a cowboy is easy—taming him isn't!

In February:	**LOVER, COME BACK!**	Diana Palmer
		Lisa Jackson
		Patricia Gardner Evans

It was over so long ago—yet now they're calling, "Lover, Come Back!"

In March:	**TEMPERATURE RISING**	JoAnn Ross
		Tess Gerritsen
		Jacqueline Diamond

Falling in love—just what the doctor ordered!

Available at your favorite retail outlet.

REQ-G3

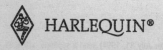 HARLEQUIN®   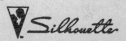 Silhouette

My Valentine 1994

Celebrate the most romantic day of the year with
MY VALENTINE 1994
a collection of original stories, written by
four of Harlequin's most popular authors...

MARGOT DALTON
MURIEL JENSEN
MARISA CARROLL
KAREN YOUNG

Available in February, wherever
Harlequin Books are sold.

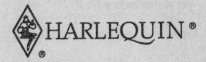

HARLEQUIN ®

VAL94

MEN MADE IN AMERICA

**Fifty red-blooded, white-hot, true-blue hunks
from every State in the Union!**

Look for MEN MADE IN AMERICA! Written by some of our most poplar authors, these stories feature fifty of the strongest, sexiest men, each from a different state in the union!

Two titles available every other month at your favorite retail outlet.

In January, look for:

DREAM COME TRUE by Ann Major (Florida)
WAY OF THE WILLOW by Linda Shaw (Georgia)

In March, look for:

TANGLED LIES by Anne Stuart (Hawaii)
ROGUE'S VALLEY by Kathleen Creighton (Idaho)

You won't be able to resist MEN MADE IN AMERICA!

When the only time you have for yourself is...

Christmas is such a busy time—with shopping, decorating, writing cards, trimming trees, wrapping gifts....

When you do have a few *stolen moments* to call your own, treat yourself to a brand-new *short* novel. Relax with one of our Stocking Stuffers— or with all six!

Each STOLEN MOMENTS title is a complete and original contemporary romance that's the perfect length for the busy woman of the nineties! Especially at Christmas...

And they make perfect **stocking stuffers,** too! (For your mother, grandmother, daughters, friends, co-workers, neighbors, aunts, cousins—all the other women in your life!)

Look for the STOLEN MOMENTS display in December

STOCKING STUFFERS:

HIS MISTRESS Carrie Alexander
DANIEL'S DECEPTION Marie DeWitt
SNOW ANGEL Isolde Evans
THE FAMILY MAN Danielle Kelly
THE LONE WOLF Ellen Rogers
MONTANA CHRISTMAS Lynn Russell

HSM2

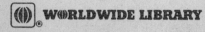 **W❉RLDWIDE LIBRARY**